Breaking Light

Karin Altenberg

W F HOWES LTD

This large print edition published in 2014 by
W F Howes Ltd
Unit 4, Rearsby Business Park, Gaddesby Lane,
Rearsby, Leicester LE7 4YH

1 3 5 7 9 10 8 6 4 2

First published in the United Kingdom in 2014
by Quercus Editions Ltd

A CIP catalogue record for this book is available
from the British Library

ISBN 978 1 47127 497 8

Typeset by Palimpsest Book Production Limited,
Falkirk, Stirlingshire
Printed and bound by
www.printondemand-worldwide.com of Peterborough, England

FSC Mixed Sources
Product group from well-managed
forests, and other controlled sources
www.fsc.org Cert no. TF-COC-002641
© 1996 Forest Stewardship Council

PEFC Certified
This product is
from sustainably
managed forests
and controlled
sources
www.pefc.org
PEFC/16-33-495

This book is made entirely of chain-of-custody materials

Till mamma och pappa
migliori genitori

Memory believes before knowing remembers.

William Faulkner, *Light in August*

Michael he whistles the simplest of tunes,
And asks of the wild woods their pardon.
For his true love is flown into every flower
  grown,
And he must be keeper of the garden.

Richard Thompson and Dave Swarbrick,
'Crazy Man Michael'

PROLOGUE

He stops for a moment, turning the keys in his pocket. A single car creeps past and his gaze follows the beams of its head-lights until they pick out one of the oaks at the bottom of the street; its bare branches are veins feeding blood to the dusk. Then the car is gone and gloom settles again over the village. He listens into the drizzle. Nothing.

He turns back into the fractured light cast from a couple of old-fashioned lanterns on either side of the door. Somewhere above, the wooden sign hangs heavily from its chain. He can't see it now but remembers well the painted hare and fox. He pushes the door open and steps inside, on to a sludgy carpet. To his right, a fire is failing in the grate. There's a faint smell of wet dog but the space in front of the hearth is empty now, where normally a beast or two would be resting after a walk on the moors. A thin man enters from the room behind the bar and for a moment, as the door swings open and shut, there's the glare of strip lights and the hum of a dishwasher.

'Evening.'

'Can I have a pint of your local draught, please,' he says, placing one arm on the polished wood of the bar.

The barman pulls the beer. 'It's very quiet this afternoon; must be this God-awful weather.'

'Yes,' he agrees.

'Here you go, sir.'

'Thanks.' He takes his first sip of the bitter and looks around the room. It's as good as empty, except for a lonely figure in the corner, reading a paper. A TV with the sound turned off is flickering above the bar and both men stare at it as the news comes on. There's a photo of a man in his mid sixties. You can tell he is heavyset, although the picture is only showing his face. It's a bit grainy and the eyes look dull. There's nothing much to him.

He hears a rustle of paper as the figure in the corner looks up at the screen. It's a woman – quite small and plump, he notices, but he cannot make out her features.

'Good riddance,' the barman snarls. 'He was an unpleasant fucker; came in here a few times. Never liked the look of him.'

He takes another sip from his pint.

'They sent him down for ten years. Apparently a new witness came forward. About time, too.' The barman shakes his head.

'Yes,' he agrees, 'it was about time.'

The barman looks at him. 'You from around here, then – or just visiting?'

2

'I've just acquired a house down the road.'

'Oh, yeah? Which one would that be?'

'Oakstone.'

'I see.' The barman falters and looks at him again, more intently this time.

Something touches the air between them, something damp and chill. He hears a dull thud behind him and turns towards the door. Then he stares into the corner again; this time there's only a shadow – and a newspaper lying open on the table. There was something vaguely familiar about the woman, he realises now that she is gone.

He sighs. The clock behind the bar says five o'clock; two arms reaching out from the heart, one slightly shorter than the other, stunted, damaged.

'I should get going,' he says and feels in his pocket for some change.

'Well, welcome to Mortford. I hope you will drink here again soon.'

He smiles and nods and then looks at the clock again. Five o'clock does not look right, he thinks for the first time; not quite balanced, slightly askew.

CHAPTER 1

Mr Askew looked up from the bed into which he had just pressed a row of scillas and snowdrops – the fragrant kind. Normally he would have planted the bulbs in the autumn, but there had been little opportunity until now. He stretched his back and looked at the neat track of tender blue and white. Like the skin on the inside of a young woman's arm, he thought. He had decided to divide the small allotment into two parts of unequal size: the larger area would be dedicated to aesthetics – to colour and scent – and the smaller patch to produce, if only for the satisfaction and comfort of the sprouting. He loved the show of stealth and secret strength as the fingers and ears of tender vegetables stretched up through the crust of earth. The previous allotment holder had planted a couple of roses and a viburnum. The latter for a bit of evergreen, he suspected, but he did not care for it – it was a crude plant with little elegance and it had a sweet scent borrowed from more distinguished cousins. The roses were another testament to his predecessor's lack of imagination.

A woman was working in the allotment next to his. She wore a pea-green veil, partly covering her face, and a red dress with matching leggings showed from under an ugly padded jacket. She worked silently, methodically turning the fragrant soil. Every now and again she would reach for a bucket at her side and fetch a handful of orange peels, which she scattered over the hummocks of earth. Her movements were gracious as she balanced and swayed like a line dancer between the ridges and furrows of her miniature field. The frail February sun that had come out to warm the earth, taut and exhausted by winter, picked out the flowing fabrics around the thin woman. It played with the folds of her green veil for a moment before swathing her in a shawl of warm light. Mr Askew blinked once and cleared his throat.

'Ahem, excuse me, madam,' he mustered, although his voice sounded hoarse. 'What's that you're planting?'

The woman seemed to hesitate in her movements but did not look up, pretending she had not heard. Mr Askew felt the chill of the ground seeping into the bones of his fingers and stood up stiffly to warm his hands in his armpits. He was a tall man with long, heavy limbs and large feet. One shoulder somewhat lower than the other, it was as if he was leaning ever so slightly away from something looming over him. The face revealed less. Unknowable. And the eyes, too dark

6

to read, quickly averted, as if from a mirror. His hair was dark too, almost black under a Coney Island baseball cap, and he wore a neatly trimmed silver moustache that seemed curiously out of place – as if from another era; a forgotten joke. At his age, his joints were a consideration but they had not yet become major indignities and there was no sign of real weakness running through his bones.

She was in her mid fifties, he reckoned, but surprisingly girl-like in her movements. There was a sapling in her lot – a young rowan tree – so tender it was barely distinguishable against the marbled winter sky.

The frosted caw of a crow lanced the air and broke. He cleared his throat so suddenly that she looked up for a moment and the cold light seemed to expand. 'Did you know that the moor used to be forested, thousands of years ago?' It was a remark rather than a question. 'Where are all the trees now? Gone, I tell you.' Yes, he *was* telling her and it surprised him. His life was mapped in silence these days. If he had left it unexplored, it was less from idleness than from not wanting to know. Like a box packed long ago and left unopened, the string still tightly knotted.

Now, he thought instead of how the trees had been cleared by prehistoric farmers and how what remained had been used up later as firewood in the blowing houses for smelting the tin, or as timber for shipbuilding. The subject interested Mr Askew, the relationship between human industry and nature. He might have been grinning as he took a shuffling step towards the woman. She pulled her veil closer around her face, tucking in an escaped strand of black hair.

'So, you see, Dartmoor forest was a wood without trees. You couldn't see the trees for the forest, aye?' The joke made him snort but then he grew thoughtful. 'When it comes to nature, man has only got himself to blame.' It was the truth as he knew it.

But truth was a tricky concept – one that he had never learnt to enjoy. He was used to being less certain. It was the state of trying to understand that possessed him. Perhaps this was why he persisted in wanting to tell this silently flowing woman about trees. 'Do you know,' he continued ardently, 'that it takes two hundred years for an oak to mature?' He could feel now that she despised him and that she wanted to leave but wouldn't; for some reason of her own, she needed to know what he had to say. He said it quickly, as if reading aloud from a book. 'So it grows for two hundred years, then it sits still, it rests, for another two hundred years and then it dies for three hundred years.' He was gasping but could not stop himself. 'I wish we were more like trees, you know. There's so much in our lives we have to endure – and always in a hurry.'

She had stopped in her track and he knew she

had listened. Yet, when he finished talking she gathered her tools into the bucket that had held the orange peels and turned to go. Her movements were soft and floating, defined by the loose fabric under the dull jacket.

'Ah, well,' the tall man muttered to himself. He bit at his moustache and pulled down his cap, hoping it would hide his inadequacies.

They had seen him, although he was so insignificant against the bleak air, and now Billy Dunford and Jim of Blackaton were leading the chase. Normally, he would escape quickly – or hang back at the end of the lessons and wait until the others had left the classroom, then he would saunter down the hill and sit on the riverbank where he could be alone, concealed by willows and alder. As the river whispered to him, he imagined other children like himself – ones that were *different*. The ones who, as Uncle Gerry would put it, were not to everyone's taste. The wrong kind. He would speak to these playmates as softly as the rustle in the leaves and he would use all the words that did not fit into his normal talk: cheerful words like 'want', 'pretty' and 'party', and more complicated and brittle ones like 'me' and 'father'. Once, after having looked around to make sure no one else was there, he said the word 'love'.

But today, as Miss Simmons rang the hand bell, the underside of her large arm swinging like an

9

udder with each flick of the hand, he had not been fast enough. Thoughtless, he had stopped in the middle of the yard as a flock of geese sculled north over his head.

'Jump, Bunny-boy! Go on, you ugly freak. I said, "jump"!'

He looked around in panic and knew what was by now inevitable. Going back into the school-house was impossible – it would only make it worse if they thought he was running to Miss Simmons for help. There was a gnarled oak by the furthest wall. He took a deep breath and started towards it. But his legs were not moving as fast as they should. It was like running in a dream, when you run and run until you're exhausted but your legs do not follow your brain and you realise you're still in the same place. He could hear them closing in. Part of him just wanted to lie down right there on the tarmac in the yard and let them gather around him. Let their winter boots thump into his flesh and smash his teeth until the pain was so intense it would block out the fear. *To be rid of the fear.* But he was not brave enough and so he ran. He stumbled once, grazing his bare knees and the heels of his hands against the loose gravel on the tarmac, but he was soon up again and the tree was getting closer.

'Look at him run, the ugly shit! We are the foxes, coming to get you, Bunny-boy.'

He reached the tree and stretched to grab hold

of the lowest branch but his hands were shaking badly. He was sobbing and wiped his wet face on his sleeve as he looked over his shoulder to see his pursuers closing on him. Whimpering with his mouth open, he managed to gather enough strength to swing himself on to the branch, hanging like a koala with his arms and legs clutching the limb of the oak. It made him feel even more exposed and, with a last, desperate effort, he managed to sit up and pull himself, hand by hand, towards the trunk. From there it was easier, so that, when the first of the boys reached the tree, he was already out of reach. Tears and mucus ran into his mouth through the open gap under his nose. It was appalling and made him want to throw up. He knew he was disgusting.

'Look, he's crying,' he heard from below. 'Bunny-boy is drinking his own snot again. What's the matter with you? Why don't you close your mouth like normal people?'

He hugged the tree, his cheek pressing against the bark, which smelt of lichen and dog shit. He closed his eyes, trying to imagine another place – a place where someone would keep him safe.

'He's so horrid, his own father couldn't stand him – he just stayed away when the war was over so that he wouldn't have to see his freak-boy again.'

Where was the whisper of the river?

'Why don't you stay up there until your face grows human?'

'He'll stay for the rest of his life, then!'

'Yeah, that's right. Let him stay there until he learns to speak properly.'

They all laughed at that and pinched their noses with their fingers, mimicking his voice, their tongues pressed to the roofs of their mouths: 'Ga, ga, ga.'

'Hey, gimp, tell us something funny. Ga, ga!'

They were looking up at him, the discs of their awful faces grinning. He might have thrown something at them, an old acorn perhaps, or one of his boots. He could have taken off one of his boots and thrown it down into one of those faces, smashing it so that there was blood everywhere and teeth and pulpy flesh. He would have, if it hadn't been for Jim of Blackaton, bigger than the others, blond, handsome, holding back, watching over their heads, staring silently with that smile. Looking straight at him and yet somehow avoiding meeting his eyes. It made his skin creep, as if little black beetles with curly legs were walking all over it. What did Jim of Blackaton *see* when he stared like that? He whimpered again, although he had decided not to, and hit his head against the tree to make it stop making those revolting, vile noises.

'Well, do you want to say something, eh? Ah, go *ooon*.'

There was the bell again, and the sound of the boys departing, their laughter and their feet kicking at stones and dry leaves. But he could no longer hear the river. He let himself down from the tree.

There was a chill in the air, as if winter had turned on its heels and come back, when he walked down the lane towards the cottage. The façade had been pebble-dashed to give it a durable finish. It made it look harsh and uninviting – like the kind of surface that would rasp your knees if you were pushed on to it. He would have found it less threatening if it had been washed in lime, like the other cottages along the street. He could see the light from behind the drawn curtain in the front room and knew that somehow he would be in trouble. Carefully, hoping to curtail whatever was in store, he pulled down the brass handle and pushed open the door.

Uncle Gerry was smoking in the armchair by the peat fire, a glass at his hand, his long legs stretched out towards the grate.

'Hello, Uncle Gerry,' he said with relief.

'Evening, lad.' His uncle sounded cheerful. 'Lost track of time?'

The boy shrugged and dumped his satchel by the door.

'Good day at school?'

He shrugged again.

'Hungry?'

He couldn't say.

'Isn't this music sublime?'

He listened to the voice on the wireless. It was

a big band and an American woman singing; she sounded beautiful and jolly. Every now and again she repeated, 'Put the blame on Mame, boys.'

'Perfection!' sighed Uncle Gerry and leant back his head so that the lank hair stuck to the antimacassar. The boy's hair was thick and dark, not fair like Uncle Gerry's.

He nodded; he trusted Uncle Gerry to know about good and bad.

Then Mother was at the door. 'Look at you. Do you *have* to get yourself into such a state every bloody day?'

He sighed.

'Well?' Mother sounded tired and he knew it was because of him.

Reluctantly, he turned his attention away from the American lady's singing and back into the confined room. 'Sorry.' He tried to smile at her with his eyes, as his mouth was no good for it.

'You fell out of a tree again, right?' Uncle Gerry suggested.

He nodded again, too vigorously. There was blood, he could taste it but wasn't sure whether it was coming from his nose or his mouth.

'Aw, don't let it drip on the floor,' Mother wailed. She left the room but returned a moment later with the dishcloth. 'Here,' she said, thrusting it into his hands. 'And look at those clothes – do you expect me to mend and clean them every night?' She did look tired; her eyelids were pink but there was something disturbingly colourful about her too, something to do with the lips and the cheeks.

Holding the vile cloth over the hole in his face, he looked down at his clothes. He couldn't see anything immediately wrong with them, but the wool of his socks had dark patches where his scabbed knee had bled through the yarn, and the bark of the oak tree had settled like dust over his shorts and school blazer. Mother took a step towards him; for a moment he thought she was about to stroke his hair but her hand took hold of his shoulder and turned him this way and that. She pulled the cloth from his face and scrutinised the damage. She avoided looking into his eyes. He let his own eyes drop to her feet. Her ankles in the beige stockings had swollen and bulged over the side of her courts. He felt very tired suddenly and wished he could have rested his head.

'Filthy!'

The force of her remark made him blink.

'For pity's sake. Can't you see that the lad's hurting?' Uncle Gerry's face looked scrubbed and his eyes did not quite seem to have the room in their sights. It was like that sometimes in the evening. 'You're a bloody bitter bitch these days, do you know that? Where's the old Celia I used to know? She was a really nice girl, and it wasn't that long ago . . .' he faltered.

'Finished?' She turned her back to them, smelling perhaps of rose water.

15

Uncle Gerry sighed and pulled a face; the boy smiled quickly, to make him feel better.

'Right,' she said, briskly, over her shoulder, 'take those rags off and put on your pyjamas. There's some stew on the stove.'

He ate his bowl of stew standing by the stove, his bare feet aching against the flagstones. The memory of blood in his mouth made the lamb taste of rusty bog water, of dark caves, perhaps of death. He shuddered every time he swallowed a mouthful.

Afterwards, he returned to the front room. Uncle Gerry's chin had slipped on to his chest, but he recovered it as his nephew knelt to put some more peat on the hearth. The fire glowed and glowed, smelling of earth scorched in battle.

The boy spoke first: 'Uncle Gerry, trees are good, aren't they?'

'Yeah, they are good, all right,' said Uncle Gerry.

'Nothing bad about them?'

'No, not that I know of.'

They were quiet for a while as they pondered this; the only sounds the breathing of the peat, the wind in the chimney and the subtle wash as Uncle Gerry sipped his Bell's. Mother's resentment persisted in the scullery, as quiet and dense as packed snow. The boy moved closer to the armchair, cautiously resting his head against the older man's leg.

'Hey, lad.'

The boy looked up at his uncle, whose face had grown vague in the dull light.

'You must learn to stand up for yourself, you know.'

Whatever could he mean? The boy was stunned and stared in disbelief. 'What?'

The uncle cleared his throat and looked deep into his glass. 'You know what I mean – not take any rubbish from them.'

'Who?' Suddenly he felt the old anxiety rising inside him, tightening its grip around his throat. It wasn't meant to come in here, not into this room where he sat with Uncle Gerry by the fire, where sounds were low and words were soft.

'Don't play the fool; you're a smart boy – the other kids, of course. Don't give them any opportunity to be nasty to you.'

He felt hot behind the eyes. Was he about to cry? What a freak he was. Repulsive. How much did Uncle Gerry know? Had he guessed at something? Somehow this made it all worse and he wished he were back in the tree. He was choking and stared hard into the fire. He must be better; he must try harder to be normal. Don't give them any opportunity. He could feel Uncle Gerry looking down at him and shifted away from the armchair.

'I saw a lot worse in the war, you know,' Uncle Gerry muttered. 'At least you have never known another way.'

Never known another way? He had heard them talk about him when they thought he wasn't listening.

'Poor kid, used to be so carefree,' they would say. 'So anxious and withdrawn lately. Stiffening like a cat when you walk past.' Stiffening? No, I'm just vigilant. Mustn't let the guard down. Not now. Not ever.

A few weeks later, he was eating grass again. This was one of their favourite games. Billy came up from behind on the playing fields and tripped him so that he fell on to all fours. Jim then put his boot on the back of his head and hissed, 'Go on, Bunny-boy, eat your grass, it's the only dinner you'll get today.'

From where he lay, his cheek pushed hard into the grass, he could see the new boy in the class below his own, watching from a few yards away. There was nothing unusual about this – their play often attracted an audience – but the look on the new boy's face was different. There was no smirk; instead, his features were closed and unflinching. His eyes were dark, which made his face look very pale. Suddenly, he started forward. He was quite a small boy but his feet were fast and he reached Jim and Billy in a few steps. They were both taller and much bigger. The new boy pushed Jim of Blackaton hard in the side. 'What are you doing?' he shouted. 'Let him go!'

They were all stunned but there was something about the new boy's gaze at that moment which made Jim of Blackaton lift his foot from his head. Jim spat on the grass, only just missing the new boy's polished boots, and muttered some obscenities. 'Ah, how cute. Look at them, Billy. Bunny-boy has got himself a fluffy little friend,' he leered, but he was more uncertain now and, when the new boy continued to glare at him, he spat again – the corner of his mouth was a bit unsteady – and motioned to Billy. Together, they moved off towards the other boys who were playing football nearby.

During all this, he had stayed as he was, flat on the ground, but now the new boy bent over him and pulled him up by the arm. The new boy looked at him, intrigued rather than accusing. 'Why did you just take it? Why didn't you try to get away?'

He shrugged and shook the new boy's hand off his arm. He looked around quickly. The others would not approve; they must not see.

'Why were they trying to make you eat grass? It's disgusting, I tell you. Even my dog wouldn't eat it – he tried once, but it made him throw up. You should have seen the colour of the puke. He's dead now.'

He would have liked to have a dog. He averted his face but knew that the new boy had seen it already.

'I would have kicked back at them, if I were you,' the younger boy persisted. 'Right here.' He pointed at his shins.

He didn't know what to say but dug the heel of his boot into the lawn. Then, because he had no better alternative, he scrambled after the new boy, who was now walking back towards the school-house. The situation was altogether unsettling and he did not know what to make of it. The boy had seen for himself; he must know by now that he was a freak.

'I'm Michael.'

He looked up and then quickly down again. What did it all mean? He could feel a warm patch where the boy's hand had rested on his arm.

'What's your name?' the boy who called himself Michael asked helpfully.

'Gabriel,' he whispered.

'What?'

'Gabriel—' this time a bit louder – 'but my uncle calls me Gabe,' he managed and at once regretted revealing the nickname. It sounded awful. And his voice.

'What happened to your face?'

'I am a mutant,' he volunteered, in case this was what was wanted.

'A what?'

Did this new boy, who looked so normal – pretty even – really not know what a mutant was? It amused him and he decided to take a more scientific approach.

'I am a harelip. That's why I have the face of a bunny. My palate is cleft. That's why I speak like an idiot. Sometimes.'

'Oh,' Michael said, and after a moment's hesitation, 'Can I see?'

Gabriel recoiled as Michael's face came up close to his. No one, apart from Mother and Uncle Gerry, had ever been that close to him before. He tensed as Michael looked at the hole that ran like a dark gutter from his mouth and into his malformed nose. Suddenly he wanted to protect Michael from it all.

'It won't happen to you,' he assured him, and added, 'I was born this way.'

'Fab!' said Michael.

They started walking again. A group of daisies had opened their eyes to the grey day but the March wind was chilly. Gabriel glanced sideways at the boy who walked beside him across the grass. His school uniform seemed very clean and he had thick brown hair that curled a little at the temples. It was like a tight woolly hat or like the painted-on hair of Pinocchio, Gabriel thought. His eyes were brown, almost familiar.

Michael looked up and smiled. 'Would you like to come back to my place one day after school? You can try my friendship machine, which decides whether we can be friends or not.'

'I'd like that very much.'

'Tomorrow then,' he said and started running.

Gabriel remained, dumbstruck, but suddenly remembered: 'Where do you live?'

'Oakstone,' Michael called back without stopping.

Then all was quiet again, apart from the river, which whispered to Gabriel. 'Stick to your own kind,' it sang. 'He is too good for you.'

Mr Askew pushed open the metal gate in the low wall that surrounded his new home. He had left the gardening implements in the allotments, as he hoped to be back after lunch. He didn't really need an allotment, of course – the garden at Oakstone was so large – but he preferred to keep the lawn, which stretched from the house to the garden wall, intact. It was the kind of lawn where gazebos were raised and ladies got their heels stuck after too many glasses of Chardonnay and where you couldn't find your mini gherkin when it fell off the canapé. To Mr Askew, it served as a barrier and kept him apart from the community, perhaps even safe. It was fringed by a screen of ancient elms and oaks, which rustled gently in the summer and creaked hesitantly throughout the winter. He walked up the gravel drive and recognised that his old, beaten-up Skoda looked out of place. There were weeds in the gravel and the house itself looked curiously unlived in. The green door, so familiar by now, opened up on to the lovely hallway with its floor of diagonal limestone tiles inlaid with black marble diamonds. He sighed as he looked around at all the boxes still waiting to be unpacked. He lifted one, marked 'my books', and carried it into the drawing room. The drab winter sun filled the room with an acceptable light. He pulled out his penknife and cut the Sellotape around the box. There it was, the backlist of his academic career, thirty years of research, his only defence against the 'publish or perish' device. He smiled as he read their titles – how ridiculously pretentious and wide-eyed they all seemed now:

We Who Are Not Like 'the Other'
Physical defects in England, 1250–1600
Once We Were Stars – changing perceptions of
  malformation
Display of Abnormality – malformation and the
  self
The Bequeathing Beauties of Biddenden – charity
  in the twelfth century
Duality – a social construct

He opened the last book at the title page, where he saw his own name: an apparent achievement. He hesitated briefly before moving on a few pages; there, solitary in the middle of all that whiteness, was the dedication. He could see now that it looked wrong, exposed and exposing. He shut the book and dropped it back into the box, pushing it into a corner of the room where he might forget about it.

He felt drained suddenly and settled into one of the armchairs by the cold fireplace. He might have nodded off for a moment and the room seemed bleak when he opened his eyes. No, my world is not dull, he thought to himself. It is alive with the thoughts I feed into it. In the shallows of my mind I paddle in the pools of memory. Will somebody come and find me here or have I been abandoned, left behind at the end of the day? Sometimes, he realised, he could not distinguish between the floating of his dreams and the wash of the wind across the moor.

A bird was singing outside the French windows,

perhaps an optimistic blue tit or a blackbird showing off. He thought about what to have for lunch. His appetite was no longer what it once was and food now bored him. Ah, well, he thought, I'll have some soup from a tin. Retirement didn't bother him – in fact, he relished it. All those years of commuting on the bus from his flat in Swiss Cottage through the congested capital had been hateful. The bodies of strangers, pressed against his, their morning breath on the close air. He had been a timid teacher and the various institutions, departments and centres that had hosted his subject over the years had realised that they would be better off keeping him on research grants. He had never been ambitious in the way his colleagues were. Nor did he feel that his time in academia had been wasted – his focus had always been on *finding things out*. And it was so much simpler to live in the intellect. His accomplishments, which were largely based on an early experience of what his colleagues called 'field-work', had been achieved over a long time. His reputation had initially only been acknowledged within the small group of academics who shared his interests and so he had somehow managed to hold on to his privileged position as a relatively vague, easily forgotten and anonymous figure on the periphery of academia. It was easy to convince others that he lived for his research, so that no one ever asked the question, 'What else?' His natural curiosity and urge to *understand* had resulted, almost accidently, in an international reputation.

Mr Askew smiled grimly as he thought of his leaving party the previous year. It had been held in the senior common room at his latest hosting institution. A bewildered group of staff and a few postgraduate students, whom he may or may not have come into contact with, had turned up to slump against the wood panelling. A selection of drinks had been put out on a table, closely monitored by Mrs Bail, the secretary who was unusually good with figures. The furniture was the usual mix of standard-issue convenience and mock medieval. On entering the SCR, he had shuffled straight to the drinks table and asked for a glass of red wine.

'Will that be Cabernet Sauvignon or Chardonnay, Professor Askew?' asked Mrs Bail, pulling at her cardigan to cover her large bosom.

He looked down at the dismal array of bottles and Tesco juice cartons and sighed. 'I'll have the Cabernet Sauvignon, please.' Lowering his voice, he suggested, helpfully, 'The Chardonnay is white, my dear.'

Mrs Bail looked up at him with steely eyes. 'Is it, now,' she muttered. 'I can't quite see why one has to make a fuss about it.' She poured the wine. 'The nibbles are over there.' She pointed towards a table at the other end of the room where a couple of the postgrads had lost themselves over plastic salad bowls of salt-and-vinegar crisps and Bombay mix.

He thanked her and looked around for somebody

to speak to. Professor Bradbury, the current head of department, was being talked at by Dr Chatterji, an eager visiting researcher specialising in transvestites. Bradbury, who was a head taller than Dr Chatterji, was looking far into another world where people did not bother him. He had a great vision for the department but no one quite knew what it was. His near-black hair was permanently tousled, as if his *gebiet* was adventure sports rather than the early history of leprosy.

Dr Rochester, wearing ostentatious red corduroys and a green tweed jacket, was sharing a joke with one of the male research assistants, Mr Wilson, who wore a low-cut T-shirt, showing some of the hair on his chest. Rochester was the current star of the department. His professorship would not be far off, although he was still in his thirties. He had written a book on the interbreeding of Neanderthals and Homo Sapiens, which had been made into a TV documentary by Channel Four. Rochester himself had presented the documentary, striding tall along dried-out wadis in Jordan. He had worn a linen suit and a panama hat, which, at the time, struck Askew as pretentious, but which had earned him – Rochester, that is – quite a following amongst the postgraduates. Presently, he was leaning over the handsome Mr Wilson, whispering something very close to his ear.

'Professor Askew?' Askew recognised one of the postgraduates he had supervised on occasion. Was it Catherine – or Kate? He smiled at the young woman, who could helpfully be described as frumpy; he thought he recognised in her dress his own efforts at indistinctness.

'I just wanted to say that I'm very sorry that you're leaving.' She said it quickly, but could not prevent the blushing spreading from her throat.

'Oh, well, that's . . . that's very nice of you.' He was taken aback. 'Thank you, but I'm sure this will be a livelier place without my dead freaks.' It was meant as a joke, but Catherine or Kate looked up, appalled.

'How can you say that? Your research has changed my life,' she said earnestly.

Askew didn't know what to say; she looked like a normal enough person. Was she mocking him? He frowned and she saw it.

'Now, I'll have to deal with him.' She nodded towards Rochester.

He followed her gaze. 'Dr Rochester is a man of some standing now, you know—' he did not know what else to say – 'and of such positive colours,' he managed.

She suddenly looked close to tears and, to soothe things, he added, 'Quite on the make.'

'Well, exactly,' hissed the earnest girl. 'He's a self-obsessed, narrow-minded prat who sleeps with everything in trousers.'

'Oh.' Without thinking, he looked down at her full skirt and sensible shoes.

'You, on the other hand,' she continued, 'are an awkward dear with no ambition and that's why you have never been of much interest to anyone except people like me.'

'Oh,' he said again.

'And I mean that in the best possible way,' she added.

'Yes, yes, of course you do,' he said politely, but wasn't quite sure.

'Ah, well, I must dash,' she said, suddenly cheerful. 'Mustn't miss my karate class.'

He nodded; he had obviously got her wrong.

'Anyway, it was great talking to you – I feel a lot better now.'

He watched with a sinking heart as she left the room, her wholesome canvas tote bag bumping heavily against her thigh. Too enclosed from the beginning, the senior common room seemed further reduced by his sudden loss of poise. Yet he could not bring himself to leave; something was expected of him. He needed to stay so that they could settle their minds and do their reluctant duty towards him. He swallowed the rest of the wine and looked towards Mrs Bail, who was still guarding the drinks table, her face and body blown up with the importance of her task. Fortunately, he caught the eye of Dr Lamont, a sweet man of insubstantial presence, red hair and intelligent gaze. Lamont winked at Askew and picked up two glasses of red from the table.

'That Bail woman is a fearful old brute, isn't she?' said the wizened Scotsman as he handed Askew a drink.

Askew raised his eyebrows and took a sip of the wine.

'So, do you think the Dark Lord will make a speech?' Lamont nodded towards the head of department, who had managed to detach himself from Dr Chatterji and was currently training his opaque eyes on Caroline Manners, an American postgraduate with ample endowments, including a healthy grant from a Midwestern college.

'I'm afraid he might . . .' Askew sighed unhappily.

'Ach, cheer up, old pal; you're out of all this now.'

He frowned.

Lamont clinked his glass against Askew's in a solemn toast. 'Congratulations. You have survived thirty years in the beehive of academia.'

'Yeah, well . . .' Perhaps he and Lamont could have been friends; the thought made him feel sad.

'What are you going to do with yourself?'

'I'm going back to where I started to try and figure things out.'

'Ah, this is what we all hope to extract from retirement: an end – a conclusive end – to the long wait for fulfilment; a revelation of truth . . .'

Askew laughed. 'Well, it's either that . . . or I'll go for long walks on the moor and sit down and look at it as I imagine one would look at the sea.'

'You're lucky to have learnt how.' Lamont looked at him closely with curious blue eyes. 'I imagine our childhoods to have been quite similar,' he tried. 'How did you grow up?'

29

Askew didn't answer, but the wine trembled in his glass.

'Where were you at school?' Lamont pressed on. This was a common enough question and one that could even be expected between two people who had been acquainted for several decades.

'I cannot remember where I was taught – or what – only what I have learnt.'

'Aye.' The dried-up Scotsman nodded, but still he would not give up. He tried another avenue: 'Anyway, you protected yourself well; your strategy of integrity is one of the most successful I have ever witnessed.'

He looked up, surprised.

'How do you do it?'

'It takes some practice,' he said vaguely. He never wanted to fail Lamont.

It was the Scotsman's turn to laugh, but kindly. 'Yes, I imagine it does.'

They were quiet for a moment, looking into their wine.

'Would you have wished it otherwise?' Lamont asked softly.

'There was no other way.'

'There always is, in the beginning,' he proposed.

'There was never a beginning.'

'What about later on? You had a wife . . .'

'Well, no,' he admitted, because Lamont was the only person he had been this close to. 'That is, never in any proper way. There were girlfriends . . . early on. Not that many.' Very few, in fact – if any.

It was not that he wasn't *able*. No, nothing like that. Nor was he *disinclined*; he still woke with an erection most mornings. It was just that time had passed him by, so that now, when he was asked what he had been doing with that time, *his* time, he could not answer. It was as if he had taken a running jump forty years previously and never landed.

'Well, conventions are of little importance these days.'

He could not offer more, but Lamont was bolder.

'The important thing is that you loved.'

'Yes,' Askew agreed elusively.

'Not everybody is that fortunate.'

'No,' Askew realised, and looked up at his friend. 'Were you never in love?'

Lamont shook his head slowly. 'I'm not sure . . . but I did get married and we had a couple of children – they make it all worthwhile, you know.'

Askew looked miserable and Lamont tried to compensate: 'I used to envy you so; you seemed always to have some other purpose – what was it . . . a hobby of some kind?'

'Oh,' he hadn't realised that anyone had noticed. *What else?* He looked around the room as if he might find an answer. 'I was . . . gathering information for a while . . . Private research, if you like – trying to clear some old debts,' which was more to the point than it sounded, he knew.

Dr Lamont looked surprised but did not press on. He searched instead for safer ground. 'Any other relatives?'

At one stage there had been suddenly many. 'There is someone—' this was more than he had admitted before – 'somewhere,' he added.

'Well, I may drive out to see you some time. It'd be good to get out of the city,' said Lamont, who had finally realised that this was as far as they would go.

Now, in the armchair at Oakstone, Askew thought that perhaps he should ring Lamont and ask him to come down for a weekend. He sighed – it was so difficult to know about friends. How did you know for sure that somebody was your friend? It was not as if it happened by general agreement; there was no certificate or decree to make it credible.

Suddenly he remembered something from long ago and got up from the chair. His limbs were a bit stiff, but no worse than could be expected at late middle age. As he climbed the stairs to the first floor, he was glad of all the running he had done as a child – all that exercise had kept him fit. Another flight of stairs, not as grand as the first, brought him on to the second floor, which had once housed the servants. He faced a narrow corridor of closed doors, each one opening on to an identical small room, but he knew which one to go for. He hadn't been up here since he moved in – there was no need with so much space to heat up elsewhere. He turned the handle but the door did not give. He put his shoulder to it and tried again. This time the door budged and opened on to a dark room with a single, curtainless window facing the moor. The paint on the windowsill was chipped and there was dust and dead flies on the floor. There was no hint as to what the previous owners had used the room for – if at all. He looked around, almost expecting to find a superhero poster on the wall. And the broken club chair as it had been on that day, pulled into the middle of the otherwise-empty room. *The friendship chair.*

'Right,' said Michael brightly, 'this is where you sit.' He gestured towards a large leather chair in the middle of the room. The seat and armrests were torn in several places, but it was still an impressive piece of furniture and Gabriel hesitated.

'Go on; there's nothing to be afraid of. I assure you that the procedure is very safe.'

Gabriel wondered where Michael had learnt to speak like that. 'All right,' he said and sat down in the chair. It engulfed him and his feet did not touch the floor but stuck out at an awkward angle.

Michael looked sceptically at his plimsolls that were dangling in mid-air. 'Ah, well,' he said, 'it would have been good if your feet touched the floor so that you were earthed, but there's nothing we can do about it now.'

'Earthed?' Gabriel asked anxiously.

'To ground the current if something goes wrong,' Michael said with all the confidence of his age and added, 'Not that anything will, of course.'

Gabriel swallowed and wished he could hear Michael's mother somewhere in the large house. Michael was rummaging about close behind him and Gabriel climbed on his knees to look around the high back of the armchair. A *Little Electrician*'s kit box lay open on the floor. There were red and black leads scattered around it and next to them a black box with buttons on it and some metal clips.

Michael raised his head and frowned. 'You're not supposed to look – it may ruin the experiment,' he said with a hurt expression.

Gabriel settled back into the chair, his heart beating harder now. The palms of his hands were cold and clammy.

'If you pass the test,' Michael was saying from behind, 'we can have some pancakes for lunch.'

'I'd like that,' Gabriel said in a small voice.

'Well, then you need to do your *very* best.' Michael was standing next to him now.

'Yes.' This was always the case.

''Cause you do want us to be friends, don't you?'

'Yeah.' He nodded and, because it suddenly felt very important, he added, 'Yes.'

'Put your arms like this,' Michael instructed and pulled Gabriel's arms along the armrests, 'and your legs should be apart, like this.' He stood bowlegged like a cowboy who had just got off his horse.

'That's it; hold it like that and remember not to move, as that may mess up the results.'

Gabriel nodded carefully so as not to move his body.

'And, by the way, you must keep your head still.'

He tried to sit absolutely still while Michael attached one of the red leads with a metal clip to his finger. It nipped a bit but did not hurt. Michael looked up and smiled encouragingly. 'There; it's not too bad, is it?'

He blinked his eyes as a signal.

'Good. I need to put the electrodes all over your hands and feet and ears and chest 'cause these are the best places to measure.' Gabriel was aware of his heart beating harder and he had a thick sensation in his throat. Michael was leaning over him and he could feel his warm breath as he tried to attach one of the electrodes to his ear. He smelt of buttered toast and sand. 'Hmm—' Michael stood back and held his chin – 'I think I'd better use some tape to attach it to your temples. That's how the guy did it in *Frankenstein*.'

Gabriel had never been to the cinema, but Uncle Gerry had told him that *Frankenstein* was a horror film. He frowned involuntarily.

Michael patted him on the shoulder. 'It's nothing to worry about; it'll just make it a bit more *real*. Just wait here for a minute – and try not to sweat; water and electrics don't mix.'

But Gabriel *was* sweating now. In spite of the chill in the unheated room, he could feel his flannel shirt under the slipover sticking to his back and a bead of sweat was trickling along his temple. He

35

breathed deeply and tried not to move. There was a Captain Marvel poster pinned to the wall in front of him and he wondered where Michael had got it; he had never seen a poster like that at Wilkinson's. The poster showed Captain Marvel, the gold flash glittering on the chest of his red bodysuit, fighting against a giant spider. Gabriel looked away quickly and his eyes fell on a low stool on the floor below the poster. There was nothing special about the stool – Michael had probably stood on it to attach the poster to the wall – but something about it made Gabriel feel peculiar. It was painted light blue with a slit in the middle so that it could be carried around. In a flash he saw an image of himself trying to climb on the stool and heard laughter as somebody picked him up and carried him away. It was an odd sensation and he wondered if it had anything to do with the electrodes that were attached to his hands and feet. Just then, Michael returned with a roll of tape.

'All right, let's get going.' He bit off a couple of strips of tape and stuck them to his left index finger while his right hand fitted one of the remaining electrodes to Gabriel's temple. At first, the tape wouldn't stick to his damp skin but on the second attempt it worked and Michael quickly attached the last electrode to the other temple. He stood back and admired his work. 'Perfect!'

Gabriel was not altogether reassured, but remembered the pancakes and strained to smile with his eyes.

'Now, try not to swallow while I attach the leads to the battery.'

The saliva was collecting in his mouth and his throat was aching as he waited for Michael to stick a black and a red lead to each of the metal tongues of the large battery.

'There! Now I'm going to switch it on – only a little, at first – and you must tell me when it hurts; these are dangerous things to play with . . .'

Gabriel's throat made a strange sound and he stared in panic at the black battery box as Michael turned on the switch. He shut his eyes and waited for whatever was in store. But nothing happened. He opened his eyes.

Michael was looking up at him expectantly. 'Well?'

He could not answer.

'Blink once if it hurts and twice if it doesn't.'

Gabriel hesitated and blinked twice.

'Darn!' Michael muttered and turned the switch to the next setting. 'If you don't feel anything, it may not work and we cannot be sure to be friends.'

Gabriel wanted to cry but knew he must not. His entire life depended on this.

'Now, you ought to feel this.'

He shut his eyes again and tried to feel that sensation that would herald their friendship. It wasn't there. His eyes were welling and he shut them harder.

'Remember, blink once when you feel it.'

Perhaps there was a slight tingling in his spine?

Oh, was there? He couldn't take it any longer and, abruptly, he blinked – once.

'I knew it!' Michael shouted. 'Jolly good. I knew we could be friends.' He jumped up to the chair and shook Gabriel's hand as if they were bankers sealing a deal.

Gabriel swallowed at last and looked down at his hand where the electrodes were still attached. He hoped he really had felt enough. But, as he looked into Michael's beaming face, he pushed all his doubts aside and laughed a throaty laugh. 'Can we have pancakes now?' he asked and pulled his sleeve across his face that was still damp with sweat and perhaps tears.

'Yes.' Michael was bounding with joy, either from the success of the experiment or his new friendship. 'I'll tell *Maman* we are on our way.' He ran out the door and along the corridor, leaving Gabriel still attached to the chair. Carefully, so as not to damage anything, Gabriel picked off the electrodes one by one and put them on the floor next to the open box.

The kitchen was bright but quite chilly when Gabriel entered. The light from a single overhead bulb was grating against the weak daylight that sieved through the diamonds of a row of leaded windows.

Michael's mother was standing by an Aga cooker. She had soft brown hair, styled in waves around her face, and she wore a stripy apron over a green woollen dress. She was very pretty, Gabriel thought.

38

'Ah, there you are. You found the way on your own, then?' Her eyes were large and deep like a deer's.

He nodded. It did not occur to him that this might be odd.

'Come and sit down; Michael is just fetching the jam from the scullery. The maid is off today but I hope you will like the pancakes, all the same.'

He hesitated for a moment; he could not remember ever sitting at a table other than his mother's or Uncle Gerry's. There was a nice smell of frying butter from the stove. She looked up at him and smiled with her doe's eyes. Michael must have warned her about him but he looked down just the same, letting his fringe fall over his face.

'Hurry up – they are almost finished; you can have the first one if you sit down now.' Her voice, too, was different and beautiful – it sang at the end of each word, like some small animal might, and her lips pouted in pronunciation. He thought of his own mother's lips that grew thin and white when she scolded him.

He pulled out a chair and sat down. 'Thank you, ma'am,' he whispered at the table.

'I'm Mrs Bradley, but you can call me Amélie, if you like. Michael told me that you're his new friend at school. I'm glad you met; it's not always easy to move into a new area.'

He was baffled. She wanted him to call her a name he couldn't possibly articulate and she was glad that Michael was his friend.

'What are your parents called?' she asked and put a measure of batter on the frying pan. It frizzled for a moment.

'My mother's called Cecilia.' It felt strange saying a name he used so rarely.

'And your father?'

'I don't know,' he said truthfully. 'My father went away before the war and didn't come back.'

'I am very sorry to hear it. So many died in that awful war . . .' She had turned away from the frying pan for a moment and her eyes looked at him in a sad way. It worried him and he wanted to put things right.

'Oh, but he didn't die,' he tried to explain. 'He didn't want to come back because of my face.'

She looked at him oddly. 'Who told you that?'

'I don't know . . . Everybody, I suppose.' He couldn't remember who first told him.

She was quiet for a moment. 'What does your mother do?'

'She works as a secretary for Dr Lennon,' and, in case she did not know the word, he added, 'She answers the telephone and takes notes on a pad and pops to Wilkinson's for the milk.'

Mrs Bradley put a plate with a beautiful golden pancake in front of him. It smelt delicious and he suddenly remembered: 'I have an uncle – he's called Uncle Gerry, but his real name is Gerald Askew. He used to be a doctor too, but he's no good after the war and now he does odd jobs on the farms, taking care of sick animals. He lives up on the moor in a cottage, but often comes to see us.'

He heard a clattering as she dropped the spatula on the floor. 'Askew, did you say?'

He nodded with a mouthful of pancake and got off his chair to fetch the spatula that had left a greasy skid mark on the tiles, but she had already stooped to pick it up. When she stood again, she took a step closer and looked carefully at his face. He felt uncomfortable, remembering he looked a fright when eating, and backed a little towards the table, but her eyes held him. Suddenly, she reached out her hand and stroked his cheek. So soft. He flinched and looked up at her in alarm. Just then, Michael burst through the scullery door with a jam jar in his hand. There was some jam on his face too.

'I tested all of them,' he said earnestly, 'and this is the best one.' He looked from Gabriel to his mother. 'Honestly, it is.'

'Is it, now? Well, that's just splendid.' His mother laughed. 'Why don't you two sit down and eat your pancakes before they get cold?' She seemed normal again and Gabriel was greatly relieved.

When they had finished their pancakes, Mrs Bradley asked, 'Does your mother know you're here today?'

He shook his head. It was a strange question; he rarely told his mother where he went after school. 'Where're you going?' Mother would some- times ask. 'Nowhere,' he would answer, and it was usually left at that.

'Tell her you're welcome to come here and play with Michael at any time, will you?' she said, her eyes ablaze again.

He was beginning to feel a bit sorry for Michael, who had such a strange mother, but then he remembered her warm touch on his face and the flash of the deer. 'Thank you, Mrs Bradley, I will,' he said, knowing he wouldn't.

But of course, Mother found out anyway. Gabriel had just got back from Michael's on a damp evening a few weeks later when it was made clear, as he had always dreaded, that Michael's house, with its strange and yet familiar feeling and the soft, beautiful mother, was too private and positive an experience to last.

'You're never to go to that house again, do you hear me?' Her hands were hard on his shoulders and her face was too close; he could see the pores around her nose and smell the frustration on her voice.

'But why?' For once, he felt he needed to assert himself. 'Michael's my friend.' He was careful not to say, 'my only friend.'

'Your *friend*?' A drop of her spit landed on his chin. 'He cannot be your friend – it's . . . unnatural.'

This was an argument he had heard before, although never from her. Suddenly, he wanted to shout, 'It's all your fault – you're the unnatural one, giving birth to a freak!' But he didn't; he had learnt to control his impulses and never blame anyone else for his shortcomings. Instead, he stamped his foot and bleated, 'But he is! He is my friend – he has said so himself – I passed the test.'

She sighed and let go of his shoulders to cover her face with her hands. 'Have you met Mr Bradley?' The anger had gone from her voice, but he could sense that this was somehow more important, and it frightened him.

'No.'

'Mrs Bradley?'

He hesitated; she was the most private part of it all – he did not want to give her up.

'Answer me, Gabriel. What is she like?'

Her body is still and her face is alive. She moves like a tree in the wind . . . or like a deer with the moon in its eyes. 'She's lovely,' he whispered. How easy it was to betray under such threat. And still the blow, when it came, surprised him. She had never hit him before. His cheek burnt and he tried to swallow down the tears. He was trembling now and could not make sense of it all. In what way was he wrong *now*? He tore away from her and out of the house.

As he turned off the road, it began to drizzle and the lane was soon muddy underfoot. He didn't stop to open the gate on to the moor, but scissored over it, supporting himself with one hand. The turf and heather squelched as he ran. The wind that was blowing into the hole in his face resonated with his panting. Sheep huddled uselessly amongst last year's bracken, scattering off with empty panic in their inane eyes as he passed. He crossed a river that sang of the sea and hurried its white water under a clapper bridge. He climbed a tor and the rain seemed to lift for a moment as he crested the hill and dug his heels into the slope on the other side, where Uncle Gerry's cottage came into view. The longhouse was built into the hillside, facing a narrow valley of enclosed paddocks. A dirt track passed the cottage along the valley and connected it to the Stagstead and Mortford roads on either side. Uncle Gerry kept a few sheep in a pen and chickens in the yard, which had left it mucky with dung and wet straw. Gabriel didn't stop to knock but burst through the door, which opened straight on to the parlour. A peat fire was fading in the large flagstone fireplace and a kerosene lamp stood in the globe of its own light on an oak table in the middle of the room. The stone walls were lined with books and a dark oil painting hung over the mantelpiece. A stuffed buzzard, perched on a peg, watched the door, flanked on the other side by a set of stag's antlers. The gramophone was turning without music.

Uncle Gerry had been asleep in his chair, but woke to the commotion.

'Evening, Gabe; what's new, lad?' The bottle of Bell's on the side table was still half full.

Gabriel didn't answer. He dropped his damp

44

mac over the back of a wooden chair and fetched a couple of turves from the wicker basket and stoked the fire. Flames danced in his eyes as warm light fell on to a rug of deep colour. The sudden heat made his cheek pulse again. His damp shorts reeked like dog's fur. Uncle Gerry rose to put on a new record. The jazz filled the small room but did not shift the silence between the man and the boy.

'Go on, tell me what's wrong.' If he slurred the words it was because he had been woken from a dream of how it might have been. He smiled, his eyes still sentimental.

'Mother says I can't play with my new friend.'

'Why ever not?'

'She says it's unnatural for me to have a friend like Michael. Is it, Uncle Gerry? He knows what I am and he still wants to be my friend. Honest – he tested me and I came out all right.' He tried not to blink. 'I *did* feel the current,' he added, hoping it was the truth.

The smile waned from Uncle Gerry's face. 'You know your mother's nerves are frail and she gets very tired at times. Perhaps she's having one of her headaches?' he suggested.

The boy, who had hoped for an alliance, sulked.

'Who's your new friend, then?'

'He's called Michael and he lives in a big house surrounded by trees and he has a Captain Marvel poster and a dead dog and a mother with a ring

45

that sparkles.' He could have gone on, but stopped – and reddened.

'That would be a diamond, lad. It seems you're mixing with posh folk, Gabe.' He poured a stiff drink and frowned. 'But your mother never held *that* against anyone. Does this boy not have a father?'

'Oh, yes, he does! One that comes at weekends. He works in London, for the government. He was a hero in the war and met Mrs Bradley in France when there were lots of Nazis around.'

Uncle Gerry put down the glass with a clink and looked straight at Gabriel – his eyes suddenly quite focused. 'Does Michael live at Oakstone?'

'Yes – how did you know?' Gabriel was amazed; his eyes shone with admiration. Uncle Gerry knew everything.

The boy's uncle cleared his throat and looked away. 'Oh, I just guessed; it's the only posh house around here, apart from the manor.' His voice was sharper now.

'Do you know Mr Bradley, then?'

'What? No, not really . . . That is, I might have done, a long time ago.' He stood up and turned to inspect one of his bookshelves, his index finger trailing the leather spines. 'Have you met him yet?'

'Who?' Gabriel was not too concerned about Mr Bradley.

'Mr Bradley, of course.'

'No, but Mrs Bradley says I *really* should.' He

picked up the tumbler and smelt it. 'Was he a nice man, when you knew him?'

'Leave that alone!' shouted the uncle and snatched the glass out of the boy's hand.

'Sorry, Uncle Gerry; I didn't mean to . . .'

'Ach, never mind, boy. You shouldn't touch the stuff, though; your soul's not strong enough for it.' He reached out to appease the boy, but he had moved away and was again squatting by the fire, playing with the poker.

'Is *your* soul strong enough?' he wanted to know. He had not appreciated, until now, that he failed in this aspect too.

'Me? I haven't got one.' Uncle Gerry laughed – but his eyes stayed the same.

'Why not? Did you never have one?' A tooth was coming loose somewhere in the trench of his mouth and he wriggled it with his tongue.

'Oh, yes, I suppose I did once, and Lord knows I tried to hold on to it . . . but I finally sold it for a bottle of booze after Monte Cassino.'

'Why?'

'Eh? Never mind – it's just a figure of speech . . .' His voice trailed off as he turned to sip at the last of the drink.

They were both quiet for a while. Gabriel felt the repulsive taste of blood from the loosening tooth.

'All right – let's get you back to your mother; she will be worried by now.'

'But—'

'Come on – put your mac on.'

'Will you speak to Mother, Uncle Gerry? *Please*.'

'Yes, I'll have to speak to her about this.'

They walked the track back to the Mortford road, which was slower than going across the moor. It had stopped raining but it was getting late and Gabriel was beginning to tire. He was falling behind and stumbled on stones and fallen twigs. They were passing through a plantation where a senate of bearded firs stood silent and ancient under a new moon. Uncle Gerry had stopped somewhere ahead and was waiting for him in ghostly contrast at the end of the dark colonnade of trees. He took his nephew's hand in his and pulled him along. They walked like that for a while without talking, floating through the night, each one drawn to his own thoughts, until they were startled by the call of a hunting owl. Gabriel was not afraid of birds but drew closer to his uncle just the same.

'Gabe?'

'Yeah?'

'I was thinking that you and Michael could come over to my cottage sometimes after school . . . No one needs to know. You can help me feed the chickens and suchlike.'

'Oh, thanks – that'd be grand.' He smiled in the dark and squeezed his uncle's hand a bit harder.

It was almost midnight when they reached the cottage in the lane behind the church. As they stepped on to the path leading up to the porch, the door opened and a rectangle of light fell over them. From inside the light, a dark figure with fuzzy contours seemed to reach out and topple towards them, as if overthrown by its own shadow. Gabriel held back and pulled at his uncle's hand, but realised at once that the shape was Mother, lit from behind by the overhead electric light in the front room. He was too exhausted to prepare himself for the reprimands he was sure would come or to be surprised when they didn't. Once inside the front room, he could see that Mother's face was puffed and raw, but he had no time to reflect on it as he was ushered upstairs to bed. Then Uncle Gerry was in the narrow room, helping him off with the boots and unbuttoning the shorts and finding the pyjamas under the pillow. The room was chilly and Gabriel shuddered as he was helped into the flannel jacket that was so cold it felt damp against his skin. And then there was the nauseating wash of the first waves of sleep – the sinking in and out of folds of velvet and the island of emerald green in blue behind his closed eyelids. And somewhere, nuzzling up against the beginnings of his dreams, their underwater voices:

'Well, Cecilia, I'm very sorry, but it was inevitable that this would happen – sooner or later.'

'I suppose, but why now?'

'I don't know, sis, but let's be reasonable. Let's try to keep the children out of it.'

'He must never know. Do you hear me? *Never.*'
'But Cecilia . . .'
'No: it's my final decision.'

It was well into the afternoon, the feeble sun barely reaching over the hedges, when Mr Askew set out for his allotment again. As he shuffled along the street, past Wilkinson's, which was now the deli, and a group of Gore-texed ramblers outside Rowden's, he wondered whether he needed to employ a woman to come and do a bit of cleaning for him; somebody who could come – and be gone – while he was out for a walk or at the allotments. The thought was unsettling but he had to keep at it, unflinchingly. However, his mind soon slipped towards more pleasant thoughts. He quickened his steps as he remembered the plan he had worked out during his after-lunch doze. He was going to plant an herbaceous border on the side of the allotment that faced the silent woman's plot. He could already see it in his mind's eye: the taller achillea and delphiniums at the back and then anemones and sea holly at the front. Perhaps a few poppies. Lapis lazuli flanked by gold, white, purple and red – a rainbow of goodwill and neighbourly consideration.

As he turned on to the path to the higher ground, he could see a glimpse of colour in the dull field. 'Ah, good,' he said to himself. 'She's back.' Leaning into the wind, he stumbled towards her, waving his hand and shouting, a bit too eagerly, 'Ah, I thought you might come back this afternoon – it's such a nice day for it, isn't it?' He had made his mind up and would not have it otherwise, although the wind did bite and the sky was darkening over the hills in the west. A few gulls, having detoured from the coast beyond the horizon, scattered reluctantly from the beds of fat worms as Mr Askew charged up the broken path, his coat catching briefly on last year's brambles. He was suddenly uncertain whether she had heard him – the wind was still against him – and threw his words at her with renewed force. 'Lovely afternoon, wouldn't you say?' He faltered as he saw that she had stopped digging and was looking at him. In the flurry of the afternoon, she seemed remarkably still – the kind of stillness learnt in solitude. She was younger than he had thought at first, perhaps in her early fifties, and her dark gaze, as it finally settled on him, was more intense.

'Not necessarily.' Her voice was clear, the pronunciation distinct but foreign.

He was taken aback for a moment, then murmured, 'No, I suppose you're right. Weather is always a matter of opinion – quite subjective, really. What is fair to one may be quite foul to another.' How stupid he sounded.

And yet her smile was without irony, or so it seemed. The headscarf had slid back to reveal her black hair, streaked with a few strands of silver. 'Our nature makes it difficult to reach absolute certainty and consensus . . . but some things are

51

indisputable—' her eyes were the colour of reeds in a river – 'such as, a rectangle has four corners, or, if I sow, I will reap.'

The wind was fretting with his hair, lifting the fringe, which he kept long out of habit, and blowing it about. He tried to hold it down until he remembered the cap in his coat pocket. Putting it on gave him a moment to recompose himself. 'I plant because I want my day to be a little bit more beautiful, if possible,' he admitted, and dared look her in the eye.

She looked at the snowdrops and scilla at his feet and nodded. 'These flowers are new to me; they are very pretty. You're lucky to have such insouciance. I sow vegetables because they offer me a sense of belonging—' she pushed her spade harder into the earth with surprising strength – 'and something to tend to,' she added.

He nodded. And then he remembered what he had come to tell her. 'I intend to plant an herbaceous border.' His hand indicated gently where. 'It will be very . . . colourful in a few months. You see, it was you who inspired me, this morning.'

It will become her beauty, he thought to himself, and the flawed day seemed suddenly perfect.

CHAPTER 2

'I do not drink, take drugs or get caught up in trafficking,' the strange woman on his doorstep said defiantly, and added, 'I want to make it clear that I'm not like one of them Eastern Europeans.'

Mr Askew only stared.

'I wouldn't normally answer an ad, you understand—' she tried to look under – and then over – his arm which held open the door – 'but, as there's less to do up at the farm these days, I thought I might be charitable and help a neighbour who's new to the community.'

She was waving a piece of paper in front of him, a piece of paper, he realised, with his own handwriting on it. It was the note he had put up on the board at the post office, advertising for a cleaning lady. How he regretted it now. But it was too late for that, quite clearly. He looked beyond her, towards the canopy of green leaves that fringed his property. At least I still have the trees to myself, he thought, and lowered his eyes to her. She was a short and compact kind of woman and, if it hadn't been for her bum, which presented itself in too-tight denim, she would have been altogether unremarkable.

'It's only for a couple of hours a week, you do realise?'

'Most respectable homes around here are normally cleaned for at least four hours a week.' She was beginning to sound impatient.

'Oh. All right; let's agree on three hours, then,' because he would always compromise.

'Fine. I'll start on Friday,' she said, thinking it was her own triumph.

He sighed and began to close the door.

'Ah-ah-ah!' She might just as well have put her foot in the gap.

He looked at her again.

'I insist that you supply me with rubber gloves and cleaning products. Mr Muscle do the best ones.'

'Oh, yes, yes, if you say so . . .' He sounded nervous and hoped she didn't notice.

'See you on Friday, then.'

'Yes, yes.' Closing the door at last, he tried to offer her a smile with his mended mouth.

As he leant his forehead against the closed door, he could hear her footsteps departing on the gravel outside. He realised that she had been wearing a pair of very white trainers that looked as if they had just been taken out of their box. The whole thing unsettled him. Why had he thought it would be a good idea to have somebody come into his home to move around his things – bounce her large bum against his furniture? He imagined the soles of the white trainers squeaking on his parquet and winced. You stupid fool! Well, it was done now. He hadn't even asked her name. He felt damp and his shirt was sticking to his back. He waited a little longer before walking into the drawing room, where he could watch the gravel drive and the lawns from behind the curtains. Grabbing at the worn folds of green velvet, he squinted at the light, which seemed suddenly to have turned against him. She was nowhere to be seen – but still he imagined her spying on him from the bushes by the road. What had she made of his face he wondered. Had she noticed that it was badly sewn? At once, he felt the urge to go for a walk.

He stepped through to the kitchen and opened the back door on to the porch. His walking stick was leaning against the glass and his leather boots were caked in mud from their last outing. I wish I had a dog, he thought as he put on his boots, if only to feel the softness of its ears.

As he walked through the fields and paddocks, the sun came out from behind the clouds and warmed his face. A few young lambs idled amongst daffodils while their mothers grazed matronly nearby. Somewhere above – too high to cast a shadow – a couple of ravens were soaring and carousing in a courting game, their wedge-tails stencilling cuneiform on to the spring skies. As soon as he left the enclosed land behind, a breeze rose from the high moor, eager to greet him with coils and twists. Further away, on the horizon towards the coast, its freshness had already been trapped by a flotilla of wind farms: giant scarecrows in a field of barley. Mr Askew hunched his shoulders against the challenge as he started climbing towards the summit of the tor. As he trudged on, the clitter scraped at the sheep's dung which had stuck in the pattern of his rubber soles. He tugged at his cap in an effort to keep the wind out of his head but it would not let him alone. 'It will ease once I reach the valley,' he said to himself in order to clear his mind. From this high position, his eyes swam out across the expanse of land that was still untamed by plough and unbound by road or dyke. Man had come here for centuries but, although groups of settlers had tried to manifest themselves in the landscape, what remained were signs of struggle and submission rather than of conquest and triumph. Cairns and standing stones, chapels and stone crosses and other monuments to the living and their dead were deftly mirrored in grafts of peat digging and mining and small patches of ridge and furrow where somebody once tried to grow a crop.

A cloud, which had rested over a small lake for some time, decided to move on, silently detaching itself and bringing with it its own shadow that was the exact shape of the lake. Mr Askew followed its drift with his eyes until his gaze could no longer avoid the small cottage in the valley below. Even from this distance he could see that the thatch was tidy and the stonework in the barn was new. The yard was paved with slate and, where Uncle Gerry's henhouse had once stood, somebody had parked a four-wheel drive. The cottage looked very pretty where it nestled in the green valley – some would have called it picturesque and expected roses and honeysuckle to climb up to the eaves in summer. But Mr Askew, as if this had nothing to do with him, blinked and looked away, averting his mind from the hospitable smoke that once escaped from the chimney and from the proud rooster and his harem that used to fritter in the yard. He felt a bit tired and sat down with his back against a rock. In front of him were the remains of a cairn, which marked the summit of the tor. Every summer, ramblers would add to the pile, each one carrying a stone to the stack for luck, and every winter the storms would tear at the stones, scattering hope and fortune. And then he laughed, remembering Michael on the moor on a day of strong winds: 'It can blow the flesh off your bones, if you let it. Honest, Gabe! So what you need to do is either open your mouth and let it blow right through you or, if it's really bad, you must lie down and hold on to the grass with your hands and teeth – like this,' and Michael had thrown himself on to his stomach, biting into the moor. Mr Askew laughed again and opened his mouth wide to let the wind blow through him and fill his lungs.

★ ★ ★

All through that first summer, their friendship stretched and tightened like a cat sunning itself on a stone wall. The end of the school year saw many of the other children returning to work on the farms and smallholdings, so that Gabriel, who had no such duties, was suddenly out of harm's way. They no longer met at Oakstone but, every morning, whilst the tracks of snails spelled their silvery messages across the path, Gabriel would run under the trees, through lozenged sunlight, towards the moor gate – the last port before the open wash of grass and bracken. Red kites watched him with their yellow eyes and swifts raced like arrowheads through the high skies. A hare would stop in her tracks and listen to the threat of the thump, thump of his plimsolls on last year's heather. Michael would meet him, breathless, at Hart Cross, one of the stone crosses that had marked the trails across the moor since the monks first walked into the wilderness. Each such morning brought new excitement as their uncurtailed curiosity widened their world – there was nothing and nowhere they would not explore. They would twirl like shamans across the heath and dance with the petrified maidens in a stone circle, rest for a while on grass beds in the remains of an ancient settlement, or take aim at each other across the muddy trenches left behind by tin miners.

They followed a tin mining leat for hours until they reached its source. Here, they took their clothes off and jumped into the water. Holding on to a rock or digging their hands into the silt at the bottom of the stream, they would let the current hold them still as trout as they opened their eyes to the unparalleled beauty of an under-water world – a world that would inevitably disappear at the end of each breath. These tiny deaths would make them thoughtful and edgy for a while, irritated by each other and themselves because, by now, there was little to distinguish one from the other. Once, they watched a cow drown in a mine pit. Powerless and grief-stricken, they clung to each other as the terrible head roared in panic and the once-kind eyes dimmed and rolled back into the blood dark. At such times, Gabriel was comforted only by the warm-sand smell of Michael's temples or the tanned skin at the back of his neck and the familiar crests of dirt under his fingernails. Sometimes, when they were tired and lay down to rest together, keeping each other warm, out of the wind, Gabriel could no longer tell to which body his head belonged or whose heartbeat was pulsing in his ears.

Only hunger would drive the boys off the moor and into the valley where Uncle Gerry's cottage sat, irreversibly, in the hillside. They would come tumbling down the slope behind the house or trudging wearily like crusaders along the road, their broken swords beating at hedgerows. On one occa-sion, they returned to see Uncle Gerry speaking to a tall man in the yard. Uncle Gerry was leaning on his shovel, so that it seemed as if the other

59

man was looking down on him. The tweeds, too, made the stranger look important against the muck of the yard, although he did take off his hat in an effort to lower himself a little.

'It's my dad!' Michael shouted and quickened his step.

But Gabriel held back and pulled at his dirty fringe.

'C'mon, Gabe,' he called. 'Let's go and meet him.'

Still he hesitated and stepped into the shadow under the hedge; the light out there was the warm gold of midsummer.

'Don't be such a drag.' Michael, too, had stopped.

Gabriel wanted to shout and stamp his foot in frustration, but only pulled at a twig of bramble. This was what he'd dreaded. 'He won't like it if he sees us playing together. You know we are not supposed to.'

'My dad never said so . . .' Michael insisted, but stepped into the shadow just the same, so that they were standing, hidden, a few feet apart when they saw the man who was Michael's father hand over a thick envelope to Uncle Gerry, who took it – but uncertainly.

'What's that?' Gabriel hissed.

'No idea. Do you think they've met before?'

He did not reply, but stared in wonder at the two adults as they shook hands and smiled at each other before parting. The two boys watched in silence as Michael's father strolled casually along the lane towards the main road. The sun shone off the brilliantine in his dark hair and, as he walked, he loosened the knot in his tie.

'Perhaps Dad came to offer to help Uncle Gerry repair the old shed – he's very strong, you know,' Michael said, thoughtfully, and added, 'Honest – he is.'

Gabriel believed it and suddenly he hated his friend. Michael's father was no longer the absent Mr Bradley but this *dad* who had come between them. The hedge stank of rank sweat, he noticed, and he started to itch where a nettle had stung his shin the previous day. It was hateful. 'I don't think he could build a shed,' he lied. 'His hands don't look big enough.' A weevil was crossing a patch of sunlight at his feet and he crushed it with his plimsoll. It made him feel better – but only briefly. His despair had not crumpled.

'But they are!' Michael protested desperately. 'They're as big as a bull's hooves.'

'Bulls' hooves are sometimes quite small,' he said brutally and laughed.

The other boy looked at him incredulously. 'You're just being mean. Anyway, you don't know what my dad's hands are like – only I know that,' he said, sulking.

This was true, of course, and it only made it worse. 'And you're just stupid!' he flared, to shield himself.

Michael looked at him with dark eyes – and went away.

'Yeah, just go away!'

Gabriel remained for a moment, but trembled as a bumblebee bounced off a cluster of violets.

The shadows were longer and flies had gathered around the crushed beetle when Gabriel dared to venture out from under the shadow of the hedge. Michael was drawing on a piece of paper at Uncle Gerry's oak table when he entered the cottage. He could see that Michael had been crying – there were dirty streaks on his cheeks – and this made him cautious, as if he had just entered a room where somebody lay sick in bed. Michael did not look up but continued to push his crayons hard into the paper, the grain of the oak showing up in the drawing where the boy had coloured in. Gabriel went over to the sideboard and fiddled with some fossils that were displayed there. Just then, Uncle Gerry entered from the yard.

'All right, boys, let's try to make up, shall we?'

Neither boy looked up but Michael stabbed his drawing with a red crayon.

'Come on, you two; I'm sure this is just a misunderstanding. Tell me what happened.'

Still they kept their silence.

Uncle Gerry sighed. 'Well, whatever it is, you'd better get over it now. I need your help staking up the old shed for the chickens.'

This offered a welcome distraction for the two boys, in whose minds the cause of the argument was already beginning to fade. But the hurt on the one part and the shame on the other lingered a little longer as they helped to dig supporting poles into the ground at the back of the shed. Until Michael suddenly remembered: 'But wasn't my dad going to help you build a new shed, Mr Askew?'

'Mr Bradley? Whatever gave you that idea?' He sounded genuinely perplexed.

'Well . . .' He hesitated. 'It's just that we saw you talk and shake hands.'

Uncle Gerry laughed briefly but composed himself. 'Two men shaking hands does not necessarily indicate that they will build a shed together.'

'But why—?'

'Your father was just out for a walk and greeted me in passing.' The tone of his voice seemed to be closing the subject.

This sounded logical enough and the boys dared to glance sidelong at each other. After all, they did not yet know what it takes to build a shed. But then Gabriel remembered: 'But what was in the envelope?'

'What envelope?' This time he sounded less casual.

'The envelope Mr Bradley gave you!'

'He did not give me an envelope – you're imagining things.'

Gabriel stared in disbelief. 'But I saw it. He did. He *did*!' He was close to tears; everyone seemed to be against him today.

'It's true! I saw it too.' Michael was just as agitated.

Gabriel took a step closer to his friend and was rewarded with the sand smell of his skin.

Uncle Gerry looked at them in a strange way. 'Ah, bugger it,' he swore and kicked at one of the poles. 'All this secrecy – it's ridiculous – idiotic!'

The boys were silent and wide-eyed as the man put an arm over each of their shoulders and led them back into the house. He poured himself a drink from the Bell's bottle and took a sip before clearing his throat. 'Mr Bradley has very generously decided to fund an operation.' There: it was said.

'An operation? Are you sick, Uncle?' Gabriel was suddenly scared.

'No, Gabe, I'm fine . . .' He took another sip. 'Listen, my lad; ever since you were a little boy, your mother and I have been wanting . . . hoping . . . to mend your face. But it has not been easy; there was the war . . . We both lost a lot in the war and it has taken a while for us to get back on our feet. Your mother has been working very hard but there's never enough to put aside . . . and I . . . I have been rather useless lately. Not particularly reliable.' He laughed coarsely and drained his glass.

Michael took Gabriel's hand in his and the warmth of their palms protected them.

The man would not look at them as he poured another drink. 'Anyway, that's of no consequence now that Mr Bradley has come back.' He seemed to snarl the name, but Gabriel only noticed the last bit.

64

'Come back? Has he been here before?'

But Uncle Gerry ignored this question and continued: 'The long and the short of it is that Mr Bradley has offered to pay for your operation. He came here to discuss the details . . . You will be taken to the hospital in Exeter at the end of the summer – and your face will be as good as new by Christmas.'

'But why would my dad organise the operation? He has never even met Gabe.'

'Your father is a rich man, Michael – and that explains a lot. He can afford that which we fail to offer.'

But Gabriel, on his part, was not surprised. Hadn't he always known that he was not in charge of his own life? That things relating to him could be passed around in brown envelopes? That he was the wrong one that needed mending? Even Michael's dad knew it. And so Gabriel gravely accepted this telling of an operation, which he understood was offered as a form of kindness. And yet, at this hour of sunset, when the obscure light that fell through the window of the cottage was further dulled by the rose that climbed outside, Gabriel realised that there was another mystery to his life. Because, although his intuition told him that he was quite alone in the adult world, he knew that in a parallel existence, where he was expected to have a purpose, there *were* things that could be relied upon – insubstantial things, perhaps, but still reliable: the song of the river and the rustle of the trees, for instance, and the smoke of blossom through the hawthorn, the broken shadow of the standing stone and the watching eye of the red kite. And there was that other part which would make him whole. There was Michael.

Mr Askew found himself in Rowden's, lost amongst bird feeders, scented Hello Kitty stickers and Barbour oilskins. The hardware store catered for the gentleman farmer, burnt-out banker and stay-cation tourist alike. With a rising sense of panic, he slogged past stacks of purple-glazed pottery, sheepskin slippers and New Age calendars, only to bump his foot on a sit-on lawnmower, conveniently parked at the end of an aisle. He whimpered damply but soldiered on until he reached the homeware section where he was faced with a dizzying array of cleaning products. Their names seemed negatively correlated to their chemical content, so that, on reading the label, one would realise that 'Spring Fresh' was slightly more poisonous than 'Fields of Lavender', whereas 'Footprint' was not quite as filthy as it sounded. There was even a washing-up liquid dispenser shaped like a toy gun, called 'Sani-girl'. Mr Askew looked anxiously along the shelves until, at last, he found the 'Mr Muscle' section. Quickly, he grabbed a few bright coloured bottles and looked around for some rubber gloves and sponges. Thus fully armed, he started the retreat towards the till. Apologising profusely, he squeezed past a couple of equestrian-looking women – who stepped aside, as if to let pass the great unwashed – and a Japanese tourist studying a doorstopper in the shape of a skimpily-dressed fairy bending over unnecessarily to smell a flower at her feet.

The shop assistant had not yet grown out of her puppy fat, and her breasts bulged alarmingly out of a tight top, which read, 'BRAIN FIRST, BODY SECOND'.

'You get one of these half price with any purchase over ten quid,' she said, as her text-trained fingers stamped the figures into an old-fashioned till.

'I beg your pardon?'

She looked up at him then, but without interest, and gestured towards a rack of neon-coloured plastic key holders to one side. 'You get to choose one of them with your name on it.'

'Oh.'

'Only half price – it's a bargain – and they glow in the dark.'

He looked in despair at the names on the plastic rectangles. Gabriel did not appear amongst the Beverleys, Olivias, Alfies, Mohammeds and Dylans. 'That is—' he hesitated – 'most kind, but no thank you.'

'Are you sure?' She looked unaffectedly perplexed, one of her acrylic nails hovering uncertainly over the *enter* button.

'Yes, yes, quite sure.'

'Ah, well, you're really missing a bargain.' She was good at her job, and disappointed in him.

★   ★   ★

It had started to rain by the time he got out into the street and a mound of horse manure was disintegrating into the cobbles at his feet. He took a deep breath, holding the bag with his shopping tightly against his chest. He could no longer face going to the allotment today, and yet he could not stay at home – the new cleaning lady was expected at noon. How he wished that he had not let himself be inconvenienced in this manner. But this, he realised, like so many other things, was something that he would just have to endure. He started shuffling along Market Street, his mac flapping around his calves and his downturned gaze recognising every pebble, curb and dent along the worn-out route.

Outside Wilkinson's, something colourful stirred in the corner of his eye and he looked up to see the woman from the allotment holding a box of root vegetables in her arms. He was surprised, almost shocked, to see her there, out of their common element. Suddenly he was aware of the sour smell from under his pullover and held his arms closer to his body. She had spotted him and smiled as if about to say something. Just then a young man opened the door of the shop and exclaimed, 'Wow, look at that. Thanks so much – that's an amazing crop for this time of year.'

'Yes,' she laughed, 'I'll say it is.'

He saw that her wrists were too thin inside a cuff of gold bangles and wished he could have helped her carry the box. But the young man had already taken it from her and was turning back into the shop, gesturing for her to follow. He walked on then, but heard them behind him: 'Who was that? A friend of yours?'

'He lives up at Oakstone, I believe.'

'Ah, the famous *professor*.'

'I didn't know he was a professor.'

'Nah, he doesn't look it, does he?'

'Look it?'

'You know . . . clever.'

'No?'

'Don't get me wrong, he's a nice-looking geezer, but he seems a bit . . . well, peculiar – as if he needs looking after.'

'Don't we all.' She laughed.

'Well, now, you see!'

The door closed behind their gay voices and Mr Askew trotted on along the wet street, once again safely out of reach.

He had barely got into the house when she rang the bell; the floor was still wet where his mac had dripped. 'Oh dear,' he moaned. 'I'm not ready yet.' But there was no going back and there she was when he opened the door. She was peering out from under a clear umbrella dotted with hectic-looking ladybirds. Her blue eyes were the kind that would scan a room and not miss anything – and yet not quite *see*. He noticed that her face at that moment looked quite callous. He smiled at her and she looked appalled.

'Afternoon, Mr Askew. It's me, Doris Ludgate, come to clean the house.'

'How do you do?' He didn't quite catch her name, but politeness was always a form of protection.

'Can I come in, then?'

'Yes, yes, of course.' He stepped aside to let her pass. She was wearing a pair of wellingtons, but fished out the same white trainers from a plastic bag and put them down on the checked tiles in the hall. She kicked off the rubber boots with surprising agility and bent over to put on the trainers, her behind bulging dangerously and forcing him to take a step back until he was pressed against the wall.

She stood to face him. 'There. That's better. Now, where shall I start?'

This too was something he had failed to contemplate. Somewhere in a far corner of his mind, he heard his mother's voice: 'Don't you dare come in here and mess up my kitchen!' And just then, he remembered Michael's mum dropping the pancake spatula by the old Aga – and the greasy skid mark on the floor tiles. For a moment, he could smell her beauty in the room – the perfume on her skin – something sweet intermingled with the woodiness of iris. She knew all along and she did nothing. And yet I can't hold it against her. It was the first time I was persuaded by beauty in a person.

'Eh?'

'Oh, I beg your pardon, I was miles away.' He wondered whether there was dandruff on the back of his jumper.

'Were you, now?' She looked at him in dismay and he could see that the blue in her eyes had hardened into slate. 'Well, that's no good, is it? I have never been employed by somebody like you before but, as a new member of staff, I believe that the very least I can expect from the management is that they *listen* to me.' Strictly speaking, she had never been employed, of course, other than very briefly in a café and then by her husband, if you could call that employment. In the beginning, he had sometimes shouted at her to make herself useful and fix him some proper food for his tea and once or twice he had laughed hard and said that, if she hadn't been his wife, he might still have hired her as his whore. At the time, she thought that was quite flattering, meaning that she was good at *it*; he wasn't normally one to pay her compliments. But the thought of having a proper job again, like before she was married, had always been tantalising. Only last year, she had found a DVD in the *Gazette* with a free interactive induction course to corporate management for small-scale entrepreneurs. She had taken it into the village hall and put it into one of the computers. A nice young man from the college had helped her start it all up and then all she had to do was push the big button to the right. The young man had asked her if she was about to start her own business and she had

71

said no, not really, but perhaps she would become employed one day.

'Oh dear; but I'm not really your manager – I have just asked you to do some cleaning for a few hours . . .' His voice trailed off as she turned to glare angrily at him, but there was no way he could recoil further into the corner by the door.

'You may call yourself whatever you like, but what I mean to stress is that I still have my rights.'

'Yes, yes, naturally . . .' He nodded, albeit still hesitantly. 'But what exactly are they?'

'What?'

'The rights.'

'Oh.' She was beginning to sound – and feel – rather impatient and she spoke very slowly and clearly. 'As I said before, I expect you to listen.'

'Ah, of course . . . What was it that you said again?'

She sighed deeply and shook her head. '*Where* would you like me to start?'

'Didn't I say?' He blushed and laughed briefly. 'In the kitchen, please, if you wouldn't mind. The floor needs washing; it's a bit greasy, I believe.'

Once he had shown her to the kitchen and laid out a smorgasbord of cleaning products, brushes and sponges, he retreated upstairs to the small room he had chosen as his bedroom. His armpits were clammy and his heart was beating so hard he could see his chest juddering as he lay down on the narrow bed. Through the floorboards, he could hear the anger in her limbs as she moved around downstairs. The white trainers squeaked against the floor and her arms clanked a brush hard on the sink. *Crash!*

He winced as he remembered the weight of the sledgehammer in his hand as he flattened the woodlice against a stone.

'Let me try. Please, Gabe, let me.'

'No!'

Thud! Thud!

It was a day towards the end of that endless summer, the sun still warm; Gabriel was waiting outside the post office, where they had agreed to meet that morning. The plan was to make a new dam in the millstream under the bridge where the water was shallow and could easily be waded. Only Gabriel had been up early to buy a present for Michael in Mr Rowden's shop. It was a little boat with a cotton sail that could be tacked and fastened to nails at the aft. The hull was dark blue and the keel was red and Gabriel thought it looked quite authentic. He had been eyeing it in the shop window for weeks. He had used all his savings, but he reckoned it was the right thing to do – to make up for making Michael cry that time when Mr Bradley had come to see Uncle Gerry.

He had been waiting for a long time already; the sun had moved a little and he was now in the shade, so that he felt cold and a bit forgotten. He kicked a pebble across the tarmac and watched it settle in the middle of the road just as a car passed, coming in from the moor road. Then it was all quiet again. Waiting sometimes made him feel queer and he shuddered a bit. But, just then, he saw Michael on the other side of the street by Mr Rowden's shop and he stepped into the sun, raising his arm, shouting, 'Hey, Michael!'

Michael looked up and waved. Then he turned and looked back over his shoulder once, before crossing the street towards Gabriel.

'Hey!' Michael said, skipping a few steps. You could tell he was in a good mood.

'Here, I bought this for you.' He handed over the little sailing boat, gently. 'It can sail for real if you tie the sails to one corner. I thought we could try it in the stream today . . .'

Michael took the boat and looked at it. 'Wow!' he said, and it made Gabriel feel good.

'You like it, then?'

'Yeah, it's brilliant . . . But look, Gabe, I only came over to say that I can't come to the bridge today.'

'Oh?' Gabriel shrugged.

'Dad's taking me to the beach. And afterwards we're having fish and chips for supper, by the harbour, where the fishing boats come in.' Michael was beaming.

'All right,' Gabriel said, and looked down at his shoes. Why should he care about the fishing boats?

'Thanks for the boat, though. I'll test it at the beach and let you know how it works.'

'That's okay. I don't even like sailing boats. I prefer motorboats.'

The words rolled out over the road as hard as the pebble before. Gabriel frowned and bit his lip. It was not what he had meant to say. He wanted to say something else. But Michael was in a hurry, already crossing the street to where Mr Bradley's car was waiting, somewhere nearby.

Gabriel felt cold again, although he was standing in the sun, blinking hard.

And then he saw Mother outside Mr Rowden's. He was suddenly glad to see her, although he felt he didn't really want to talk to anyone at that moment – not to Michael, not to Mother – just put his head inside her summer coat where he knew it would be warm.

'Oh, dear. But, Gabriel, what *are* you doing?' Mother's laugh sounded nervous. 'In the middle of the street.' So that he felt he had to pull away from her and, when he did, he saw Mr Bradley's car parked just a few yards away and he saw Michael standing next to it and Mrs Bradley opening a door to put a hamper in the back seat, and he hoped that Mother hadn't seen but he knew by her body, by the way she held her breath, that she had. Suddenly, Mrs Bradley looked up, and Mum looked too, and Mrs Bradley's smile went strange and, for a moment, Gabriel thought she was going to say something – to call out to them. Only, he didn't want her to. He felt a vague sense of panic rising inside him and he took Mother's hand and pulled it hard and, for once, they both pulled in the same direction – away from the car where the Bradleys were getting ready to go to the seaside; away from Mrs Bradley, who wore a pale yellow short-sleeved summer dress. Her arms looked lovely and her dark brown hair, shining in the sun, was tied loosely with a yellow ribbon at the back. Because Gabriel had time to see all this before he pulled Mother away.

As they turned their backs on the car and started in the other direction towards the church, Mother's hand felt rubbery and strange, as if she too was cold and forgotten like he had been in the shade. He felt he ought to say something but he could not say anything, because of his mouth, the dryness that would smell stale and the feeling of *alone* that he remembered still, and what was there to say, anyway? It was very warm and the sun made sharp geometries of the world, triangles of light and dark, and Gabriel held on to Mother's hand all the way back to the cottage, even though he was already nine.

Perhaps the memory of the incident in the street still lingered somewhere in Gabriel's mind as he found himself at the back of Uncle Gerry's cottage a few weeks later with the big sledge-hammer. The summer was weary by now and so were their games. The weight of the sledgehammer felt good in his hand as he flattened the woodlice against a stone, his own desolation diminishing with each perfect thud. Michael was there, of course, a frantic shine in his brown eyes and his dirty fingers eagerly feeding more woodlice for the block. 'Let me try! Please, Gabe, let me!'

'No!'

Thud! Thud!

Michael with his rich dad, a father who afforded where others failed – and his hands the size of bulls' hooves.

Thud!

Fish and chips by the harbour.

Thud!

And then Michael's fingers were on the block, trying to steady a woodlouse for its sacrifice, but he did not pull his hand away quickly enough. Surely Gabriel would not have let the hammer fall on to those thin fingers? And yet this time there was a different kind of thud and a terrible scream. Gabriel stared at the fingers, which, for a brief moment, seem unharmed and abnormally white before there was suddenly blood everywhere. And, in all that bright panic and howling, there was a strange and terrible warmth inside Gabriel.

And so, at the end of that first summer, they ended up in hospital together – Gabriel having his face fixed and Michael three of his fingers. Because they were the best of friends, they were allowed to recover in the same ward. And, although they were not allowed to lie together like they used to up on the moors, behind their closed eyelids they would dream the same dreams of roaming and adventure. The green and blue dreams that race along serpentine roads with eight cylinders or merge thickly out of underground caves. Although they were supposed to be asleep – and the nurses, with their beautiful, cool hands smelling of soap and their kind, kind smiles, had pulled the curtain around each bed – Gabriel could still feel the warmth of Michael's heart against his, smell the nearness. Brothers in arms. Blood brothers.

The house was all too quiet. He must have fallen asleep but he was convinced that Mrs Ludgate was still downstairs. She would not have left without making herself known. He sat up on the bed and felt with his feet on the floor for his shoes. The room was cold and he rubbed his hands together and shrugged his shoulders before getting up. He pulled his cardigan down over his stomach but, to his dismay, this only made it ride up at the rear, exposing his lower back. How come my clothes are shrinking? he thought to himself as he started down the stairs. Yet another addition to the general catalogue of indignities. He found Mrs Ludgate bent over a framed photograph in the drawing room. It had been taken on the front steps sometime in the late forties or early fifties. He could feel an unreasonable anger rising inside him. 'What are you doing? I thought you said you were here to work.'

She stood back quickly, her throat reddening. 'I was just admiring this photograph,' she confessed. 'Is that your family?'

He glanced at the photograph, quickly. 'Yes.'

'Aww! Then that cute little boy must be you, is he?'

'Yes . . .' He was beginning to hate her.

'So you actually grew up in this house?'

'I . . . I lived here for a little while when I was very young,' he said, cautiously.

'I can't quite imagine a family living here – it seems so quiet . . .' and, after a second's thought, she added, 'It's a huge house for a single man, isn't it?'

'I wish you would mind your own business and get back to the cleaning.' He could not stop himself any longer – and they were both a bit frightened.

'All *right*, all right.' She pulled at her fleece jacket so that the border of sheep bounced along her hips. 'No bother; I was on my way, anyway. It took me all this while only to clean the kitchen – it was that filthy.' Suddenly she snorted. There was a lot at stake here – something she had realised when she saw the advertisement on Mrs Edwards' notice-board. Yes, she had known straight away and she had ripped it down quickly, in case anyone was watching, and hurried out of the post office without staying for the gossip.

'Good thing you hired me – you clearly can't cope on your own,' she said now, knowing it wasn't quite true. In any case, she wasn't particularly good at putting things in order. She gave a laugh, as if for emphasis.

Mr Askew frowned. He wasn't really listening,

thinking instead about how he'd got himself into this situation. There was something vaguely familiar – although unkind – about her face. He realised that there was no preventing her from coming back. If only, he thought to himself as he watched her puffed face laughing, she could dissolve in a pit of cow urine and quicklime, her tongue shrivelling up in her throat.

As she was leaving the room, her trainers making a squelching sound against the parquet, she looked back over her shoulder at the photograph. 'Anyway, you were a very lucky boy to grow up with all this. You look like a happy child.'

He went stiffly into the hall and opened the front door for her.

'Perhaps you knew my husband back then? He would be about your age – a few years older perhaps.' Her voice was too insistent, driving into his head like a screw.

'Goodbye, now,' he said, painfully, and, because she did not seem to have heard, he added, 'Bye-bye.'

When she had left, he stood for a long time in the doorway of the sitting room, looking at the photograph – at Michael's brown eyes smiling back at him.

CHAPTER 3

A single pink rose had come out since his last visit to the allotment and he was at once grateful for the lack of horticultural creativity in his predecessor, who had planted the roses – because the blowsy pink flower *was* pretty and, on this sunny Sunday in April, his equilibrium restored after Doris Ludgate's Friday visit, he could allow himself to be at peace. The herbaceous border was coming along fine, its green shoots stretching eagerly towards the warming sun.

'Good morning, Professor Askew.'

He had not noticed her approach and blushed for everything about himself that might be wrong when caught unawares.

'Good morning, Mrs . . .?'

'Sarobi,' she answered gaily.

'Oh, how do you do?' He might even have bowed.

Then they were quiet for a moment, not quite knowing how to proceed. She smiled at him and he remembered: 'I saw you deliver the vegetables to Wilkinson's the other day – they looked beautiful.'

'Wilkinson's? Oh, you mean the deli. Yes,' she

confirmed, 'I sell him most of what I produce and can't eat myself.'

He frowned. 'But you can't grow it all here?'

'No—' she laughed – 'I've got a small garden with a greenhouse behind my cottage.'

'Where's your cottage?'

'At the bottom of Church Lane.'

'Oh.' He did not want to know, all of a sudden.

'You'd recognise it straight away.' She laughed again. 'It's the only one with a pebble-dashed front – you know, that horrible gravel stuff.'

He tried to swallow.

'Are you all right?' she asked.

'Yes, yes, I'm fine.'

She looked at him closely for a moment before continuing, 'I'd love to have a small croft but, until that happens, I rent the allotment. There aren't many of my kind farming the land around here – let alone owning it.'

This was more than she had ever said before and he tried to take it all in. 'Your kind?' he mustered.

'Yes, you know – aliens.'

'Pardon?'

'I'm only kidding.'

And so she was, because her laugh was real and the bright colour and merriness of it made him laugh too and then an unexpected warmth inside him made him laugh a little more. She didn't seem to mind, so he said, 'I have a garden as well – but this allotment makes me feel particularly alive.'

'Yes, I know what you mean.' She was suddenly serious.

He could see that she was holding the skeleton of one of last year's leaves in her hand. She must have picked it up along the lane, where large elms grew in stately rows. It looked so fragile; the way she held it made him think of the wing of a butterfly.

She noticed him looking and said, 'Isn't it gorgeous? It reminds me of those Italian anatomical tables from the seventeenth century, where the spinal cords and nervous systems of humans have been laid out on an oak board.'

'Oh, yes! There are a couple in the Royal College of Surgeons in London.' He could not contain his enthusiasm. It was a place he knew well. He had often studied the anatomical boards and marvelled at how, in order to remove the nerves in one piece, those early physicians had placed the whole body on the board and dissected it slowly and methodically to leave just the nerves. At the end of the operation, the nervous system seemed to merge with the veins of the oak.

'I'm sorry,' she said. 'You probably think they are disgusting . . .'

'No,' he replied with emphasis, 'not at all.' He thought of the way the nerves grew from the spinal cord like the branches of the tree of life.

They smiled at each other again.

'Once, when I was a student, I was allowed to visit that museum alone, after hours.' He wanted to offer something back, for their sharing to continue. The building had been dark, he remembered now, but the display cases were vaguely lit from behind. He had stood there, and felt so reduced, in front of the bones of a giant. 'There's this giant – do you know the one I mean? – it's this sad freak who had to stand and be displayed in both life and death.'

'Yes, yes.' She nodded and he felt encouraged.

'And then, in one of the galleries, I came across all those specimens floating in glass jars.'

There had been the ovary of a cow, a lamb foetus, the beak of a cuttlefish, the foetus of a walrus, ventrally dissected. He shuddered as he remembered them now, but they had meant nothing to him then – nor had the embryos, tumours and placentas. But then . . .

'There were these pickled punks – you know, bottled babies, neatly arranged in rows according to size, starting with the very small. The labels would say things like "A female foetus, estimated to be in the ninth week of gestation" or, even worse, "A female foetus, about the time of birth". Quite hard to take, really . . .'

He had stood there, watching over them as they sank and sank in their drunken sleep. A still life of five siblings, two hundred years old and still floating blindly in their shared aquarium. Their tiny bodies gently bent as they slotted into each other – head to foot, back to front – like an imprint of the way they had lain together, nesting.

84

Their doll's hands were softly gathered and their mouths were open, their eyes closed, unseeing, as if they were singing in chorus – and not drowning alone.

'It's so sad when you look at these things without a scientist's mind . . .' She spoke very softly.

'I'm sorry. I didn't mean to depress you. I have never told anyone before . . .'

'No, no; I'm glad you told me. Somehow.'

He glanced at her and it was true: she did not seem depressed. There was a brightness around her and it made him feel lighter too.

'Your English is very good,' he said, to change the subject. 'Have you been in this country for long?'

'No, only a few years . . . But I studied medicine at Cambridge in my youth.'

'I'm sorry; I didn't realise that you were a professional.' He frowned again.

'But I'm not. My father died while I was at university and I had to go back to Afghanistan to marry – and after that I could not practise.'

'Is your husband in England too?'

'No, no, I was widowed many years ago – my husband was a lot older than me.'

'I'm sorry.' He bit at his moustache out of habit.

'Not at all.' She laughed again but this time the sun did not settle in her eyes. 'Are you married?'

'Me? No, no . . .' he said, keeping it soft.

She nodded and studied his face for a moment, so that he had to look away. High above their heads, bands of cirrus rode in from the west, slicing the skies as they went.

'Anyway,' she said, 'I must get on with the weeding.'

'Yes, yes, it's a good day for it,' he said, gratefully accepting her gift of escape.

That afternoon, Mr Askew walked down the hill and turned left at the old twill factory to follow the millstream to the river. He stood for a while at the top of the stone bridge, looking at the still waters. A carpet of white anemones pulled itself across last year's fallen leaves. There was a whisper of green in the trees and Mr Askew closed his eyes and trained his senses to the sounds and smells of spring. The song of a young warbler ascended and descended in the willows and a rodent fretted in the undergrowth, trying to get ready in time for it all. He walked on, following the lane up a small hill until he reached a hamlet. A dog barked from behind a fence but apart from that there was no indication that anyone was living in the cottages and barns, still farming the land and enjoying their ancient rights of pasture on the moor. He continued along a path strewn with small rocks and wondered why it had not been better paved, as it was the main access to the commons. Just before the moor gate, he passed the remains of an old chapel that had once served as a comfort and warning to travellers about to leave the civilised world behind and venture out into the untamed wilderness. It seemed odd on a day like this that anyone should ever have been so terrified of the moors, he thought, as he lifted the latch of the cattle gate.

Back in the Middle Ages, people around the moor would have wondered at the unknown that lay outside the boundaries of the cultivated land. During the summer months, they would follow their stock on to the hills and downs in the morning and look at the remains of earlier settlers. But standing stones and ruined prehistoric settlements would mean little to medieval Christians who saw life as a journey in time and space, from the cradle to the grave. They would have little concept of history, and the monuments on the moor would have been unsettling. Uneasy minds explained them as the works of giants or saints, and chapels and stone crosses were erected along the routes around the moor to ward off evil and establish the good force of Christianity. How much braver the prehistoric settlers were, thought Mr Askew to himself as he started out towards the tor on the horizon. The coconut smell of the gorse sieved through the air and, in the distance, sheep seemed to grow out of the turf like champignons. He straightened his back as his feet found firmer ground again. It was an easy stroll on this high ground and he was soon at the foot of the rock. From this angle, the tor looked like an ancient stone fort of the crusaders in the Holy Land. But rather than being constructed by holy warriors, this pile had been shaped by ice and storms over thousands of years – the forces of nature, coming together in a clash of wills.

The views from the summit on this spring day were of gently rolling hills and pasture, lush with fresh grass. Below him to the west the early-evening sun was resting in the ridge and furrow of a long-forgotten field. But Mr Askew knew only too well that, with a change in weather, the same view could turn into a lunar landscape of barren ground: a landscape that threatened and terrified.

He started scrambling around the rocks, his mottled hands smoothing their rough surfaces, until suddenly he found what he was looking for: a large rock basin, perfectly eroded out of the granite. It was filled with rainwater that darkly mirrored the torn fleece of scattered clouds. To any observer, the stone bowl would appear bottom-less – an opening into the underground or a well of the unknown. He shivered as he looked at the still surface and remembered a distant day, so very unlike this one – a day in autumn when the summer had already died and low clouds of Atlantic mist stroked the hills and downs, removing the skies.

Some might have expected that mending the wrong would take away the evil. Anyone would have thought so; it was like when something was killed it went away forever. And it was, after all, what everyone had been taught. But Gabriel knew better. Or, if he didn't know, he had come to realise – a bit like how, now that he was nine and a half, he understood certain things that he hadn't understood when he was only seven, say, or eight. Yes, he knew that mending was just mending, a simple fix of the physical, or a new set of clothes, or a stupid sailing boat with a red keel. Mother didn't realise this, nor did Uncle Gerry or Mr Bradley, who could afford. Not even Michael, whose face was the dearest thing.

But, when school started again, Gabriel knew that nothing had changed and that he still had to run.

And so he ran with the blood taste in his mouth. His plimsolls were black with bog water and muck, his sunburnt legs streaked with dirt. He knew no one would follow his run through the bull's paddock, where hooves had pitted the turf into mud and puddles. Panting, he reached the firmer ground of the commons, the landscape pulsing in his eyes as he looked towards the summit of the tor. He was treading on his own shadow now and slipped once on fresh sheep dung. He hurried up the slope on hands and knees, the scree cutting into his palms. The great rocks of the tor were like a band of awful giants, resting at the close of the day. He found the solid embrace of one and settled in the crook of its arm. Pulling his knees towards his chest, he felt in his pocket for comfort. His hands were shaking as he pulled out a sticky wand of liquorice. Gradually, his breathing settled and the blaze in his eyes dwindled. His shoulders loosened and his legs stretched out on the kind grass. Far below, the village, as small as a world, made the shape of a swallow's tail in the newly harvested fields. He looked west, towards the high moor; chafed by the ice sheet and polished by wind, it was smooth as fur. He touched the granite at his back. It was not altogether cold, although the sun was no longer strong enough to heat it during the day and put that lovely smell in it. He knew these rocks by heart: the strange piling of stone, the nooks that were large enough for him to hide in but small enough not to be found, the large rock basin, perfectly eroded out of the granite. It was filled with rainwater, the surface as blank as a mirror.

'You're still a freak, you know,' they'd told him, so that the rock basin, when he looked into it, threw back Gabriel the freak.

And yet he loved this place, perhaps more than any other. It was his castle. How could he have known that it would all start to go wrong when he agreed to bring Michael there one day after school?

It was a sodden day in autumn. The mist heaved. Michael was leaning over the rock basin, his dark fringe falling like a curtain in front of his eyes and his right hand, the damaged one, reaching for the gloomy pond.

'Careful, you wouldn't like to fall in.' He could hear his own unnatural voice in the misty void.

'C'mon, Gabe; this is terrific.'

Gabriel leant over the basin and peered at the blank disc of water. Both their faces were reflected there, side by side. They looked remarkably alike.

'I can hardly tell which face is yours and which is mine,' he said, and stretched out his hand, as if to touch each of the faces in the pool. 'Apart from my scar . . .'

'Yeah, well, we are the same, aren't we?' Michael laughed and continued, 'If we had a long stick with a hook at the end, we could fish out all sorts of things.'

'What things?'

'You know, sacrificed stuff, like virgins and chopped-off hands.'

'Virgins?'

'Yep, they'd be in there.' He knew that for sure.

'What, like the Holy Virgin?'

'No, stupid! Other ones like . . . Well, you know – naked ones with silky skin.'

'Wow!'

'Yeah, I keep telling you.'

'But why would they be in there?'

'*Because* this is where the Druids used to sacrifice to the pagan gods.'

'Would there have been lots of blood?' Gabriel asked, stepping anxiously on to a boulder.

'There was *soo* much blood that the whole tor would light up like a red lantern at sunset. Even ships off the coast could see it and would sometimes run aground, thinking it was a beacon.' He would not have it otherwise.

'No!'

'What? You don't believe me? I'll show you.' He started to scramble over the rocks on his hands and knees.

'You look like a goat,' Gabriel sniggered, but he felt uncertain as Michael disappeared into the mist. 'Hey – where did you go? Wait for me.'

'Hurry up, then!'

He was somewhere nearby and Gabriel followed the echo of his voice into the damp blanket. He was suddenly afraid. Dark figures, cloaked and hooded, seemed to be stepping out of the fog like silent sentinels as he stumbled past the strange rock formations. Everything had gone ghostly quiet – even his own breathing seemed muffled; the only noise was the blood raging in his ears. He swallowed hard and called hoarsely: 'Michael?'

There was no reply. In order to calm himself down, he started singing under his breath: 'Put the blame on Mame, boys . . .' It helped a bit and he sang it a little louder, the same line over and over again. 'Ouch!' He cried out in pain as he hit his knee on a boulder.

There was a burst of giggles from only a few feet away as Michael appeared from behind a rock, vaguely at first, and then as his usual self. 'Ha! You were really frightened, weren't you?'

'No, I wasn't.' His face was burning, his skin all prickly under his clothes.

'Who's Mame, eh? Is she your secret girlfriend or something?'

He started to protest, but Michael interrupted: 'Never mind; I don't care. Come here, though. Look at this.' He kneeled and looked over the side of a large rock which fell vertically down into the mist. 'Look!' He pointed at a streak of rusty red on the face of the granite.

Gabriel gasped. 'What *is* that?'

Michael moved closer to his side and whispered in his ear, 'This is where the blood used to run, after the Druids chopped people's heads off . . . You can still smell it, if you get close enough.'

They both leant over to smell the rock.

'Do you smell it?'

'Yeah . . . It smells a bit like metal.'

They sat up then, huddled together with their feet sticking out over the edge, each drawn into his own imagination. This mutual silence was warm and close. Then there was a faint draught coming up from the valley to the west and the boys trembled slightly in the damp cold. But there was something else too, something in the air that had not been there before. It sounded like a distant moaning or chanting, which drifted back and forth on the breeze. The sound would grow weaker for a while, only to return with unexpected intensity. *Ho, ho, hooo,* it sounded.

And then, suddenly, something large came swooping up out of the mist – and, as soon as it was gone, it reappeared from the other direction. At once, there was a great din of noise, horrible howling and screaming, as a number of hooded figures came out of the mist and hurled themselves at the boys. Gabriel let out a protracted sound of agony as he realised that they were no longer hidden by the mist but terribly exposed – and completely trapped. Michael, on the other hand, was kicking and making the sort of noises a mountain lion might make. But to no avail. The hooded creatures were soon dragging the boys over the rocks, back towards the basin. Gabriel was quiet now, letting himself be pulled along, removing himself into that familiar space where he could not be hurt, but Michael was still furious. 'Let go, you bullies! Bloody Nazis!' he screamed. Then he looked up and fell silent as, out of the murkiness, they saw Jim of Blackaton standing stiffly by the basin with a large knife clasped in his raised hands. Just behind him was his faithful lieutenant Billy Dunford, standing with his legs apart, hands on his hips, his ginger hair pasted to his head in the mist.

'Bring forth the prisoners who are to be sacrificed!' boomed Jim, in the voice of Reverend Colthorpe reading the sermon on Sundays.

Gabriel was pulled up straight by a couple of the faceless bullies, his arms fixed behind his back, a hand tugging painfully at his hair to force his head up.

'Why are these prisoners being sacrificed?' thundered Jim of Blackaton.

Billy stepped forward and cleared his throat, as if he was a herald about to make a proclamation. 'This one—' he pointed at Gabriel – 'is about to be sacrificed because he went and mended his face, pretending he's no longer Bunny-boy, thinking he could escape his fate.'

There was some hooting and cheering at this.

'And him—' he turned and pointed at Michael, who was pale and drawn in the arms of his captors – 'he's being sacrificed because he's an irritating little twat who protects Bunny-boy.'

Gabriel could see that the hooded creatures holding on to Michael were just some of the boys from school with their blazers pulled over their heads. He wanted to tell Michael this to make him feel better, but Michael would not look at him.

'All right; bring the first prisoner forward.'

If only, Gabriel thought, as he was pulled forward towards the basin, they had not been so trapped in the fog; if only he could see the sky and hear the river, he would be able to let a part of himself slip away and fly against the sun, across the heath and into the trees. Then his head was pushed down over the basin, where he saw his own eyes mirrored in the still surface. He saw in that standing pool his own dark eyes, so deep with dread, and the new scar running from under his nose like a zip fastener, ready at any time to be pulled open.

Jim came forward, the knife terrible in his hands. Its steel hard and dull in the damp, dirty light. So cold where it touched his neck and pressed against his skin. And the warmth of the vomit that came out of him into the basin – not blood, but vomit – smelling sour and sticking to the inside of his nose, making him cry and choke, and all the time Michael's voice in his ears, screaming.

Screaming, 'Let him go! Don't hurt him! I'll give you anything you want. You can have my brand new Captain Marvel poster – he's from America and much cooler than Superman.'

The steel of the blade was still cold against the goosebumps: aching, shaving.

'Just say what you want – I'll give you anything!'

'Really?'

'Anything.'

'Okay, Fluffy, you will give me anything I want at any time – and you're not allowed to deny me.'

'Yes, yes; just let him *go*!' Sobbing now.

'And the Captain Marvel poster.'

Just a nod.

'Well, you can have your filthy Bunny-boy to yourself, then. A deal is a deal.'

The icy blade no longer chafing and the others gone – just the two of them, as usual. He knew it was all his fault. None of this would have happened if it had not been for him – if it hadn't been for him being a freak.

'I'm sorry.'

Michael shrugged.

'I'll get you a new Captain Marvel poster. I'll ask Uncle Gerry—'

'Can't you see it's not about the stupid poster? I don't care about the bloody poster. It's about so much more.'

And, although he knew in his heart that from now on it would never be quite enough, he said it again: 'I'm sorry.'

I am remembering too much, Mr Askew thought to himself. Is this really necessary? I had managed to forget so well. He looked around. The basin was no longer a sacrificial pool, the red lava on the rocks no longer thickly flowing blood, and the fog had cleared over the years. There was no longer anything to see – and yet he shivered. He looked out across the gentle heath, where the setting sun was painting its last impressions of the day. He slept badly these days, afraid to be dragged down into those nightmares where bright faces flashed in the dark, and more afraid still to be swooped back from the depths of sleep and wake into a dawn of dirty light. For a while, since his arrival in Mortford, he had assured himself that the forgetfulness of old age would filter his dreams and protect him from the worst of it. But, whilst looking for his reading glasses or fretting over escaped names in the crosswords on a Sunday, he knew that he was only safe as long as he managed

97

to keep his mind above the surface of the pool of memory.

For the irony of an ageing mind is that it opens itself as brutally and unflinchingly to the hidden depths of its own past as the eye of a snowy owl to the night's prey.

CHAPTER 4

There were days when Doris Ludgate felt a little low. Nothing much would improve things and she might allow herself to lie down on the couch for a moment and be a bit dizzy. She would never try to question or explore this melancholia. Once the heavy feeling around her head had passed, she would brush it away, as one might a fly, because she must go on being what she was – the person she had become. It was no use to fancy otherwise. If a brief nap did not help, daytime television certainly would. There was so much to learn from it. The talk shows alone were *so* improving. Sometimes, when there was a number to ring, she would call up to offer her opinions. She liked chatting to the operator. She did not like to be on her own – she had always been a sociable person. But circumstances had made her lonely.

On other days, she would arrange ornaments on the mantelpiece – there were two Royal Doulton Bunnykins and a row of hand-painted plaster kittens – and dust the china that was displayed on the Welsh dresser. The dinner set was one of the better things that had come from her husband's side, collected by his mother. It *was* Wedgwood, although not one of the better patterns. However, one of the more recent pieces, a side plate displayed in the centre, bore the signature of the Duchess of York on the back. These objects would cheer her up, even on the days when bittersweet memories of life before marriage would make her mouth go long and ugly.

She had grown up on the coast to the north, an only child in a cold house. Her bedroom window faced the sea. All year round the changing light in that room would help her understand the world outside – it whispered of the hurt blue of winter, the blush of spring, the heavy green of summer and the harmony, the symmetry of autumn. Sometimes, she would sit for hours looking out of the window; her reflection stared back at her then, so that she looked double. When she was little, she would imagine that there was somebody sitting next to her, in silence. A sister, perhaps.

Even now, she would sometimes dream about being back in that room. Her feelings in the dream were very different: light and warm. When she slept, the room came back and, when she woke, she had to start looking for it all over again.

After school, she had gone straight to the Harbour Front Café to work as a waitress. She had wanted to do this for as long as she could remember – that and be married. The waitresses all wore pink frocks with American-style pink-and-white checked aprons. It suited her complexion, as she had always known it would. She met her husband in the café. He walked in one summer afternoon with a group of friends and put his hand on her bum as she leant over to place his order in front of him. It was fish 'n' chips and a pint of cider. So she married him shortly after her eighteenth birthday and went away to live at his farm, where her parents-in-law still lurked in the corners and she had a baby who grew up and went away.

Her husband had always maintained that her arse was her greatest asset, but then he had never really got to know her properly, and rarely from the front. She recognised that this was not his fault; she had never fully opened up to anyone, let alone herself. She had enough trouble trying to find out what other people were thinking and doing; she began to thrive on their embarrassments and misfortunes, as they would lessen her own.

But when it came to her new employer, the *professor* up at Oakstone, however much she prodded, she could not get to the information she wanted. He remained closed to her and, for this reason, she felt she must defend herself against him – or even begin to attack, as she did that day in May.

He had not been at home when she called in for duty and she had waited outside the front door, feeling hot and bothered. When he finally turned up, he did not seem at all perturbed but bumbled on in his usual manner about some blue poppies in his allotment garden.

'Poppies are red,' she informed him, 'or possibly pink.' She was determined not to let him know that she had minded being made to wait.

'These ones are special; they are Himalayan poppies and the most beautiful, tender things you have ever seen. Mrs Sarobi says . . .' But he stopped himself in time.

Her smile was more like the grimace of a gargoyle than an expression of a human emotion – but she smiled and smiled.

He looked at her strangely. 'Are you all right?' There might have been actual concern in his voice, if he had cared.

'Why should I not be fine? Anyway, perhaps you could open up so that I could get on with my work?'

'Yes, yes,' he muttered and fumbled with the keys in his pocket.

He held open the door for her and she went inside. The white trainers squeaked her contempt on his tiled floor.

'Who's this Mrs Sarobi, anyway?' she probed.

He winced. 'Nobody . . . Somebody I have met at the allotments.'

'Ah, that colourful one. What is she, anyway? Indian?'

'I believe she's Afghani.'

She sucked her teeth thoughtfully.

'She grows vegetables for that young man at Wilkinson's – she's his main supplier.' Why did he feel the need to justify?

'Supplier,' Mrs Ludgate murmured. It *was* a hateful word. 'That might be useful, of course, but an Indian one is never quite as refined, is it?'

'Afghani,' he corrected.

'Anyway, the foreign lady isn't the point here; the point is that my husband told me once about this other guy who used to live here – some oddball called Bradley,' she hinted, her voice casual enough.

'Did he, now?'

'By the way, why are all these boxes standing here in the hall? They are really in the way.'

'In whose way?'

'In *my* way. It's very difficult to clean a house full of boxes. Why haven't you unpacked them yet?'

'It didn't feel necessary.' He no longer noticed them; the shadows had their furry arms around them.

She let out a sniff of disapproval. 'Anyway, this Bradley person used to play the organ in the Moor Cross Inn. But that's not all of it—'

'Look, I'm not interested. Hadn't you better get to work?' He could hear his own unnatural voice – and the tremor in it. He was beginning to feel sick, in spite of the blue poppies.

She looked at him with searching eyes, her bosom heaving in its fleecy folds. He was relieved she was not literate enough to read his face. But she caught the look in his eye and sensed that she had the upper hand.

'Mr Ludgate told me him and Bradley were quite friendly, growing up. The Bradley boy would do anything he asked. Anything at all,' she affirmed.

'I would prefer to be left alone – in there.' He pointed towards the door to the study at the other side of the hall.

'Suit yourself. You're used to being alone, aren't you? No change there, then.' She laughed so that he almost missed the insinuation in those last words.

But, just as he opened the door to the study, he remembered: 'What is your husband's Christian name?' There were a couple of dead flies on the floor inside the door. He pushed at them carefully with the toe of his shoe, sweeping them to one side.

'Jim. But he called himself Jim of Blackaton, after the farm.'

The light in the hall seemed hard, metallic almost, as he stared at the woman he had brought into his house.

'Ah, well. No more dilly-dallying. Time to muck out this pigsty – you'd better stay out of my way,' advised the ardent cleaner.

'You said you would do anything I asked.'

Gabriel could see that Michael was in serious trouble but did not know what to do. He stood a few feet away, paralysed like an animal presented with a threat, as the boys gathered around his only friend.

'You got my Captain Marvel poster, didn't you? It's from America – my dad brought it back.'

Gabriel heard a dull thump, like when a satchel is dropped on grass, and then a choked cry from Michael.

'You think I care about a silly poster? I burnt it.'

'No!'

There was a new pitch in Michael's voice, a tone that Gabriel had never heard before. It was more like something he had once seen in the upturned eye of a rabbit, caught under the claws of a Harris hawk. And still he could not move.

'Anyway, I'll only ask you one last time, Fluffy – or I'll pull at your fingers and break them all again, got it?'

No reply.

'OK, this is the last time I ask you: eat this toad.'

Through the guard of bodies, Gabriel could see Michael shaking his head furiously whilst pressing his mouth shut. Billy was standing in front of him with a dead toad in his hand. Long legs were hanging limp from its warty body and its stomach was swelling with post-mortem gas. Gabriel was sweating now. What should he do? What would Michael have done if the situation had been reversed – like it used to be? Michael would have done *something*, but Gabriel was unable to move. Always unable to move. He opened his mouth. His throat was dry, choking with fear. 'Stop!' he squawked. But nobody seemed to hear – or, if they did, they no longer cared.

He was watching a snail make its way across the kitchen window. There was something vaguely perverse about the way it pressed itself on to the glass, leaving a slimy trail in its slow wake. Something lighter flickered past at the edge of his vision – a moth, perhaps, or a butterfly – and was lost. The snail, in the meantime, hadn't progressed. Pathetic. *Disgusting*. With some force, he opened the back door and pulled on his boots. Outside, he threw the snail to the ground and crushed it under the heel of his boot. There! It was done. Fragments of hard shell squashed into the pale flesh. He was breathing hard, satisfied with the virtues of this tiny murder. Satisfied, yes. And then, once more, he felt the pain in his heart and looked away.

From then on, they would not leave Michael alone. There were to be countless other times over the years, like the day Mr Bradley had given them each five shillings to spend at the travelling fair, which had come to the banks of the river. They were still the best of friends, but they were both taller now, Gabriel's scar was no more than a pale parenthesis over his lip and Michael's damaged hand was strong again. But Michael had changed in more ways. The river-green glint of mischief was no longer in his eyes; he had been wearing himself to a shadow. Where before he would have asked why, he was now gravely accepting. And whereas only a few years previously he would have tossed the sun out of his hair and laughed bravely at the open skies, his smile suddenly seemed as brittle as glass. And, more importantly, he was no longer able to conjure up that parallel, imagined world which had been their own, the world that had protected them – in the beginning. But then all best friends – friends of a certain age – must lose something along the way.

On that day of the fair, at the hour of sunset, when the fairy lights turned their backs on everything that was grey and porridgy and opened the door to a world of mystery and strangeness, even Michael seemed to regain something of his old self.

'Look, Gabe – look at that!'

Illuminated dragonflies, as large as cows' heads, were hovering over the reeds at the riverbank and, standing amongst them, dressed only in a black corset, a young woman was swallowing arrows lipped with fire. A tattoo of a snake curled around her upper body.

'Wow!' said Michael, but Gabriel, impatient for more, pulled him along towards the main entrance of the fair. Wide-eyed and open-mouthed at the wonder of it all, they strolled along to the cheerful tunes of the fairground organs. People from villages as far away as Ramland swarmed around them, their bodies hidden in the shadows, their faces weirdly brightened and clown-like amongst the colourful lanterns suspended overhead.

There were a couple of rides with gaily painted horses or flying saucers going round in a circle, but those were for kids and the boys quickly ignored them in favour of the games. At one stall, you could throw balls at the china on an oak dresser, the plates scattering in heaps at the feet of the small, dark man behind the counter. The boys liked to watch the destruction, but would not spend their own coins, as there were no prizes to be won. Mainly grown men would come up to throw balls at the china, their faces red and furious. The little swarthy man would laugh and call out in an accented voice, 'Come along and relieve your frustration. Only three-pence for some longed-for peace of mind. Yes, sir, that's it! Give it to them! Better than hitting the wife, eh?'

Michael had stopped in front of a cork-rifle stall. The background was a painted desert landscape with scattered cone-shaped hills and cacti. When the game started, Red Indians on horseback would pop up and disappear and, if you hit enough of them, you got to choose a trophy. Michael was staring hard at the row of trophies at the top of the stall.

'Look at that, Gabe,' he said in a husky voice and pointed towards a small vase in blue glass with little forget-me-nots painted on it. 'Isn't that pretty?' His eyes were strangely intense as he looked back at Gabriel.

'Yeah, it's okay, I suppose . . .'

'I'll try to win it for my mum.'

Gabriel had almost forgotten Michael's mother. He had not been around to Oakstone much for a couple of years and Michael's parents were rarely seen in the village; they had a maid to do their shopping. But now he recalled her doe's eyes and soft hands and felt a warmth spreading from his stomach. 'Yeah, we can take turns.' He too wanted to win the trophy for Mrs Bradley.

Michael looked at him feverishly and said, 'No, I want to win it myself,' and each word was rolled into a perfect marble in his mouth, knotted inside with all the things he did not say.

'All right.' What did he care, anyway?

Michael paid his threepence, took aim, shot – and missed. The rifle looked real enough, the Red Indians were bright and fierce, but the dull pop of the wasted cork was disappointing. But Michael was not deterred. His eyes were fixed on the painted desert where the Indians would appear out of its single dimension. He did not miss again, but he needed a full score to win the blue vase.

'Come on, Michael; let's move on. Don't waste more money on that silly game. The Indians don't even look real.'

But Michael was calm now. 'I *need* to win it,' he said, 'but you don't have to wait – I'll catch up.'

There was something about the situation and Michael's determination that made Gabriel stay. And suddenly he too wanted Michael to win the trophy. He saw quite clearly why his friend needed to present his mother with the cheap blue vase – the grail that cupped all the joys and all the sorrows of his childhood as he left those enchanted, cruel years behind and climbed the first step of adulthood.

The air around them went still as cork after cork hit its target. Gabriel kept his fingers crossed in his armpits and, once, he even closed his eyes; perhaps he said some kind of prayer. And, when all the Indians were slain, Michael flicked a 'Yippee!' into the sparkled night as his child's pleasure soared once again and for the very last time.

The spell was broken and Gabriel laughed and hugged his friend. The man behind the counter smiled and congratulated Michael on a terrific shot as he handed over the trophy and a bonus sheriff's star.

'Yeah! I'm the best sheriff this side of the Rio Grande,' he jeered and fired an imaginary revolver out of his free hand. Gabriel smiled and boxed his friend's arm, because he dared not hug him again. And Michael smiled back at him, his strength renewed with the achievement.

And so they tumbled on deeper into the magical night until they found themselves in front of a sign reading *Dr Buster's Sideshow*. Gold-painted boards had been mounted in front of a red tent. Gabriel stared in fascination at images of giants and dwarfs, a lady with a long beard, a seal-boy with flippers instead of arms, a half-man, half-woman, naked above the waist, which looked down from the golden boards. Presiding over them was the smiling figure of Dr Buster, with a tall hat and red bow tie. A speech bubble emerged from his mouth with the text *Alive! The thrill of thrills! The world's strangest freaks!*

Gabriel pulled at Michael's sleeve. 'We must go in there.' His voice could hardly make it out of his mouth.

'No, I don't want to,' Michael said and stepped back.

He was dumbstruck. 'Why not?'

'We don't know what we might find in there.'

'But we do, don't we?'

'Yeah . . . Perhaps that's why I don't want to go in.' His voice was clear as water and he seemed to stand alone in the grey light.

'Don't be a chicken; come on, now.'

He moved forward and Michael followed reluctantly. They paid sixpence each to a man with no arms. They stared in disbelief as the man, who sat on a high stool, collected the money with a curled foot and put it into a tin box. He rolled his eyes in a crazy grimace and gestured for them to enter through a red velvet curtain.

Inside was an anteroom with curtained openings into a number of passages. A chandelier with dripping wax candles was suspended from a metal hook in the canvas roof. They heard a noise to their left as a midget, dressed in a tuxedo, stepped out of the shadows to greet them. 'Good evening, gentlemen! Welcome to the house of Dr Buster.'

Just then, a fully-grown man entered from one of the covered passages. It was the man with the tall hat and red bow tie they had seen on the board outside. 'You're most welcome! I have been waiting for such fine company as yours. And you shall not be disappointed. My menagerie consists of some of the most celebrated and wonderful freaks of nature that you will ever have seen.' The man's eyes looked very dark, as if they had been lined with kohl, and his face had been painted white. He had a broad American accent.

Michael moved a step closer to Gabriel. From somewhere inside the passages, they could hear laughter and music from a piano.

'You have already met Alfred, "the bust that speaks and moves its goggling eyes". Not bad, eh? I found him in Montana. It seems like an unfortunate soul is born every minute in Montana. That backward state alone keeps me in business, even in these hard times.'

Gabriel did not quite understand and swallowed hard.

'But I am sorry,' the American doctor continued, 'you will find me boring, talking about myself. You seem like clever English boys, all raised on lamb, choral music and poetry, no doubt. Well, I have got some poetry for you!' He tilted back his head, closed his terrible eyes and recited in a booming voice,

'All out-o'-the-way, far-fetched, perverted things,
All freaks of nature, all Promethean thoughts
Of man, his dullness, madness, and their feats
All jumbled up together, to compose
A Parliament of Monsters.

'Ha! Can you tell me who wrote that, then? No, I thought not. And yet it was your own precious William Wordsworth.'

'Let's get out of here,' Michael whispered in Gabriel's ear, but Gabriel did not seem to have heard.

'Ah, you're impatient, I can see. Would you like to step into my house, then?'

'Yes, sir,' Gabriel managed, and, with a bit of courage, 'I mean, yes, please, sir.'

The doctor laughed and the midget at his feet giggled and skipped around in a strange dance. 'Okay, you may choose your passage, but you may not choose the same one.'

'Gabe, I don't want to go on my own,' Michael wheezed.

'It's okay, Michael; it's not dangerous, just weird. It won't hurt you, I promise,' he said, being the older of the two. And then he suddenly remembered:

'Anyway, it won't happen to you – you have to be born this way.'

Michael was not convinced, but nodded, holding the blue vase to his chest.

'I'll go in there—' Gabriel pointed to a passage on the left – 'and you can go in there, and then we meet on the other side.' He ushered Michael towards the passage next to his own.

Looking around, he saw the American lighting a cigarette and chatting to the midget, who had stopped dancing. They looked quite normal all of a sudden, but, as the doctor caught Gabriel watching them, he transformed his face back into the crazy mask again and shouted, 'Go on, my boy. Go on.'

Gabriel smiled encouragingly at Michael, then he turned to the passage he had chosen for himself and pushed aside a curtain of silver-foil tassels. Inside was a corridor of mirrors. They lined the walls, the ceiling and the floor. He stepped hesitantly and was immediately met by myriad versions of himself. 'Oh!' he said, and held out a hand, which touched nothing. It was hot and suffocating in the passage and he began to feel uneasy. He walked on and the mirrored path seemed to fork and curve. It was as if the space was a lot larger on the inside than on the outside. He followed one of the forks and was immediately lost. He tried to look down at the floor, but the path had divided into a maze of possible offshoots and he could not tell one apart from the other. Ever since he was very young, he had avoided mirrors and now he was suddenly faced with a thousand reflections of his own image and none of them recognisable. He could feel a deep dread rising in his throat and smiled uncertainly, perhaps apologetically, at one of the strangers – only to be met by his own horrid, mended grin, copied a thousand times. The eyes which watched him from every angle looked like pieces of broken glass. But there was something else in all the faces that surrounded him, something quite familiar. At first he could not put his finger on it, but, as he stared harder at the reflections, he recognised the features hidden in the mask of his own face. 'Michael?' he whispered in surprise. 'Is that you?' He could hardly breathe now and stepped quickly towards one of the characters, which blurred as he moved, and inevitably hit his face hard on a mirror. 'Ouch!' He was convinced it was a nightmare and he closed his eyes tightly in an effort to remember the tree by the river that had comforted him so many times in the past. His hand seemed to stroke it and he could smell the muggy green of its bark.

'Gabe!' Michael's voice shouted from somewhere nearby, breaking the nightmare – and the dream.

'Yes, I'm here.'

'Well, hurry up – there are some grand people here!'

Keeping his eyes closed against the nausea, carefully placing one foot in front of the other and feeling along the mirrors with his hands, he slowly made his way out of the glass labyrinth.

The doctor was waiting outside, smiling his terrible smile. 'Well, my boy, what did you find in your little maze – the monster within? Or were you perhaps the young Theseus, come to slay it, eh?' he asked, chuckling.

Gabriel shrugged and looked around for Michael. They had exited into another dimly lit room, which looked like a small cinema with six rows of soft chairs in front of a raised stage. A few people were scattered around on the chairs and it took a moment before he spotted Michael, who gestured for him to sit down next to him. But, just as he moved towards Michael, he noticed another boy, not much older than himself, who was standing in the shadows at the back of the room. Something made him stop and turn towards the boy, who seemed to be looking straight at him, grinning. He was dressed in a strangely old-fashioned three-piece suit in a shiny green material and, at the neck, he wore a loosely knotted red and white polka dot cravat. His face seemed ghostly pale under a shock of reddish blond curls. For a moment, Gabriel couldn't take his eyes off the boy, who looked to him like a character out of a Dickens novel. Just then, the boy winked merrily, cunningly, as if the two of them were sharing a secret. Gabriel looked around quickly to make sure there was no one else there. There was not; the gesture of complicity had clearly been meant for him. He turned back, wanting to ask the strange boy a question – any question – about how he came to be there, but the boy was gone. Gabriel shook his head in disbelief; he squinted into the shadows, but the boy was nowhere to be seen. Just then, he heard Michael calling for him again.

There was an organ on the stage in front of a pair of curtains of gold brocade. A large woman with long black hair was playing a jazzy tune. As Gabriel sat down, the woman started singing slowly, in a man's voice.

'It's a man dressed up as a woman,' Michael whispered, excitedly. 'And he's wearing make-up. Look!'

Gabriel had never seen anything like it and could think of nothing to say.

And then the heavy curtains parted to reveal a couple of young girls in figure-hugging sequined dresses, standing face to face in a strobe of blue light. The girls were absolutely identical and their blond curls gleamed like the ribbons of gold scattered on to the lake by the breeze on a sunny day.

'Oh!' Gabriel gasped. Somewhere behind, he could hear the doctor laughing softly.

Then the twins turned slightly to smile at the small audience and started singing in harmony to the music from the piano. Their separate keys made a perfect union. They started moving softly to the music, each with one arm around the other's shoulder and the other arm stretched out like that of a prima ballerina. Their movements were slow and fish-like; the sequins sparkled like the scales of mermaids. Suddenly, Gabriel realised that they were stuck together. Their dresses were attached somewhere below their chests so that they could not move away from each other.

After a couple of songs, the music stopped abruptly and the stage went dark. When the lights came on again, the mermaid twins were gone and Dr Buster was on the stage, his arms stretched like a V towards the ceiling and his face turned upwards so that the light fell in its hollows until it looked more like a skull than the head of a living man. Gabriel shivered and Michael jumped in his seat when the doctor burst out in one of his strange laughs.

'He's weird,' Michael whispered. 'Let's get out of here.'

'That was Mary and Anne – or Maryanne, as we call them,' the doctor boomed. 'The beautiful Siamese twins from Louisville, Kentucky. And aren't they the prettiest things you have ever seen!'

The boys looked at each other. 'What is a Siamese twin?' Gabriel hissed, but Michael only shook his head.

'And please give your applause to one of the most talented musicians in the sideshow business – straight from Eindhoven, where our boys found him wandering around the ruins after the liberation – half man, half woman: Carl by day, Vanessa by night.'

The boys clapped their hands absentmindedly.

And then the overhead lights were turned on, chafing on the worn velour of the seats and on the magic, which was at once lost to the electricity. The boys squinted in confusion and stood up from their seats. The midget in the tux was standing by the side of the stage, ushering the few people in the audience out through an opening where the canvas had been rolled up. 'This way, ladies and gentlemen! This way!' he was shouting in his tiny, childlike voice. 'The show is over!'

'Excuse me, sir. What are Siamese twins?' Gabriel dared to ask as they passed.

The midget looked up with an irritated expression. 'They were born like that – stuck together. Can't pull them apart,' he said and pushed at the boys. 'Shoo! Shoo! Get a move on, now – we haven't got all night – another lot is coming through!'

Outside, it had gone chilly and the fairground music seemed distant and unreal. Michael was still clutching the blue vase to his chest. He seemed stunned. 'Wow, Gabe, that was weird,' was all he could say.

Gabriel nodded. He looked around one last time for the strange boy in the green suit.

'What are you looking for?'

'Nothing.' Perhaps it had just been his imagination.

'That woman . . . That character at the piano played really well.'

'Yeah.'

They were both silent for a while as they strolled back towards the main part of the fair.

'I wonder what it's like . . .' Gabriel said, thoughtfully.

'What?'

'To be so close together as those girls – to be so connected . . . as if you were one and the same person.'

'Yeah, and how do they go to the toilet?'

'Hmm.'

Michael shook himself as if shaking off the strange experience and felt in his pocket for change. 'What shall we do next? I still have a shilling left.'

'What? Oh, I think I'd like to go home now.'

'Already? There's so much more to do. We haven't done the Ball in Bucket yet.'

'We can come back tomorrow; the fair will still be here.'

'Oh, come on.'

'No, I just don't feel like it anymore.'

Michael sighed. 'Okay, then; if you promise we'll be back tomorrow?'

'Alright.'

The meadow outside the circle of caravans and tents was very dark and the grass was wet with dew. There was a deep scent of sleeping greenery on the night air. A dog barked in the distance.

Suddenly, Gabriel remembered something he had forgotten to ask: 'What was in your corridor?'

Michael, who had been sulking since they left

the fair, had almost forgotten. 'Oh, just some boring corridor with a couple of mirrors – one that made me look like that midget and one that made me look like a stick insect. What about yours?'

'Nothing special. Just a lot of mirrors . . .' He did not want to talk about it now, not even with Michael.

Michael, who may have heard some unusual tone in his voice, looked across but could not see his face in the dark. They had reached the road now and the gravel under their shoes brought them back to reality – but too cruelly. Heading towards them out of the dark was a group of boys.

'Who's there?' somebody called, and Michael and Gabriel froze.

'Fluffy, is that you?'

'Oh no,' Michael moaned.

'It is, isn't it? What have you got for us tonight, then? What will you do for us?'

Jim and Billy were standing in front of them with a couple of older boys from another village. The greenish light from the full moon made their eyes look like dark holes in their pale faces. They look a bit like the American doctor, Gabriel thought to himself, and felt the old prickling of the skin under his clothes. Michael was holding back, looking around for somewhere to run.

'You know there's no use in running, Fluffy; we're a lot faster than you.'

It was true, as proven on many previous occasions.

'Let's see now . . . What's that in your hand?'

Michael tried to hide the blue vase behind his back.

'Now, now, you know the deal.' Jim tutted and smiled with his head to one side. 'Give us that thing.'

'No!'

'No? But you promised to give us everything we asked for, didn't you?'

Michael stared down at his white plimsolls that gleamed back at him like the eyes of a large cat.

'Just give it to them, Michael,' Gabriel whispered. 'We can get another one tomorrow.' *Don't give them any opportunity*.

'Yes, listen to Bunny-boy; he says some good things from time to time . . . now that he's got a mouth to talk with.'

'Ugly bloody mouth, though!' Billy echoed and spat at the gravel.

'Yeah, well, that's a shame . . . but it doesn't matter what kind of mouth a poofter has because we all know where he puts it.' The other boys laughed at this and Jim looked around, pleased with his gag. 'Anyway, I suddenly got a better idea,' he continued. 'You give me that thing now and I'll give it back to you tomorrow, if you meet us at the Giant's Table at noon.'

Gabriel nudged Michael in the side with his elbow. 'Go on; give it to him.'

'But I won it for my mum – what will I tell her?'

'She won't know and you'll get it back tomorrow – it's either that or we get a real bashing . . .' He was terrified.

Michael hesitated and then stretched out the vase towards Jim. 'You promise I'll get it back tomorrow?' he bleated.

Jim laughed. 'I promise. Why would I want to keep such an ugly thing? Anyway, it's only a ransom for your free passage tonight.' And, at that, the tormentors retreated back into the dark.

'Shit!' Michael kicked at the gravel. 'Shit, shit, shit!'

Gabriel didn't say anything. He felt that his whole life was about to take a new turn and it frightened him more than anything had ever done in the past. He swallowed. 'Let's go home and get some sleep before tomorrow. We need to wake up early in order to get to the Giant's Table by noon.'

The following morning was bright and breezy. Neither boy had slept very well. The lack of rest was gritty in their eyes and lumpy at the back of their heads and the bothersome wind pulled at their thoughts like a young child wanting attention. Their separate experiences of the freak show had faded for the time being. In front of them lay the bitter sweep of the downs and the looming threat of the day and the appointment at the Giant's Table. They walked in silence, the

123

tall bracken sharpening against their shins, their hearts heavy with dread.

'We don't *have* to go,' Gabriel suggested.

Michael glared at him and trudged on.

'Michael?'

'We are not some bloody cowards, are we? My dad says the cowards were the worst culprits in the war. They deserved to die.'

This was enough to shut Gabriel up. He had no heroes in his own family. Uncle Gerry had often said of himself that he was not to be relied upon. Had he been a coward in the war? Gabriel felt the bracing wind on his bare arms and wondered whether bravery ran in the blood. His own tactics, worked out in his early years, had always been escape. At least, in this way, he had stayed alive.

'And, by the way, we're in this together, right?' Michael demanded.

'Right,' Gabriel answered weakly.

The Giant's Table was a large stone slab perched on three megaliths. Legend said that it was where the giants of the moor would gather at summer solstice to feast on bulls stolen from the paddocks at night. They would use the discarded bones as toothpicks and drink from a nearby pond until it was almost dried out and took an entire year of rain to fill up again. The dolmen stood by itself in a remote field about two and a half miles from the village, but could be seen from some distance. As the boys approached, they could make out four people hovering under the upright stones: Jim and

124

Billy and the two bullies from Hogleigh, who had been present in the lane the night before. They were laughing and drinking bottles of pop. Perhaps it will not be so bad, Gabriel thought to himself. He glanced sideways at Michael, who stared straight ahead. His face was closed and white and you could not tell what he was thinking at that moment.

'Hello there!' Jim shouted cheerfully as they approached. 'Would you like a drink?'

Gabriel suddenly realised that they were not drinking pop at all, but real beer. He shook his head. Jim of Blackaton seemed taller, as if he had grown overnight – blown up, over life-size, by the wind and the beer in the brown bottles. He was holding a wooden stick in his hand. When he had finished his beer, he lobbed the bottle into the air and smashed it with the stick so that tawny shrapnel splintered over the grass around them. Billy and the Hogleigh boys cheered and clapped.

'All right, give me my vase.'

Gabriel closed his eyes as he heard Michael's defiant voice beside him.

'Alright,' said Jim, convivially. 'But first we'd like to carry out a little experiment.'

Michael sighed and was about to say something when Jim interrupted him.

'Lads,' he said and gestured with his stick towards the two boys from Hogleigh. They all put their bottles down on the ground and fetched a bucket that had been hidden behind one of the stones.

One of them was carrying a thick rope. 'I'm sorry, I haven't introduced you properly,' said Jim. 'This is Pete, and that's Ash.' He nodded towards the boy with the rope. 'Lads, I believe you already know Bunny-boy and Fluffy, the Poofters of Mortford.' Everyone laughed, apart from Michael and Gabriel, who did not know what a poofter was.

'Now,' said Jim of Blackaton, 'we all know that poofters are dirty little pigs that need to be scrubbed, and we are going to help you with our special concoction.'

'Michael, let's get out now, *please.*' Gabriel could hear that his voice sounded pathetic. But just then Billy Dunford and the two Hogleigh boys grabbed Michael and pulled him towards one of the stones. The three of them held him tight as Billy and the boy called Ash wound the rope twice around Michael's upper body and arms and then around the stone, where it was pulled into a tight knot, leaving him limp and lifeless. Gabriel remembered Michael's voice from many years ago, on that first day in the schoolyard: 'Why did you just take it? Why didn't you try to get away?' Now he wanted to ask the same of Michael; he wanted to scream at him and wake him up, but a little part of him knew what Michael was doing, that he was leaving his body so that whatever was going to happen to him would happen in another reality – a reality where acceptance becomes a long, dreamless sleep. Gabriel's knees had begun to tremble and he felt like sitting down. But, for the moment, nobody seemed to mind him.

Jim of Blackaton stood again, like the towering executioner, perfect within his limits, contained and hard like a marble statue of an ancient tyrant or a medieval knight in armour, lance in hand – immaculate, irreproachable and safely surrounded by his henchmen. Suddenly, he opened his flies and started pissing into the bucket. A thick steaming line of urine streaked through the sunny morning. When he was done, he buttoned up his trousers and burped.

'Right, now it's your turn,' he said, casually, and pointed at Gabriel – who could not refuse. Nor could he obey, because, however much he tried, nothing would come. He held his aching penis over the bucket, knowing that, if he didn't do this, things would only get worse, and knowing at the same time that it did not matter. That it was already done. All the badness was already out in the air around them and there was no way of stopping it. It was too late to be brave. He should have been brave five minutes ago, ten minutes ago – an hour ago. Then he might have been able to save his friend, but now there was nothing left but his betrayal, which made his skin prickle in the wind and his penis shrivel up between his fingers. And, in all the horror of it, there was a terrible, irresistible warmth deep inside his stomach and a tightening in his testicles. He was no longer the victim – or was he?

Gabriel was looking deep into the bucket, his neck reddening under the strain. He could see that it was half full of rosehips, which had been crushed into a mush with the seeds – which would make your skin itch – exposed in the red pulp. Billy Dunford was impatient and pushed him aside to urinate into the bucket himself. Gabriel noticed that Billy's dick was large and there were ginger hairs around it.

'Now stir it,' Billy said, and gave Gabriel a push. Gabriel looked around for something to stir it with, but Billy shouted at him again: 'Just use your hand and give it a good old stir.' Gabriel did as he was told while the others watched in silence.

'Urgh!' exclaimed the boy called Pete. 'It stinks!'

'That's right,' confirmed Jim, smiling broadly. 'Now get his pants off.'

Gabriel thought, at first, they meant to take his own trousers off, but realised that they were moving towards Michael, who was slumped against the stone, temporarily forgotten. But, when they started to unbutton his trousers and rip off his pants, he came alive again and started screaming and kicking.

'Gabe! For Christ's sake, help me! Don't let them do this!'

'The pig is screaming. We'd better scrub him quickly before anybody hears,' said Jim, and he slapped Gabriel's back rather hard. 'You, rub this stuff into his cock and then pour the rest over him – it will give him a real itch.'

The others laughed and jeered as Gabriel grabbed the bucket and walked up to Michael.

'Don't do it, Gabe. Throw it back at them. Or pour it out at my feet – please.' The words came slowly and painfully through Michael's mouth.

Gabriel looked around at Jim and Billy, who had made his childhood hell. He could hardly remember it now. It seemed like a long time ago.

'Are you a little poofter, too? Would you like a good scrub yourself, perhaps?' they yelled.

Gabriel swallowed and closed his eyes as he reached into the bucket for a handful of the stinking mush. Michael did not flinch as Gabriel pushed the muck on to his genitals and rubbed it in, almost tenderly, making sure every inch was covered and reaching behind to push it in between the cheeks of his bum, where he knew the itch would be particularly bad. He did not look at Michael's face, but kept staring at the small prick and the red testicles between his own fingers. He closed his eyes but his eyelids no longer protected him. There had been a time when Gabriel could not tell their bodies apart – when they had been one and the same. But now they were completely separate, like strangers who had just met for the first time.

Michael's body was still and tense, but Gabriel could hear him sobbing and felt some wet drip on to his arm. He looked down at the shattered tear drying into the skin that had tanned all through the spring of their shared childhood. He stood back then, heaved the bucket up with both arms and poured the rest of the content over Michael's bent head. He was aware of the clapping and jeering behind him, but did not turn round. He stood straight and looked at Michael, who spluttered and spat and finally raised his head so that they stood facing each other, the best of friends, each in his own space, and Gabriel knew that there was more than a world between them. And to have Michael looking at him like that with his eyes . . .

He was hardly aware of Billy Dunford slapping his back before untying the knot at the back of the stone. He saw Michael stumble forward with the red rosehip mush still in his hair and the white seeds too, and his trousers curled around his ankles so that he could not walk properly but fell on to his hands and knees so that Gabriel saw the stuff on his bum that would itch and itch, and he did not notice the others until Jim hooted again and threw something into the air, splitting it with his stick, so that the parts fell hard on to the grass, and it was the blue vase for Mrs Bradley, breaking, breaking.

He thought, for a moment, that there was nothing left to destroy. For one wonderful moment he believed that their shared shame, his and Michael's, could not be any greater. But, when he breathed in, when relief made him try the air again, he knew at once that he had been wrong. There was a new threat all around them, blacker than before and denser, smelling of bull and something sweeter, like red carnations.

'I'll teach you fucking bum boys to do as I say.' Blackaton's voice had changed, too. It was deeper. The image of the cow drowning in the mine ripped through Gabriel's mind. It made him flinch.

'Hey, Billy, help me hold this bastard down. Put your foot there on his neck so that he lies still.' The last thing he, Gabriel, saw before closing his eyes was Michael kneeling, the trousers trapping him at the ankles, with his head pushed down into the grass and his bum in the air and Jim of Blackaton stooping over him, gripping the stick hard in his hand. 'And you two, make sure Bunny-boy sees all of this. Make sure he hears the piggy squeal.'

Gabriel felt their arms reaching across his body from behind, like tentacles. Hard fingers tensed around his upper arms and pulled at them and locked them behind his back so that he cried out in pain.

'Shut up, you freak, and watch Jimmy play with your sweetheart!' His head was jerked back. It felt as if the hair was coming out of his head.

'This is how you take it, you filthy bum boy.' Hissing, panting between his teeth. 'Up your arse. Like. A. Fucking. Beast!'

Keeping his eyes shut, he couldn't close his ears to Michael's screams, tearing at the air. *No, no, no, no*, came from inside his own head and, almost as close, the quickening of somebody else's breath and the *pick, pick, pick* of his captor's heart, beating against his own back. *To think that there's still a heart somewhere in all of this; that hearts are still beating.* And, outside, what was happening was the singing of a blackbird.

And then his eyes opened to blackness and he knew that he had become the black beetle, looking out.

'Bloody hell, Jim – leave it, now. We'd better get out of here, quick.'

Soon, I shall break the thin thread that's still holding us together, he felt, as it was happening. I'm doing it now, he thought, as he managed to break free from those arms, which were not so sure of themselves anymore, and started running, stumbling blindly across the moor, with only the shadows from the stones chasing after him this time. The shadows, and that look in Michael's eyes.

Who would know that he was responsible? Who would even recognise him? He was no longer the same, after all. The solid, immovable lump above his stomach was not his heart, the wordless noises that came out of his mouth were not his voice, and his own face was replaced by the face of betrayal.

He felt the pain stabbing his side, but ran on, leaving Michael behind. Leaving Michael alone.

That night, he could not cry but, as he lay face down on the aching bed, tears fell like rain in his room. All through the night he could hear it falling. 'Please, Gabe, don't do it,' Michael said again, and he answered from the darkness: 'You're safe with me. I'll protect you, like you protected me in the beginning.'

He lay there in the grieving dark, trying not to breathe, and thought that perhaps this was true – that it was still somehow possible to turn it all back and start again. And then he would be right as rain.

CHAPTER 5

Mr Askew stood in the hall, wearing his gabardine coat, and listened to the pendulum of silence swinging backwards and forwards. The boxes in the corner were covered in a fine layer of dust, but the tiles, at least, were still perfectly geometrical and their contrast of black and white was comforting. There were only two outcomes, two ends, Mr Askew felt: either he would be destroyed or else maybe he would be completed. Yes, there was still that chance.

He shrugged and recalled his purpose for the day, which was the village market. Sighing, he felt for the keys in the prolapsed pocket of his old trench coat and looked around a final time, hoping that there might still be the possibility of escape. He caught a glimpse of himself in the dark mirror and looked away at once. Reaching to switch off the lights, he remembered that the bulb had blown and needed replacing. Once again, he patted his pocket to make sure the keys were there. He took a deep breath, almost choking on the smell of dust and something brown and gloomy – a dead mouse, perhaps – but it was faint enough that it could be dealt with at some later date. He opened the door and stepped out into the blustery wind. The trees at the end of the garden were agitating against each other.

Parked cars were lining the street in the centre of the village and the narrow pavement was congested with young women pushing prams and herding children. Mr Askew stepped into the road and waited next to a parked Land Rover. He looked on, appalled, as a family of holidaymakers pushed past. They were each dressed in what looked like the gear a pirate, stripped of his finery, would wear on the way to the gallows: beige knee-length trousers, thong sandals and cotton vests in fearful colours. One of the children was carrying a toy gun, as if he was still prepared to defy the law.

Continuing to avoid the pavement, Mr Askew hobbled along the street, past the churchyard with its old, reassuring stones that watched wisely over the valley to the east. The market was held indoors, in the Jubilee Hall by the pay-and-display car park.

He cursed himself for having agreed to help out at Mrs Sarobi's organic vegetable stall. What had possessed him? He had, at least, washed his best shirt in the bath the previous night and pressed his trousers under the mattress. The jacket was still good and the tie . . . The tie might be quite wrong for the occasion, but that idea had only just struck him. He pulled it out and looked at it

135

closely. There was an old spot of grease – a vestige of a college dinner – béchamel, perhaps, or just ordinary gravy. Putting it back inside his jacket, he sighed and pulled at the belt of his trench coat. He wanted to look good today. At least my breath does not stink of cigarettes or some awful gum disease, he thought to himself as he entered the hall.

There were women everywhere and the decibel level was high. One or two prosaic-looking men hovered amongst the stalls, timidly waiting to give their opinion of some object they generally did not care for – or pull out a wallet. Children, balancing dangerously on the cusp of eagerness and boredom, were cluttering the passages and Mr Askew was beginning to feel quite keenly that his being there was a mistake. Just then, he heard somebody calling his name. He looked up to see Mrs Sarobi waving at him from a stall at the back of the room. Her voice had given his name a gentle but distinct substance, for which he was grateful. She made it sound like a river, sleeked with silver and green.

Apologising as he went – but managing to avoid unnecessary attention – he made his way through the crowd towards Mrs Sarobi's table. There was sweat on his brow when he got there, but he achieved a smile. 'This is quite something . . .' he said, feeling slightly less outlandish.

She laughed, but without irony or malice. 'Yes, almost like a souk. You'd better come behind the

136

table, where there's a bit more space.' She was wearing a white linen tunic and black slacks and her hair was swathed loosely in a bright ochre-coloured scarf.

He followed her advice and squeezed past the adjacent stall. Her vegetables were laid out in plastic baskets and labelled neatly with wooden plaques. To one side, there was a vase with posies of pink and white poppies. He admired them closely and smiled at her. 'They are the simplest of joys, aren't they?' Her eyes, he saw, were very dark out of the sunlight.

She nodded. 'Yes, they can be . . .' But sometimes, she felt, they represented the greatest of threats.

He looked at her curiously. 'You're not so sure about them?'

'Sure about them?' She laughed. 'Oh, I don't know . . . Where I come from, the poppy fields used to be the most beautiful things you have ever seen.' She could see them now; each poppy was so fragile, but together they bled like silk through the valleys – a natural beauty that contained a threat so deadly and so powerful that a succession of soldiers took charge of the cultivation, tainting it with the smell of metal. It was the greatest of ironies and, for a moment, the thought of it threatened to draw her back into that sheath of darkness. She felt she was losing herself. Not here; not now. These vegetables in their baskets protected her against all that.

'Mrs Sarobi?' he said. 'Are you all right?' He touched briefly the white fabric of her tunic, his hand resting on her back. That warmth.

'Yes,' she said, steadying herself against the table. 'Yes, of course.' She laughed brightly, feeling the touch of his hand.

He did not quite understand, but he had seen the shadow on her face and wanted to say something consoling. Instead, he uncovered himself, as if offering a kind of gift.

'Last week, when I was up at the allotment . . . It was a very blowy day, if you remember?' He did not need a reply, but she nodded just the same. 'One of my pink poppies had just come out – it was the first one – and it frightened me. Every gust of wind tore at it so that I expected it to lose all the petals.' He glanced at her to see if she thought him ridiculous, but her hands were busy with a broad bean, which she had snapped. 'It was so unbearably fragile.'

Like the shapes we sometimes mistake for love, he thought. It had made him feel quite sick that day – the way one was repeatedly presented with a lesson in the symmetry of beauty and death. As if one needed to be reminded.

A cool breeze meandered through the room and brought them back to the Mortford village hall. But this was no longer isolation. They were standing in a patch of light and it was clear that their minds had touched. Mrs Sarobi realised that she had been holding her breath. She felt she needed to say something pleasant and clever. Anything, as long as it seemed thoughtful; it was always easier, in a situation like this, to operate in the clarity of her intellect.

'There's so much in Western culture which repeats itself,' she said. 'Take Helen, for example – sister of the *Dioscuri* – although utterly unique, she too had a double: a phantom other.'

'You know a lot about Western culture,' he interrupted, admiringly, feeling suddenly very awake.

'You have to, when you don't belong.' She smiled. Surely he must realise that trying to understand the culture – and the mind of one's neighbour – is the first task of the exiled? 'Anyway, my point about Helen is that she too was into poppies. She extracted opium from the pistils and mixed it with wine so that anyone who drank it would be prevented from crying and feeling grief for an entire day, even if their most beloved family and friends died in front of their eyes. This was all she had to offer: beauty and deception – and yet she shaped the course of history as we know it. As *you* know it.'

'Real power is often based on something as insubstantial as beauty – or fear, for that matter.' He knew this for a fact, as he had been under the spell of both. 'This is what the poppy represents.'

'Yes—' she nodded sadly – 'and there are, of course, the fields of Flanders . . .'

'Yes, yes,' he agreed, 'obviously.'

There was an embarrassed silence between them,

as if they had become too intimate, too quickly. Mrs Sarobi started fidgeting with the baskets, rearranging and tidying away a pea that had fallen out of its pod.

'They are not buying your vegetables.' He had only just noticed.

'No, I know. Perhaps they are too expensive?'

'Perhaps . . . although they are good vegetables.' He wished he had more to offer.

'Yes, and they sell for more in the deli . . . They probably think that I have poisoned the carrots – or that I'm going to blow myself up if they come too close.'

He looked up at her nervously, but saw that her eyes were smiling.

'I think they are afraid of standing next to you, where their looks would inevitably be compared against your beauty,' he said, and reddened.

'Ah, Gabriel, you're a true gentleman,' she said, laughing.

But he only heard his Christian name. He could not remember when he'd last heard somebody say his first name, but now it made him feel warm around the chest. Her mouth was pink inside, he noticed, like a kitten's – or a cat's, at any rate.

Just then, he heard a familiar voice cutting through the general babble and looked up to see Mrs Ludgate debating loudly with a woman who was cowering behind a small table of bric-a-brac, embroidered cushions and crocheted babies' booties. Doris Ludgate stood deliberately, squeezing an oversized beige patent-leather handbag in her armpit. 'Are you trying to tell me that this is an original Royal Albert plate?' She was waving a piece with a pattern of flowers at the owner of the stall, who muttered something inaudible in grumpy defence of her produce.

'Well, I'll tell *you* that you won't sell *me* some old dross, pretending it's the real thing. Look – can't you see that the flower of the month is misspelt? It says *Decembel*.'

The bric-a-brac woman tried to protest, but Mrs Ludgate would not have it.

'Ha! You have to give it to them, the Chinese – they are pretty excellent copyists, but, if they can't get their child labourers to spell properly, they are not going to fool *me*. Do they not teach them to read and write in China, eh? What about all those school books and pens we used to send them? Have they not been using them, eh? Eh? Or perhaps that was Africa . . .' Her cheeks were glowing; she could have been a painting by Caravaggio, had she not got herself so worked up. 'Anyway, bloody waste of good charity, no? Somebody ought to tell the government. *Decembel!* Yeah, *right*.'

Several people had turned to watch the scene. The woman at the stall seemed quite intimidated and tried her best to appease Mrs Ludgate, if only to make her lower her voice somewhat.

'At this rate, there will soon be nothing English

141

left in this country. *Royal Albert*, my posterior,' Mrs Ludgate muttered loudly and clattered the offensive piece of crockery back on the table.

She was wearing a boat-neck top and, from behind, Gabriel Askew saw that her neck was bulging over her vertebrae, like something cetacean. Oh dear, he thought, I do hope she does not come this way.

But, of course, eventually, not even the Jubilee Hall was large enough to keep them apart. Mr Askew felt suddenly too hot and dabbed his brow with a large handkerchief, which might once have been clean. Mrs Sarobi noticed. 'Why don't you take your coat off?' she suggested.

'Yes, yes,' he muttered, self-consciously, once again regretting the tie. He turned his back to the hall, as if he was preparing to undress for bed, bundled the coat on to a chair and patted his hair.

When, at last, he turned back to the room, he was dismayed to find himself face to face with Mrs Ludgate. However, for once, she did not seem particularly interested in him. She was sucking her teeth, looking doubtfully at Mrs Sarobi, as if she too somehow belonged to the category of fake crockery. 'I have always been told,' she said, pronouncing every word slowly and with care, 'that the people from Afghanistan – the real Afghanistanians, that is – wear those blue tents. Are you sure you're not Indian?'

'Quite sure,' Mrs Sarobi answered sincerely.

Mrs Ludgate frowned. 'Anyway,' she said, 'I hear

you're a *supplier* – a fruit and veg supplier . . . like Mrs Thatcher used to be . . . But you're not like her, are you?' The idea had only just sailed up in her mind and it bothered her. Nor could she remember if Mrs Thatcher had actually been a supplier – or the daughter of a greengrocer. Same difference, anyway.

'No, I would certainly not like to think so.'

'Nah, I thought not.' She exhaled, relieved. 'Anyway, just so that you know, I am all for it.'

'For what?' asked Mrs Sarobi carefully, and cocked her head.

'You being a supplier and all.'

'Okay . . . Um . . . Well, thanks.'

'You know, there are a lot of others – others like you – who don't supply anything, if you see what I mean.' Doris Ludgate winked in order to convey the kind of understanding she liked to believe existed between intelligent women – of all colours.

'No. I'm afraid I don't.'

Mr Askew glanced anxiously at Mrs Sarobi, but saw that she was so composed, she could have been carved out of marble. He cleared his throat and took a step forward.

'Oh, hello; I didn't see you there. I don't usually notice men who skulk,' said Mrs Ludgate, coldly, and turned back to Mrs Sarobi. 'The *professor*—' she nodded towards Mr Askew – 'will have told you that he's my employer. That is, I am an employee in his household.'

'You don't say?' said Mrs Sarobi, and glanced

sideways at Mr Askew, her eyebrows slightly raised.

'Um, Mrs Ludgate comes up to Oakstone to do the cleaning on a Friday afternoon,' he explained, scowling with embarrassment, and was rewarded by a brief smile from Mrs Sarobi.

'That's right. Oakstone is a big old chunk of a house – it's grade two listed.' She looked up to see if Mrs Sarobi had taken this in. 'It's important that somebody – somebody professional – keeps it in check and makes sure it doesn't get itself degraded. We wouldn't want it to slip down that list to a one, would we?' She was so pleased with herself, she had to chuckle.

'Hello, Doris; I'm pleased to see you so cheerful today.' A small, plump woman had come up to them. She must have been in her mid fifties, but her skin was as smooth as milk and prettily aglow. She had very pale blue eyes but her friendly smile put warmth into her gaze. 'I was very sorry to hear about . . . everything.' As she put a smooth doll's hand on Mrs Ludgate's arm, it was clear that she really was sorry. Mrs Ludgate flinched, pulling her arm away and, for a moment, Mr Askew thought he saw something vulnerable swim through her gaze, like a detached duckling crossing a pond.

'Not sure what you're on about. I'm just fine, myself.' She laughed hoarsely to emphasise.

'But I heard—' The doll-woman suddenly stopped herself; perhaps she too had detected the flaw in the armour. 'I must have got the wrong end of the stick,' she said, jovially.

'I'd say so.'

'Anyway, I actually came over to introduce myself to Mrs Sarobi.' She turned to face the Afghani woman, who had retreated somewhat, in spite of her previous stoicism. 'My name is Ann Chandler; I'm the chair of the local Women's Institute.'

'Nice to meet you.' Mrs Sarobi smiled softly.

'And . . . Professor Askew, is it?'

'Ahem . . .' He nodded and shook her outstretched hand. It was surprisingly firm, but moist like a child's.

'I heard that an elegant gentleman from London recently bought Oakstone. Pleased to meet you.'

He had noticed her flattery and was grateful for it.

'Such a beautiful old house,' she continued. 'A pity more people around here can't see it . . .'

'Yes,' he said, feeling somewhat ungenerous. 'Yes, that is, I prefer to be on my own, if at all possible.'

Mrs Ludgate snorted and pressed her lips together.

'Yes, I can understand that. Village life can be a bit intimidating at first,' said Ann Chandler, smilingly, and turned back to Mrs Sarobi. 'I was wondering whether you would be interested in joining the Mortford WI? Most of us are members now . . .'

'Oh, well, what a surprise . . .' She seemed

genuinely taken aback. 'I mean, I'm honoured, naturally, but are you *sure* you would like me in your group?'

'Yes, of course. Why not?'

'Well, it's just that I thought the WI was mainly for the home-grown . . .'

Ann Chandler laughed so that her rosy cheeks shuddered. 'I'm sure that used to be the case, but we cannot afford to be so narrow-minded anymore. Where would that leave womankind, eh?'

'Yeah, but just the same, perhaps we ought to have a vote about this?' Mrs Ludgate interrupted, staring intensely at Mrs Chandler.

'Nonsense. We don't vote people into this community. And we are in dire need of a Skills Coordinator.'

But Mrs Ludgate was not entirely convinced. 'No one,' she said and looked at the other three, each one in turn, 'can say that I'm not an open-minded person.' She stretched her neck a little, like a turtle, and added, 'At least, not when it comes to skills . . . and coordination. But, for somebody to take on such a major role right from the start, it seems, well, out of order . . . or at least not quite proper. Wouldn't you say, Mrs Chandler?' She turned, deliberately, to the plump woman standing to her left.

'Well, my dear, let's not argue about it, shall we?' The chair of the WI smiled so that her doll's face took on a radiant, globe-like quality, like a very small moon.

146

'There's no need to worry,' Mrs Sarobi said firmly. 'I'm not one for groups, really, and I haven't got time at the moment to get too engaged . . . I'd be happy to come for some of the meetings, though.' She seemed calm enough as she spoke, but then something inside her flared. She turned to face Mrs Ludgate. 'It's not a competition, you know – life. It's just about trying to be *decent*. To other people. And to oneself, for that matter.'

Mrs Ludgate sulked and Mrs Sarobi rearranged some courgettes in a basket.

Mrs Chandler, sensing some discomfort, turned back to Mr Askew. 'Anyway, I'm delighted you're putting some new life into Oakstone. It's been empty for a while. I remember it from when I was a child; it seemed a jolly place . . . until . . . There was a boy. They said there was something not quite right about him – in terms of the mind. I forget what he was called—' She stopped abruptly and looked down at her feet.

'Bradley! I told you, didn't I?' Mrs Ludgate said triumphantly and gestured at Mr Askew. For a moment, they looked at each other, intently, each measuring the other.

'Yes, that's right; Michael Bradley was his name. But he disappeared at some point – never came back. After that, Oakstone was quite dreary. There were rumours something terrible happened to him as a young boy. But it's all such a long time ago now . . .'

'A scandal, no doubt,' Mrs Ludgate suggested, cocking her head.

'Mr Askew, are you okay?' Mrs Sarobi asked, her eyes alive with concern. She reached out to touch him, but something, a look on his face, held her back.

'Yes, yes,' he mumbled, 'I'm quite all right. I need . . . just need to get out. Some fresh air.' As he pushed past the table and the astounded women, a few petals detached themselves from one of the white poppies and fell on to the floor.

To always remember those eyes.

After Michael, there were no friends, or, if there were, they were of no consequence, easily forgotten. In their place – or absence – Gabriel went for walks on the moor. He walked and walked. The rhythm of his steps pounded on his mind.

In between the walks, during the hours and days when he outwardly lived his own life, he sat at the back of the classroom and listened to the drone of Miss Simmons' voice as it listed Latin verbs along with the kings and queens of England and the rivers of Europe. Often enough, as the grey yarn of boredom was knitted into the afternoon, he wondered what the point of it all was. At least nobody bothered him anymore – he was left alone. After school, he would still go to Uncle Gerry's cottage. As the twilight waned and emptied itself into evening darkness and the blackbirds in the trees were silenced, one after another, like gas lamps going out along a street, the cottage filled with what was no longer there. While Uncle Gerry slept off the day's drink in his armchair by the fireplace, Gabriel would sometimes look up from his homework or his book with a sense that something had been left behind, like a ball on an abandoned playing field where the cries of the players are still ringing in the air. The emptiness in the cottage was full of Michael's breath and, if he listened closely, he could still hear Michael's voice and, sometimes, in his mind, he would answer.

'Honest, Gabe, Biggles knew how to fly both Hurricanes *and* Spitfires! And he flew a lot faster than the Focke-Wulfs and Messerschmitts. Although they are actually quite good planes too . . .'

'Yeah, I *know* that. But Algy was a really good pilot as well – they were best mates.'

'Um, they were related, actually – cousins, I think.'

'Or like brothers, even?'

'Yeah, perhaps a bit like brothers.'

Shortly after the travelling fair visited Mortford, Michael had been taken out of the village school and sent to a private school in Ramleigh, which was only a few miles away. Mr Bradley had bought Michael a bicycle so that he could cycle to school. Gabriel only knew this because Uncle Gerry had told him. He had not seen Michael since the day

149

at the Giant's Table, but Uncle Gerry would some-times meet Mr Bradley in the pub on a Saturday evening. Mr and Mrs Bradley must have known that *something* had happened, they must have noticed, but it was clear that Michael had not told his parents any details, and Gabriel was greatly relieved by this. Relieved and puzzled, because it must have shown on Michael's face, like he was sure it showed on his own. And the dreams that ripped opened the night – the dreams where he was the one pushed to the ground. Once again, he was the one eating grass. And Jim of Blackaton in iron armour. There were nights when he dared not fall asleep at all and the days that followed such nights were yellow and full of pain from a place somewhere behind his eyes. And yet, no one seemed to notice. But sometimes, when he was sober, Uncle Gerry would look at him strangely and ask why he would not play with Michael. He would shrug and mumble something about them not having so much in common anymore, but, while he spoke those words, shame would open its terrible, stinking jaws and breathe into his face so that he went all red and hot. At such times, Uncle Gerry looked very sad and shook his head.

One Sunday in early September, when Gabriel reached the cottage, Uncle Gerry was in the yard oiling the chain of a rusty old bike, which was standing on its saddle. He looked up when he heard Gabriel approaching.

'Hello there, Gabe; look what I got for you.' He stood back, beaming.

'For me?'

'That's right – Mr Green gave it to me in exchange for some stuff I did for him up at Chidcombe Farm.'

Gabriel blinked and stared at the bike, which looked as if it had been dug out of a bog.

Uncle Gerry noticed the look on his face and frowned. 'I know it's not new, like Michael's bike, but, believe me, once I've straightened out the back wheel and cleaned it up a bit, it will be as good as any bike around here.'

'It's very nice, Uncle G. It's just . . . well, I don't know how to ride a bike.'

'Easiest thing in the world, lad. Trust me, you'll learn it in less than an hour.'

'But where would I go?' For some reason Gabriel felt that the bike was going to be a problem and he struggled to keep his sinking heart out of his voice. 'I . . . I wouldn't know where to ride it . . .' His world had shrunk that much.

'Now you sound like an old bag. You should go around with Michael, of course,' Uncle Gerry replied, with genuine surprise. 'Gives you a new interest to share with him, doesn't it? Boys your age need a bit of adventure and freedom, eh?'

There was a thickening in his throat and he felt hot behind the eyes. 'I can't go cycling with Michael,' he muttered and kicked his heel at the gravel in the yard.

'Come on, now, Gabe; you should be ashamed of yourself. I have never known you to be ungrateful before . . .'

'No, it's not that. I like the bike; it's just that—'

'I know it's not a new bike, like Michael's, but I was going to give it a lick of paint. I found some tractor paint in Green's barn and he said I could have that, too.' Gabriel could tell that Uncle Gerry was very upset – there were spits of saliva coming out of his mouth as he continued. 'I was quite excited about this, you know, quite determined to make something good out of it, and now you have spoilt it . . . Metallic blue is what I was going to paint it. But you can do the bloody work yourself, if you think you can do it better.'

Gabriel could feel weeks of dammed pain and frustration welling up inside him. 'You don't get it!' he screamed and kicked the bike so that it fell over. 'You don't get anything. None of you do!'

'Whoa! Hang on a minute. I think you'd better tell me what it is that I'm supposed to understand. I'm no mind reader, you know, and you never speak to me these days.'

Through his tears, Gabriel looked up at Uncle Gerry and, for a moment, he hoped that there was perhaps a way, after all, to tell his uncle about the badness, about the *wrong* that lived inside him like a black beetle in a tree stump. But as the moment stretched – thinner and thinner – he realised that it was not possible, that it would never be possible, and that Uncle Gerry would be better off going back inside the cottage to his bottle of Bells than staying here trying to understand Gabriel.

'Go on, lad. Is there something you want to tell me about?'

'No, there's nothing,' he muttered and managed a smile – which did the trick.

'Ah, well, in that case I think I'll go inside . . . to read for a while,' Uncle Gerry said vaguely, and turned his back on the failed bike project.

As the boy watched his uncle's departing back, a ray of sunlight found its way through the canopy of trees and got entangled in the spokes of the wonky back wheel, which was still spinning, although ever slower, on the upturned bike.

In the end, Gabriel painted the bike himself and, although the back wheel was never to be quite right, he learnt to ride the bike in Uncle Gerry's yard on a sunny Sunday morning. The early autumn dew made the grass in the nearby meadow look as fresh as spring and the brightness of that morning would forever be linked in Gabriel's mind with the exhilaration of freedom. Once he had got the hang of it, Gabriel wobbled towards the lane, where the very first of the fallen leaves stuck to the tyres and attached themselves to his sodden plimsolls. The bike was too large for him and he had to stand up in order to reach both pedals but, after a while, as he got more confident, he would sometimes sit on the saddle to go down gentle slopes, and let the pedals turn on their own.

For a while, the bicycle offered boundless delight and, as the boy looked upon the world anew from the elevated position of the saddle, the wind smattering through the red and green ribbons he had tied around the handlebars, it all seemed fine – as if he was part of life's adventure, after all; as if he actually deserved to be. Once or twice, like on the day when he first dared to let go of the handlebars, he cycled past Oakstone, slowing down in the place where the large trees opened on to the gravel drive. One afternoon when he made the detour past Oakstone after school, he thought he saw Mrs Bradley in an upstairs window, her soft shape further indulged by the smoky glass. But Michael was never to be seen. Gabriel could not stop thinking about Michael's bike. Uncle Gerry, who had seen it, had told him that it was a Raleigh in racing green with three gears. Gabriel did not have any gears, but he had the streamers that Uncle Gerry had helped him make, and the blue metallic colour *was* unusual.

Deciding to make the streamers for Michael was certainly part of bringing to life that magnificent Raleigh, which he had never seen but which, in his mind, had taken on extraordinary properties. He set about the task with unusual fervour. He found the fabric in a pile of clothes at the back of his mother's wardrobe. There was an old skirt or slip of a soft crimson silk. It was the kind of thing Uncle Gerry's American singers would wear while singing in their soft, husky voices. He had never seen his mother wear the garment and reckoned that it would be okay if he cut the fabric horizontally along the hem – he did not need much, anyway. It proved more difficult to find the gold fabric needed for the project, but then he remembered the old sofa in Uncle Gerry's cottage. It was dirty now and piled with stuff which Uncle Gerry had once left there and never removed, but once, a few years ago, when Gabriel had looked under the sofa to retrieve some lost object, he had been struck by the colour that the fabric had preserved out of the light. Turning over one of the seat cushions, he was thrilled to see that the deep golden colour was still there. He hesitated for a while before cutting into the sofa cushion, but reasoned that Uncle Gerry never had seemed too bothered about it and the cut-out area would not show unless you turned the cushion over. Once Uncle Gerry had fallen asleep in his chair, Gabriel started shredding the two pieces of fabric. 'Just like Captain Marvel's uniform,' he breathed, as he cut into the crimson and the gold. And, as he tied the ends of the bands together, he was again consoled by the simplicity of things.

Hiding in the undergrowth on the periphery of Oakstone late one evening, he waited until he was sure the house was asleep. Then he ran through the shadows like a pathfinder until he reached the end of the lawn. Here he stopped for a moment, panting, and listened beyond his own heartbeats; there was only the wind in the elms and the sound of a small animal fidgeting under last year's leaves. He walked slowly now, softly through the smell of mushroom and ivy, but his footfall on the gravel seemed to cut through the blackness. Arriving by the porch at the back of the house, he stubbed his toe on something rubbery, which could only be one of the tyres of the Raleigh. A rattling confirmed this. It was too dark to make out the colour, but he knew exactly what shade of green his hands touched as they felt along the frame for the handlebars, trembling ever so slightly. Quickly, he tied the streamers to the handles, one on each side. He knew that it looked great: just right. As he ran back to the road, he did a few skips and took a flying kick at a pebble or a fir cone that disappeared into the night.

For days after, he felt a tingling thrill in his stomach as he pictured Michael finding the streamers hanging from the handlebars of his three-speed Raleigh. In his mind's eye, he saw Michael riding to his school in Ramleigh in the morning with the red and gold flaming either side of him. For once, he felt quite proud of something he had done. But after a couple of weeks, when he had still not heard anything from Michael, he began to despair; because, deep in his heart, he realised that he had made the streamers as an offering of atonement – or at least in the hope that he might see Michael again. But, when he finally did, it was in circumstances that he could never have imagined and would never have wished for. As he eventually stood face to face again with Michael, after over six months of separation, it was to the sound of a door closing on their shared life.

In the classroom, the light which spilled through the tall windows was thick with dust that refused to settle. From the back, Gabriel watched as a patch of sweat spread slowly, like a continent, over the silk of Miss Simmons' blouse. He tried to imagine what her armpits must smell like. Even at thirteen, he knew that she might be the kind of drab woman who kept a collection of old lipsticks, never having found quite the right shade. He was so deep in thought, he did not hear the knock and, when he looked up, all the children's heads were turned towards the door, where Uncle Gerry stood talking to Miss Simmons. Gabriel got up to collect his things before the adults had time to address him. Uncle Gerry held open the door for him, but did not speak until they were out of earshot.

'There has been an accident,' he said, not looking at Gabriel. 'Mr Bradley came off the road in his car.'

'Oh,' Gabriel said, not knowing quite what to feel about it.

'You need to go and fetch Michael from Ramleigh straight away and bring him back to Oakstone. I'll stay with Mrs Bradley.'

'But—'

'He's dead, Gabriel. I'm sorry.'

'Mr Bradley is dead?'

'Yes. I'm terribly sorry. You never got to know him. It's . . . just awful.'

Gabriel did not answer this. His mind was confused. What did it matter that he had never got to know Mr Bradley? And then he thought about Michael, who had just lost his dad. Never having had a dad, Gabriel found it impossible to imagine what it would be like to lose one.

'Hurry up! You need to cycle as fast as you can. Mrs Bradley needs her son by her side and we don't want Michael to hear from anybody else.'

'Alright,' he said, and started running towards his bike, which he had left leaning against the willow by the river. 'I'll ride as fast as I can.'

He raced along the lanes, where the hedges had grown thick and tall all summer. It was like going through a tunnel and he leant into every bend like a Tour de France champion. It was exhilarating and he soon forgot the purpose of his outing. Not until he skidded to a stop outside the school in Ramleigh, his cheeks flushed with the wind and the speed, did he remember that, on this day, he was not a racer but a grim messenger. It was a small school with only two classrooms, both on the ground floor. Hesitating in the yard outside, Gabriel tried to look in through the windows where classes were in progress. Suddenly, he saw Michael, who was sitting next to one of the windows. He raised his hand in a greeting, but at the last minute he stopped himself from calling out. Luckily, Michael hadn't spotted him yet. He paused to think. How could he tell Michael about his dad's death? Would he be upset? Gabriel suspected he would. He himself would have been very upset if it had been Uncle Gerry who had crashed his car into a tree and died. Perhaps there would be a scene. He did not want that to happen. And anyway, hadn't Michael made it quite clear that he did not want to see Gabriel? If he had wanted to talk to Gabriel, he could have come and found him at Uncle Gerry's cottage any time during the past six months. But he hadn't.

Carefully, trying to avoid attracting attention from any of the other children, he sneaked up towards the window where Michael sat. They were all crouched over their books. The teacher, at the front of the room, was marking papers with a red pencil. There was no dust in the air and the desks were of polished wood. The boys wore blue blazers with a crest on the pocket. All these details registered in Gabriel's mind as he peered through the window. One or two of the boys had spotted him by now and glanced up uncertainly from their reading, keeping an eye on the teacher at the podium, but Michael was still absorbed in his book. At once, Gabriel realised that he did not know how to deliver his message; there was no way to do it. He turned to go, but stopped again and kicked angrily at a pebble by his feet. He was suddenly cross with Michael and Mr Bradley and

Uncle Gerry for putting him through all this and he despised the other boys in the classroom with Michael. They were quite hateful, he decided, the boys and their combed hair. But somehow he knew that he would be a coward if he didn't carry out his task and Michael's dad, who was now dead, thought that cowards deserved to die.

With a beating heart, he walked right up to the window where Michael sat and breathed at the cold glass. Michael looked up from his book in astonishment but Gabriel did not meet his eye. He breathed again until the glass was all misted up and then he wrote with his finger, *Your dad is dead.* Michael stood up from his seat, but Gabriel breathed on a new patch of glass and continued without looking at him: *Mrs B upset*, he began, but realised that he had to do it back to front for Michael to be able to read. He started again, breathing on a new patch, writing in reverse, whilst biting his mended lip: *come home at once.* By now, several of the boys had run up to the window to see what was going on. They were crowding around Michael, pushing at him to get a better view. Michael did not move; he stood alone amongst the shouting boys until the teacher cleared them away and, reading the fading message, took hold of Michael's shoulders and led him out of the room. Neither of them paid any attention to Gabriel, who was running now, back towards his bike, which he had left by the school gates. As he ran, he saw something out of the corner of his eye: there, neatly parked on its prop-stand, was Michael's green Raleigh with three gears. Gabriel hesitated; should he go up and have a proper look at it? He glanced over his shoulder, back towards the school building, and ran on; he did not want to be there when Michael appeared. But, as he mounted his own bike, he felt again that lovely warmth inside him – a warmth that was reflected in the flaming gold and crimson ribbons he had noticed attached to the handle-bars on the parked Raleigh.

It is odd, thought Mr Askew to himself, a few days after the village market, as he passed the little churchyard on his way to the allotments, how memory leaves long gaps – black holes in one's own mind. Years and years are lost in thick folds of time and then tiny details come back with such clarity as to give one a headache. He closed his eyes for a moment, feeling quite dizzy. It was Mr Bradley's funeral that had suddenly surfaced in his mind. 'Why now?' he asked himself, grumpily. Things had been so different after that. Since leaving, all alone, to put that world behind him, his life had been an endless odyssey – until now.

It was a rainy day in October, he remembered, as he sat down to rest for a while on the low wall that surrounded the churchyard. 'No, I'm wrong, quite wrong,' he muttered aloud. 'It was a sunny day, and there was still dew on the grass in the shadow of the gravestones.' He grimaced in concentration. 'I must at least try to get it right.'

A lot of people whom he had never seen before turned up to the funeral, people from outside the village. Their faces looked wrong, like Uncle Gerry's after a bottle of Bell's – all vacant, with big, blubbery lips. Others looked stiff, their white, pinched faces strangled by their black ties. These strangers avoided your eyes, staring instead at their newly polished shoes, frowning.

But what he remembered most clearly was the fury hidden under the masks of the people he did know – of Mrs Bradley and Michael, and even his own mother. Fury at the injustice of it all and fury at the absence of the main character – the terrible forlorn weight of what was not there. Fury that they should have been left behind in this way. Uncle Gerry, too, was furious, although quite why that was, Gabriel could not understand. Not then, anyway.

The church was lit only by the sun, streaming through the south windows. Sitting between Mother and Uncle Gerry in the pews, Gabriel looked at the bosses on the oak beams that curved above him like the hull of a ship. There were images on the bosses, he realised – little animals, which he had never seen before: a pelican dipping her long beak towards her heart and three hares running in a circle, with only three ears between them. They were comforting and he was relieved that he could look at them rather than at the people around him. The minister, however, could not be ignored. Gabriel noticed his thinning hair and large protruding ears; it was as if the ears had been growing to make up for the loss of hair. The minister's voice suggested truths with the frail conviction of a believer: 'I am the resurrection and the life. He who believes in me will live, even though he dies.'

What did it mean? Could it be that Mr Bradley was not quite dead, that there was still a chance that he might live? One could never be quite certain, could one? After all, no one had been allowed to look inside the coffin. Perhaps it was a ploy; perhaps the coffin was empty or perhaps Mr Bradley was inside but not dead. He shivered in the cold church when he thought about what it must be like to be left inside a box like that.

'. . . neither death nor life, neither angels nor demons, neither the present nor the future, nor any powers, neither height nor depth, nor anything else in all creation, will be able to separate us . . .'

Gabriel was beginning to feel quite annoyed with the minister. Why was he saying those things when they clearly weren't true? Everyone was quite separate, sitting in the pews, as if on a bus, each one staring in front, into their individual pocket of space. Even Uncle Gerry, who was sitting so close Gabriel could smell his aftershave and the sharper, fetid alcohol smell it was trying to hide, was distant. He kept his eyes closed but Gabriel knew he was awake, as he would open his mouth every now and again to mumble in unison with the minister.

Michael was sitting next to Mrs Bradley across the aisle on the first pew. He looked shrivelled up inside his new suit and there was a white band at the back of his bent neck where his hair had been cut to reveal skin that had not been exposed to the sun all summer. He was looking down into his lap. Gabriel wished he could whisper to him not to worry about what the minister said, but to look up instead, at the pelican and the hares.

Then they all stood to follow the coffin out into the graveyard. Six men, wearing uniforms laden with medals, carried it slowly, high on their shoulders.

'Who are *they*?' Gabriel whispered to Uncle Gerry.

'They are men who fought with Mr Bradley in the war.'

'Are they heroes, like him?'

'I suppose so, yes.'

'Uncle Gerry?'

'Hm?'

'Were you a coward in the war?'

'Hush now,' he answered, and put a finger to his lips.

At the graveside, the minister announced that he was committing Mr Bradley's body to the ground. That would be the flesh and blood, Gabriel reckoned, but what about the soul? What happened to the soul? Perhaps it was committed to the Holy Ghost, who otherwise seemed to have little purpose in the overall scheme of things. Or perhaps it just faded after a while, he thought to himself, like the fabric of an old deckchair.

The minister's large ears were sunlit from behind now and, as he bent to make the sign of the cross, Gabriel could see in them the veins where the minister's lifeblood was running through him in its own circuit, which made him quite separate from anyone else and so much more alive than Mr Bradley, who had been committed to the ground and was already beginning to fade under the earth which was being thrown on top of his coffin.

There was a gust of wind, honeyed air bringing the sweet scents of autumn's gentle decay. Or were they the scents of death? Gabriel looked at Michael, who was staring mutely, intently into the filling grave. Suddenly, he looked up and his eyes met Gabriel's. Grief flowed across Michael's transparent face, but his gaze was dark and bottomless. And just then, for the first time, Gabriel felt that this loss was also a terrible and strange thing in his own life. He felt a sudden great emptiness inside him, which was not quite hollow because it was beginning to fill with a pain that was mirrored in Michael's dark eyes, looking away now. Michael, who was a year younger than himself and yet seemed to understand so much more, as if he had already lived a life to the end of its course and started all over again.

Once Gabriel had awakened to the pain inside, he could see it in other people too. It was in the straight backs of the men in uniform, it was in the bloodless, tensed face of Mrs Bradley, the softness all gone, and, more surprisingly, it was in Mother, who was weeping soundlessly, tears seeping down her cheeks and falling from her jaw on to the collar of her best dress. How could it be that he had not seen it before?

Several times during the afternoon, as the mourners gathered in the drawing room at Oakstone, where tea was poured and cucumber sandwiches served by well-meaning ladies of the parish who had come to help, Gabriel's face reddened as perfect strangers – whose faces wouldn't open – came up to him and offered their condolences. Some of these strangers even put a damp hand on his head or on his shoulder, as if to steady him or paste him to the cold shadows next to the empty fireplace where he was skulking. The dense air was full of displeasure and it took a while for the room to fit; the atmosphere was too close, the company too strange – like waiting for a thunderstorm. But after a while, once sufficient tea and brandy had been poured, it all settled and the afternoon began to warm some of the guests through the French windows. Portraits of ancestors – government officials and imperial minor officers – seemed to straighten in their gilded frames. Somebody, perhaps one of the aproned ladies of the parish, had brought a bouquet of red and purple dahlias and put them in a crystal vase on a rickety console by a window. The light, which sieved through the petals, cast a shadow the colour of forbidden fruits on to a crocheted tablecloth.

Above the starched collar of an otherwise undistinguished suit, Uncle Gerry flamed. Gabriel could see that he was drinking gin, as clear and innocent as a child's face. With the new insight that the unexpected pain had brought, Gabriel also noticed that subterranean rivers of despair flowed under Uncle Gerry's grey stubble. The uncle looked at the silent nephew who had sidled up to him.

'If one can't have a drink at somebody's funeral . . .' he said, as if to explain why he seemed to be only half there.

But the boy did not answer.

'I'll just pour a little one for the dead,' he slurred apologetically and inclined his head.

And still Gabriel remained silent.

'Ah, don't look at me like that, Gabe. It's late – late in my life – and things haven't exactly gone according to plan.'

And Gabriel watched Uncle Gerry's shaking hand as it steadied itself around the re-filled glass.

'There,' said the man, 'that's better.'

They stood in silence for a moment. People around them had turned their backs, and their shoulders seemed to be slowly solidifying into a black screen.

'Why are all these strangers telling me that they're sorry for my loss?' Gabriel asked, at last.

The room seemed to have gone quiet around them as Uncle Gerry turned slowly to face him. The man rocked a bit on his heels, trying to focus his gaze into the open eyes of his nephew, which were of warm, brown soil with small black seeds for pupils.

For a brief moment, Gabriel detected a spark of clarity and intelligence in Uncle Gerry's eyes. I shall know now, he thought. At last, they will tell me. And then his uncle blinked and looked away, smiling vaguely at the guests.

'All this contemptuous flesh.' he raved, and flicked his arm, spilling gin on to the parquet floor.

'Tell me, please. I need to know.' He had gripped his uncle's arm, his nails digging into the sleeve of the black jacket.

'Look, Gabe, I would never do anything to hurt you. Do you understand me?'

'No, I don't. You're never straight with me.'

'You'd better speak to your mother about this. I have sworn to her . . .'

'Sworn what?'

'Never mind.'

'But why, Uncle G? Why did you swear about something that's to do with me? Why would you do that?'

'Oh, well, one does sometimes, eh?'

He realised this was true. Hadn't Michael sworn to do anything at all? But still he insisted: 'What, though, Uncle G? What did you swear?'

'Oh, forget about it,' the uncle said over his

shoulder, already pushing his way through the crowd towards the door.

Alone again by the marble fireplace, Gabriel could not determine the exact reason for his sudden sadness that was quite separate from the pain inside. He longed to be outside. His arms felt too long, his polished shoes too narrow. Slithering past the thick black bodies, he made his way towards the refuge of the kitchen, where Mrs Bradley had once served him pancakes.

The door to the kitchen was ajar and a rectangle of light, slightly askew, leaked from it on to the floorboards of the dark corridor like spilt milk. Gabriel stopped abruptly as he heard his mother's voice from inside.

'I don't believe in your compassion,' she said, her voice thin and hard.

'I'm sorry to hear that . . .'

Gabriel gasped as he recognised Mrs Bradley's voice shaping the soft words out of her round mouth. Holding his breath, he pressed his back against the wall and edged a bit closer to the door, crabwise. From his new position he could glimpse Mrs Bradley's back and, facing her, his mother, clasping her elbows across her chest, her shoulders narrow and sharp. Her face was red and puffy and it suddenly struck Gabriel that he had never seen his mother laugh; her unhappiness was like tinnitus in the walls of their house. But what was she doing now, crying in Mrs Bradley's kitchen? A wave of shame on her behalf reddened his face.

'Here we go again,' his mother snarled, 'but it's a bit late for you to say sorry, don't you think?'

Mrs Bradley sighed and turned slightly towards the window so that Gabriel saw now that she was smoking a cigarette. He couldn't remember having seen her smoke before and he looked in fascination at her white hand with its elegant fingers as she put the cigarette to her red lips. Her other hand was supporting the smoking arm so that she too seemed to be protecting her chest. The arm, Gabriel noticed, pushed up her breasts ever so slightly and he could make out their bulging round shapes through the thin fabric of her black dress. He had a sudden, dark, exciting urge to run up to her and put his head against her cleavage and smell her woman's smell. His head was hot and his temples were pounding, his heart beating faster and faster. He struggled to keep his breathing in check.

'I have been wanting to speak to you for a long time – ever since I realised that the two of you were still in Mortford – but George told me that you wouldn't let me anywhere near you or the boy.'

Gabriel's mother snorted in reply and followed Mrs Bradley's gaze out of the window. The sunlight fell through the leaded windowpanes from the left and illuminated their faces, as if they had been painted by Vermeer.

'Can we at least try to be reasonable for the sake of the boys?' Mrs Bradley's voice sounded tired and sad.

'Reasonable. Who are you to tell me to be reasonable? You're not the one who has had to raise a boy on your own. You haven't had to do a menial job to keep a shitty little household afloat at a time when rationing has made it almost impossible to find decent food anyway. You're not the one with a mental cripple of a brother.'

'I understand it must have been hard, horrific . . . but we did offer you money – George did.'

'As if I would accept his filthy money.'

'You're upset; can I get you a drink to calm your nerves?'

'Why, of course I'm upset! What do you expect?'

Mrs Bradley vanished from Gabriel's view for a moment, only to return with a bottle of brandy and a single glass in one hand, the cigarette still in the other. She poured the drink and handed it to Mother before she cleared her throat and spoke again. 'Believe me, we were both devastated at the hurt we caused you, but the war changed everything. You cannot imagine what it was like on the continent.'

'Oh, so now it's my own stupid fault for hiding comfortably in Britain whilst the war raged in Europe, is that it?'

Mrs Bradley sighed again. 'No, that's not what I mean at all. All I wanted to say is that everything becomes black and white in a war – in some ways, life seems suddenly so simple – things are either good or bad – good or evil. And love . . . love in such circumstances is . . . it's hard to explain, but it's all-consuming. It offers itself as the only possible salvation . . . George was my life, my destiny. It was as simple as that. And now he's gone.'

This was followed by a silence and Gabriel stretched his neck in order to get a better view. His mother was crying soundlessly, but her stiff shoulders were shaking now. Her face looked different, thawed, as if a layer of skin had been dissolved by the tears and drained away. It gave her features a tenderness. Years later – however much he tried – he would never be able to remember what she looked like at that moment, his own mother. And yet, even at the age of thirteen, hiding in the dark corridor, he realised that he was seeing his mother as she once was, as she might have been.

'I used to love this house,' he heard her sob. 'I think we might have been happy here, if it hadn't been for . . .'

Mrs Bradley, too, was crying now, softly, but with a quiet passion which made her even more desirable in Gabriel's eyes. He was confused. Confused by his conflicting emotions and by the two women's strange conversation that still did not make sense to him. He was torn between the loyalty towards Mrs Bradley, with whom he realised he was in love, and the loyalty towards Mother, whom he clearly ought to love. And then suddenly he felt a great lump growing in his throat and silent, hot tears started streaming down his face.

For the second time that day he was overcome by a great sadness. In hindsight, this moment – this hot, breathless hiding in a dark corridor – was his coming of age. This moment, so full of longing and lust for clarity and unity. As he eavesdropped into his own past, into his own beginning, and the meaning of their words slowly started to dawn on him, he realised too that every event in his life so far had brought him to this knowledge.

And, for a brief moment, he saw them all clearly in front of him: the two women crying in the kitchen; Mr Bradley, who was suddenly so much more to him and yet already cold in his grave; Uncle Gerry, slurring and stumbling through his drink; and Michael and himself, separated now by an unfathomable distance.

He closed his eyes and relived once again that fateful day of Mr Bradley's funeral. And then there was that other occasion, not as upsetting, perhaps, but still disturbing enough for him to have pushed it to the back of his mind for all these years: the reading of the will.

He saw, quite clearly, the lawyer, Mr Turnpike, who was sitting behind an enormous desk. He had never seen such a desk in Mortford before, not even at Oakstone. He, Gabriel, had been at one end of the desk and Michael at the other, his head bowed. He too had glanced down at his shoes, the shiny black ones he had worn for the funeral. They had been hurting in all the wrong places. Mrs

Bradley had been sitting behind Michael, and he remembered now how he could feel, rather than see, Mother sitting behind him, her back straight and her lips stiff and stretched like the mouth of a fish.

'All right,' he heard her say impatiently, 'let's get this over with, shall we?'

Mr Turnpike frowned. He was dressed in an expensive-looking dark suit with a thick, stripy tie and a yellow silk handkerchief in the breast pocket. 'I understand,' Mr Turnpike began, without looking up from the desk, 'that you have not yet been told of the full extent of your . . . ahem . . .' At this point he cleared his throat and pushed his half-rimmed specs further up his thin nose. 'Of your . . . connection. Your blood connection, that is.'

Gabriel noticed a tuft of coarse grey hair sprouting out of Mr Turnpike's ear, and wondered why the lawyer's hair was growing from his ears rather than on his head, like most people. He looked at Michael again, to see what he was thinking, but his side-on face gave nothing away. Was Mr Turnpike's hair growing out of the ear on Michael's side too? he wondered.

'Well?' Mother's hardest voice sliced through the room.

Mr Turnpike was beginning to look decidedly unhappy. He kept fidgeting with some papers in a file, which lay open on the desk.

'Well,' he repeated, without looking at Mother

or Mrs Bradley, 'I'm afraid I am obliged to read the content of the will with all three benefactors – that's the wife and the two sons and their . . .' He hesitated again, stroking the wood of the desk now, as if it was a giant pet, offering reassurance. 'Yes, with their guardians present.' There were beads of sweat on his brow. Behind Gabriel's back Mother made a noise as if blowing her nose, and Mr Turnpike looked up from the desk, his eyes falling instead on Mrs Bradley's chest.

'You boys,' he soldiered on, 'won't fully appreciate the details . . .' He brought out a silver cigarette case from the inside pocket of his jacket and, leaning over the desk, offered one to Mother, who sneered, and to Mrs Bradley, who accepted but had to stand up and lean forward to reach the case. Mr Turnpike's hand trembled a little as Mrs Bradley's blouse billowed. Gabriel, too, couldn't take his eyes off her as Mr Turnpike lit her cigarette. He sensed Mother tightening in the chair behind him. Then Mrs Bradley and Mr Turnpike both sat down and order was restored in the stuffy room, where the air was suddenly as heavy as the desk. But it was an order threatened by the crimson marks that Mrs Bradley's lipstick left on the filter – delicious little cherries where her lips had kissed.

Mr Turnpike cleared his throat again and began reading out the will. Gabriel could feel the lump in his own throat growing and swallowed to push it down. For this reason he wasn't listening, at least not consciously. There was a small allowance from the age of twenty-one and then, later on, there was Oakstone, shared by the two sons, although Mrs Bradley would have the right of residence for as long as she lived.

Gabriel looked across at Michael again – at his brother. How had this happened? He felt strange and wondered if Michael felt the same now that they were not just Gabe and Michael anymore, but brothers. Michael's thin hands were fidgeting, playing back and forth on the edge of the desk, as if it were a piano. His healed fingers were beautiful – slender, like a girl's. *Thud, thud.*

'Are you boys listening?' Mr Turnpike took an ordinary handkerchief from his pocket, not the silk one, which stayed immaculately where it was, and dabbed at his brow. 'I understand this must be hard for you . . .'

Gabriel said nothing and Michael murmured something and shrugged, because this was just the kind of thing, without any point or direction, which adults said to children.

'Stop picking, Gabriel,' Mother's voice wheezed from close behind, which made Michael stretch his neck to get a better look at the scab on Gabriel's knee, where a drop of blood was now visible under the crust. The attention made Gabriel want to pull it all off, just to show Michael. But, when he reached for the scab again, Mother's hand came suddenly forward and grabbed his wrist hard – so hard it brought tears to his eyes, which made the whole thing – a comforting, good thing – turn just awful and embarrassing.

Michael gloomed again and refused to look up. Mr Turnpike stared rather hard at his manicured hands, as if the buffed nails might be about to convey a coded message. 'There's something so sad about this . . . this business when children are involved . . .' he suggested.

'You don't say,' Mother replied dismissively, so that the hair at the back of Gabriel's neck stood out. But then Mrs Bradley looked over at him and smiled. Her eyelids were pink, he saw, and her face a bit blotchy, but he reddened all the same.

'There's just one more thing, then . . . You need to supply me with details, bank accounts . . .' Mr Turnpike said, vaguely.

Just then, Michael looked up at Gabriel. They were looking at each other. Without knowing why, Gabriel made a face – pulling out his ears and squinting his eyes. Michael's eyes were darker than ever, made darker by the smoky, brownish gloom in the room, but a light turned on somewhere deep inside and flickered once. Michael's lips were very red and slightly pouted, like Mrs Bradley's, and he looked very thin inside his best suit, as if his ribs might show through the fabric. Gabriel, on the other hand, was jam-packed in his own suit – he could feel the fabric in his armpits and his crotch, and the shorts were hitching up his thighs. Too much going on at once. He was ready to burst – must let it all out somehow. The air in the room was unbreathable. He might have been swimming underwater. Michael might have had the same thought because he suddenly blew up his cheeks like a puffer fish and let the air out in one long, perfect raspberry fart.

That was it; they burst, snorted, shrieked with dammed-up laughter, grunting like sea lions in the closed room. It was awful, horrible and wonderful at the same time.

Mr Turnpike's mouth fell open in his red face. 'Well, I have never . . .'

'Shush, *chéri, s'il te plait.*' Mrs Bradley sighed and sucked at her cigarette. 'Try to be a grown-up boy, for your father's sake,' she said, which made Michael howl even louder.

'Right, that's it!' Mother said, and stood up. 'I knew the whole thing would turn into a farce.' She grabbed Gabriel by the back of the neck and forced him to stand up, pushing him towards the door.

Gabriel slithered and managed to look back once at Michael, whose eyes were alight with a feverish flame.

Did he realise, as he was pushed away, that the heavy oak door closing on the room, still ringing with Michael's hysterical laughter, was also the door closing on their childhood? Had he realised?

Now, as he rose from the churchyard wall, Mr Askew remembered something else which he had chosen to forget: he remembered Mother's hand closing hard around his wrist as she pulled him out on to the street, how she had been leading him just as much as she was leaning on him, and the tears streaming down her face. Poor Mother; he had loved her then and felt bad about loving – about being in love with – Mrs Bradley.

And he remembered how, when they got home, she had suddenly dropped to her knees in front of him, her hands cupping his face, her eyes looking into his eyes.

'I'm so sorry, my darling,' she had said to him. 'I'm sorry about it all, but I was trying to keep our dignity – yours and mine. You see, it's *all* we have.'

His heart had bumped funny then. He had wanted to touch her cheeks, which smelt of crying. He had been bursting with love, but then the moment had passed.

'What about love, Mother?' he wanted to shout now, down into the tunnel of time. 'What about the love that should have warmed my childhood?'

At least that childhood had ended in laughter.

CHAPTER 6

Mr Askew had just congratulated himself that Mrs Ludgate might, by now, despise him enough not to turn up this Friday afternoon. The sound of the doorbell brought him back to reality.

'You all right?' She looked him up and down, reproachfully.

'Yes, of course; why shouldn't I be?'

'You were looking peeved; a bit . . . lost, you know.'

He didn't reply, but noticed that *she* was looking different. She was wearing summer gear: a thin-strapped dress in the kind of floral pattern which would forever separate English women from their continental sisters. Her bra straps were, by all measurements, broader than the dress straps, so that it looked as if she was wearing her lingerie on top of her clothes. He shuddered involuntarily and let his gaze sink to her feet.

'What?' she demanded.

'Eh?'

'What are you staring at?'

He honestly could not have told her, but suddenly

realised that she must have had some kind of accident and decided to take a softer approach.

'Have you had an operation on your feet?' he asked, hopefully.

'No.' She was beginning to sound quite snappish. 'Why?'

'Oh, I'm so sorry.' This wasn't going well, he realised. 'It's just . . . Well, those things on your feet . . . I thought they might be orthopaedic.'

They both looked down at her feet, which had finally escaped from the white trainers, only to be fooled into the cul-de-sac of a pair of bright green rubber clogs. Her toenails, which could be glimpsed through large holes, had been painted sky blue, as if they were about to sing solo in a children's pantomime.

'Yeah . . . and what's wrong with them? They are *Crocs*; my daughter sent me them from Exeter for my birthday.'

'Crocs? But what are they *for*?'

'They are like flip-flops, only more fashionable. And the nail polish is the same colour as Kate Moss.'

'Kate who?' He couldn't believe he was having this conversation.

'Supermodel.'

'A supermodel wears those . . . *things*?'

'Nah, probably not,' she realised, not without disappointment, ''cause she needs to wear heels – not as tall as the other models, poor love – but she does wear this colour nail polish. It's called "denim".'

'Oh, I see.' He sighed, realising that Mrs Ludgate was just too loud for his world. 'I suppose you'd better come inside. I was just about to make myself a cup of tea.'

'So, do you like the sea, then?' she asked, casually, as she followed him through to the kitchen.

'Pardon?'

'The seaside – I saw your car parked up by the rocks at Edencombe the other day. Reckoned you must be one for staring at the sea. Sunsets, and all that. Nothing there apart from the beach and the flipping sea and that old loony home up on the cliffs.'

He could feel her eyes on the back of his head. 'No, that can't have been my car you saw.'

'There's no one else around here who'd drive a car like that. It looks like it's from East Germany or the Cold War or somewhere like that.'

'Czech Republic, actually,' he corrected.

'Yeah, whatever . . . It was your car I saw and it was empty, which means you must have gone for a bit of a romantic stroll along the shore—'

'Look,' he flared, 'I honestly can't remember. I must have stopped off to sun myself for a while on the way back from the garage.' He could feel the prickling of sweat and his shirt was sticking to his back. He wished he had not been wearing the lambswool slipover. It was too hot a day.

'Only it was raining. Pissing it down, actually.' She would not let it rest.

'So what were *you* doing there in the rain, then?'

She had pushed him far enough into a corner and he realised it was time to strike back. But, as it turned out, it was too late.

'Just going past on the bus. Family stuff; none of your business.'

'Well, no—' he had not seen it coming and it made him crude – 'but *your* business is to clean this house, so you'd better go to it, don't you think?'

Defeated, he turned to the kettle and busied himself with a cup, whilst craving for the comfort of chocolate. Just then, the doorbell rang again. 'What now?' he barked, and threw the teaspoon on the worktop, from where it fell on to the tiled floor, clattering. Like that spatula, all those years ago.

'I'll get the door!' cried Mrs Ludgate cheerfully, celebrating her triumph.

'No, you most certainly will not,' he replied, adding 'bitch' in his mind, as he pushed past her to get to the hall.

The sunshine collapsed like a wave into the cool hall as he opened the door to the bright day. He blinked at the sudden light before seeing Mrs Sarobi standing there, smiling.

'I am sorry to intrude. I understand you prefer to be on your own, but I wanted to give you these to say thank you for helping me at the stall the other day.'

He looked at her thin, brown hands, which held out a basket of strawberries. It seemed, at that moment, to be the loveliest gift he had ever been offered.

'How delightful. Thank you.' His hands touched hers briefly as he accepted the punnet.

She laughed. 'It was the least I could do, after—'

There was a sudden noise from the hall and they both turned to look at Mrs Ludgate, who was about to speak. 'Ah, Mrs Sarongi, is it? Are you bringing *supplies*?'

'It's Mrs Sarobi,' Mr Askew corrected coldly.

'Oh, it's okay,' said Mrs Sarobi, calmly. 'I'm used to people getting my name wrong.'

'It's not *that* difficult; you have to be pretty bloody stu—' Mr Askew began, but was stopped by Mrs Sarobi, who put a hand on his arm. Such a slender, beautiful hand, it reminded him of something – something lost in time and memory.

She smiled at Mrs Ludgate and said, 'I had forgotten you would be here today; please, don't let me interrupt your work. I must leave . . .'

Mrs Ludgate shrugged evasively.

But Mr Askew could not stand Mrs Sarobi leaving. 'No. Please . . . That is, perhaps you would like me to show you the garden?'

For a moment, she looked surprised, but composed herself. 'Oh, yes, I would like that very much.'

'Excellent. We will bring the strawberries and something to drink. Wine, perhaps?' He seemed to pose this question to himself more than to anybody else, uncertain as to whether it would be proper. Did she even drink wine? Perhaps her religion . . . His thinking was cut short when he heard Mrs Ludgate laugh behind him; he was quite certain he did, but, when he turned round, he saw only a fixed smile on her face.

He turned back to Mrs Sarobi. 'You wait here; I won't be a second,' he said, handing her the punnet of strawberries to hold. Anxiously – eager, like a child – he went, knowing that, if he did not seize the moment, quick, quick, it might be gone. She might be gone, tired of him. As others had tired of him before.

Pushing past Mrs Ludgate for a second time, he rushed to the scullery next to the kitchen and grabbed a bottle of Sancerre from the rack. It was one of his follies, the rack. Had he seriously imagined that he might be entertaining on his return to Oakstone? That he would somehow suddenly turn into a host, after a lifetime of shying away from entertaining? He sneered at his own vanity and returned to the kitchen to pick up a couple of glasses. For an instant, he saw his own image reflected in a leaded windowpane: that moustache, its main feature, a disguise. Would it hold? The wine was not cold enough and the glasses were not altogether clean, he noticed, but there was nothing he could do about it now. Returning to the hall, he heard Mrs Ludgate's voice, triumphant:

'. . . So I said to Mrs Edwards, "She looks Indian enough to me, as if she ought to be wearing one of them sarongs," I said, "but she ain't, is she? 'Cause she's Afghanistanian." But I don't think she believed me. Looked at me oddly, all dark in the face, like she'd just turned Indian herself, she did.' She laughed, throwing back her head to show the creases on her neck.

'Is that all, Mrs Ludgate?' he asked, coldly. She stopped laughing abruptly and looked at him.

'What?' she barked.

'If you could just get on with hoovering the drawing room today and perhaps water the potted plant by the window, that'd be grand,' he said, closing the door on his self-appointed housekeeper.

It had rained during the night and the vegetation was still glittering in the afternoon sun. There was a mild summer wind blowing through the boughs of the old elms, making the leaves rush like small pebbles in the shallows. He stood stiffly in front of her, holding the bottle in one hand and the stems of the glasses in the other. His dark slipover and white shirt, neatly buttoned at the cuffs, gave him the look of a waiter.

'I am sorry,' he said in a strained voice. 'Please don't take any notice of her.'

'Oh, she's just curious; she cannot make us out, that's all. And I can't say I blame her.' She smiled up at him and the wind caught in her headscarf, gently moulding it around her face like a carved Madonna, just come alive.

186

He nodded. He realised that, at times, she made him feel calm, almost at ease, as if she was surrounded by an aura of harmony – like some kind of magnetic field or a wash of sleep. They walked quietly side by side for a while, following the gravel path around to the back of the house. He kept stealing glances at her, on and off, and wondered if, in a different life, he might have been walking with her like this *for real*. A rush of nostalgia – for something that had never been – touched his heart like sticky sadness.

Just then she looked up and saw him watching her; she gave him an oddly quizzical look, as if something had just dawned on her.

He cleared his throat, desperately trying to think of something to say. 'You have grown,' he blurted and immediately blushed at his own stupidity.

She too blushed, gorgeously, and answered, 'I'm wearing heels. I don't, normally . . .'

He looked down to see her naked feet in a pair of canvas wedge shoes. Next to them on the sunlit gravel, pointing slightly towards each other, were his own shoes, the ones he would normally only wear around the house. The brown leather was worn and scuffed, like the bark of an old tree. Quickly, as if to hide his shame, he took a step into the shadow next to the wall. The breeze brought a sweet scent of milk and honey. For a second he thought it was the scent of her skin, before realising that it came from the large buddleia that was in full bloom. Perhaps it's a tolerable shrub after all, he thought to himself, at least at this time of the year, before the panicles start to turn. A red admiral was hovering on one of the purple cones, not quite settling, as if it was still deciding whether the flower was worthy of its grace. It was the kind of shrub that you would see on derelict sites and at the back of warehouses, he realised, looking quickly around the garden. The grass urgently needed mowing and the beds were completely overgrown. He gathered that she too had noticed the lawn.

'I have neglected the garden in favour of the allotment,' he explained, apologetically.

'Well, it's too large for you to manage yourself. You should pay a boy from the village to cut the grass . . .'

He nodded and muttered, 'Yes, yes, perhaps a boy. Just one, though – not too many people. I would rather have the grass grow like a prairie.'

But she ignored him and continued, '. . . and I could help you with the beds, if you like.'

He looked at her, startled. Around them, the light was growing a deeper green.

She laughed again. 'Don't look so frightened. Would you not rather have me crawling around your garden than some gardener?'

'Oh, yes. Any time,' he twittered, trying to sound light-hearted. It was such an awful thought, and beautiful at the same time.

'You would have to give me a hand, of course; I can't do it all on my own – and it's your garden, after all,' she said, casually, and sailed on along the gravel.

He released himself from the shadow and followed a step or two behind. If I could trust this woman, he thought to himself as he watched her slight back where the end of a black braid showed from under her headscarf, perhaps my burden would be reduced. But she has got her own weight to carry, surely. It would not be fair of me to increase her load. But it's so tempting . . .

'I was thinking,' he said aloud.

'Of what?' she asked, looking back at him quickly and away, her cheeks still aglow.

Oh, well, he thought, if she was willing . . .

'I was thinking,' he said again, 'that it feels like we have known each other for a long time.'

This is so easy, he thought, and smiled sadly at his hapless shoes that seemed to symbolise something more.

But she was too clever to fall for such flattery. 'What are you doing here, in this place – this house?' she asked, as if to force open a new avenue of honesty. She had stopped, and stood facing him.

He sighed and, in order to avoid her eyes, stepped off the path on to the grass. She followed and he led her towards the dappled shade of a bright green acer.

'I started dreaming about Oakstone. I grew up around here, you know,' he answered, surprising himself with such honesty. 'I came back to be completed – to try to become whole, but I don't

189

know how to achieve it. And also, there was some old stuff I needed to sort out.' He bent down to feel the grass with the hand holding the two glasses. It felt dry enough and he sat down heavily with his legs sprawled in front of him. He frowned at the sight of his mottled white skin, which showed in the gap between his beige socks and charcoal flannel trousers. Putting down the Sancerre and the glasses, which immediately fell over in the tall grass, it suddenly occurred to him that he hadn't brought a bottle opener.

'Oh, I am such a dimwit!' he cursed.

'Forgot the bottle opener?'

He nodded miserably, whilst rolling up his shirt-sleeves. How could she have known?

'Ah, never mind. We'll drink it some other time. Have a strawberry instead.'

He liked the way she said it: *some other time*. He listened to her words and loved their clear lightness. He let them trickle across him like summer rain on a windowpane. They were both quiet for a while then. Once or twice, their hands brushed against each other as they reached for the strawberries in the punnet. The bangles around her wrists chimed. Leaf shadows moved on the ground.

'So you imagined,' she said, eventually, 'that, just by coming back to this house, by buying this old wreck and all of this—' she gestured with both her arms around the garden – 'you would find some kind of sense?'

'I belong here.' He must try to keep this private conviction.

'Do you, now?' she said, with a kind of flat irony.

He laughed loudly at her absurdity. What did she know?

'I mean,' she continued, but without the irony, 'can we ever belong again, once we have been uprooted?'

'Do you not miss Afghanistan – would you not like to go back?'

'Of course I miss it. But the memory of it's pure nostalgia. The world I grew up in does not exist anymore. And neither does yours. There's no way back.'

He stared at her in disbelief. In the rapt afternoon, he could feel the old tingling above his lip and pressed his index finger across his moustache. There was always the danger, he felt, that the seam would open up again – the live wound, the old wound.

'Where did you grow up?' he asked, obscurely, in order to gain time.

'In Herat.' Her mind returned briefly to where the Silk Road takes a breath and rests by the river before entering Persia. 'My childhood was full of the scent of pines and roses, and I used to play in pomegranate orchards and terracotta-coloured courtyards,' she continued in the voice of someone declaiming Byron. But he could see clearly that the satin pink and crimson of the roses and the dusty terracotta had all been woven into the scarf, which shaded her face now in a lovely blush.

'That sounds wonderful.' He even thought he could smell the roses in the air around them. And those pomegranate blossoms.

'Precisely; it's an image distilled from nostalgia,' she replied with vehemence.

'How can you be so sure that there's no way back?'

'It's difficult to see a bright path when the past is so dark. When the last thirty years of memory have reduced a nation . . .' She shook her head. 'Anyway, my point is, we all have to move on. Even you have to move on.'

'I want to die in the place where I was born.' It sounded a bit childish, he recognised.

'Does it matter *where* we die?' She did not seem to register the offered key to his past. 'Isn't it better to focus on how to live?'

He had never really thought of it like that. 'Well, I . . .' He was suddenly taut inside with the fear that they were not similar at all. He looked at the strawberry punnet on the grass between them – it was an empty, aching thing.

'I am sorry. I have hurt your feelings,' she said softly, and reached out to put her hand on his bare arm. He flinched, but kept staring at the blades of grass. 'Look, Gabriel, I have an obtrusive way at times; you mustn't take too much notice of what I say in the heat of the moment.'

He did not look up, but she bent forward to look into his face.

'You see, I was quiet for too long and now I

have this constant urge to express myself,' she said jokingly, trying to coax him back out of himself.

He did not reply, but shook his head sadly.

As if she had been reading his thoughts, she said, 'You know, us having an argument is a good thing – it means that we are getting closer. A unity is always made up of at least two parts, and we will never get close if we can't accept each other's differences.'

He looked up then, at her warm eyes surrounded by a silky cobweb of lines, but in his mind it was Michael's twelve-year-old face he saw in front of him. And those eyes looking back at him. He turned his troubled eyes away from her and pulled at a trouser leg. Feeling the dark beetle turn inside him and the old anxiety rising, he realised he was trapped. There was no protective corner into which he could remove himself and hide from her knowing gaze. He needed to strike out, if only to create some space. 'Well,' he said, his voice gone hard, 'fortunately, you have no idea about my "differences" – not to speak of my shortcomings – and I daresay that, if you did, you would find them difficult to accept.'

'Feeling sorry for ourselves is never going to help, you know.' She was fed up, he could tell.

'That's easy for you to say,' he retaliated, and, because he had never really grown up, he added, 'What do you know about anything, anyway?'

She made a strange noise then, out of her throat, but she did not answer. Her light body shifted on the grass, stirring up a scent of camomile.

And then, all of a sudden, the beauty had gone out of the day, as if something had dirtied the air. The jasmine gave off a smell of urine. His heart wobbled as if it was not his young self he was remembering, reflected in Michael's eyes, but some other dear child, lost and vulnerable – an orphan, perhaps; somebody he ought to reach out to and comfort – save, even – before it was too late. Smiling palely, he turned to apologise, perhaps not so much for what he had said as for who he was, but she had already left. The grass next to him was empty, save for a blackbird that had hopped out from under a shrub and looked at him now, sideways, with beads of unseeing jet.

When Mrs Sarobi first saw the pebble-dashed cottage towards the bottom of the lane, she had been disappointed. The estate agent had described it as picturesque and Edwardian, but the drab, roughcast front of the house had made it stand out from the other cottages in the lane, which were limewashed and chocolate-box charming. The interior, too, had made her heart sink. An old woman had lived there alone, she was told, and the cottage had stood empty for years after the woman's death, as the only son, who was living in London at the time, had not been able to decide what to do with it. In the end, several years later, the grown-up son had made it clear that he was no longer interested in the cottage or its contents. The agents had handled the whole business. It had been put up for sale and the price had been low enough for Mrs Sarobi to afford the deposit with the money her lawyers had eventually managed to get out of her former husband's family in Herat. She had been living in a council flat in Bethnal Green at the time. That was where they put her when she arrived, not quite knowing what else to do. It seemed to surprise the authorities that she had a plan for her life in this country. They warned against it, saying that she might struggle to fit in. But she had had enough time to think about her plan. She was impatient and so she had bought the cottage in a hurry, without viewing it first, making the fatal mistake of trusting an estate agent.

It was true that somebody had made a half-hearted attempt to tidy the place up, but a couple of decades or more of neglect had left their mark. The old woman's furniture and other artefacts had been included in the sale, but Mrs Sarobi suspected the place had been looted before she moved in. There was very little left of value. The carpet in the front room had once been maroon, but years of unbroken traffic had worn it down so that patches were frayed and the floorboards showed through. A torn leather armchair, once of high quality, stood by the dusty grate. Any ornaments or pictures had been removed but, in a low, built-in cupboard opposite the window, Mrs Sarobi found an old record player and a handful of seventy-eight records from the forties and fifties. In the kitchen, the linoleum had been cut away around the Rayburn to reveal the original flag-stones. Mrs Sarobi decided to expose the flagstones completely and put down one of her thick woollen rugs on top. Above the sink hung a yellowing calendar from 1974; a few illegible pencil marks spelt out a fading existence amongst pictures of furry ponies grazing on the moor. Only one date had been clearly circled in red: a Sunday in July. For some reason, Mrs Sarobi had felt compelled to keep the calendar in a drawer.

The two small bedrooms upstairs were cold and draughty, but the beds, which had miracu-lously been left in place, were of antique inlaid mahogany and bore witness to their owner's former station. Mrs Sarobi decided early on to do the place up, room by room, on her own. In the larger of the two bedrooms, taped to the back of an attractive chest of drawers, she found a number of letters. She held the small bundle carefully in her hands and sat down on the bed. A ribbon had been tied around them and Mrs Sarobi hesitated, as its fading red suggested their content. She had a strong sense that she was trespassing, and her heart was beating harder as she untied the ribbon and let it fall next to her on the stripped bed. There were eight letters, all still in their envelopes; the love of a lifetime in eight letters, each cautiously weighted word browning in fading ink.

She pulled out the first one, dated 1936, and blushed as she read that initial rush of agony and lust: *Your eyes, the softness of your lips, your naked skin, I want, can't wait, oh my love, when?* A man called George had signed the letter to his darling Cecilia. She herself had never received such a letter. She could not imagine what it would be like to read those words addressed to her – if it had been her eyes, her skin as soft as silk . . . She could not bear it; it was all too much. She put her hand to the bed and thought of Cecilia sleeping there. It made her shudder. But it was for that reason, for the empty bed, that she could not resist the last letter. Her hands were shaking as she held the envelope in her hands. The stamp was dated 1942 but, as she pulled out the letter, another, smaller envelope fell out. It was unstamped and, to her great surprise, unopened. The same hand, that only a few years previously had written about flesh and heart, had marked the letter, *To my son, on his eighteenth birthday*. She contemplated the sealed envelope, turning it over in her hands. She was at a temporary loss. Opening the sealed letter seemed to be going too far. She put it back in with the other letters and retied the fading ribbon. After a moment's thought, she put the bundle in her pocket; she would decide what to do later.

However, she soon forgot about the letters; it was another find, from the smaller bedroom at the

197

back, which was to keep her awake for many nights. She found the cache by chance. It was hidden under a loose floorboard, which in turn had been covered by a marble-topped bedside cupboard, left behind with the bed. The cache held a child's treasure hidden in an old tin case, the size of a shoebox. As Mrs Sarobi opened the lid of the box, kneeling on the floor by the bed, her body was prickling as if tiny ants were crawling all over her skin. There were a few pebbles, polished on a riverbed, a feather from a raven, still with a blue sheen to the oily black, a small metal clip with flaking red paint, which looked as if it might have something to do with electronics, and, wrapped in a soiled white handkerchief and placed carefully into a corner of the case, a collection of blue glass shards, some of them still showing a pattern of tiny painted flowers. Mrs Sarobi held the shards in her hands and felt at once a peculiar sense of purpose. She carried the handkerchief and its contents carefully downstairs. Gingerly, almost tenderly, she laid out the pieces on the oilcloth on the kitchen table and stood back to look at them. They were from some kind of vessel, she reckoned, and, without knowing why, she decided to try to piece them back together.

Over the following weeks she made slow progress, what with her daily work in the allotments and still sorting out the house at night. But gradually, piece by broken piece, the vessel began to take form. It was a cheap, ugly thing, she realised, but for some reason a child had treasured it, guarding it along with the things that mattered most, protecting it wholeheartedly against the giant world – that baffling hugeness that the child was just venturing into.

Mrs Sarobi had been a child once – with a child's name. She used to be Nahal – young plant. Her father gave her this name. He had been a keen gardener. 'Once life has been given,' he used to say, 'growing is its most fundamental occupation.' This name was the most significant gift she would ever receive. It carried the weight of a life born out of another, tied with the silken thread which stretched from her mother's heart – the heart which stopped shortly after Nahal was born.

A leggy girl with thin plaits and a cotton smock the colour of canaries, Nahal would play in the courtyard with her cousins. In the alchemy of late afternoon, the terracotta walls turned to red gold. Later, she would sleep, sedated by the scent of evening jasmine. Listening to her father's slippered feet on the stairs in the morning made her warm.

'You must study, you must read,' Father would say. 'Illiteracy is the greatest threat to this country and our culture – because, in the end, ignorance always makes us cruel.' By then, she was aware of threats. She felt tranquil inside her father's words, but around them tension was mounting and coarse twines of it found their way into her body. She felt them, knotting into a ball in her stomach.

They had to leave and they went to England,

where the rain curved across the landscape like a strung bow. In Cambridge, that first evening, she picked a white flower and held it under her nose – but it had no scent and she was embarrassed to have been found out in that way. She was lost for a while.

Gradually, she grew accustomed to her new home. She was intelligent, they told her with astonished admiration, as if no one expected her to be. She was different in so many ways, after all. She learnt and the young plant grew. It thrived in this rich, well-watered soil where it had taken root.

When her father died, she could have cried; she could have fallen to her knees and cried, 'My life, my love is dead.' But she was too dry, sapped. She was uprooted, her growth stunted. It was as if she had been whole before and now she was only half and so she had lost twice as much. Her grief was doubled. The burden of her own life was too heavy for her flesh, her breath, her single heart.

With no time to lose, her uncle in Herat brought her back and, using the small inheritance from her father as a dowry, married her off to one of his associates. It was a favourable arrangement, she was told. As her new husband's property, she was pushed into silence and lost herself once again. She withered behind closed shutters, although, sometimes, tender fingers of sunshine would reach through the slats to touch her face and, from time to time, a scent of jasmine would carry along the street over the car fumes.

When she did not conceive, her husband grew impatient – angry, even. He was much older and time was running out. 'Give me a son,' he demanded, but she willed herself to stay barren because she knew that no life would be able to grow in that place.

She supposed he did it to increase the odds – or perhaps it was a punishment. They – the men her husband brought to the house – entered her body and she withdrew her life, her secret life, into a protective corner of her head. Her body became irrelevant – an outlandish tumour, attached to her in some obscure way – until she wondered if it had ever served a purpose – if she had ever served a purpose.

He died shortly after the Taliban took over. With the help of a foreign organisation she managed to escape before his relatives closed down on her. The almost comic irony of that did not escape her; she was saved, just as an entire culture went under.

For a while, once she had reached Britain, the country where she had once been happy with her father, she wanted there to be somebody to whom she could say, 'I will tell you everything.' But no one asked. No one ever asked. But she had a plan and, in the end, she just wanted to go where she had never been. She went to Middle England.

Although she had no religion and it was no longer demanded of her, she continued wearing a headscarf. She withdrew into the veil and its folds of silence. All she wanted was a small piece of English ground where she could bring things to life – and let them grow.

There was something about him on that first day at the allotments that reminded her of her father. It was his eyes that convinced her. They were very dark, giving nothing away at first, but then they had started to shift. He too had things to tell, she could see, things that he was used to keeping to himself. He had great strength under-neath all that vulnerability and she felt at ease in his company; there was a clear affinity. At times, she wanted to reach out and touch his warmth. She liked their shared silence, which was more than words. They understood each other, without knowing each other; they could tell each other everything, she felt. She hoped. That was all.

CHAPTER 7

The house had been built some time in the early eighteen hundreds; its graceful symmetrical lines and generous proportions epitomised the kind of harmony and elegance that was the reward for imperial service. In the garden, glossy rhododendrons, blazing acers and a single, spiky-branched monkey-puzzle tree, fostered from seedlings in a new, harsh climate, were further testaments to its connections with the rest of the empire. It was only natural, then, that it should be set slightly apart from the rest of the houses in the small stannary town on the edge of the moor.

It was Mr Bradley's father, Colonel Bradley, who, on inheriting the house from his father, had decided to call it Oakstone – a masculine, solid and, above all, English name, which signified everything he believed in. He died of a massive stroke, which, to his friends at the club, seemed altogether appropriate. The colonel and his wife only ever had one child and, although the fact that the child was a son lessened the stigma, a couple of their standing was really supposed to breed better.

Mrs Bradley left life quietly, facelessly, and slipped into obscurity without much fuss and to the inconvenience of no one – something she might have been quite proud of in life.

The fortune, most of it originally from the wife's side, was considerable – or so it was thought. But, by the time of Colonel Bradley's death, it had dwindled. There might have been an ill-advised investment, or a mistress or two with expensive tastes. That was the thing about wealth – even the kind acquired abroad: one could never be too sure about it. By the time the house was passed on to the only son, young Mr George Bradley, it came with a much reduced inheritance.

And now, Mr Askew stood amongst his unopened, dust-covered boxes in the high-ceilinged hall with the checked tile floor, and frowned at a memory. There was a musky, brambly darkness in the corners, as if the house itself carried in its walls a clammy bafflement at life and human emotions – as if it too wondered how to live a decent life.

He dreaded this particular memory, he averted his mind from it, but, irritatingly, it followed him closely, like an unfed cat slinking between his legs. Annoyed, he walked into the kitchen, trying to shake off the past. The kitchen where Mrs Bradley had once served him pancakes and where, years later, he had been forced to come of age – where everything that he had previously taken for granted, all the warm comforts, mundane secrets and sorry little truths, had been twisted like a kaleidoscope, forever changing the colour and the play of light. Mr Askew was feeling increasingly anxious. He moved heavily towards the back door and, pushing it opened, stepped out into the misery of the day.

They were about sixteen or seventeen when they met again, for the last time, before Michael vanished and Gabriel escaped.

It was the summer before Gabriel's last year in school. The skies were high and the evenings were powdery blue, and there had been a rumour going around for weeks: there was an underground pub up on the moor where farmhands and vagabonds would meet to drink and gamble. Gabriel had heard the rumour too, although he was never anywhere near the boys at school who knew about such things. He asked Uncle Gerry about it once, but something dark came into the latter's eyes as he told his nephew to keep away from such places. He should have known better, of course, than to tell a teenage boy to stay away from a secret. Gabriel became obsessed with finding the pub. For a fortnight, he spied on his schoolmates and their older brothers, straining to overhear something that might reveal the secret location. Until, one evening, cycling back from Stagstead over the moor road, he saw, on a ridge on the horizon, two figures struggling westwards against the wind. Without hesitation, he turned the bike off the road and made for the ridge, riding across firmer ground and pushing it through mires and up the scree. It was a beautiful evening and it would stay light for many hours yet. The bog rush was in bloom and the tiny orchids wore their green bonnets. Once, he came across a carpet of dog violets growing out of the wind and the scent of fresh, elusive mystery made him stop for a moment and fall to his knees, as if answering a prayer.

A buzzard soared overhead, away from the sun, but Gabriel ignored its invitation and continued westward along the ridge, the bike rolling more easily now on the firmer ground. He had lost sight of the two figures he had seen previously and, after a couple of miles, he knew that he was lost. This was a part of the moor he had never been to before. The wind was rising. He had gone too far. Something told him he ought to turn round and follow the watchful buzzard back towards civilisation. He hesitated. There was a swift chill in the June air; he could feel it now and he wished he had brought his pullover. A single sheep bleated forlornly somewhere nearby and was answered from afar. He felt with the tip of his tongue along the fine fuzz of his upper lip and sighed. At times such as this, his natural instinct was to give up, to walk out and pretend it didn't matter. No one ever asked him to explain his actions. Gabriel's relationship with his mother had grown even more distant lately. Most things about him were either conveniently forgotten or brushed under the carpet, and so he reckoned that what he did or didn't do was of no real consequence. Slipping away was easy. And yet, on this particular evening, he felt a sudden urge to explore the moment – just as he would have done as a boy, charging over the moor with Michael at his side. He was aware that Michael had once made him braver and that the weakness inside him was all his own doing. He was the wrong one, the one who must try to set things right. And yet he seemed utterly unable to better himself – he remained a coward.

Cycling on, he felt a rush of excitement. His new-found bravery was followed by that familiar tightening in his groin and he had to brace himself not to reach down to his fly and touch *it*. There had been other times on the moor. Hardening. The smell of gorse flowers – sweet, sticky. The shame of it. Why would it not leave him alone? Instead, he pushed on over the heathland. The exercise felt good and eased the compulsion for the moment. The wind found its way into his cotton shirt, filling the fabric over his back like a spinnaker. He stopped and listened. He could hear music on the air. Turning his head, he followed the failing notes off the high ground and into a narrow valley where a stream had once been chan-nelled away to leave a dry riverbed. There, hidden in a grove of stunted oak trees, was a dilapidated granite farmhouse. It surprised him that he hadn't seen it before, it had been so close, but then the moss-covered walls merged seamlessly into the surrounding vegetation, and the roof, a muddle of turf and rusting corrugated iron, further camouflaged the building. The small windows were all boarded up, but the notes from a piano escaped through a gap between the wall and the roof, where a small part of the drystone wall had crumbled. A dribble of damp smoke leaked from a broken chimney.

Gabriel felt confused. Why hadn't he smelt the peat on the wind? He did not usually miss signs like that. Just then, he heard a noise to his left and drew in his breath as a large Alsatian bared its teeth in a snarl and growled at him, its tail stuck out like a standard. 'Shush! It's okay,' Gabriel whispered in his broken voice, holding up both hands as if threatened with a gun. The dog stood tensely and looked at him through narrow eyes. Thankfully, it was safely tied to one of the miniature oaks and, perhaps for this reason, realising it was mastered, it decided not to bark. Gabriel lowered the bike softly into the tall grass and walked up to the house. The door hung loosely on its hinges and, as he pushed it open, a gust of wind forced its way through the narrow passage to announce his arrival.

The single room was dim with smoke and thick with alcohol fumes. Vague grey light sieved through the broken roof in places and a couple of hurricane lamps were hanging from the rafters. Rough-looking men, hardened by years of labour and drink, were seated at a couple of trestle tables made out of old doors. Cards and dice were spread in front of them. Others were slumped on mismatched chairs – probably brought along by the drinkers themselves – drawn up to a damp hearth where a peat fire was struggling to take hold. Still others seemed to be leaning against the wall, asleep or too drunk to move. A few men looked up from their drinks with a flicker of interest as Gabriel entered, but most continued their silent gaming as if nothing had changed. There was only one woman in the room, no more than a girl, really. She moved through the shadows carrying a tray, picking up ashtrays and abandoned glasses. She was pretty in a freshly scrubbed sort of way – a pink and white waitress uniform hugged her small body. She looked dangerously out of place, like a pastel toy dropped on a motorway.

Gabriel was stunned. His eyes were drawn to the source of the music – an upright piano in the middle of the room, a burning candle melting on to the polished wood. He might have seen a ghost. Draped over the piano, hardly able to stand up, was Uncle Gerry, wordlessly humming along to a hectic ragtime dance. Clinking away at the battered keys, dressed in black tie, the suit too large for his thin frame, and with kohl painted around his eyes, was Michael. Gabriel recognised him straight away. His dark hair was pasted back with water or oil and his feet, which tapped frantically to the rhythm of the music, had been squeezed into what looked like the shoes he had worn for Mr Bradley's funeral. Surely they couldn't still fit him? Sweat was trickling down his temples and there was something manic in his eyes. The two figures at the piano seemed to be isolated from the rest of the men, as if they were part of the room itself; they might have come with the rest of the interior of the dilapidated barn, the same way a good pianist becomes part of the furnishings in a high-class cocktail bar.

Abruptly, the music stopped. A couple of the men applauded absentmindedly. Uncle Gerry had slumped forward over the piano, like a marionette with cut strings, and Michael sat motionless, dazed and panting and looking down at the keys as if they might reveal to him what was going on. Suddenly, he stirred and looked up, straight at Gabriel. A crazed smile spread across his tragic face, where the kohl had melted on to his cheeks. 'Gabe, my man!' he shouted in a high-pitched voice. 'Come over here and dance with me.' He held out his arm, as if for a waltz. A couple of the men laughed and jeered. The shame of it made Gabriel shrivel up inside. Why had he not followed the buzzard?

Michael stood up, steadying himself with a hand on Uncle Garry's shoulder. 'C'mon, have some moonshine,' he said elatedly, pulling a grimy bottle from out of Uncle Gerry's coat pocket. 'It will soften you up . . . You have become so . . . wooden.'

'No, thanks.' Uncle Gerry and Michael – together – here. Why hadn't they told him? For how long? Without him.

'Ah, go on,' Michael pleaded jovially, taking an unsteady step closer to Gabriel. 'It'll do you good.'

At that moment, Uncle Gerry groaned loudly and slipped rather elegantly on to the earth floor, where he remained, curled up like a foetus. The soles of his shoes were worn through, Gabriel noticed, and then, as he looked on in horror, a puddle slowly formed around his uncle.

Michael turned, precariously, to follow his gaze. 'Oh, dear me,' he slurred. 'Looks like Uncle G has pissed himself again.' He swayed around again and, leaning closer to Gabriel, whispered conspiratorially out of the corner of his mouth, 'He's such an awful lush, you know.'

'Shut up!' Gabriel wheezed, clenching his hands against the tears. 'Just shut up, will you?'

'Oh, dear *me*,' Michael said again with emphasis, looking suddenly downhearted.

'Why are you doing this, Michael? Why are you dressed like that?' Gabriel asked in a thick voice.

Michael shrugged his shoulders. 'They wanted me to.'

'Who are they?'

'King Herla and his roaming demons.'

'What are you talking about?' Gabriel felt a great wave of irritation. He noticed a cluster of angry spots on Michael's chin and, for a moment, he felt relief that his own pimples were not as bad as that. *They wanted me to.*

Michael smiled charmingly and nodded towards

one of the gaming tables. There, seated at the head, in a crude carver chair, was Jim of Blackaton. He was leaning back into the seat with his arms crossed over his chest like a medieval king. As Gabriel met his gaze, he grinned and raised his eyebrows. It was obvious that he had been observing them for some time.

Gabriel turned back to Michael. 'Are you still doing everything they tell you to do?' he asked with a mix of horror and contempt.

'Yeah, why not?' Michael answered defiantly and took a deep swig from the bottle. 'And why should you care?' he added with force.

Gabriel ignored him. 'Let's get out of here. We must get Uncle Gerry out of here *now*. Please, Michael . . .'

Michael stared at him, dumbfounded. 'But I can't; I only just started playing.'

'Please. He might die here. Can't you see he's not well? How long has this been going on for?'

As if that was the next cue in a terrible tragedy, Uncle Gerry groaned again and rolled over on his back, blinking once, like Lazarus. There was a streak of vomit down his shirtfront. He might have been hurled back from Hades.

'Ah, a gathering of old friends – how *nice*.'

Gabriel felt a chill along his spine at the sound of the familiar voice. He had not heard it in years – not since Jim of Blackaton dropped out of school shortly after the incident at the Giant's Table. He froze inside and the old terror gripped his heart and tightened around his throat. Involuntarily, he raised his hand to his upper lip and touched the seam, but was rocked forward as Jim of Blackaton clamped a heavy hand on his shoulder.

'Hello, Jim,' Gabriel muttered, trying to sound offhand, and then, his eyes swivelling back to Michael: 'Let's go, Michael; you don't have to stay here.'

'Oh, but that's where you're wrong, Bunny-boy; Michael is under contract, you see. He has signed up for the whole summer. *All* of his precious posh-school holiday.' Jim strolled over and put a protective arm around Michael's thin shoulders. 'He seems to like it well enough though – as long as we supply him with moonshine and a tuned piano – don't you, Fluffy?'

Michael tilted his head meekly and smiled a coy smile at his tormentor.

'And precious *maman* thinks that you're back at school, revising for your exams over the summer, doesn't she?' Blackaton laughed and patted Michael's back. 'We send her weekly letters back to Frogland, no?' Turning back to Gabriel he said, 'It's good for business, you see. My customers like knowing that there's somebody in the room making a bigger fool of himself than they are. Makes them feel good about spending their money here. And, my God, they spend it – the Moor Cross Inn is one of my more lucrative side businesses at the moment.'

Gabriel cast a dubious glance around the room

and frowned, desperately trying to make sense of it all.

'You have grown, Bunny-boy,' Jim of Blackaton said, gaily, menacingly. 'I like that thing . . . your moustache – suits you.'

Once again, he felt the tremor in his upper lip. He wanted to touch it, but held back. He turned to look at Jim of Blackaton. They were the same height now.

'Let him go.'

'A deal is a deal,' Jim replied in a tone that indicated boredom and perhaps bafflement at the simple-mindedness of the demand.

'We don't mind, do we, Gabe?' Michael asked, anxiously, in a small voice.

Gabriel looked at him miserably. He stared at the angry pimples, but could not face those brown eyes. He could not think of anything to say.

'Gabe?' Michael seemed suddenly weakened and grabbed hold of the piano.

Why hadn't Uncle Gerry told him that Michael was here? Why had they left him out?

'Oh, how sweet. The dumb brothers are of the same mind!' Jim bawled to the rest of the room and was rewarded with a few laughs.

At that moment, Gabriel's mind went black. He could feel the chill spreading though his arteries towards his heart. 'He's not my brother!' he shouted, desperately, through the swoop of darkness. 'He is . . . He is a freak!'

'And how easily they deceive each other. Again,

and again . . . and again.' Jim of Blackaton sighed and tutted theatrically, shaking his head deliberately from side to side.

Gabriel stumbled. The room was awful, suffocating. Something in there was strangling him. He needed to get out. As he made for the door, he stumbled over a bundle on the floor. He kicked at it in order to get free. He kicked and kicked into the soft mass until he realised it was Uncle Gerry he was hurting. He kicked some more. Tears were streaming down his face now. The drinkers and gamblers had grown quiet. They were watching this new spectacle with vacant excitement, the way they might watch a soft-porn movie or a second-rate dogfight. From the corner of his eye, Gabriel glimpsed something bright in the sullied room. He looked around and met the eyes of the waitress girl; they were round and of an unusual violet blue. For a brief moment she returned his wild stare with a look of such sadness and compassion that it made him sob.

Then everything was silent – the only sound the dripping of damp soot from the rafters and the oil hissing in the hurricane lamps – until Michael cleared his throat and grinned apologetically. 'I think I'll play another tune – a soft one this time,' he said, lugubriously, whilst continuing to smile away his sanity, love and faith.

And so, as Gabriel escaped at last into the light evening, Michael played; he closed his eyes and played the secrets in his closed heart. He played the firmness of the Giant's Table, the infinity of the sacrificial pool, a blue hull over a red keel, the wind in the great elms and the flimsiness of the streamers of gold and scarlet, which had once flamed from his handlebars; and, at the end, he played the death of the gods in a night full of sharp-edged stars and a sickle moon slicing the sky in two.

CHAPTER 8

Mrs Sarobi decided to take the bus, as if by chance, to Stanton's Cross one afternoon. It was a Tuesday, which somehow made it seem less conspicuous. As the bus climbed the steep hill out of the village, she wondered why the idea to pay Doris Ludgate a visit had come to her. She fingered the small brown paper bag in her lap; it contained two jars of blackcurrant jam. She didn't care for the stuff herself, but she had had an abundant harvest of blackcurrants that summer and jam was, at least in her own opinion, preferable to jelly, so it seemed an appropriate offering. One jar would have been meagre, three slightly over-enthusiastic.

In the seat in front of her, a couple of teenage girls were sharing the earphones to an iPod, swaying in unison to the inaudible music. It was obvious that they were bunking off school, but they were content in their girls' world, linked by the earphone lead as if by an umbilical cord. Mrs Sarobi sighed. What did it matter if she befriended that preposterous woman Ludgate? Could it be that she felt a need to be liked by one and all?

The thought made her smile. No, she was long past that kind of sentiment, she realised. This was a different kind of compulsion – at once emotional and inevitable. There was something about Mrs Ludgate that she could not quite put her finger on . . . Something which had made her cook that jam.

As she stepped off the bus at the crossroads and walked down the track, which was signposted to Blackaton, Mrs Sarobi felt that she could at least afford to look at the landscape. It was bleak. The bracken had already started turning to rust and the granite outcrops were steely-grey structures, abandoned there by some conflict of nature. An image surfaced in her memory: driving with Father through the pistachio forests around Qala i Naw. They too were gone now, of course, replaced by the tragic faces of deforested hills.

After a mile, the tarmac track petered out into gravel and the wind increased. With no hedges to stop them, the gusts seemed to want to push her off the track. Sheep huddled against each other with bewildered looks in their yellow eyes, as if this was all new to them – a cruel trick they had never been prepared for. She wound her scarf closer around her head and tucked the ends into the neck of her Gore-tex jacket. She was pleased to have it on a day like this; it made her feel strangely invincible. Come rain or shine. Just then, she saw the farm in the valley below. A small stream passed behind it and the whole area looked waterlogged. At once, she wondered if it was not the right place; after all, there was such a withdrawn air about the lonely granite house. The small windows were dark and unseeing and the gate to the yard was swinging in the wind. It might have been creaking, but wasn't. Mrs Sarobi shuddered involuntarily. As she drew closer, she saw a pink rose climbing towards the eaves. An overgrown orchard flanked the house, the gnarled trees protecting it from the worst of the westerly. She noticed a patch of blackcurrant shrubs amongst the trees – and a black crow snatching at clusters of rotting fruit.

She held the brown bag with the jam jars against her chest and entered the yard, closing the gate behind her. A dog started barking somewhere inside the house and she thought she saw someone move in one of the windows. She noticed that moss covered the damp thatch in places where the sun would never reach. Uncertainly, she took a deep breath and walked up to the porch.

The door opened almost immediately after her hesitating knock. There was nothing unusual about Mrs Ludgate, except her hair, which looked as if she had recently been lying down, and there was something else, to do with her eyes. They looked bare, Mrs Sarobi realised, not prepared for the outside world. Mrs Sarobi thought she saw a bruise on the other woman's chin, but it might just have been the way the light fell.

'Hello,' Mrs Ludgate offered, huffily, and put a hand to her hair, trying to make it right.

'You must wonder,' Mrs Sarobi began, 'why I have come.'

Mrs Ludgate only stared.

'You see,' the foreign woman continued, 'I wanted to introduce myself properly, seeing as we have a common acquaintance. And to bring you these.' She held out the little brown bag. It dangled helplessly from her fist.

'Oh,' Mrs Ludgate said, a glint of avarice in her eyes, and she took the bag from the outstretched hand. 'I suppose you'd better come in for a while; the wind is a bit harsh today,' she said as she withdrew into the shadows of the house, leaving the door open.

Mrs Sarobi followed her into a low-ceilinged sitting room dominated by a large, old-fashioned fireplace and, next to it, almost on the same scale, a heavy black TV on a stand. The mantelpiece was crammed with pastel-coloured figurines, she noticed, as Mrs Ludgate tidied away some magazines and crumbs from a tired couch with a garish pattern. The two women sat down, awkwardly, at either end of the sofa, and Mrs Ludgate looked into the bag.

'Blackcurrant jam,' she observed.

'Yes,' Mrs Sarobi had to admit.

'Ah, well,' Mrs Ludgate sighed and they were both quiet for a moment.

Mrs Sarobi cleared her throat. 'Perhaps this wasn't

such a good idea . . . I should leave,' she said, uneasily, wondering if her voice, if her accent . . .

Mrs Ludgate looked up. 'No,' she said, abruptly. 'No, why don't you stay for a cup of tea?'

'Are you sure?'

'Yeah, why shouldn't I be? It's the time for it.'

'The time?'

'For tea.' And it was decided.

While Mrs Ludgate went to the kitchen to make the tea, Mrs Sarobi looked around the brown gloom of the sitting room. The furniture seemed to have been bought as a suite, some time in the seventies. The flowery pattern, in green and mauve, had been worn away into a greasy shine on the armrests of the couch and two matching armchairs. She placed her hands in her lap and sat delicately on the end of her seat. A low table of polished pine in front of the sofa was marked as if a dog had gnawed at it. An opened can of peaches stood on the table, the handle of a fork or a spoon sticking out of it. Syrup had trickled down the side of the can and hardened into a ridge of grime on the wooden surface. In the unlit fireplace, leaning against the iron grate, was a broken vodka bottle, shards still swimming in a pool of liquor. She wondered why she hadn't smelt the alcohol on the air as she walked in. Just then, Mrs Ludgate returned with two tea mugs – one featuring an insane-looking purple cow and the other a bright yellow cat that looked as if it had been electrified.

221

'Is Mr Ludgate not at home today?' Mrs Sarobi asked, sipping her milky tea. It was as drab and tasteless as the passing of time in this house.

'Nah, he's not around just now,' Mrs Ludgate replied vaguely and languidly but, somewhere in that casual voice, Mrs Sarobi detected a familiar note – a note from a long time ago, when violent men had ruled her own life.

They drank their tea in silence for a moment, staring ahead into the darkening room.

'Shall I switch it on?' Mrs Ludgate asked, hopefully, nodding towards the TV.

'Oh, no; not for my sake, no,' Mrs Sarobi answered in alarm and added, 'Thank you.'

Mrs Ludgate sighed audibly.

Looking around in desperation, Mrs Sarobi's eyes fell on a framed photograph of a child on the mantelpiece. It was partly hidden behind some plaster kittens, so that Mrs Sarobi had to stand up briefly to get a better view. The child was a little girl, she realised, and the Technicolor had started to bleed in the corners. The frame was made of seashells stuck together with glue, and it had a little plastic sign shaped as a scroll at the bottom saying *Ilfracombe*. 'What a sweet little girl' she said, rather unconvincingly, whilst peering into the tightly unsmiling face that seemed to have been pasted on to a stripy roll-neck jumper. 'Who is she?'

'It's my daughter,' Doris Ludgate answered. Her voice sounded tired.

'I did not know you had a daughter.'

'No reason why you should. She lives in Exeter.'

'Does she visit often?'

'Sometimes . . . but only when my husband is away. She sends me cards for my birthdays, though.'

'Really? That's nice.'

'Yeah, every year. But she hasn't been to visit for a while now. Not for a few years . . .'

'Oh . . .' Mrs Sarobi had to sit down. 'Why?' It was all she could muster.

'Dunno. It's just the way, isn't it?'

'Yes, I suppose . . .' Mrs Sarobi had to agree.

'She's that busy.'

'I see.'

'A visit would be nice, though. Perhaps sometime soon, she will come . . .'

'Yes, perhaps.' Mrs Sarobi nodded, feeling helpless amongst such sadness.

Suddenly, Mrs Ludgate stood and walked across to the mantelpiece to rearrange some of the plaster animals around the photo frame. It was as if she had to put this gesture between herself and the child in the photograph. 'Her name is Celestine,' she said with a dry laugh. 'I named her myself. Silly, really, giving a child a name like that. What was I thinking?'

She remained standing with her back to Mrs Sarobi, who tried to console: 'It's a pretty name.'

'A bit too pretty for these parts, wouldn't you say? Don't know what came into my head. It was just one of those moments . . . She was sleeping in my arms and her face was so pretty and peaceful, I could hardly breathe. She was so beautiful, I wanted to cry – I could feel it like a pain in my heart, you see.' She turned abruptly to face Mrs Sarobi on the couch. 'She was my darling girl.'

Mrs Sarobi nodded again, knowing that her voice wouldn't hold if she tried to speak.

'Mr Ludgate hated the name, of course. He wanted to call her Jessica, so that's what she was christened. But I still call her Celestine, in my head, like.'

Mrs Sarobi sat silently on the edge of the couch. She was aware, of course, that too many words had been spoken today and that, in amongst those words, too many secrets had somehow been revealed. She sighed and hung her head, sensing a swoop of grief going through the room.

But it was too late. Mrs Ludgate realised that she had been lured by a rare and unexpected kindness into letting her guard down. And now she had to protect herself from this compassion, this foreign goodness that threatened her battlements. Her guest was smiling a sad, still smile, as if she knew, as if from the very beginning she had known, so that Mrs Ludgate had no choice but to hate her too, like she hated that Professor Askew.

'It's a shame, isn't it?' she said with a sneer.

'What is?'

'That you didn't meet that Mr Askew twenty years ago, so that you could have had a child of your own, rather than gawping at other people's daughters.'

Mrs Sarobi only shook her head uncomprehendingly.

'Barren women always do that – gawp at other people's babies. Not saying you in particular, love – just barren women in general.'

'I don't . . . I mean . . . Why are you saying this?' she answered, faintly, feeling exhausted and oddly fragile. She tried to remember the means that she herself had once used to defend herself against cruelty – and that sticky kindness, which threatened to expose the shame of it. But she could no longer remember the defence, only the hands that had held her down and pushed her face into a pillow.

'So starved for love that they have to make fools of themselves in front of babies – or older men.' Mrs Ludgate stumbled on with a strange fire in her eyes – panic mixed with Schadenfreude, perhaps.

And Mrs Sarobi, who had dried up all those years ago, was once again close to tears.

'Ah, well, such a shame . . .'

But Mrs Sarobi was no longer listening. She had got up from the couch, her legs shaking a little. 'I must go,' she mumbled.

'Really? Won't you stay for another cuppa?'

'No,' she answered. 'Thank you.'

'Oh, well, I thought I should offer, seeing as you came all the way.'

But Mrs Sarobi was already making for the door. Doris Ludgate was alone.

Hoping to escape the destruction she had caused, she went into the kitchen to feed the dog, which had been locked into the conservatory. He was a big brute who only listened to her husband. She scooped some dog food out of a tin into the bowl and hesitated before unlocking the door. The dog was growling at her through the glass panel. Quickly, she turned the key and pushed down the handle at the same time as she rushed out of the kitchen, slamming the kitchen door behind her. She could hear the dog in there, devouring his food, his claws rasping against the linoleum.

If Mr Ludgate had ever laid hands on their daughter, if he had ever touched her, it was something Doris Ludgate had chosen to forget. The alternative was impossible. How would a mother be able to stand in front of such a thought and face it unflinchingly? It was more than she could endure. That's how I lost her, she thought to herself now. She deserved that absence and those non-committal cards; they were not gifts of love or even duty, she realised, but constant reminders of how her daughter perceived her. Her own daughter. Sometimes, just after having woken up in the morning, before reality had arranged itself properly around her, she would try to think about how it had been, early on. She tried to remind herself of moments of awkward intimacy, of a small hand in hers or tiny socks hung up to dry on a line strung between the trees in the orchard, in pairs, like a string of DNA. The building blocks of a kind of life.

Evening had fallen outside and the sitting room was gloomy as she returned to the couch. Still she did not switch on the lights. She sat in darkness, waiting, listening for the sound of her husband's engine on the drive. Once or twice, she flinched as she thought she heard his footsteps on the gravel outside, but it was only the mounting wind off the moor. He would not come. There was no need for fear. Her heart was racing; her hands were cold. I am pathetic, she thought to herself. I must not be afraid. I must not. No.

CHAPTER 9

Uncle Gerry's death was awfully plain. He just slipped away one day, sitting in his chair. A coward sneaking out of the back door without saying goodbye. It was an aneurysm, Dr Lennon confirmed, and, rather unimaginatively, blamed the bottle before adding that it might just as well have been the liver. 'Quite rotten through,' he said. 'Must have been in excruciating pain.'

To Gabriel, the episode was disappointing. He had been cheated of what was supposed to have been the most devastating and significant moment of his life. It did not occur to him that the loss had already seeped into him and that he had lived with the anger, grief and absence for almost a year, ever since the episode in the pub on the moor. He had carried the unbearable for so long. The actual death – the stiffening corpse in the surviving armchair – was just something that had been left behind, a somewhat awkward legacy that one didn't quite know how to deal with – like the cottage with the books and records and stuffed birds and the old tweed jacket, which Gabriel took to wearing.

At the funeral, as he carried his wreath to the newly filled grave, Gabriel was struck by the futility of this conventional gesture; it did not seem to match the shadows in his own heart. The whole thing had been confusing – too confusing to know exactly what it signified.

The memory of Uncle Gerry still enraged Mr Askew. It had occupied his mind for days now. *Why* could those blasted memories not leave him alone? He stomped along Market Street with anger in his step. 'What if I, too, had taken to the bottle, like the two of them? What then, eh? Eh?' he muttered to himself, making a couple of schoolchildren step off their scooters to giggle and point. And then, halting at the street corner, he stood, shaking his head like an old horse, and said, 'I suppose I am to blame. I should have done something. But no one told me what to do. No one ever told me *anything*.' How easily we betray each other, he thought. And, most frequently, most devastatingly, we deceive those closest to us. Was there supposed to be some kind of awful symmetry to it? That kind of betrayal was like suppressing one's own origins, like detaching our life from its force and context. That's when we split in two, so that we can never be whole again. Never be one. 'And yet,' he muttered aloud, 'we are told we must learn to forgive, to overcome, to bridge and create order out of chaos.' When I try to imagine harmony, all I remember is a palm pressed into mine like a gift – or an offering: the unexpressed loyalties and tenderness of my childhood.

Suddenly appalled, he straightened himself up; in another minute he might have cried – there at the corner of Market Street and Gorse Lane. A grown man like himself. He looked around. The children had long lost interest in him and moved on, shooting on their scooters towards that Aladdin's cave of Rowden's. A dog ran past, sniffing the hedgerow at the other side of the street, and then, a moment later, its master appeared, dressed in loden fabric and plus fours for the moors. The man with the dog looked at Mr Askew a fraction too long but, deciding not to get involved, he nodded briefly at the rather elegantly dishevelled man, standing hapless and red-eyed inside his battered trench coat. Mr Askew sighed with relief and pulled at his collar. He did not like being addressed by strangers. Especially not the kind who dressed to kill. And those red socks. He had always been suspicious of red socks. They seemed to want to express individuality in a person without character. Not that he would know about these things, of course. Fashion had never been for him and, as he had never really fully known who he was, it would have been difficult to dress accordingly. He liked to think, however, that he had had some aesthetics. A saving grace. That *was* important, he realised, as was having taste. Taste was an indication of integrity, he reckoned. He might be judgemental, but only when it came to vulgarity. Take Mrs Ludgate, for example: was it not within his full right to loathe her? The thought of her made him shiver with discomfort. Or was it fear? There was a novel idea. Perhaps he was afraid of Mrs Ludgate. It wouldn't surprise him. The truth was that she seemed to know too much. She was not at all the fool he had taken her for in the beginning. And somewhere inside that knowledge lived a kind of danger – the threat that he would have to face up to it all. He was a coward, after all. There, it was said. It made him feel better, relieved, to think that the blame – and the bitter shame of it – self-inflicted, perhaps, but still *his burden* – might be eased, lifted for a moment.

Fortified, he lumbered on along the lane towards the bridge. A single sparrow chirped like a bad phone line in the hedge.

After Uncle Gerry's funeral, leaving was easy. There was a time of waiting, of course – a few months of confusion and frustration, until school finally finished – but all those sliding moments just served to increase the separating distance. So that, in the end, it *was* easy to leave; the lifeline, such as it was, had already been cut. He knew he must go away, but he had no idea where to – nor what his going away might lead to. Mother talked about university, but he could not think what to study. He had sent off all the appropriate forms, but could not remember what subjects he had listed, or what institutions. The whole idea seemed

231

so utterly alien to him, as he had never yet believed in himself enough to take anything seriously.

Deciding on going west, as far as the coast, was directed as much by a romantic idea of the sea as by the practicality of being able to afford the train fare there. And he relished the challenge of walking the distance back, camping along the way.

'Now, listen to me . . .' Mother would demand, and he would sigh and say nothing.

'A young man like yourself needs to have a plan.'

'Like me?'

'All I'm saying is that you're not the kind of person who can fall back on the goodwill of other people – or a large family. Not at this time, at any rate.'

'Well, then.'

One summer evening, when he was still building up the courage to leave, he was sitting at the kitchen table, hunched over *The Times*. Idly flicking through the pages, he considered, for once, his mother. She was busying herself by the cooker; her back was slightly bent these days, her features somewhat blurred or distracted – the way features become when you stop looking at them. She was wearing what looked like a man's cardigan over the plain navy blue dress she wore for work, and he noticed that she had been biting her nails. Whose cardigan could it be? He didn't dislike her or resent her – on the contrary, they were vaguely friendly towards each other these days. It was just that he didn't know her – he didn't know who she *was*. How could he, when she had always kept things hidden from him? Over time, and through the loss they should have shared, the distance between them had become too vast, too arduous to cross. He realised that she was probably quite lonely. Just then, she looked up – not at him, exactly – and asked something or other, but vaguely.

'Mm?' He pretended to study the pages more intently, and that was when he saw the article. The title caught his eye first – *The Last Freak Show in Europe* – and then, below it, he saw the photograph, slightly blurred where the printer's ink had smudged, of the smiling showman in a tall hat, standing in front of a circus tent, his arms extended, palms facing up. Gabriel recognised him straight away – he hadn't changed much since Gabriel and Michael had visited Dr Buster's Sideshow on that night before the incident at the Giant's Table. He leant over the paper, oblivious, once again, of Mother, and looked closer at the photograph. There, at the back of the shot, barely visible, were those two golden girls – the Siamese twins that had fascinated him so all those years ago.

Gabriel began to read:

In many cultures today, a monstrous birth amongst humans is still blamed on the mother. In Europe, there used to be a common belief that a woman could imprint on her unborn child her own impure fantasies, so that the deformity of the child mirrored her wickedness. A source from seventeenth-century Germany tells of a woman who quarrelled with her neighbour, and butted her head against the other woman in fury – she subsequently bore a child with two heads. A loose woman may give birth to an hermaphrodite child who would be able to fornicate with both men and women. A woman who told lies and was never to be trusted might find herself mother to a two-faced Janus. It has been said that the mother of Joseph Merrick, the Elephant Man, was frightened by an elephant during pregnancy. Today, of course, we know that physical malformation is programmed in the genes long before birth, and the exhibition of so-called freaks has long been banned on humanitarian grounds. But Dr Buster's Sideshow is still in business. The show last visited Britain ten years ago, but has since been confined to southern Europe, where laws are more relaxed.

Gabriel looked up from the paper. He was vaguely aware of Mother addressing him, but he ignored her like one would a summer breeze. He frowned, unable to fully comprehend what he had just read – or, rather, why such an article would have been written now. It seemed somehow to be directed at him alone.

A message delivered *aux mains*, for his eyes only. He wondered if anybody else would have noticed. Surely it must be a sign? He read on:

> Recently, an increasing number of the performers, who would, by current standards, be classed as disabled, have been removed from Dr Buster's Sideshow and put into institutionalised care.

The feature had been written by a professor of medical anthropology in London, who was carrying out a research project on the last freak shows in Europe and the States. A *professor*. So somebody was actually studying the mystery he had once experienced? It seemed an incredible thought.

Suddenly he heard Mother's voice again, this time quite clearly:

'I wonder, Gabriel, if you really know what you want?'

'Look, Mum,' he groaned, irritated to have been disturbed, 'did you know what you *really* wanted at my age?' He stood up and crossed to the sink to get a drink of water.

'Actually, yes, I did.'

This surprised him and made him turn to look at her. She was watching him and he detected a look in her eyes that he had not seen before – something that flared once and settled. For a moment, he was confused to be looking down at her – he was so used to looking up.

'What was it that you—' he began to ask, but she interrupted him.

'What about your university applications? What if you're accepted – how will I be able to reach you?'

'Don't worry; I won't get a place,' he replied, but not with such certainty this time, as he thought of the professor mentioned in the paper.

'Oh, Gabriel. You're a clever boy . . . and you have such imagination.'

'Oh, yeah? I thought you didn't like my *imagination*.'

'Let's not argue,' she sighed.

'All right,' he muttered, cheeks aflame.

'I found Gerry's old sleeping bag and this rucksack.' She gestured towards something that was hanging from the handle of the kitchen door. 'I thought they might come in handy for your trip.'

'Oh, thanks, that's really great.' He felt the purpose rising in him again and, for a moment, he thought that he could perhaps tell her after all – tell her what it was that he wanted, or, at least, what he hoped to find.

'I *do* know what I want,' he tried. 'I want to find out about things. I can't explain it very well. I want to know if there's something else. You know, something I haven't understood yet, some mystery that needs to be solved, that kind of thing . . .' His voice faltered as he heard, for himself, how ridiculous he sounded.

Mother smiled then, but sadly. He was older,

she noticed – his body had hardened and the cuts on his knees had healed – but not old enough.

'*Mystery*,' she said, shaking her head slowly. 'A mystery is just an imitation of something we carry inside us – the urge to explore something we can never discover.'

'But . . .' He was shocked and appalled by what she had just said. He had never heard her speak like that before. Perhaps he had misjudged her, thinking her stupid and irrelevant. 'No, I won't accept that.' He winced at the hollow sound of his own voice, which somehow managed to fill the kitchen.

'Ah, well,' she said then, without much emotion. 'You'd better start packing.'

As the train left the platform at Exeter and Gabriel shoved his backpack on to the luggage rack and sat down on the hard seat, it was as if Mortford no longer existed – although part of him realised that things might carry on as normal: Mother would get up in the morning, finding the milk bottle on the doorstep, boys would be taught in dimly lit school rooms, a farmer would be looking with jealousy at somebody's new tractor and the buzzards would soar over the moor, keeping an eye on what went on down there.

Oakstone had stood empty for a few years. Michael had been sent to boarding school shortly after Mr Bradley's funeral and Mrs Bradley had left at about the same time – no one knew where, but some thought she might have crossed back to the continent. A few times, he had sneaked into the gardens and peered through the French windows where there was a gap in the curtains; the furniture and the paintings of glorious ancestors were still there, but there was an empty feeling about the place, as if the house had been stripped of any significance so that all that remained was a set for a film or perhaps a staged tragedy.

But all that was no longer relevant – all Gabriel's roads were leading away from there. He put his hand on the seat next to him as if its polished wood might offer some kind of reassurance that this was reality. If Mother had been upset about him leaving, she had not shown it. But she had washed and ironed his shirts carefully and helped him pack the rucksack on the eve of his departure. A few times, as these preparations went on in the small cottage, they had brushed against each other and once, when they met in the doorway to his bedroom, she had held her hand to his cheek for a moment, and he had let her.

Where was Michael? Gabriel could no longer picture him – would he even recognise him if he saw him? He too might have left school now. The posh school. Had he gone to his mother in France or was he still in England? For a moment, Gabriel closed his eyes and tried to imagine Michael at Oxford or Cambridge, as this was most certainly where he would have been expected to go. But, however much he tried, he could not conjure up an image of him amongst the Gothic limestone and the soaring stained glass. Nor would he let his mind turn off the safe path of memory to face again the Moor Cross Inn, where they had last met.

But no, he convinced himself, this was no longer relevant; his quest was altogether more personal. He rested his forehead against the cool surface of the train window and looked at the landscape. All through the south-west, the pastures were rinsed and silky after a summer rain that had sailed ahead of the train earlier that afternoon. The skies opened high now into an impossible blue and the waning breeze combed softly through fields of barley. As he travelled into evening, towards the sea, the setting sun warmed his face through the window and he relaxed. Grey towers of ancient churches reassured and time loosened its reins, bringing him further away. The sky – the vanishing sky – seemed to swell and swallow up the horizon and he let his shoulders sink, his hands slacken and relax.

This is how the journey began. He was travelling away; he was travelling towards. Looking for . . . Looking for what? What sort of a quest was this, and what did he hope to obtain as he set forth from Mortford?

Amongst the strangers on the train, he was a stranger to himself. He had no idea who he was and, as he looked into his own eyes reflected in the darkened window as the train raced through a tunnel, he found no clues. He was back again in that corridor of mirrors where this quest had first started.

Although it was a short journey, a few hours at the most, because it was his first passage of this sort it felt endless. And, through this distance, the deepening countryside outside the window tried to convince him of its possibilities.

Travelling west, the engines of the train laboured on through the landscape that gradually lost its familiarity. At dusk – one of those numb nightfalls that make the landscape look sluggish – he was relieved to cross a great river. As he watched the dark waters from the bridge, he knew that it was too late to turn back.

He had few belongings. His backpack held a handful of shirts, socks, underwear, a wool cardigan, an anorak and some books he had taken from Uncle Gerry's cottage but never looked at. The sleeping bag was tied with straps to the bottom of the rucksack, along with a small primus stove and a water bottle. Mother had packed a stack of sandwiches and given him a five-pound note, which he kept in the otherwise empty wallet in the inside pocket of Uncle Gerry's tweed jacket.

As he stepped on to the platform at Penzance, he knew at once that this was different, that the adventure could begin. A lonely gull laughed overhead as he stood for a moment, taking in the scent of the sea – not the close stink of the shore, but the breath, the sigh of ocean – the salt breeze, the deep, deep water, the oysters in their shells, the metallic, the cold. And there were other smells too, connected with the seaside: deep-frying, rotting fish waste, and something else that he couldn't quite pin down.

He shouldered his backpack and walked along the quay into town, having decided to spend the first night in a B & B. The quay was dark but, here and there, tentative light sieved through thick curtains and painted the cobbles in smoky grey. A fine band of pink still rested on the horizon and the sky out there was the same colour as the night skies of the illustrated Bible he had read as a child.

It took him a while to find a place with a vacancy, and the woman who let him in was brusque rather than friendly as she showed him to a tiny room at the top of a rickety staircase. She was a large woman, almost as tall as he was; her abrasive dark grey hair was tied back in a strained bun and her skin was a strange pale yellow. He smiled, wishing that he had kept the little moustache he had been growing over the scar. She left him alone then, closing the door before descending the stairs. He could hear her steps for a long time, as if the room was in a high tower, rather than in a harbour house.

It was more a ship's cabin than a room, he felt, and it suited him just fine. He could feel, rather than distinguish, the sea outside the window, resting in the harbour after a long day of worrying and fretting amongst the hulls of fishing boats. He lay down on the narrow bed without undressing and fell sleep almost immediately.

He woke early to the smell of bacon fat and realised how hungry he was. After groping around a while in the browning gloom, he found a narrow kitchen at the back of the house. The woman was wearing a calf-length skirt of a coarse material and a fisherman's jumper that was a few sizes too large. He watched her for a moment as she stooped over an old-fashioned cooker, which was black with soot and grease. Stepping into the kitchen, his boot slipped on something, which melted into the linoleum floor.

'Good morning, Mrs . . .' he said gallantly, trying desperately to remember her name.

'Morning,' she muttered, without turning. 'You can seat yourself at the table, there.' She indicated with her head towards a Formica-top picnic table set up in the opposite corner. A single chair had been put in front of the table, which had been laid for one under a naked bulb. He fidgeted for a moment with the cutlery, which was not altogether clean.

'So, you must be very busy in the summer. Do you get many guests?' he tried.

The woman muttered something and he wasn't sure she had heard his question. However, he thought better than to ask it again.

Instead, he sat politely and, when she placed a

huge plate of stringy bacon and eggs in front of him, he finished it all quickly and with good appetite. This seemed to cheer her up somewhat. She chuckled as she poured him another cup of tea. A large dog, its pelt the colour and texture of the woman's hair, entered the kitchen and pushed itself under the table to settle at his feet. The stink was almost unbearable and he was relieved that he had had time to finish his breakfast before she let the dog in. He could feel the woman studying his face closely and he hoped that his revulsion wasn't showing. For once, he was grateful for the scar that would divert her attention, he hoped.

'So, what brings you here, then?' she asked at last.

This straight question took him aback somewhat and he had to think hard.

'I wanted to meet the sea where the land ends,' he said at last, and blushed. He wasn't even sure this was what he wanted to do, but it sounded good. He had come there for no better reason than his foot had stepped on to the train.

'Ah, I see; a quest to the end of the world,' she said, and he thought he could detect some irony in her voice. 'Well, it's not much to look at out there, you know – just rocks and sea. Same as anywhere else.'

'Oh, well . . .' He glanced with some horror at the unkempt woman.

'The paths around here are ancient, I'll tell you. You're not the first pilgrim to come this way.' She had a broad, fleshy mouth, which gave her the expression of a large fish that prefers to consume huge amounts of tiny things. She was formidable.

'Pilgrims?'

'Pilgrims, knights-errant: young men trying to set the world right.'

He hated the way she made him sound common. 'Oh, but—' he tried.

'I hope you find whatever it is that you're looking for,' she interrupted. Then her lips closed with a damp sound.

Grateful to get away, he walked in the morning sun to the little harbour and on to a pier, where he sat with his back against the smooth, fortress-like walls of the jetty, the backpack by his side. By now, the sea was as blue as the sky he had been watching the previous afternoon. No, it was bluer, more innocent, and the houses in the town looked like children's building blocks, stacked against the hill-side. Soon, tourists were milling around the quays in the harbour and their constant chattering soothed Gabriel's mind. He closed his eyes to the sun and listened to the little noises of the world – to the swell, which rustled the pebbles in the shallows, and the sea breeze, which intrigued the masts and tackle. Somewhere, a dinghy pulled at a rope, whining like a spoilt child. The sun turned around the harbour until, in the end, it handed his hot face to the shadows. He fell asleep and dreamt that he was a child again, resting against the rocks of the tor.

But he did not allow himself to rest for very long. His journey must begin here, at the end of the world.

Resting his elbows on the weathered stone of the bridge railings, Mr Askew watched the stream below. Transparent, it had only one purpose, which was to flow. It was possessed by this motion, un-restrained, un-helmed, immaterial. It held nothing and wanted only freedom. Freedom from what? The prospect confused him. It was a fluid state, which could only be achieved in opposition to something more solid.

What freedom had he hoped to find as he set out on that first journey? He had no work, school had finished, and there was no love to hold him. Loveless, he had lost an uncle, a father, a brother, and his mother had at last set him free. 'You'd better start packing,' she'd said, as if freedom was a thing with which to rap his knuckles one last time. 'You'd better find out for yourself.' And yet she was the one who had always kept knowledge hidden away and chained in dark dungeons.

Loveless? A vague image flickered in his mind. He remembered a market; he moved with Mother through legs of people and stalls. The crowd heaved around them until all he could hear was the blood pulsing in his ears. He could not pene-trate the forest of legs. And then, an opening, a glen and light and air. 'I thought I had lost you!'

he cried, as he turned and looked up into her face – Mother's face, smiling.

'I was right behind you,' she said.

In a sudden flash, he realised that she had really wanted to be, that she had tried to, at any rate, and that the intention reflected a kind of love.

No, he realised now, it was not escape that compelled me. He stood back from the railings and continued across the bridge. Not a search for freedom, then, but for the opposite – the eternal hope of belonging.

He started walking then and, directed by some locals, he found an ancient inland walkway that led across the peninsula to the coast on the north. There were cornfields dotted with the red of poppies, hedges fragrant with insect life, and fields of green grass where lambs still tilted against their mothers. When he looked back the way he had come, he could still see the bay and the cone of a strange island, which he hadn't noticed before. It sat on the horizon like the mirage of a citadel. For a day and a half, as he walked across that upland, he would turn to see this island shrinking behind him.

But mostly the landscape around him looked like a reflection of itself: glossy and still, like a photograph. He wished he could have told somebody about it, but realised also that real beauty is something best enjoyed alone.

If those summer days above the sea enchanted

him, the nights unsettled him. Quite often, he would sleep out in a field, making a lair for himself in the high grass, like some kind of a beast. When he pressed himself against the ground, he could feel, through the wad of the sleeping bag, the earth's heart beating against his own – *thud, thud, thud*. He would sometimes look up at the stars, picking them out as they hung alone or in comfortable clusters. His favourite was the two heads and locked hands of the Gemini.

Dozing, straining not to wake himself, he would fill up with the absence – the loss that was so familiar by now. Trying to be whole, he listened to the unfamiliar noises that filled the darker end of the night. The sea breeze would often rest all night and stir with him in the morning. Then the sun would rise and pick out pearls from the surface of the sea.

Once, well above the tidal mark at the beach near a small town, on a night of such semi-consciousness, a shadowy couple stumbled across the dunes without seeing him. They passed so close by that he caught the trailing scents of alcohol and powdery perfume. Gabriel held his breath and, after a moment, the woman giggled as the man made urgent noises, fumbling around her body. Soon, Gabriel heard their quickening breath and little animal noises from just a few yards away and pressed his hands against his ears – but it did not help; he could not shut out what was happening; it was as if he was there, too. He might have moaned as, behind his closed eyes, he tried to picture the girls he had fantasised about during his teenage years in Mortford: Suzy Hill, with hair as black as the river at night and long white arms, and Dolly, who worked as a maid at Daunton's farm and was a bit dim. The boys at school had called her an easy ride, but he had never known quite what that meant. He had associated the hot, overwhelming urge with all that was repulsive and shameful. Touching himself in bed or up on the moor, he had felt only revulsion and eventually release. An image of Mrs Bradley in a tight-fitting dress surfaced briefly in his mind, but he pushed it away with such force that his arm hit the sand and the couple on the dune stilled for a moment, listening into the night – but their moaning soon started again. Gradually, Gabriel's body relaxed until he was no longer in it, but freed at last, and the shadows seemed to take on individual shapes and stand out like statues of icy marble – even though he himself was burning.

Afterwards, he tried not to think about this episode. The next morning, he stood and glanced over at the place where the couple had lain. The sand was disturbed but there was no other trace of their lovemaking. Later, Gabriel wondered if it had happened at all – or whether it had just been another one of his lewd fantasies.

And yet something had changed in him that night. It was as if his eyes had opened for the first time to the image that had been drawn in dark contrast on the inner wall of his heart on that day by the Giant's Table. As he looked out from the depths of his sleeping bag the next day, the sky looked different, as if something had dirtied the air. In this dull grey light, Gabriel could sense that witnessing the sexual act on the beach had merely put a faint smudge on his heart where that other dark memory had been lurking for so long. But, instead of fear or disgust, he felt a strange surge of euphoria and gratitude and he smiled to himself, wishing that there had been some way of telling Michael that there was nothing filthy between them, that the badness was all Jim of Blackaton's, and that what Jim had done to Michael that day on the moor was in no way related to the lust and yearnings that had begun to stir inside him soon afterwards. Touching another person could be forgiven; it was different from the thing that Jim of Blackaton had done to Michael – an act of such violence that it had split the skies open and let the darkness into the world, an act so powerful that it could tear two friends apart like a bolt of lightning cleaving a tree. How deluded they had been to fall under the spell of shame. How little they had understood about the nature of things. He wanted to tell Michael that he could be clean again and that the beauty that had gone could return.

While he was walking, constantly moving, his feet creating their own rhythm, his past seemed weightless and distant. He was a stranger in the past and the present was moving, moving. He reeled through this present – he had a purpose at last, if only just to keep on walking.

He walked north along by the sea now, through the ludicrous beauty of those summer days. He walked to the rhythm of everything that had come before and everything that lay ahead. And, all the time, it – all of it – was singing inside his head, *dum, dum, dum-be-di-dum.*

Sometimes, he had to make his way into a village to buy some bread and eggs. It did not worry him particularly that he was running out of money. He would find a way, he was sure. People addressed him along the road; some wanted to ask and others wanted to tell. It didn't matter much. It was all the same in the end. As long as he didn't give too much away.

But, for the most part, he kept his eyes downcast so that he was unaware of any effect he might have on other people. And, often enough, he wondered why he was there at all.

Not long after the episode on the beach, he was crossing a meadow and passed a lamb sleeping alone. He stopped to watch it for a moment, wondering why it was not with its flock. He looked around and saw the rest of the sheep moving slowly, like a patch of bog cotton, in a field further up the slope. Just then, the lamb woke and raised its head to the bright day. It looked so fresh, so new to the world, that Gabriel had to laugh. 'You'd better hurry up, if you want to catch up with your friends,' he said. His voice frightened the creature, which struggled to stand, and, as it did, he saw with dismay that an extra pair of legs was sticking out from its belly. Gabriel flinched, and looked away.

After reaching the sea again, he began to weary of walking and sat down, resting his head between his up-drawn knees by the side of the road. The road was not busy, but every now and again a lorry would drive past at high speed, churning up clouds of dust in its wake. He whistled between his teeth. Birds looked down from a wire. Soon, a lorry slowed down and stopped beside him, spewing fine road dust and car fumes.

'Where're you headin', boy?' the driver shouted out of the window.

Gabriel got on to his feet and brushed down his trousers. 'East,' he replied with insouciance.

'Hop in. I'll take you as far as the bridge at the old ford.'

Gabriel thought for a moment, looking around, before he picked up the backpack at his feet and climbed up into the passenger seat.

'I'm Bob,' the driver said, cheerfully, putting the lorry into gear and releasing the clutch. He was a small and plump man. Almost bald, he wore his shirtsleeves rolled up, as if to show off the mat of ginger hair that covered his arms and hands.

'I'm Gabriel,' the hardening boy replied over the

engine noise, and decided that that was as far as he would go.

Then they went. The road began to move, faster and faster, into a tunnel of high hedges – too fast for his mind, which had walked at its own rhythm for over a week. He felt nauseous and closed his eyes hard. The wind tore at him through the open windows. He leant out and opened his eyes. A raptor circled in the empty passage of sky above the road. That's when he noticed a peculiar smell from the back of the lorry.

'What's that smell?'

'Roses.' The man chuckled and hunched over the wheel as they turned a sharp corner. 'You like it?'

'Oh,' said Gabriel. 'Yes.' But he wasn't so sure. There was something disturbingly musky amongst the heady sweetness, something that made him think again of the couple on the beach.

The driver was whistling some jaunty tune.

'I love my job. Driving around in a lorry full of roses, thinking of all them women.'

'What women?' Gabriel wondered.

'The gorgeous ones, son. The sort of women who are given roses. Perfect, milky-skinned, red-lipped . . . Phwoah!'

Bob gripped the wheel harder so that his knuckles whitened under the ginger hair. For a while, Gabriel too tried to imagine these women, but it was no good.

'Have you ever seen a lamb with six legs?' Gabriel

asked instead, not to show off, but just because he could not get the sight out of his mind. It sat there, even when he tried to conjure up a milky-skinned woman.

'Ha!' The man who called himself Bob laughed. His eyes were clear as mirrors. 'If I saw a freak like that, I'd wring its neck.'

Gabriel did not know what to say.

'Bloody scandal that such creatures are still being brought into the world today. You would have thought that they'd have bred them out by now.' Bob shook his head violently and spat out of the window.

'They are mutants,' Gabriel tried to explain. 'It just happens.' He thought of Bob's spit dribbling down the side of the lorry.

'Yeah, well, it's not gonna happen in my world; I can tell you that for free, son.'

Gabriel frowned at that and looked away. How bright was the day and how dark it was in amongst the hedges.

They went on and did not speak much for a while.

'It's a nice day,' Bob said once.

'Yes,' said Gabriel. 'It's nice.'

His legs were beginning to hurt and he tried to move them, but his rucksack was in the way.

At last, the lorry stopped and he found a new path and followed it into the woods. He walked for an hour or so between oaks and beeches, the nettles high on either side of the path. And that was where he stumbled upon them relaxing in the sun – the prop gang.

It was midday and the woods were empty. The road he had just left passed by a hundred yards to the south and, to the north, beyond the valley, was the sea. Gabriel remembered that he had not eaten for a while and he knew by the throbbing at his temples that he was dehydrated. He looked down at his clothes; the leather boots and flannel trousers were covered in dust and his cotton shirt, open at the neck, was pasted to his back. Somewhere, far down the road, earlier in the day, he had removed the woolly jumper and stuffed it into the backpack that he carried now, slung over one shoulder. He threw down the backpack on the ground. He mopped his brow with a handkerchief and pulled his hand through his hair. A few beads of sweat had caught in the downy rag that attempted, once again, to cover his upper lip. He wiped his face with the damp handkerchief. His head was pounding still after the lorry drive and the light that sieved through the canopy of leaves was beginning to hurt his eyes. I need a drink, he thought to himself. I really need a drink. He looked around again but the place offered no clues. A whiff of air, as stale as his breath, brought the scent of moss and rotting leaves. Somewhere a dog barked and the sound carried like a gunshot through the slow air.

With a sigh, he decided to walk on along the

ridge of a deep ravine. Far below, he could hear the purling of water amongst rocks. Some small animal, a mouse, perhaps, stirred in the under-growth of last year's leaves and spiky twigs as his tread crackled on the hard path. He had not walked for long when he heard mumbled voices from somewhere nearby. Straining his ears, he followed the sound off the path towards a small clearing.

Three young men, somewhat older than him, were sprawled out, resting in the dappled shade of the shrubs. A few empty bottles were lying in the grass around them. One of the youths seemed to be telling a story, but fell silent when he spotted Gabriel. The other two, who had been facing the storyteller, turned lazily to see what was going on. As they watched each other across the silence, Gabriel could hear his own heartbeat. The summer heat seemed to be pushing towards him, sipping the air out of his throat. His tongue had swelled and he felt like opening his mouth and letting it hang out. Instead, he swallowed and tried to speak, but the noise that escaped sounded more like the croak of a rook. He tried again, his dry mouth rasping on the words. 'How do you do?' he said, and, realising how ridiculous he sounded, like Stanley on the shores of Lake Tanganyika, he tried again. 'I wonder if you have a drink? I'm thirsty . . .' His words trailed off as he watched the glassy faces of the young men on the ground. They were casually dressed; the one who had been telling the story wore a soiled string vest and baggy cotton trousers, held up by braces; a battered straw panama had been pushed to the back of his head. The other two were similarly shabby in collarless shirts and faded denim trousers. One of them was smoking a cigarette and the third one, sitting slightly apart from his friends, resting his back against a tree trunk, was lithe and athletic, with a remarkable head of reddish blond curls. Gabriel thought for a moment he looked familiar, but he could not place him. Their eyes were a bit glazed and they seemed to look at him with sluggish remoteness rather than with hostility, as if they expected the cue to come from him. The smoker took the cigarette from his lips and spat on the ground. Gabriel watched as a string of dribble hung in suspension from his lower lip.

Suddenly, as if somebody had turned over a page, the storyteller whistled between his teeth and spoke: 'Well, well, well. If it ain't a tinker.'

Gabriel frowned. He did not like being called a tinker, but he was not quick enough to answer back. He could feel his face going a little red and hated it. Pointing with his thumb over his shoulder in the direction of the road, he said, inanely, 'No; I just came from the road. I have been walking for a week now.'

'Go on. You don't say,' the guy with the braces said with flat irony and the others laughed.

'Hey, Charlie, give this guy a beer; he's as dry as a desert.'

It was the youth with the copper curls who had spoken and, when no one moved to get Gabriel a drink, he scrambled to his feet and pulled out a bottle from a canvas bag that was sitting in the shade. He tugged the cap off and walked over to Gabriel, who had not moved. 'Here you go,' he said with a hazy smile, and handed the bottle to Gabriel. 'I'm Reynard and this—' he pointed towards the storyteller and smoker in turn – 'is Charlie, and Stan from the States. You can call me Rey.'

Gabriel only nodded and put his head back and drank from the bottle. The three youths watched him attentively in silence until he had emptied the bottle. Rey chuckled, as if he found the situation particularly funny.

'So, have you got a name, then?' asked Rey, his eyes merry.

'Gabriel,' he said, looking down at his boots, which were partly covered by dry leaves. It occurred to him that Rey's voice did not sound local. There was a slight twang to it that he could not place; perhaps it was from the east. He looked up and blinked once against the faded gold and green of the woods around them. 'My name is Gabriel Askew.'

'Gabriel,' Rey repeated, thoughtfully. 'That's quite a mouthful. Do you mind if I just call you Gabe?'

Gabriel stared at the stranger in surprise. Something eerie and intent flickered in Rey's gaze now, he noticed, and he saw that his eyes were green and a bit slanted, although perhaps this was just on account of the sun, which had suddenly found its way through the leaves of a great oak behind them. 'No, I suppose not,' he said, hesitantly.

'You been on the road for a while, then – spent all your money?'

Gabriel blushed and nodded.

Rey regarded him keenly for a moment before turning to the others. 'What do you say, guys? Do we want to help this kid to a decent meal?'

This resulted in a round of laughs. The man called Charlie spoke first: 'You've got to work for your food in this world, boy. You'd be better off hanging out with us for a while. Here, have another beer.'

'I'm not sure . . .' Gabriel hesitated.

'Ah, go on, Gabe,' Rey sniggered. 'Relax a little; you look like you have come far, or perhaps you just don't know where you're going . . . I think you're due some good times, don't you?'

'I suppose I could stay for a while, until it cools off . . .'

'That's the spirit!' Rey called, triumphantly, and nudged the smoker with his foot. 'Hey, Stan, move over; make room for our new friend.'

Stan stabbed out his cigarette on the grass and shifted reluctantly to one side.

'Come on, guys; we may just as well finish off all the drink – we'll get paid again tonight,' Charlie said, hoisting four bottles out of the bag.

'What is it that you do?' Gabriel asked and accepted another bottle. He sat down in the grass.

'We are the prop gang for a travelling show,' Charlie explained and inclined his head towards the distance. 'We got a day off today . . .'

There was another round of laughs at this.

'That is,' Charlie continued, 'we *took* the day off. Thought we deserved it, as we've been slaving our guts out lately.'

'So, you see, we need to fortify ourselves; the boss can be pretty mean, if he finds out.'

'Yeah, that's right; the cheapest, grubbiest boss in the world,' Stan muttered wryly, and lit another cigarette.

'Depends what you're prepared to do for him,' Rey remarked, casually.

'Oh, yeah? Like what?' Stan seemed suddenly interested.

'What?' Charlie tutted in mock bafflement. 'Are you saying that three shillings a day is not a high enough wage to keep Stan the Stabber safe on the deserted roads of the Old World?'

'Shut up, Charlie. I'm warning you . . .'

'Oooh,' Charlie cooed like an old woman. 'Now you're making me *scared*. Perhaps you would rather go home to Oklahoma, where I'm sure you'd get a very warm greeting. I bet they'd all be lined up to welcome you back – sheriff and all.'

Rey regarded Gabriel with an eyebrow lifted. He winked, but Gabriel looked away. Where had he seen Rey before?

'I told you to fucking shut up!' Stan shouted and threw an empty bottle at Charlie's head. It missed by half an inch and fell on the grass with a dull thud before breaking with a chinking sound against a stone. The sound reminded Gabriel of something – a moment suspended in his memory – an instant of clarity and darkness. He tried to hold on to it, but it was gone, lost in a blue haze. He frowned and looked up at the others, who seemed to have fallen asleep on their backs in the grass, as if under a sudden spell. A deep green shard of glass caught a ray of sunshine and reflected it back into the sky, as if from under water.

Gabriel took another swig from his bottle. And another. He was beginning to feel quite drunk. He was not used to alcohol, especially not on an empty stomach. He looked back towards the path, where the sunshine was dancing in the air. It looked like the path of a road in a fairy tale where you would expect the highwayman to appear, all dressed in green. He contemplated getting up and walking away, but his head was too heavy. The song of the wind in the treetops was suddenly deafening, as if waves were tumbling on to a shore nearby. How had he not noticed it before? It was as if the insistent noise had just been switched on in his brain. He boxed the side of his head lightly, as if to get rid something lodged inside his ear.

He heard another noise from nearby and looked

up to see Rey sitting with his back against the tree trunk again, laughing softly at him.

'Dear, dear . . . Has the drink gone to your head?' Rey whispered gently and tilted his head so that the copper locks stirred.

Gabriel stared back at the golden youth, but his head felt too heavy for his neck. He tried to keep his eyes open, but the world seemed to be moving and he felt nauseous. For a lingering moment, he was sure the world had shifted; like a mirror, it had been set at a different angle, the two of them the only witnesses.

He woke into a warm, furry dusk. For an instant, he could not remember where he was. There was a dull pain behind his eyes and a metallic taste in his mouth. Then sound started to return through the thick night: at first, the sound of the under-growth, and then another noise – an engine being revved. He closed his eyes again to the dark and breathed deeply. The air was heavy with scent: the moist smell of moss and herbs, the thick scent of honeysuckle and the earthy stink of animal shit. It was all coming back to him: the tunnel of time that signified his journey, the lorry drive, following the path into the woods and the drink in the glade . . . Abruptly, he sat up and looked around. Black limbs of trees seemed to reach up towards patches of violet-white sky, recently abandoned by the sun. The others were gone; there was no sign of them apart from a slight impression in the grass around him. He was suddenly afraid. On his hands and knees now, he searched in the gloom for his back-pack. He found it only a few yards away, where he must have dropped it earlier in the day. 'Okay, calm down,' he said to himself and stood up. Brushing dry twigs and leaves from his clothes, he looked up to see a couple of lights through the trees; they seemed to stare at him like the eyes of some forest beast. Taking a step towards them, he realised they were the headlights of a car, about a hundred yards away. This made him laugh. The car was parked, but with the engine running.

'Hey, Gabe!' somebody called through the woods. 'Hurry up, if you want a lift out of here.'

He moved towards the lights – the dark around him and the blinding beams made it difficult to see where he was going, but when at last he felt the gravel road underfoot, he hesitated. He looked back over his shoulder at the path that disappeared into the forest. Well, he had come this far – he'd better walk on.

As he approached the car, he could feel a feverish energy rising inside him. The failing dusk had melted away and in its place was this car of bright wonder.

'Hey, tinker.'

Gabriel stopped and turned to face the man they called Charlie.

'Come to join the prop gang, have you? You're looking a bit sprightlier than you did this afternoon . . .' Charlie was eyeing him up and down.

'Yeah, well, I had a nap,' Gabriel replied and shifted the backpack from one shoulder to the other.

'A nap. Do you hear that, Stan? Tinker just had a nap.' He laughed and turned to Stan, who had just stepped out of the shadows, smirking.

'I'm *not* a tinker,' Gabriel said sourly, but with emphasis.

'Hey, cool it,' Rey interrupted in a friendlier tone. 'It's just the way we talk . . . Anyway, do you want to earn some cash?'

'Sure . . . What do I need to do?'

'One of our gang is . . . sick. There was an accident . . . Anyway, we could use an extra pair of hands at tear-down tomorrow night.' Charlie was looking at him again, critically, and Gabriel wished he were taller, older, stronger, and perhaps altogether different.

'Where is this place?'

'Not too far – up on the moor.'

Gabriel felt something touch him, something like a cool wind, and swallowed once.

'Okay, no problem,' he said, stretching his back a little. 'Shall we go, then?'

And so he was back on the road, moving further away from the sea, across the ancient uplands. Rey was driving and Gabriel was sitting next to him in the passenger seat. The other two were asleep in the back. He could sense rather than see the landscape, which flowed into the night. This terrain was veined, compact and fleshy; sometimes the road bumped under the car. In the wedge of light slashed by the headlights, strange shapes seemed to gather at the edge of vision. A fox slinked across the road and escaped, but Gabriel would remember the amber gleam of its eyes – a fraction of time in that long night. And yes, once or twice he wondered why he was there at all, until they reached it at last, as he had known they would: Dr Buster's travelling sideshow.

Wrenched out of the memories of childhood and exposed in the unforgiving light of a summer dawn, Dr Buster's Sideshow looked pathetic, almost ashamed of itself. The sign above the entrance to the main tent, which had glared at Gabriel and Michael all those years ago, had been repaired once too often and the image of the smiling Dr Buster was so caked in paint that it looked as if he suffered from some kind of exotic skin disease. The stalls, which encircled the circus tent, were bleached by time and weather, their loose canvas awnings flapped in the wind, and without the adornment of the fairy lights, the whole lot reminded Gabriel of bunting left out and forgotten after a village fête, stirring every now and again over a communal hangover.

Rey drove slowly through the lot and parked at a distance from the other caravans and trucks. Stan and Charlie stumbled out of the car and disappeared without a word.

'You can stay with me for a night or two,' Rey said. Gabriel was too tired to object and followed him to the back of the site, where an old-fashioned caravan was parked well away from the others.

Rey opened the door with two keys and stood back to let Gabriel duck through the narrow doorway. Rey entered behind him and rustled around for some matches. Soon, a soft, golden light from a hurricane lamp, swaying gently from the ceiling, framed the scene. The caravan looked larger on the inside. There were a couple of bunks on either side of a table and a small gas stove on a bench in a corner. The bunks were covered in thick crimson mattresses, like something you might expect to find amongst a band of gypsies or in the tent of some desert sheik. Ledges had been fitted along the curved walls to form shelves, which were filled with books. From somewhere, a faint draught was blowing through the cabin, which was surprisingly cool. Gabriel stared in disbelief.

'Can I get you anything?' The sound of Rey's voice made him twitch. 'A coffee, perhaps? The absence of tea in these parts is regrettable, of course, but at least it's not ersatz.'

Gabriel hesitated.

'Sit down, please.' Rey gestured to one of the bunks. Gabriel dropped his backpack inside the door and slid in behind the table. He sat down carefully on the edge of the bunk and picked nervously at the sleeve of his shirt. The crimson mattress was filled with horsehair and he felt its coarse texture through the thin fabric of his trousers.

Rey smiled and wriggled past the table to light the stove. He pulled back a red and white checked curtain that had been strung up above the cooker. Behind it was a little larder with a couple of army-issue enamel mugs and plates, some mismatched cutlery and a few waxed-paper packets of groceries. He brought out the mugs and put them on the table. He scooped some water out of a bucket on the floor and poured it into a small brass pot, followed by coffee from one of the bags. His long curls seemed to come alive as he busied himself with the pot over the blue gas flame. 'You should be a bit careful around Charlie; he's not always as benevolent as he seems.'

Gabriel nodded slowly. 'And Stan?' he asked.

Rey laughed gaily. 'Stan's a bit of a crook, all right, but at least you know where you stand with him.'

'Oh, I see,' Gabriel said, but was not quite sure. He remembered the dusky, shifty gaze of the smoker.

The pot started to wail and Rey killed the flame. A rich, seductive scent filled the cabin and Gabriel began to relax.

'And stay away from the boss, too, for that matter.'

'Why?'

'Never mind; just stick close to me and you'll be okay,' Rey said and poured the steaming coffee into the brown enamel mugs. His gestures were casual; there was an ease in his limbs, as if he had never been required to consider his own body. His face was smooth and his cheeks were brushed in bronze. They sipped the hot coffee in silence for a while.

'Where are you from?' Gabriel asked suddenly, surprising himself. He would normally avoid the great awkwardness of questions. He never wanted people to ask too many of him and he had become accustomed to supplying only half answers.

Rey looked up and his eyes filled with a strange mirth again. 'Oh, you know, here and there. I have been on the road for so long, I cannot remember. The steps I have taken have hardly been determined by myself. And you?'

'Same here . . .' he replied, quickly.

Rey laughed again. 'Good man, good man; that's what we like to hear,' he said and winked.

Gabriel ignored the note of sarcasm in his voice and looked around the cabin. 'You read a lot, then?' he asked. The books, he noticed, were in a variety of languages, only a few in English. They looked expensive, with proper leather binding.

Rey frowned. 'Yeah, well, you know, you get fed up, at times,' he said and waved his arm evasively, as if to indicate some wider meaning, which did not make itself clear. Instead, he turned to reach into a recess in the wall and pulled out a brown paper bag stained with grease marks. 'I expect you're pretty hungry. You haven't eaten for a while, have you? Here, have some bread and cheese; it's still fresh,' he said, as if Gabriel would have expected better.

Gabriel realised that he hadn't eaten since morning and broke the bread with great enthusiasm. Rey watched in silence. He was rolling a pellet of bread between his fingers. There was something almost humble about his presence. Or perhaps 'graceful' was a better word. From outside came the muffled sound of a brawl. The two youths listened for a moment, but it died away.

'Are you not having any?' Gabriel asked through a mouthful of bread.

'Nah, none for me.'

Gabriel swallowed the food. He could hear the joints in his jaw.

Rey pulled out a pilot's watch from a pocket in his denim trousers and strapped it around his wrist. 'Well, I need to get some sleep. We start at dusk.'

Gabriel nodded and looked around.

'No facilities in here, I'm afraid – we have to piss outside,' Rey continued, and moved towards the door.

'Fair enough,' Gabriel said, getting to his feet. He felt remarkably well and rolled up the sleeves of his shirt. He could smell the boyish odour of sun and dust on his own flesh and it reminded him of adventure. The two youths stepped into the twilight that seemed suddenly warmer. They stood for a moment, side by side, the light and the dark blended into two tall shadows. Gabriel touched briefly the faint scar that linked his upper lip to his nose like a silver chain. A rope of exhilaration coiled in his guts. The prospect of this new adventure warmed many past failures. He realised that he had no idea what the job would entail. At least it would be something happening. They walked back towards the light from the door of Rey's caravan and the last remains of night seemed to loosen. In the waste beyond the site, something shrieked – a fox perhaps – but only once, and the sound faded fast.

As morning finally broke, milky and damp, the two youths crawled into their bunks and slept.

CHAPTER 10

It was on returning from his morning walk one day that Mr Askew suddenly knew he had to find Mrs Sarobi. He needed her. Thrilled with this new purpose, he turned off the lane and made for the path to the allotments. As he passed through the cluster of chestnuts and oaks and climbed to the higher ground of the fields, he saw her from afar, holding a watering can without pouring. He stopped and stood, weighing on his heels, quietly, silently. It was a gentle moment. Far away, a plantation of firs was hard against the horizon but, here by the allotments, the world was softly quilted. He had stayed away for too long, he realised. His herbaceous border would be overgrown and unkempt. Quickly, he smoothed his fringe to one side with the palm of his hand. His hair was still dark, with only a few strands of grey in it, but his moustache was all silver. Perhaps I should shave it off, he thought, with a pang of anxiety, as he started towards the lonely woman in the field. No one else seems to wear them these days.

Mrs Sarobi jerked and looked up as he approached. 'Oh, I didn't see you coming. What a nice surprise.'

She looked genuinely pleased, he realised. Perhaps she had forgotten the episode in the garden.

'Yes, I thought I ought to do some weeding and watering. I've not been here for a while. So many other things keeping me busy . . .'

'I see.' She looked intrigued, but did not ask. 'Don't worry; I've kept it in good shape for you.'

He could see now that she had. The flowerbed that separated their lots still looked beautiful. A couple of the delphiniums had flowered a second time and their spurs of lapis lazuli stood to attention, flanking the proud achillea. Only a couple of the yellow flower heads had turned brown. The common asters crowded around, marvelling at the majesty and splendour. 'The Field of the Cloth of Gold!' Mr Askew exclaimed. 'Isn't it magnificent?'

She laughed at his enthusiasm. 'Well, yes, I suppose it's something for an Englishman to be proud of. You should have seen it last week when it was at its peak.'

'Yes, yes,' he muttered, guiltily, whilst scanning the plot. 'Let's see what else we have got here . . .' The poppies were over by now, of course. In their place were the dried stalks, topped by their star-capped seedpods. The Japanese anemones had opened up in amongst the other flowers. He smiled to himself and wondered if she had noticed yet. It was a clever bit of planting, if he said so himself, as the anemones would remain bright and cheerful when the other flowers withered away shortly. 'This bit may look a bit over-planted just now,' he said pre-emptively, 'but you just wait a week or two and you'll see . . .' He looked over at her allotment. There was a patch of courgette plants, adorned by orange flowers and yellow and green vegetables. And, further along, there were globe artichokes, aubergines and garlic, and the harvest moon was still a week away.

'My word! You certainly have green fingers,' he said, admiringly, sucking his teeth. 'Yours must be the finest allotment harvest in the county.'

'We all have to be good at something. I like to make things grow – gives me a sense of harmony. There's such wonderful symmetry in nature.'

'Some would say the opposite – that nature fosters chaos.'

Mrs Sarobi did not answer. She looked down at the ground. She looked out over the fields and commons. 'I think this might be my favourite time of the year,' she mused. 'The colours deepen and all the plants have grown strong over the summer. Look—' she pointed towards a distant tor – 'even the stone seems to have grown.'

Mr Askew did not seem to be listening. He looked instead at her young rowan tree. Its frail branches were drooping with the rusty fruit.

'Isn't it odd,' he said, continuing his own strand

of the conversation, 'how some people spend their time removing obstacles to create order, whereas others keep rearranging the setting to cause chaos.'

She nodded slowly and smiled as one would at a child.

'Well, I was just remembering a story I read once in the newspaper. A zoo – I can't remember which one – was short of space and decided to house the bears and the foxes in the same enclosure. Every day, the bears would tidy up the site, collecting sticks and stones into neat piles whilst the foxes were asleep, and every night the foxes would come out to scatter the sticks and stones around again in a seemingly pointless fashion. After a while, the zoo keepers reckoned that the bears would go crazy with frustration, and removed the foxes into another enclosure. And you know what happened?'

'No . . .'

'They got depressed.'

'The keepers?'

'No, no – the bears and the foxes.'

'Oh.'

'They were dependent on one another to balance the symmetry of chaos and order. Without the other, they lost their purpose.'

'It's a beautiful story. It sort of hints at the heart of a mystery, doesn't it?'

'Hmm,' he muttered, wondering if her delight was genuine or whether she was mocking him for telling that stupid anecdote. Was he flirting?

'Would you like a cup of tea?' Mrs Sarobi said. 'I brought a thermos flask.'

'I'd love some.'

'Here.' She picked up a couple of empty buckets and turned them upside down.

They sat down, side by side, in the early autumn sun. The plastic pail buckled dangerously under Mr Askew and he tried to reduce his weight by resting only on his right buttock. They sat in silence for a while, sipping their tea and squinting against the lowering rays of the sun. There was a smell of newly-dug earth and jasmine around them and a few waning leaves, although not too many, drifted through the polished air and settled at their feet. Mr Askew was about to speak, but saw Mrs Sarobi's boots, so little, nimble and delicate, on the ground next to his own shoes and remained silent, so that, in the end, it was Mrs Sarobi who had to break their delicious silence.

'I wish,' she said, dreamily, 'that we had a wall at our backs, something to shelter us from the wind. Then this would be our bower of bliss. Just ours.'

'Bower of bliss,' he repeated, blushing and snorting through his nose. But he could not hide a smile of delight.

He was just about to add something quite schmaltzy, the kind of thing he would never normally say but that seemed to be called for at that moment, when Mrs Sarobi exclaimed, 'Oh, look. Isn't that Mrs Ludgate?' And it was, of course. 'What is *she* doing here?'

What indeed. Mr Askew blinked in bafflement. His left leg was hurting where he was straining to keep his weight off the bucket. Mrs Ludgate was wearing three-quarter-length trousers that were straining a bit over her calves as she pushed up the slope, hands on her knees. She walked with her head down, an unspeakable leopard-print sun hat shading her face. The sheep on her fleece jacket seemed to be skipping more exuberantly than ever. Mr Askew swallowed and looked beseechingly at Mrs Sarobi. 'Is it too late to hide amongst the rhubarbs?' he asked, realising that he was trapped.

'Don't be foolish.' Mrs Sarobi laughed and lifted her hand in a greeting.

If Mrs Ludgate had seen the wave, she ignored it. When she reached them, she looked up, as if in surprise, and uttered, flatly, 'Oh, it's you.' Her face was puffed up like a cow's udder before milking, Mr Askew noted.

Mrs Sarobi smiled nervously. She had not been prepared for this. 'Um . . . Hello; how are you?'

'Fine; just out for a bit of a stroll. I was about to post a card.' She removed the hat and squinted at the sun.

'I see . . . To your daughter?'

'Nah.'

Mrs Sarobi smiled again, not knowing quite what to say.

'Thought I might save on the postage, delivering it myself.'

'That's crafty of you, especially if it's for some-body local.'

'Yeah, well . . . Here it is.'

'What? For me?' Mrs Sarobi hesitated, not quite believing.

Mrs Ludgate's outstretched hand seemed to tremble for a moment. 'To say thank you for the gift – of the jam. It was better than I thought.'

Mrs Sarobi smiled in relief and accepted the card. 'I'm pleased to hear it.'

Mr Askew looked at the two women in disbelief. It was clear that something was going on between them, some new connection that he was not part of. Too taken aback to toughen, he stood up and offered his bucket to Mrs Ludgate. 'Please,' he said, 'sit down.'

She looked at him suspiciously. 'Er, thanks . . .'

Mrs Sarobi was the first to gather herself. 'Would you like a cup of tea?' she asked, refilling the mug she had just been drinking from. 'I don't have any fresh mugs . . . Hope you don't mind.'

Mrs Ludgate accepted the mug with a nod, but hesitated before drinking from it. Then she put her lips cautiously to the rim, almost not touching.

The other two watched her drink, as if she was a child doing something for the first time, a child passing some kind of test – a *rite de passage*. At once, Mr Askew became horribly aware of himself, standing there, looking down at the bare head of the woman drinking. Her head bent over the mug so that he could see the whiteness at the nape of her neck where her hair would normally sit. He was conscious of the unbearable intimacy of the scene, of the three of them, ageless in the isolation of the moment. He felt again the stickiness of his palms as he tried not to sweat in Michael's friendship chair. Nothing has changed, he thought to himself. Ageing is just the passing of time. There's nothing more to it. Nothing more. 'Honest, Gabe.'

'What was that?' Mrs Sarobi asked with a special kind of tenderness, leaning closer from her bucket. The moment was gone.

'What?'

'You said something.'

'Did I? Oh, I'm sure it was nothing. Nothing at all.'

'That's professors for you,' Mrs Ludgate confirmed to Mrs Sarobi, pleased to understand them so well. 'They've got so much stuff in their heads that it sometimes has to come out in little puffs, like steam from a kettle. He does it all the time, you know – talks to himself. Although . . .' she said, pausing for a moment, cradling the mug in both hands. 'Although, quite often, it's as if he's talking to somebody else. In the beginning, when I first started coming to Oakstone, I used to think there was somebody else in the room with him, but there never was, was there?'

'So, you live on your own up at that farm, then?' Mr Askew interrupted quickly, with feigned innocence, hoping, for a moment, that the change of subject might act as a kind of screen, densely

277

erected between them, to protect him from the onslaught of truth. 'Must be lonely at times.'

'Gabriel, please . . .' Mrs Sarobi warned, but was ignored.

'As a matter of fact . . .' Mrs Ludgate started bravely, but seemed to falter. Her hands shook in a sudden spasm, spilling some tea on her white trainers. 'As a matter of fact, I prefer being on my own.' She fell quiet and looked down at her stained shoes, frowning. The yellow tea-stain on the white leather reminded her of piss – as if she had wet herself. You disgusting pig. Wait until Daddy gets home! Sometimes, when 'waiting for Daddy to get home' in that room by the sea, everything would go quiet, into a silence dense with sadness and fear, and all she heard was the sea. All she smelt was the sea, as if it was rising up to greet her – or to swallow her up.

'Ah, one can always rely on one's own company, can't one? Less trouble that way,' Mr Askew mused, mildly, and looked at her, his head tilted to one side.

Mrs Ludgate seemed to have turned into a standing stone.

'I heard . . .' he continued softly, carefully testing the waters. 'A while ago, I heard Mrs Edwards at the post office telling some other ladies that Mr Ludgate had been losing some of his property, lately. Had to clear some debts – with some court costs thrown in on top . . . It all went for a song, she said.'

'Yes?' Mrs Ludgate stirred again, but dry as leaf. 'And you believed her, of course . . . Everyone in Mortford knows that Mrs Edwards is a gossip and a liar. Everyone. Anyway, I know things . . .'

'What *things*?'

'Well, you'll just have to try and find out. But it's relating to your family and that place, that *Edencombe*, and whatever it is you're hiding away up there.'

'Break it up, you two, will you?' Mrs Sarobi interrupted at last. 'You're like a couple of children in the sand pit.'

Yes, Mr Askew thought to himself – children. And yet I went through so much in order to come of age.

'There's still some tea in the flask,' Mrs Sarobi announced, remembering how tea seemed to work like opium on the minds of the British. The sun, too, was trying to comfort these three outcasts who appeared to be so intent on destroying themselves, but it was no good. Everything was wrong.

Mrs Ludgate trembled once. The silence around them was bulging like a blister. Ready to burst. She cleared her throat. 'I must go . . .' she suggested, and, for once, no one contradicted her.

Gabriel woke to distant piping music. Rey's bunk was empty and he wondered why he hadn't woken earlier. Picking sleep from the corners of his eyes, he stepped out to see the lights from a nearby village on the horizon; they seemed to sit in the sky like a crown of stars. Turning round, he saw the fairground, lit up now by thousands of fairy lights. He laughed out loud. The magic had returned. What different worlds inhabited the day and the night. Suddenly, he heard the piping calliope music quite clearly again, carried on a quickening breeze.

As he approached the site, he could feel a feverish energy rising inside him. The solid night had melted away and in its place was this world of bright wonder. There were people, for example, where, early the same morning, there had been none. They were milling around, young and old, alight with excitement. A band of rackety boys ran past him carrying sods of candyfloss and, as he watched their departing backs, one of them fell over and dropped his pink cloud into the dust. Gabriel moved on into the crowds.

Suddenly, Rey was by his side, gesturing for Gabriel to follow. They stopped by the big-top tent.

'Perhaps we will catch the end of the show,' Rey whispered, and lifted a sheet of canvas so that Gabriel could sneak in without being seen. The big top was not particularly large and the sideshow that it housed was more vaudeville than circus. The interior looked so different from what Gabriel remembered from his childhood; the anteroom with many doors and the corridors of mirrors were gone, as were the dripping chandeliers and crimson velvet. In their place was a grandstand facing a

circular stage, lit by coloured strobes that rico-
cheted off a number of large glass prisms suspended
from the tent roof. The light that sieved on to
the stage at that moment was incredibly lovely: the
rosy tint of a desert sunset or the heart-coloured
dawn over a snowy plain. The smell did not match
the freshness of the light; it was dense with the
sharp, not altogether unpleasant, whiff of sawdust
and the odour of a mass of bodies, gathered at the
end of the working week. But there was something
else, too: a scent which he remembered from all
those years ago. He breathed in through his nose.
Face powder, perhaps, and carnations.

He did not have time to register the act, which
went off stage just then, but, as he sat down next
to Rey in a seat on the back row, a roar went up
from the audience. Rey laughed out loud and
clapped his hands like a child. A jaunty overture
was played on a piano or an organ. Gabriel struggled to see through the crowd what was happening
on stage; the people in front were standing up in
their seats, cheering and clapping. Suddenly, they
hushed and sat down and the stage was visible
again. 'Ah,' Rey said, with a sigh. 'They are here.'

Gabriel gasped and rose up in his seat like a
meerkat. This, he felt with some certainty, was a
world within a world, where all his ages merged and
tumbled so that he was twelve years old again
and yet a grown man. The tones of the organ
sounded as if they were emerging from under water
and the audience around seemed suspended, almost

fictional, as if it was part of the silent set. He was aware only of the warm, living presence of Rey's body next to his. Recovering from his initial surprise, he realised that his hand was clasping Rey's wrist tightly; he was suddenly acutely aware of the warm, chicken-heart pulse of his new friend against his fingers. With an embarrassed mumble, he let go of the arm, blushing, and shifted slightly away on the wooden seat. But his heart had flared and ached again for that other warmth he had reached out for – the other hand – a comfort long gone. For a split second, he saw an image of two boys seated together, eager, vulnerable and dear.

The two girls who had appeared on the stage were older now, of course, and their sequined mermaid costumes had been replaced by silk evening gowns, but there was no mistaking them. Their golden blonde hair and starry eyes were the same and their bodies were still joined just below their bosoms. Mary and Anne, the Siamese twins from Kentucky. Rey chuckled and studied him sideways. 'They are the only real freaks left in the show, apart from a few midgets and a pinhead. All the others are fake, you know – gaffed freaks,' he said in a tone which Gabriel could not quite interpret.

'I've seen them before – when I was a child,' Gabriel whispered, excitedly.

'Oh, yes; haven't we all?'

'No, I mean it!'

'I believe you, my friend. They are what we – every man – have always been looking for. Don't you know the story of Castor and Pollux?'

Gabriel shook his head and worried, not for the first time, that his new friend would find him dim.

'You see,' Rey began, 'growing up, we reluctantly give up the idea that we may live forever – that childish illusion of immortality.'

Gabriel glanced to see if Rey was talking about him, specifically, but the older boy seemed lost in reverie.

'Castor and Pollux, the most famous twins of all, were born of the same mother, but Castor was fathered by a king and Pollux by a god. When mortal Castor was killed, Pollux went to his father, Zeus, and asked to share his own immortality with his brother, so that they could be together again.' Rey stopped abruptly and shook his head for a moment before continuing. 'You know, Gabe, this story amuses me; how futile to try to extend your own life through another, when being human is such a single act.'

Gabriel remembered to smile politely. But, at this moment, he was more interested in finding out about the freaks. 'There used to be a guy on the organ, dressed as a woman,' he said.

'Vanessa? He's long gone.'

'And the chap with no arms?'

'Him, too. He got involved in a sharp-shooting competition, holding the guns with his feet, and one of them backfired into his face.

283

Gabriel looked at him in astonishment, forgetting the stage for a moment. And, just then, he recognised the boy in the shiny green suit who had smiled at him as he emerged from the hall of mirrors.

'You!' he gasped. 'You were there . . .'

But Rey ignored him, continuing his lecture. 'You know, this show is merely a shadow of its former glory. This used to be one of the greatest. That was back when freaks were worthy of display. Back then, people thought we were a significant cultural institution.' Rey laughed gaily at this point, but his voice was serious as he continued. 'People like us helped the rest of society explore itself. That society felt good about itself when it could distinguish between "us" and "them" – that's how they created meaning in their world . . . But there are very few *real* freaks around these days; the ones that look particularly offensive to the world are all kept hidden away in institutions. The authorities insist it's for our own good.'

'Why?' Gabriel kept most of his attention on the stage, where the two women were dancing to a melancholy song now and singing in turns in deeper, huskier voices. He was not sure whether Rey saw himself as belonging to the world of freaks or that other world.

'Because it's considered bad taste to ogle "others" – we must not be *tempted*.'

'But – we could just look away.'

'Ha!' Rey gave a short, dry laugh and continued watching the show in silence.

Gabriel too turned his full attention to the stage, just as the Maryanne sisters unfastened their gowns at their shoulders and let them drop to the ground. There were whistles and catcalls from the audience. Gabriel felt hot all over; his throat was thick with excitement and dread as he stared at the young women who pranced on the stage, wearing only black bodices with frilly red lace around the hips and fishnet stockings. From behind the curtain, somebody handed them a tall hat and a cane each. Smiling widely, they started doing a slow cabaret dance, their legs kicking the air in unison. The men in the audience kept whistling and calling and Gabriel wished they would stop. He felt a tightening in his neck and the rushing of blood in his ears.

Rey leant closer to Gabriel. 'This is their final number,' he whispered softly, as if he could feel the anguish in Gabriel's body. The music ended and the sisters bowed to the audience before taking their leave, shaking their bums provocatively so that the red frill shuddered as they went. The lights were turned on abruptly and people started to spill out of the tent.

Gabriel wanted to get out, too; he needed to clear his head – breathe some fresh air – but Rey stayed seated. 'After the last two wars,' Rey said in a sinister voice, 'the disabled have started to be distinguished from the cripples and the freaks. You see, *they* sacrificed themselves for King and country – *dulce et decorum* and all that – so they were entitled to a good pension and medical care.'

Gabriel did not know what to say, but he listened intently.

'Nowadays, governments no longer find it desirable or appropriate to have aliens of *that* kind—' he nodded towards the empty stage where Mary and Anne had been only a moment ago – 'drifting around their countries, so the fairs and sideshows have been much diminished in favour of zoos and aquariums. We travel in the periphery, in the margins of the map, these days.'

'But is the distinction between "us" and "them" not important anymore?' Gabriel asked. It was, after all, how he had structured his own life, although never quite knowing to which side he belonged.

'Horror movies have taken over from the freaks of nature, and all in the name of moral progress or – as they call it these days – civil rights. But, if you ask me, we will always want to look at people who are different, whether it's a glamorous actress or a man without arms and legs. There's nothing more fascinating to humans than the human other – or the unknown, for that matter.'

'What, like a mystery?'

'A *mystery*?' Rey said, thoughtfully. 'Yes, I suppose so . . . At least the unknown keeps the rumour of mystery alive. That's all we can live by.'

'Yes,' Gabriel confirmed in a childish voice. 'I want there to be mysteries so that I can find things out. That's the whole point, surely?'

286

Rey looked at him closely for a moment. 'No, Gabe. It's the other way round. Exploration is the *whole point* – not what you may or may not find.' He slapped his knees and stood up. 'Enough of that; I've got some stuff to be getting on with.'

Gabriel turned to follow his friend but, to his surprise, Rey was gone.

All through that night, Gabriel travelled the world of wonder. As he moved through the fair, the calliope music guiding his step, the night was an open door and, when the last of the punters had tired of the magic and gone home to bed, it was time for the fair to move on; the roustabout gang began their shift.

They started by dismantling the grandstand, row by row, and carrying it outside to put into a pile, which was shifted by another gang on to a lorry. Compelled by the precision and symmetry of their labour, Gabriel joined in their work. He just walked up to a group of them and held out his hands in a silent gesture. The men stopped and looked at him for a moment, then one of them nodded and Gabriel fell in to the rhythm of the night crew.

Shoulder to shoulder with those silent men whose muscles stretched and ached under the hard, back-breaking labour, Gabriel felt, for the first time, that he wanted to learn what the body can do – he wanted skill.

After the grandstand had been pulled down, they

dismantled the stage, pulling it apart section by section. The rigging, lighting and sound equipment came down before the side wall sections could be detached and folded away on to another truck. The lot was full of men stripped to the waist. In the headlights from the trucks, they looked like Cretan bull leapers, bending and writhing in the night. One by one, the trailers of the performers left the lot to move on to the next site, a few miles up the coast. But the prop gang worked on and took no notice of their departure. It was three in the morning when they started pulling down the big top. The adrenaline was flowing through their blood now, washing away the evening's alcohol and fatigue. Handling the huge tarpaulin was like hoisting the mainsail of a man-of-war. The men gathered around the perimeter of the tent and each took hold of one of the thick ropes used to attach the tarpaulin to the ground. On a given signal, they walked forward, each holding back on his rope, so that the great, heavy tarpaulin was lowered slowly to the ground on the six main poles. As Gabriel's whole body strained against his rope, he imagined what it would be like doing the job in a strong wind.

Once the lot was cleared and all the trucks were loaded, the prop gang set off on to the road, travelling east. Gabriel couldn't find Rey's caravan and, too exhausted to care, he climbed on to the flatbed of a truck carrying scaffolding. Settling down amongst the metal pipes, he realised that the flatbed was crowded with men, some of them already asleep. Gabriel felt his muscles relaxing, falling away into a mass of arms and legs. The night was cool, their shared sweat steaming. Gabriel fell asleep to the roaring of the old engines and slept on as the truck came to a halt on another muddy field, much the same as the previous site.

He was woken up by Rey, who had climbed into the flatbed to find him. Gabriel stretched his aching back and pulled a leg from under a heavy weight. 'What?' he said, irritably.

'I brought you some coffee; thought you might need it before we start again,' Rey said, his voice forming an image, an outline, in the dark. Light still only revealed itself in patches: a flash of teeth, a jacket opening on to a cotton shirt.

'What? You must be kidding! We are not building the site now, are we?'

'You bet we are.'

'Shit.'

'Quite.'

'Where are we, anyway?'

He could sense Rey shrugging. 'Does it matter?'

'No, I suppose not.'

'Come on, then.'

Rey jumped down from the truck and Gabriel followed, fumbling for a moment to get his bearings. They stood silently, side by side, drinking the hot coffee as the grey light of dawn rose out of the ground and made the shadows stand up straight. Then, suddenly, there was birdsong on the air. It was not as if one bird started and the others joined in – it all happened at once, as when the needle is dropped on to a turning record.

Gabriel listened for a moment, warm inside from the coffee and a sense of satisfaction. Then he walked stiffly through the armada of parked trucks into a nearby meadow to urinate. By now, the landscape revealed itself. The pale blue sky seemed to have risen from a horizon bruised in violet and pink. A thin breeze, no more than a breath, rose over the downs and combed through the yellowing grass in gentle strokes – a mother's hand – softly. He stood for a moment, as if he was part of the field, straight and thin like a stalk, swaying slowly under the caressing wind.

Back at the new lot, everything had shifted into deliberate activity. The same men, who, only a few hours ago, had sweated in the moonless night, had been granted new energy by dawn and were currently busy pulling the folded tarpaulin and canvas off the trucks and raising the rigging again. Gabriel sighed. He was hungry and every part of him ached. Looking around for a hint of what to do next, he walked over to a group of men who were standing on makeshift scaffolding, driving rigging poles into the ground with sledgehammers.

Amazingly, the whole lot was resurrected within a few hours. The people of this village would wake in morning to colour and music, whereas the people of the previous village would wake and see it gone.

The morning was still glittering with dew as the roustabout gang set off for the cook shack. The cook was a huge man with a tattoo snaking out of the neck of his shirt and on to the back of his shaved head. His big-jawed face had a growth of dark stubble around it. Rey sidled up to Gabriel in the queue. For a moment, Gabriel felt a rising sense of irritation. Where had Rey been while they had all been working hard? What made him think that he could just come and go like that?

'That's Dido,' Rey said, indicating the cook. 'He doubles as the Iron Man. You'd better stay on his right side . . .'

'Why, what does he do?' Gabriel asked, peering anxiously at the monster cook. He was no longer irritated.

'Oh, no, no, nothing like that.' Rey laughed. 'He's the kindest soul. I just meant that he will feed you better, if you stay sweet with him.'

The fabric of Dido's cotton shirt strained over his muscles as he loaded eggs and rashers on to plates. A woman appeared from the back of the van, carrying a large thermos flask in each hand. Her hair was peroxide blond and done up in an extraordinary beehive. It seemed to be leaning a bit to the left, as if she had been sleeping on one side. Her make-up was smudged, but there was a certain strong beauty to her features. She wore shorts and a red and white polka-dot shirt, tied around her midriff. She did not seem to be wearing a bra and her breasts swung riotously inside the loose fabric as she put the coffee flasks on the counter with a bang. Placing her large hands on her hips, she shouted in a surprisingly deep voice, 'All right, ye bastards, come and get it!'

There was laughter and whistling from the queue, and some coarse shouting too. But silence and order soon settled over the trestle tables and benches on the dusty ground around the van, as the exhausted men gorged on their breakfast.

'So, how do you like our Circassian beauty, eh? Magnificent, don't you think?'

'Yeah, she's quite something. What does she do?'

'Zilda? Oh, you know . . . a bit of dancing, and she's in this double act with Dido – knife throwing, or something of that sort. That's what she does on set . . . In her own free time, she has a whole other business going.'

'What sort of business?' Gabriel wondered with elusive interest whilst chewing his bacon.

Rey looked at him with a strange smile on his face.

'What?'

'What do you know of women, Gabe?'

'Well, you know . . . this and that.' He reddened.

'Have you ever delved into womanhood, rummaged through its secret passages, tasted its ripe flesh and drunk its forbidden juices?'

'No; I mean, that is . . .'

'And the smell . . . Ah, I tell you, the smell is

divine – at once fresh and sweetly dirty. It's like nothing else in the universe.'

'I see,' Gabriel mumbled and stared glumly down at his plate. He thought of that night on the beach and tried to remember any particular smell associated with the quickening noises of the lovemaking couple. But another smell surfaced in his mind – a smell of young bulls – the smell of threat. A sudden fear gripped his heart.

'Are you okay?' Rey looked at him with concern. 'I didn't mean to embarrass you, or anything . . . You do know there's nothing *wrong* with it, don't you?'

He nodded, but uncertainly, wishing Rey would look away. But the older youth did not flinch.

'You know, Gabe, good and evil are sometimes so close that one can overshadow the other,' he said. 'That's why fear is our worst enemy.'

As if he didn't know.

'You must learn not to fear the erotic – or love, for that matter.'

'Yeah, all right,' Gabriel muttered.

Rey finally shifted his gaze from Gabriel's face and lit a cigarette. He leant back his head and blew the smoke up into the air. 'Anyway, back to the wonder of women. My real passion doesn't lie in the erotic, but in the very essence of its being—' he leant closer to Gabriel, his free hand gripping the edge of the table – 'the core of womanhood.'

Gabriel had stooped chewing, suddenly interested. 'And you know all that . . .?' He hesitated, not quite getting it. 'You got all that from Zilda?'

Rey laughed again. 'Hell, no! Zilda is a coochie girl, Gabe, and that's not all she is. No, no, I'm talking about *real* women.'

'Who are they? Where . . .?' Gabriel asked fervently, but he never got an answer as, just then, Zilda's voice thundered over them again:

'That's it, you dirty lot! Get a move on; we haven't got all day. Got to serve the gentry, now. Up you get – on your way.' She shooed with her paddle-like hands from the van, as if the men were a group of ducks frittering in a yard.

As the rugged men of the night crew shuffled off towards the trailers to find their bunks, Rey nudged Gabriel and nodded towards a group of smarter looking caravans. 'Here they come, the real aristocracy, the seediest kinkers you have ever seen.' A dark flicker went through his mossy eyes. 'Look at them,' he continued, with soft contempt, 'and the great ringmaster at the rear.'

And Gabriel stared in open-mouthed amazement at the party of show-people who strolled towards the cook shack. It was a scene from a medieval court. A Mexican dwarf in a double-breasted pinstripe suit came first, arguing with a rakishly thin man who followed a few steps behind, showing the innocent palms of his hands and blinking away tears in a mask of white make-up. This unhappy pair were followed by a bare-chested African, as black as tar, smoking a fat Cuban cigar; a man in a soiled string vest and boxer shorts, who had shaved the left part of his body whilst wearing his hair long, braided into a pigtail tied with a pink ribbon on the left side of his head; a pinhead with a lopsided smile; a midget and his wife, hand in hand; and then, the most magnificent of them all, teetering in flowing silk dressing gowns and feather boas, Mary and Anne, one pink and one blue, radiant clouds in a Tiepolo sky. A couple of yards behind them, in a frayed velvet tailcoat and skinny trousers, walked Dr Buster himself, with a considered gait, hands clasped behind his back, dark eyes to the ground, like a schoolmaster – or a vicar, perhaps – guarding his flock. Just then, he looked up at the two youths. He registered Gabriel with merely animal indifference and, turning his head slightly, a wolfish grin on his face, he winked – quickly, darkly – at Rey, who took a step back, away from him.

And Gabriel. What about Gabriel? The blood had slowed in his veins, his heart beat sluggishly against his chest, pumping, pumping. For an instant, he saw himself clearly, standing between the band of freaks and the golden boy, Reynard, recognising something in all of them, confirmed, and for a moment almost comfortable, in the familiar sense of unreality.

CHAPTER 11

Doris Ludgate was standing by the French windows in the drawing room at Oakstone. It was raining outside and the reflected light from the puddles on the patio marbled the ceiling above her. Mr Askew hesitated in the doorway, where the shadows disguised him. He was still uncertain after their last meeting in the allotments. She was holding a folio book in her arms, flicking through the pages with great intensity, lowering her face to study some of the images closely. Mr Askew tried to hold back the anxiety that was rising in his throat; he followed every page as her chubby fingers scrabbled at them. He remembered the way she had slobbered jam on a piece of toast once – in his kitchen. Finally, he couldn't take it anymore.

'Careful with that, please, Mrs Ludgate; it's one of my most precious books.'

She looked up with a start, almost dropping the book. 'Oh,' she said, 'it's you again.'

'Yes, it's me.'

She flared up. 'I would prefer it if you didn't sneak up on me like that.'

'I wasn't sneaking. It's my house, remember.'

'Pah!' She exhaled and craned her turtle neck. She flicked her hand on the open page. Dust danced in the grey light around her. 'These images are filthy.'

He shook his head sadly; it *was* more than he could take. 'They are heartbreaking.' As if it could be told in a word.

He could feel her looking at him, too closely for comfort. Raising his head defiantly, he met her gaze. He could not read her expression at that moment. It puzzled him. Was she smirking, as usual, or was there something else? In any case, he did not like her touching the book. He hated her hands on its back and her index finger, damp with her slimy saliva, on the edge of the pages – his pages.

'I would be grateful if you would put Diane Arbus back where she belongs,' he blurted.

'Diane who?'

He nodded towards the book.

'Oh, her . . . Who is she, anyway?'

'Ah, a kindred spirit.'

'A *what*?'

He ignored her; she wouldn't understand, anyway. He sighed. He used to feel so connected to Arbus; that way she had of moving amongst other people, recognising them. I too just wanted to go where I had never been – where I had left no trace.

But Mrs Ludgate was looking thoughtfully now at the book in her hands. 'It's a bit creepy . . .'

she said and he sighed, exasperated. But her voice was strange, altered, as she continued. 'She seems to find in each one of them exactly what they are trying to hide – whatever is behind those masks.'

Mr Askew stared at her in disbelief. He had not expected this turn of events. 'But you're absolutely right!' He was astonished – excited, even. 'Arbus said that the flaw was what drew her attention to a person; it's the flaw that makes a person beautiful, that makes us look at them.'

Mrs Ludgate nodded slowly and walked over to the side table where she had found the book. Putting it back gently, she said, without looking up, 'I suppose she got that right. Perhaps we shouldn't worry so much about being . . . what we are.' She sounded unhappy.

He was suddenly feeling a bit odd and realised that he was tingling all over with a sympathy that he did not know how to offer – not yet, anyway. Instead, he told her, 'When I was young, I worked on a sideshow for a little while. It may sound weird to you . . . but to me it was more of a lesson of life – a kind of rite of passage, if you like.'

She didn't let on, but he could tell that she was listening. That's when I first realised that life is a striving for unity, he thought now, a desire for completion, a search for the missing half. We all suffer under the weight of emptiness. We are afraid of being alone. Love – and desire – is all about reintegration with our other half – through love, we hope to be whole. It's no great mystery, then, that we are frightened – and fascinated – by stories of fraction and duality; conjoined twins, clones, doppelgangers, spirits split from the body, the ego fighting the id, castration – these are all threats to love.

'She knew that, too, didn't she?' Mrs Ludgate nodded towards the book.

'Knew what?' He flinched, as if she had read his mind, but noticed something new and intense about her, something that challenged the gloom around them.

'You know . . . that we are never quite . . . right – or at least not just one thing.'

'Sure, she knew . . . She knew that those of us who believe that we harbour a freak inside won't stop searching. We may be mended, but we still carry the phantom pain . . . We *are* the phantom pain.' He stopped abruptly.

'Is that what you wrote about in them books of yours?'

'Eh?' What did she know of his books? 'Yes, I suppose so . . .'

'There's stuff . . . stuff that we carry around with us inside, like, which makes us seem uncaring and cold to other people.' Her breath made a fluttering sound and he was reminded of the streamers he had once made for Michael's bike. 'But we are not!'

The fervour of her defiance made him recoil. 'No, no; I'm sure you're right.'

'I'm not educated and all that, but I still

understand . . . things.' Her cheeks were flushed. 'It's just that, most of the time, it's been better to pretend otherwise.'

With that, she turned to go, but stopped and looked back at him. 'Perhaps you would let me look at that book again sometime, if I ask beforehand?' A magpie rattled dryly outside the windows. The rain had brought on the worms.

'Yes, yes, of course,' he answered, bewildered, but it was all too sudden and he was already backing away.

'There's some unwashed crockery in the sink,' she said, vaguely, and gestured towards the kitchen, because she too needed to escape. As she passed him on her way out of the room, Mr Askew realised that something had changed. He could not put his finger on it until she stepped into the hall. He turned quickly and looked down at her feet. She was wearing a pair of slippers. Her feet made no noise.

It had been a great adventure, it was true – a rather spectacular coming of age. Mr Askew drummed his thumbs on the steering wheel to a tune on the radio and hummed to himself as he drove along the country lane towards the coast. The hedges on either side were still seething with life. It reminded him, briefly, of his allotment. He had neglected it a bit lately. It probably needed watering – and weeding. Why was it that weeds stayed so fiercely alive when the things you were actually trying to grow died so easily? Yes, I must do some weeding, he thought. The prospect made him feel good. He did love his allotment – the simple pleasure it provided. Driving on, he smiled again. 'It was a bit like running away with the circus, eh? What do you give for that? I was quite the hero, though; saved the day in the end, didn't I?' He laughed to himself, shaking his head. A car overtook him on the narrow road and he swerved to the left, rattling the wing mirror, the hedge scratching against the side of the Skoda. 'Bloody hell!' he cursed and, driving on at a slower pace, he muttered, 'It's beyond me how they are ever let out on the roads.' But then he remembered how he used to drive without a licence, in the beginning, after that summer on the moors when Rey had taught him to drive on abandoned quarry roads and dirt tracks. Rey had made sure that he would know how to drive when the time came.

He reached the hill from which the sea became suddenly visible and slowed down to take in the view. A tanker rested heavily on the horizon and, closer to the shore, a sail hung listlessly from a single mast. The light was milky, the sun hidden behind a veil of cloud. It was clammy out there, as if there might be some thunder in the afternoon. He drove along the coast road for a few miles, watching the seabirds as they lifted on the thermals only to dive again over the cliffs. Every now and again, another car would honk at him as it passed.

'Halfwits,' he muttered at the windscreen. He parked, as usual, a little away from the house on the cliff and walked the last bit along the coastal path.

'Good morning, Mr Askew. A bit sticky today, isn't it?' He was greeted by Ms Turpin at reception.

'It is, indeed; we may get some thunder later on. Unusual for this time of year, no?' he replied, smiling broadly. He liked Ms Turpin; a steely-haired spinster with a heart of gold, he had a feeling that she was the kind who did not mind silence. For no good reason at all, he felt like telling her. 'Can you imagine, I ran away with the circus once and saved a couple of damsels in distress.'

'Did you, now?' She laughed. 'I'm glad you made it back.'

'Only just.'

'Oh?'

'Yeah, only just.'

'Well, now,' Stan said, and lit a cigarette, 'isn't it lovely to be amongst friends?' They were standing around him in a semi-circle in the narrow caravan. Charlie, who had just pulled a knife, was facing a few men from the roustabout gang, who, in turn, were clenching their fists. Behind Stan, on a ruffled couch, Mary and Anne lay sprawled together; Mary had a bruise under her left eye and a mark on her neck – the imprint of a man's fingers. Rey, with Gabriel in tow, had only just entered the scene.

'What's going on?' Rey asked in a level voice.

'They pimped the twins to a couple of men from the village,' one of the prop gang replied without taking his eyes off Charlie and Stan.

'Where are those men now?'

'They ran off; Hutch and Chris are after them.'

Rey nodded slowly and turned to the twins. 'Are you two all right?'

'Fine,' Mary replied, curtly. Anne was covering her eyes and clutching at her pale blue dressing gown; her hair looked like spring sunshine against it, Gabriel noticed.

'If you ever try something like that again, you're dead men, do you hear me?' Rey said, calmly, turning to Charlie and Stan, his green eyes afire.

'Who are you to tell us what to do, pretty boy?' Stan sneered and spat on the floor. 'What makes you so bloody righteous?'

'Ever sinning, ever righteous – I embody the contradictions of human nature; hadn't you realised?' Rey replied with the ghost of a smile.

Stan, it seemed, was losing his cool. 'You book-reading faggot! How the hell do you think you can tell me what do?' he shouted, bunching his fists.

Charlie took a step closer but Rey held up his hand. 'No, Charlie, put the knife away. I know the boss put you up to this.'

'And I wouldn't come between the boss and his business, if I were you,' Charlie snarled.

'What's in it for you, then, eh, Charlie? An extra week's pay? A trial run of the goods?'

Charlie didn't reply.

'You're a fool if you think he'd let you in on the proceeds.'

Charlie gave him a look of contempt; he was not the kind who would take advice. 'Oh, yeah?'

Rey laughed sarcastically. 'You think you know him, then? You think he's just some petty crook, like you? Somebody who grabs a bit of fast cash when he sees it coming his way? Well, you're *so* deluded. Dr Buster is a greedy devil, a wolf of hell; he's been trading in people – their bodies and souls – since long before you were born. It's what he *does*. And he'd get rid of you in the wink of an eye, if he didn't need you to carry out his dirty work.'

'Oh, yeah? And how come you know him so well, then? Are you one of those abandoned kiddies he picked up at the side of a road somewhere, eh? Brought you up in his menagerie? Well, I'll tell you a thing you may *not* know, Rey. Buster's fed up with you. Do you hear me? Fed up!'

'You don't say.' There was ice in Rey's voice and his eyes looked dangerous. Gabriel had never seen his friend like this. A field of energy seemed to flicker about him and yet he was eerily composed, separate, as if he was something quite *other*. Gabriel was struck by a strange sensation that this was a game played between greater forces, a game that was already ancient, and that he, Gabriel, was just sliding past, moving quickly along the edge.

There was a snigger from Stan, but more un-certain now.

'I knew you bastards were up to something,' Rey muttered in a tone which indicated that he had already lost interest in them. Turning to Gabriel, he continued in a softer voice, 'Gabe, can you help the girls back to their own caravan?'

Gabriel nodded and tried to squeeze past Stan to get to the twins. 'Boo!' Stan exclaimed, blowing smoke into Gabriel's eyes.

Charlie laughed. 'Something wrong with your eyes, tinker?'

'No, it's the smoke . . .'

'Awww.'

Gabriel ignored him.

'Piss off, Charlie. Gabe, get those girls out of here, *now*.' There was real danger in Rey's voice.

Gabriel blinked again and, pulling a cotton cover from the couch, he helped the girls to their feet and wrapped the cover around them.

'Very neat, tinky,' Stan commented, his quick eyes glinting. 'Very neat indeed.'

As he followed the twins out of the caravan, Gabriel looked back once to see Rey, standing alone amongst the other men, like a figure out of antiquity.

Maryanne's caravan was in the other part of the enclosure, just behind the big top, where garlands of light bulbs were strung up between the colourful trailers. It was an old-fashioned show wagon, painted in red and blue with *Maryanne* printed in gold letters across the side. A silver Ford business coupé was parked behind it.

'Nice car,' Gabriel said, to break the silence.

Mary looked up at him with disdain, but did not reply. Anne buried her face deeper into the folds of the cotton throw. It was clear that Mary was in charge of their joint body; she led the way, half a step ahead of her sister, who hardly needed to see where she was going. They climbed the steep steps to the caravan and Gabriel, who could not think what else to do, followed. The interior was like the inside of a barrel – a domed fairy hut, decorated in pink and blue chiffon. Soft pillows shared a large raised bed at the back of the wagon with small fluffy toys, the kind you would win in a raffle. Above the bed, covering the only straight wall, was a large mirror. A sofa, dressed in gold velvet, bent around one wall, flanked by a matching armchair and a small mahogany table. Posies of dried flowers hung from the barrel roof and a crystal chandelier sprinkled confetti of golden light around the room. Gabriel stood, horribly reflected in the large mirror, stiff and angular in the curved room. A square peg in a round hole.

The sisters did not pay him any attention. Mary was busy boiling a kettle on a small stove in a corner near the door and Anne was folding the cotton throw, painstakingly, her hands taking care to match up each of the four corners perfectly. He thought they might be naked under their dressing gowns. Finally, Anne put down the folded throw on a chair and smoothed it once with a careful hand, as if it was a baby that she had just put to bed. Then she stood quietly with her hands along her sides, her eyes vacant. There was silence, but for the purring of the kettle.

Gabriel listened to the unsteady beating of his heart. Surely they must hear it too? He cleared his throat. 'I'm sorry,' he said, touching his upper lip.

'What for?' Mary turned on him quickly. Her accent was American, but with a slow twang to it.

'For what happened to you over there.'

'It was nothing. Don't feel sorry for us.'

'I only thought . . .' he said.

'Yeah, well, most people do,' she replied, scornfully, and poured the boiled water into a teapot.

'You have tea, then?' he asked, foolishly. 'I mean, real tea.'

'We have most things.'

Anne picked out three teacups from a small painted cupboard. The cups were bone china with a pattern of pansies. Their rims were lined in gold. Gabriel tried to catch her eye as she stretched to place them on the table, momentarily pulling Mary away from the tea-making. Mary looked around. 'Why are there three cups?'

Anne looked up mutely and nodded towards Gabriel.

Mary sighed and shook her head reproachfully.

'All right', she said and, turning to Gabriel, 'Have a seat.'

He lowered himself onto the golden chair. It was surprisingly small and he sat awkwardly with his knees close to his chin. 'I saw you perform once, many years ago.'

'Oh, yeah?' The twins sat down too, in one graceful movement.

'Yes, I have never forgotten it. You were dressed in a mermaid costume that sparkled like the sun on the sea. You were . . . You were stunning. But there was this other thing, too, this mysterious thing . . . You seemed so close, as if you were *one*.'

'No kidding,' Mary said, dryly, and poured the tea.

He blushed and looked quickly at Anne, who kept staring at something in her lap. 'I don't mean physically – that's obvious. I can't explain myself very well. It was as if you were whole – or, perhaps, as if your duality was not a dichotomy but . . . something more interesting; a mirror image, perhaps.'

'You say the cutest things.' Mary sipped her tea and turned away from him.

He turned to Anne, desperate now. 'What's your name?' he asked her, as if he didn't know.

She looked up, frowning, and glanced over at her sister, who was studying her nails. 'Anne,' she replied, shyly. Her gown had slipped back a bit to reveal a scattering of freckles on her white shoulder.

'Ah, she speaks!' he said, in mock triumph, feeling a thread of silk in his heart.

308

'She does, occasionally,' Mary broke in, 'and, unfortunately, I'm usually the one who has to listen to her nonsense.'

Anne smiled to herself, as if this was a funny joke. Gabriel couldn't take his eyes off her, the way her bobbed hair fell along her chin, as if it, too, longed to touch her soft face. He felt his flesh tightening under his skin and swallowed hard, his saliva had suddenly thickened into glue.

'Do you like it here? The show, I mean.'

'It's okay.' Mary shrugged.

'I hate it.' They both turned to look at Anne, whose cheeks wore a tint of roses.

'Why don't you leave?'

'We can't. Dr Buster secured our contract when we were just children. We would have nowhere else to go.'

'But surely he can't own you forever. How old are you?'

'Twenty-one next week.'

'Well, there you go.'

'*There you go*,' Mary mimicked his voice. 'Do you realise what happens to freaks when they are out of the shows?'

'I suppose I haven't thought about it.'

'Exactly. And now I think it's time for you to leave. We're tired.'

'Of course. I am sorry to have kept you up. I did not mean to—'

'Of course you didn't mean to – no one ever does.'

He stood up and looked at her uncertainly – at both of them. They were almost indistinguishable, apart from the gaze in their eyes, those astonishing sky-grey pools. He watched them in turn and realised with shock that it was not at all as he had thought all those years ago. They were not whole, after all; they too were unresolved – individuals, just like himself, surrounded by contradiction. He turned abruptly and walked to the door.

Mary giggled softly behind him. 'Goodnight, young hero,' her voice sang, mockingly.

'I like you,' said her sister, her other half, whose voice touched.

CHAPTER 12

After leaving the house on the rocks, Mr Askew ambled for a while along the coastal path, trying to remember what falling in love had felt like, the first time. Far out over the sea, the darkening clouds were piling into the stacking thunderstorm, dove-grey, purple and steely blue. Colours – yes, he remembered the spark of bright colours and trembling, minute details, suddenly vivid – highlighted in his mind like flash photography: a silver bracelet feasting off the pale skin of a thin wrist; the golden down on a jaw, just under the ear; the darkening in an eye, which revealed that there was so much more.

He had read somewhere that love could befall you in stages. At first, you would fall in love with yourself as the lover – that would be the vanity: natural, inevitable. Then you would fall in love with the feeling of being in love – ah, the stirring of hormones. Lastly, if you were so fortunate, you might fall in love with the other person – the subject of your love.

What about the twins, then? Had that been *love* – the tenderness he had felt? It was true, he was fairly sure, that he had first been fascinated by Maryanne's oneness – that harmony, which can only be achieved by reducing the multiple to the single. That was why he had been so frightened, at first, to discover their individuality. In them, he had hoped to reach some kind of safe ground – a deserted shore on to which he could be tossed out of the long swell that follows a storm.

Stopping for a moment to look out over the darkening waves – was this Homer's wine-dark sea? – he remembered that ardent feeling, that tender ache in his heart, wanting to give her a gift he could not afford, wanting to carry her further than his strength would bear, that overbearing wish to overcome himself and all his limitations for her sake – for his own sake. And, at the same time, always that sense of foreboding, thin and silky, like a blusher veil – French netting, perhaps, or tulle.

It was inevitable, somehow, that Rey should have known before he even knew himself. After that fateful night, Gabe had sought out the twins whenever he had the chance. He was oblivious to everything else that happened around him. The show travelled from site to site. He never knew where he was; he was not really part of what went on around him. His attention was trained on Mary and Anne. But, in his oblivion, he was aware of one thing: wherever he went, he felt Rey's watchful eyes upon him. It did not bother him. Had Rey not promised that he would look after him – that he would be safe? And he spent the nights in Rey's caravan, which made him beholden to his new friend. His backpack was still in the same place, just inside the door of the caravan, where he had put it down when he first arrived. He collected his three shillings at the end of each long tear-down night and he took his meals on the benches by the food shack.

Sometimes, in order to get closer to the twins, he would do odd performances in the sideshow. For a while, he was a ghost in the House of Horrors, a pathetic tent that had been raised over a small track with an electric train going around it. Along the track, in complete darkness, bolts of lightning would suddenly flare up and reveal a misshapen fluorescent plastic skeleton hanging from one of the tent poles, and a tape with recorded screams and horror sounds played on a loop. Gabriel's job was to jump out in front of the cart as it rattled past, his face made up in white with black around his eyes, and hoot in a ghost-like way. The House of Horrors was just next to the big top and, between carts, Gabriel could sneak out at the back and peek in at the freak show through a tear in the canvas.

This ghost-train farce came to an abrupt end one evening as a protective father lurched out in reflex and knocked Gabriel to the ground. He must have been unconscious for a while. The man operating the train noticed that two lots of carts came out looking even more bored than usual and went in to find him. Rey, who happened to be nearby, patted Gabriel's cheeks and poured some bourbon into his slack mouth from his hip flask – elixir for the poor, wounded god. After that, Rey arranged for him to do another job.

For a few weeks, he was Mr Electrico, the Human Dynamo. This was a proper act. Gabriel was strapped to a frightful looking 'electric chair' on a high stage. The caller announced the act: 'Come and see! Come and see! The boy who defies death in the electric chair! Watch the beautiful boy being seared by twenty-seven thousand volts! Will he survive? There's only one way to find out! Don't miss this incredibly risky act!' As the crowd gathered around, Gabriel pressed his arm against a metal plate, fastened to the chair, and received a current from a hidden transformer. He could then reach out his hand to light a bulb with his fingers or swing a wand of violet sparks. Sometimes, for fun, he would twist and writhe in the chair, pretending he was being tortured by the electricity. In reality, the current, although high in voltage, was low in ampere, which made it quite harmless. As his body jolted and shook, he remembered that other chair in which he had been put to the test, all those years ago. Had there really been any electricity in Michael's battery box? What would his life have been like if he had failed the test, if he had not felt the current that time? But he pushed those thoughts to the back of his mind as he saw Rey at the edge of the crowd, smiling encouragingly. Once or twice, Mary and Anne watched him from the back of the stage. On those occasions, he jerked with extra vigour, flexing the muscles in his arms against the straps that fastened him to the chair.

Then, one evening as Gabriel entered the caravan, Rey looked up from a book with cracked leather covers. The soft light from the hurricane lamp infused the copper in his curls as he shook his head slowly and sighed.

'You're in love with her, aren't you?' he asked, with a waxy smile.

'What?'

'Oh, come on, Gabe; I have been watching you.'

'Yeah, well, maybe you should stop snooping around.'

'I'm afraid that's what I do, my friend. Although, I wouldn't call it snooping, exactly . . . I'm gathering intelligence.'

'What for?'

'To bring down Dr Buster.'

'Why?'

'Isn't it obvious? I can't stand the man. He's a charlatan . . . and a full-blown psychopath,' he replied, casually, and stretched his legs under the table. 'Anyway, going back to your love, there's only one thing I have not yet worked out: is it Mary or Anne?'

Gabriel, defeated, looked at his shoes and mumbled, 'It's Anne.'

'Anne. Ah, Gabe, Gabe.' Rey tutted and shook his head, his eyes still smiling. 'Has your heart chosen wisely? Who can tell?'

'Lay off it, will you?' Gabriel flared, feeling a sudden rush of red fury rising inside him. His face closed on itself in a strange grimace. There was a faint twitch in his upper lip.

Rey studied him for a moment. 'I'm sorry, Gabe; I didn't mean to annoy you. It's just . . . Well, I'm not sure it's all that *practical*. But then, I suppose, love never is.'

'I don't care.'

'No, I can see that.' Rey sighed and continued. 'If you really care as much as you claim to do, would you be prepared to do something – anything – for them?'

'Yes, of course. But how?' He was not sure he wanted to know.

Rey seemed to be lost in thought for the moment. He was drumming his fingertips together in front of his mouth.

'Rey?'

'Eh? Ah, yes . . . Tell me, Gabe, the twins had their twenty-first birthday a few weeks ago, didn't they?'

Gabe nodded, not sure where this was going.

'Well, in that case,' he said, clapping his hands once, 'I think it's time for them to free themselves from this show, don't you? It's high time they got away, before Buster's *business* closes in on them.'

'Yes . . . Yes, I do, but—'

'You can drive a car on your own now, can't you, Gabe? You remember what I taught you?'

'Yes, sort of . . . But, where?'

'Where? What kind of a question is that?' For once, Rey looked irritated. 'Does it matter?'

'No, I suppose not.'

'Ah, I forgot – you're the boy who doesn't know where he is and who never knows where he's going . . . *Where* is important to you, isn't it?' Rey's voice was silken soft now.

'No, I don't care.' Gabriel shook his head, frowning. Rey had a way of making him feel ridiculous – like a child. He didn't want to be the kind of person who asked 'Where?' Not that he could see why that question was so laughable.

'Well, you can decide *where* later on. The first thing is to get them out of here without Dr Buster noticing and picking up your trail.'

'Okay; *how*, then?'

Rey laughed out loud. 'Don't worry, Gabe; I intend to put on a show that will keep Dr Buster occupied for quite some time.'

'Yeah? What about you?'

'What about me? I'll be gone soon enough.'

'Gone where?'

'That question again. I'll tell you where: into the labyrinth of life.'

'How will I know when to make a run for it?'

'Don't *worry*; you will know.' Rey shut the book – *Troy of the Iliad: Myth or Legend* – and stood up. 'Let's go for a walk.'

'What? Now? I just got back.'

'Don't be such a milksop. There's something I want to show you.'

It was the end of summer but the evening was warm and pleasant and millions of insects swarmed over the heather as the two youths set off across the moor. They followed a stream east with the setting sun warming their necks above their collars. The sweet, resinous smell of bog myrtle was everywhere.

'Where are we going?' Gabriel asked, regretting it at once.

Rey just pointed to a rock in the distance. 'It's marked on the map as St Michael's Chapel,' he said. 'I was there yesterday. A brilliant place – a ruin.'

The rock itself tore out of the heath like a canine tooth and, as he got closer, Gabriel began to distinguish the ruins of the chapel, which had been built into the granite, centuries previously, so that now it was almost indistinguishable from the rock. The sun cast long purple shadows, settling into its untidy bed. A single aperture remained in the chapel wall.

The climb from the foot of the rock was steep; at times, they had to use their hands. Dusk had settled as he pushed through a hole in the chapel wall. It took a while for Gabriel's eyes to get used to the gloom.

'Wow, this is great.' His voice was brittle against

the compressed shadows. He held his breath and listened. The last warm rays of the setting sun moved a breeze across the moor, which sighed in the broken battlements above. For a moment, there was no other sound.

'Rey?'

'I'm here.' Rey stepped out from behind a pile of fallen rubble. Part of his face was still in shadow. 'Isn't it marvellous?'

'Yeah . . .'

'Just imagine all the hopes and aspirations that went into building the chapel into the rock. It can't have been easy, dragging these blocks of stone here . . . and for what purpose?' He shook his head. 'This is what humanity is about: we create things against all the odds.'

'Yes, but we also destroy for no reason. This place—' Gabriel looked at the ancient stones around him; he listened to the moor wind – 'it reminds me of . . . a place up on the moors, near where I grew up. Not far from here. And of what happened there.' He hesitated, not quite knowing how to advance across such difficult terrain. 'I did something bad there. Something very bad.'

The confession hung darkly between them and would not settle. Rey remained silent, so he pushed on. 'I betrayed my only friend. My – brother.'

'Gabe, we have all done bad things at some time in our lives . . .'

'Yeah, but not like this.'

'Ah—' Rey whistled – 'you're talking of *real* shame . . .'

He was. Oh, he was – the grey sludge of it and how it threatened to swallow him up, like the mire had swallowed that cow they – he and Michael – had watched as her eyes turned in the grip of death. But, if you couldn't run away from it, you had to hide from it – always hide from it, as he did now, answering in a steady voice, 'What are you talking about?'

He could feel Rey's eyes on him and stepped back into the shadows.

'There's a certain vanity in living with shame, you know. You can wrap yourself in its filthy robes and still be quite snug.' Rey's voice was soft but it hurt.

Gabriel was awkwardly aware of his heart, which seemed to have grown too large for its cavity. He found it hard to breathe as he was back again at those other rocks, looking into those eyes. And Michael's young voice: 'Don't let them do this!' He swallowed and breathed again through the old betrayal.

'What is it that you don't get, Rey?' His jaw was stiff with frustration. 'I don't know what you're talking about.'

'Of course you don't,' Rey tutted, shaking his head from side to side, humouring him.

'Leave me alone, will you!' What did Rey know about anything?

Rey ignored him. 'It's possible to get away, you know. To shake off the filth.'

Gabriel laughed abruptly.

'Gabriel, listen to me. You're not a bad person, all right?'

Gabriel had withdrawn further into the shadows. He could smell the familiar rancid stench of self-loathing. Stay away from me. He took a deep breath.

'Gabe?'

'Yeah, yeah . . .' Gabriel felt his face twitch; in the twilight, it must have looked like a grimace. He made sure his eyes were hidden in shadows.

'No, listen to me: whatever you did, you've got to leave it behind – here, amongst these ruins.' Rey held out his hands, palms up, in a gesture which was more. It seemed to epitomise all that exasperating, blunt human striving – all the loathsome hopes of his existence. And all the possibilities, the supplications of life.

'No,' he persisted, sternly.

'No?'

'Leave it. The damage is done. Who do you think you are anyway? I don't need your bloody absolution.'

'But that's what I'm trying to tell you – it can be reversed. Doesn't this place, these ancient man-made walls, instil you with some hope, some sense of wonder and, well, just *sense*?'

At this, Gabriel felt a thickening in his throat and had to look away. He stared hard at one of the carved blocks of granite in the chapel wall. He stared, and suddenly he saw in the stone the long, steady marks of the mason's chisel. And, as he let himself be momentarily distracted by the softness of those furrows ploughed into the stone, there was a loosening inside him, a kind of falling away, and that which had been encrusted there for so long started to disintegrate, slowly turning to silt and being carried away in his blood flow.

Something swished overhead – a swift returning to its home in the walls, perhaps, or a bat waking up to hunt.

'It's time to get back, I think. Let's go,' Rey said, with unusual tenderness.

It surprised Gabriel that night had fallen so suddenly. They must have been in the chapel for longer than he imagined. A full moon had risen over the rocks and they had no trouble finding their way down and back on to the heath. They walked in silence, the dark warm between them. When Gabriel looked back after a while, the moon had moved on and the chapel was fading into the shadows, and he suddenly knew that Rey had been saying goodbye, that their friendship would remain here, while they both moved on. It saddened him, and yet how free he felt. How *light*.

Sense. The concept puzzled Mr Askew as he tried to sleep at night. Yes, he had found it in those battered ashlars in the chapel on the moor. But then, afterwards? All those years in London, had he managed to hold on to it or had he stopped striving?

You're sometimes given a nudge – like a toy boat pushed into water – and you let the push take its course. You hope that the original energy will never run out but you know that, by the laws of physics, it might already have happened and that you will be the last one to know. You go on thinking that things are generally fine. And so, for years, you restrain your emotions, relying instead on the momentum of the push. You travel the same route to work, you look down at the pavement, recognising the patterns of slabs and casually accepting the irregularities of manhole covers. Habit is your friend and it closes its doors softly, gently behind you. Then, brutally, something begins to stir and come awake.

It had been happening for some time now, he knew. The feeling was in his heart, but it was also being pumped around his whole body. *Her* face was the first thing that surfaced in his mind in the morning, and in the night . . . well.

This was such a night. He woke early out of a dream where his eyes had been wide open. Pulling on his dressing gown, he walked downstairs, crossing the hall where the pattern of white and black guided his way, and opened the front door. He stepped outside on to the front lawn and stood still, feeling the dew settling on him like the ghost of rain. He was afraid that waking up would force him to close his eyes, that, once again, he would have to walk with his eyes closed – or blindfolded. But it did not happen. On this morning, he stayed acutely aware of the significance of things around him. It's a long time since I have been conscious of these things, he thought. The world is making demands of me again. It is threatening to make sense.

Then there was a terrible accident. No one could claim that it was anything but an accident, but what followed seemed far from fortuitous. At least to Gabriel, who would later remember the unfolding events with eerie clarity.

It was the end of that long summer and the winds were gathering in the west, bringing gusts of penetrating chill and rainstorms that had gathered force on their passage across the Atlantic.

When the show finished that night, the site was a field of mud. The tear-down crew was struggling with the big top in the strong wind and the engines of the trucks revved as the wheels failed to grip in the slippery mire. Every now and again, bolts of lightning veined through the dense skin of the night, spotting men in frozen motion like searchlights over a battlefield. In the commotion, Stan was run over by one of the loading trucks. No one heard him scream, but one of the men happened to see his upper body sticking out of the mud and hurried to pull him out. But it was too late. The wheels of the truck had crushed his ribcage and, whilst this had not killed him, he had been pushed, face down, into the mud and rising water, so that he had slowly drowned in silt and his own diluted blood. Who had been driving the truck? In all the commotion, no one seemed to notice the open door of the driver's cab stuttering in the wind. The engine was still running, the headlights sieving through the static rain, eventually dipping on to another body – a body caught in flight and felled, as if by trip wire, only there was no sign of struggle or interference. When they turned him over, out of the mud, Charlie's suffocated face wore a ghastly expression. Afterwards, some would say that it was fear – others would describe it as surprise.

Dr Buster, a wild, yellow glimmer in his eyes, summoned the entire troupe and crew to the food shack for a headcount. Only one other person was missing: Rey.

'Where is that shifty villain, Rey? Get me the bastard, now!' Dr Buster roared into the wild night.

'His caravan is gone, sir,' one of the men reported.

'Gone? What do you mean, "gone"? He's under contract. Where would he go?'

There was no reply but Dr Buster bellowed on: 'Do you hear me? Has anyone seen him tonight?'

The assembled freaks and navvies all shook their heads – no, no one had seen him since that morning. No one, apart from Gabriel, who stayed at the back of the crowd now, slowly easing his way in a circle towards the twins, Mary and Anne. For he was sure he had seen Rey that night. Not face to face. No, nothing as manifest as that. He had glimpsed him out of the corner of his eye. Always at the edge of the light, Rey had appeared, hands deep in his pockets, one leg thrust forward, water dripping from a battered fedora, silently observing with a still smile on his face – like an admiral aboard his ship, preparing to engage.

Suddenly, another shout rose through the night. 'Hey, Buster, someone's broken into the safe!'

At that moment, Gabriel realised that he had to get out of there – fast. This was his cue. Sidling up to the twins, he whispered to Mary, 'Let's go.' She looked up at him and he could see that she was frightened. Anne was looking absently into the mud that covered her satin slippers; her wet hair was pasted to her skull. Gabriel thought she looked incredibly vulnerable. 'Come on, we've got to get out of here *now.*' He hesitated for a moment before wheezing into Mary's ear, 'Rey created all this turmoil so that we could escape; he wanted you and Anne free of this, just as much as I do.' And, at once, he realised that what he had just said was true – that Rey was somehow the instigator of the chaos. Could he even have raised the storm?

Quickly, he put a finger to his lips and indicated to the girls to follow him. Mary hesitated at first, but then something seemed to clear in her eyes and she put an arm around Anne and started pulling her sister into the vanishing shadows of the long night.

Behind them, Dr Buster clenched his fists and

raised them towards the streaming rain. 'Argh!' he thundered. 'I'll find that bastard and kill him! We will have police crawling all over the place, now. It will be the end of the show. Where is that fiend? The trickster has escaped again to his Maleperduis.' He flung his head back and laughed his chilly wolf laugh before suddenly composing himself and looking around the crowd with a wild gaze. 'Perhaps we should run away too, eh? What do you say? We bury the bodies and get out before dawn.' His voice was feverish, intense. 'Eh? Eh? Zilda, old pal, give me a hand, will you?' He turned to the magnificent whore, who remained silent. Turning around again, as if following his own tail, Dr Buster faced his troupe of freaks. 'Dido, old man, you have been part of my pack for a long time; give us a hand, will you?'

But Dido only spat on the ground and turned into the night.

Sliding through the mud and rain, Gabriel and the twins somehow reached Maryanne's caravan. 'Quick – into the car!' Gabriel shouted over the storm.

'But what about our things?' Mary cried back.

'There isn't much time – just grab the essentials and any valuables,' Gabriel replied with his new and unusual authority, which appeared to convince.

Someone had put a stretch of tarpaulin under the wheels of the twins' Ford. Bending closer, Gabriel saw that it was laid out so that the car would have a fairly dry passage until it reached the gravel path, which connected with the main road. This too, he suspected, was Rey's work. A rectangle of light fell on to him as the door of the girls' caravan was flung open.

'Could you help out here, please?' Mary shouted from within.

This is taking too much time, he thought to himself as he rushed up the steps and into the caravan. The girls were laden with bundles of clothes, bags of cosmetics and jewellery and even the crystal chandelier, which drooped out of their arms like a newly hauled fishing net. Annoyed, he relieved them of some of the stuff. 'That's enough,' he said, with irritation in his voice. 'Let's go.'

The girls seemed enthralled by his new command and followed quickly, leaving the door ajar as they bundled their belongings into the boot of the Ford. Gabriel had already got into the driver's seat and started the engine. A dark shape, it might have been a stray dog or a fox, released itself from the shadows under the car and passed into the night with a glint of bared teeth. Mary, herding Anne ahead of her, dived into the back seat. 'That's it,' she said. 'Drive.'

Gabriel backed carefully on to the tarpaulin, remembering what Rey had taught him. Biting his lip in concentration, he somehow managed to get the car on to the track, where he accelerated so fast the tyres tore up the gravel.

'There's something in here,' Anne protested from the back.

Gabriel swung round to see, but it was too dark. 'What is it?' he asked, keeping his eyes on the road, which was barely visible, like a ghostly ribbon, snaking into the blackness.

Anne was rummaging through something. 'It's a backpack with some men's clothes and a couple of books,' she said, with something like disgust in her thin voice.

Gabriel realised it was his belongings.

'And here's an envelope with our name on it,' Anne continued. 'It looks like . . . a wad of money.'

Gabriel suddenly laughed out loud as he realised how Rey had planned their escape, leaving nothing to chance.

'Whoa!' Mary shouted. 'You better keep us on the road. Why don't you turn the bloody lights on?' She leant across from the back seat, Anne in tow, and turned a switch so that the gravel lit up. Stunted trees, currently tortured by the storm, stretched their thin branches through the falling rain like hands clawing through metal bars, and, behind them, a darker row of hedges shook and fretted. Gabriel felt a chill run down his spine. Just then, they saw the junction with the main road a few yards ahead. It looked like they might have made it.

It was suddenly very quiet. The inside of the car could have been a submarine, one hundred feet under water. The moment seemed to float; it was as if the three bodies in the car had somehow broken free of reality, of life, and drifted away into some other state – a dream where they were weightless and the passing of time, the idea of a past, present and a future, was inconceivable.

Looking into the rear-view mirror at the twin pairs of eyes, hooded now in violet shadows as they stared back at him, he was not so much surprised at the fear in Mary's eyes as by the lack of distress or alarm in Anne's. Normally so timid, her gaze at that moment was calm and determined and there was a slight smile on her pale lips. Aware of his eyes on her, she pulled out a pocket mirror and a lipstick from a handbag in her lap and carefully, with minute precision, dabbed colour on to her parted lips. The next time he looked in the rear-view mirror, her eyes seemed to be smiling at him seductively, her lips a slit of scarlet in the flickering light. They had got away.

If anyone back at the site had noticed the car slip away, only the departing tail-lights would be visible now – a couple of sore eyes, finally closing on that wretched night.

CHAPTER 13

The fallen leaves from a silver birch stuck to the wet cobbles like golden confetti from some spectacular event that was now irretrievably over. Mr Askew stopped in his tracks and watched as a gust of wind rippled across a puddle. That's how a ghost would move, he thought to himself – parting the surface of life with its breath.

The coming of autumn was always unsettling. He did not mind the actual season, in fact he cherished that period the Americans called fall. It was an appropriate name, he thought, for the time of year when you no longer had to keep up the pretences, when you could loosen your grip and let yourself settle down into something less intense. No, he did not mind autumn itself, it was the transition – that uneasy coming-of-age as summer matured – that he could not stand. 'Let it be over with,' he muttered to himself and walked on. Fall. As in *falling in love*.

It had started to drizzle. The fog was coming in from the moor. It made the village look dirty. If it had a smell, he imagined it would be stinking – of filth and the aftermath of war. A car passed with dipped fog lamps gleaming off the wet pavement. Mr Askew trembled slightly. The car reminded him of a wolf sneaking past with all-seeing yellow eyes. His mind was not right today; he was feeling unsettled, exposed, as if he was at a turning point – just like that time when he had first gone to London, following that eventful summer after leaving school. He thought of himself as he was then: independent and strong for the first time in his life but still an innocent with so much more to learn. His body half inhabited, half suspended.

After escaping from Dr Buster's in the storm, he had driven through the night to Portsmouth. He had driven without a licence, with a couple of conjoined twins curled up in the back seat of a car that wasn't his. A pair of Siamese showgirls who he had helped run away from a nineteenth-century-style freak show that was living out its last days on the commons of England. It *did* sound like a joke. But the girls had got away all right. Once they reached Portsmouth, he had bought them two tickets with the money they'd found in the car and he had put them on to a ship bound for America – and he had never heard from them again. For a while afterwards, he kept scanning the papers for news of those spectacular twins, but it was as if they, like Rey and Dr Buster, had vanished from the face of the earth that day when they stepped on to the gangplank, turning once to wave at him. Before boarding, they had sold the Ford to a man in the harbour for fifty pounds, which they had left with Gabriel. Not knowing what to do next, he had found a phone box and rung his mother, who had given him his next cue – he had been accepted to university in London and was due to start in a couple of weeks.

On reaching Paddington, he had made his way to a room in Camden Road, which the university had allocated him. Completely alone in the world after being abandoned by Rey and the twins so abruptly, he was left with the fine sand of sleeplessness behind his eyelids and the darkness that opened the following morning, as he stirred to the smell of frying fat – a darkness that lingered long after the sun had reached his new window, fruitlessly trying to brighten the yellowing standard-issue bedclothes. But what did it matter if he slept and woke in light or darkness? The dreams and nightmares were all the same.

During those first rainy autumn nights in London, he had kept moving through the city, entering its metabolism like a thief on the run, seeing his loss reflected in green and silver on the surface of black puddles and streaming gutters. There were moments when he had begun to suspect that Rey, the sideshow, Maryanne, had all been a dream, a folly, a brief madness. Or perhaps it had all been a rather complicated plot, elaborated by some ancient and long-forgotten gods or obscure spirits of fate in order to . . . in order to do what? What was the purpose? He had managed to keep this unsettling feeling of uncertainty from his mind most of the time, but every now and again, when he had found himself alone and had time to think about it, it had overcome him, this doubt, like one of those fevers that will keep you awake all night, twisting in damp sheets.

In love.

Did he, had he ever, loved Anne? Well, he had risked his life for her, for them. He had entered another world for them and saved them from it. And, at times, in the days leading up to that last night, he had been overwhelmed by a longing to kiss Anne's lips, knowing what it would feel like and certain that just one single kiss like that would stay inside him for an entire day or more. But, just as he started to lean towards Anne's half-smiling, pouting lips, Mary would say, 'Ah, this could not have been more agreeable; aren't we lucky to be together, the three of us?' but with such steely tones in her voice that Gabriel would sit back again and draw a finger through his moustache. But love? He was not so sure. Thinking about it now, in hindsight, he was not at all sure why he had got involved. Love? That was not it, he realised – no, that was not it. He had done it because the opportunity to do something good – to do *something* – had presented itself and, for once, he had acted forcefully. He had just done it and, for the first time, he had loved *himself* – a little. Yes, he had done it. He – Gabriel Askew. *Gabe.*

And the twins, in the end, as they walked up that gangplank, had they not loved him, too – his new, assertive self? They had loved in a rather finicky way, he was sure, the way they loved themselves and their dream of a new life.

In the past, Mrs Ludgate's black eyes had often been inconveniences, a hindrance, like a stomach upset or – in her youth – the monthlies during a day at the beach. She had tried to conceal the bruising with the foundation that she had started buying years and years ago, precisely for this purpose, in the pharmacy in Stagstead. To be perfectly honest, she was quite baffled by her own foresight as a young woman – it was remarkably crafty of her to keep it to hand, just in case, for those occasions when it was needed. Lately, she had not had any reason to use it, but she did all the same. It had become a habit and she felt naked and exposed without the protective membrane. Now she was running out and had to buy some more. It had been preferable, she reminded herself, as she hurried down the lane towards Stanton's Cross, when he had not hit her in the face; the bruises on her body were more easily covered up. Even that time when her arm broke, there had been no reason for people not to believe that she had fallen down the stairs. These things happened, after all, especially on farms. But, of course, it had not been for her to decide where he hit her, in spite of the inconvenience.

The foundation was by Rimmel, which was supposed to be a slightly better make than No 17 at Boots. And yet it was not satisfactory. The colour was off – just a little too dark – and it made her skin look sodden and slightly yellow – and blue and yellow makes green, as we all know. The mirror in the bathroom up at the farm was too dark these days; she could not really see what she looked like. The window was small, just a slit in the stone wall, and the lights were no longer working – not since her husband stopped paying the bills.

She was surprised that no one had ever commented; surely somebody must have noticed the awful green bruises that would sink slowly down her face like stones caught in ice. She had become accustomed to keeping her head down, but she hated it every time she had to go back to the Stagstead chemist – the look of concern – or apathy, for that matter – on the faces of the ignorant assistants as she asked for the various items of self-medication. They were hoping to become pharmacists themselves one day, no doubt, or even beauticians, aromatherapists, that kind of thing. Hopeless, stupid girls.

The bus came around the corner just as she reached the crossroads and the driver – it was Mr Carpenter – having spotted her, slowed down and waited for her to reach the bus stop. That was kind.

'Morning, Mrs Ludgate,' he said, cheerfully, as she climbed the steep steps. 'Going for a bit of a shopping spree today, are we?'

'Shopping spree, my posterior!' she spat through her pinkest lipstick, and pulled her hat further over her face. 'There's only rubbish to buy in Mortford. If I wanted to shop, I'd go to stay with my daughter in Exeter.'

'Oh, dear; it's one of them days, is it?' said the driver, but not unkindly.

Mrs Ludgate wobbled down the aisle and found her seat at the back. The bus was empty, apart from a couple of ramblers. Foreigners, for sure – they had that smell about them. Garlic and suchlike. As the bus started moving, she held on to the seat in front with both hands, her feet in the white trainers barely touching the floor, and thought about the task at hand. Now, Rowden's sold foundation, she was quite sure of it. Not Rimmel, of course, one could not hope for that, but some other brand, surely? She wondered if the girl at the till would find it untoward if she bought two tubes at once – perhaps, if they were different shades, a lighter and a darker . . . Yes, that was the way to do it. She wondered, at times, what other women did; this must be a common pursuit, after all, as normal powder would not offer enough coverage. Over the years, she had often wished that she had a friend, somebody with whom she could discuss such issues. But it was not the kind of thing one talked about at the Women's Institute, for instance. Lately, the discussion there had mainly been concerned with the plight of the honeybee. The initial, slightly over-agitated lamentations about the decrease of the bee population had soon been abandoned for talk about recipes for honey cake. She did not care for honey cake but she didn't mind bees and, without telling anyone, she had planted a patch of foxgloves and larkspurs in the kitchen garden up at the farm. There, by midsummer, they had stretched proudly, pink and blue, against the grey stone wall, like a festival of medieval knights. One morning in July, when she was all alone – her husband away in London – she had sat for hours in the grass, her legs stretched out like a child's, watching the bees as they dipped in and out of the bright thimbles, wearing the flowers like tiny wizard's hats. She had been so overwhelmed by a sense of achievement – to think that it was her planting that dressed these creatures – it had made her cry, silly bint that she was. She liked the bumblebees best, the way their fuzzy bums would stick out of the flowers as they dipped their tongues into the nectar. Their look of dusted bewilderment as the pollen gilded their pelt reminded her of the slick and dewy meadows on the cliffs of her youth and filled her with a sudden and inexplicable longing. Identical at first, the closer she observed the bees, the more individual they appeared. Most wore the same bands of black and yellow with the soft white scut, but some had more yellow, almost red, and some were nearly all black. And the buzzing! The beautiful buzzing of the bumblebee, the abandon, the lust, the soothing softness of that summer sound as they all bumbled away, buzzing for joy in that most still and perfect of mornings.

It was November now and the moor was at its grimmest. Some of the farmers had started the swaling, the annual burning of the bracken and the gorse. There were large patches of ashy grey amongst the auburn bracken. A few sheep, blackened by the sooty undergrowth, stared at the bus as it passed on the road. She resented them and the way they threatened to draw her down into some undergrowth realm of bluebottle flies and slugs. She could not stand their mindless gaze, empty of everything but some deep-rooted instinct – panic, perhaps, or some other stinking drudge.

'It hurts me, too,' he used to say, in the beginning. 'Can't you see you're spoiling the fun?' Back then, she did not seem to have much fun – nor much of a future. Would death have been a way out? She might have thrown herself in front of the bus. It would have been easy enough, as the driver would not have spotted her as he came around the bend towards Stanton's Cross, at least not in the summer, when the hedges were high. It was a dangerous crossing, people said. But why, she had asked herself, would I do that? I am already crushed. She could have hanged herself, but her breath, she had been told, was a waste of time, so what would have been the point of that? There were other ways, she knew, to end one's life, but she had been too tired at the time to think of them

– and never vain enough. And then there had been the girl – the daughter she had secretly named for a lighter existence.

Suddenly she remembered the book of photographs she had seen in the professor's drawing room. There had been women there – and men, for that matter – wearing make-up, but the photographs had stripped them of their masks. Not in a ruthless way, but almost tenderly. That woman photographer, whom the professor liked so much, would surely have known about the use of foundation; *she* would not have wasted her time talking about the plight of the honeybee, silk-ribbon embroidery and macramé. She would have *seen*.

They had been relatively well off, at times. Not rich, mind you, but there had been enough – enough money for his weekends away along the coast or his long stays down in London. There had always been electricity and hot water up at the farm, and he had had the roof of the old barn replaced, although they no longer kept any cattle. The barn was where he stored his merchandise. He was better off as a businessman than as a farmer, he had explained to her once. Not that he ever talked to her about his business – nor of the property deals, of course – but she had managed to find out a thing or two for herself. He would buy cheaply from old widows and sell dearly to Londoners and golfing entrepreneurs. People, mainly the relatives of the old widows, would get cross with him from time to time, even upset. She knew this because they would sometimes ring up and shout down the line. But he would only put on his charms, the ones that made people afraid of him, and, afterwards, he would smile and hum to himself. 'It went for a song, Granny's bungalow did – a fucking song!' But then, a few years ago, there had been no more singing or dancing. His business had turned for the worse. He had never allowed her to work – to have a proper job outside the house. She chuckled to herself as she thought about what her husband might have said about her job at the professor's – at Gabriel Askew's – who was not just a stranger to her husband, after all. Oh, no – no stranger at all. She shivered at the thought and yet she was strangely pleased.

Suddenly, she stirred and grabbed her handbag that sat perkily on the seat next to her. She opened the oversized metal clasp with a click and looked inside, rummaging nervously through the jumble of lipsticks, old bus tickets, Kleenex, a miniature bottle of Jägermeister and a couple of postcards that she had never sent to Exeter. Then she found what she was looking for and relaxed. It was a piece of paper – a document that she had found when clearing out her husband's filing cabinet a few weeks previously. She was surprised that there were still some documents left in the house. Throughout their marriage, she had avoided knowing about her husband's business. But lately, since the professor arrived in the village, something – a sliver of a memory from the time before her fate was sealed – had made her want to find out more. She had no idea what she had been looking for, but this particular file had caught her eye immediately. It puzzled her – she could not make head nor tail of it – but, as far as she could tell, it seemed to suggest that the professor had bought Oakstone from her husband, that Jim of Blackaton had been sitting on the deeds to the house for years – just holding on to it. If he had been letting it, she had not been aware of it. As far as she knew, the house had been boarded up. It seemed almost perverse. There was an entire file just on Oakstone. How was it possible? Where could he have got hold of the deeds? There was no way he could ever have afforded to buy that house – that much she realised – not a grade two listed house. She had been thinking about it for weeks. Perhaps, today, once she had bought the foundation at Rowden's, she would bring herself to ask Mr Askew about the strange document.

The road turned off the moor and followed the stream down into the valley, where the hedges were still thick, if not lush, and the oaks and the elms, old and wise above the bus, heralded the approach with their autumn colours. This was good – it was all fine – and she could already see the tower of Mortford church ahead – solid, reassuring. And the stone in her chest began to float.

Later that afternoon, Mr Askew watched her toiling up the drive. From where he was standing

342

vigilantly by the French windows, he imagined he heard her heavy breathing – a plump person's breathing – as she pushed on up the gravel, where the potholes were mud-thick and un-drained. A green and white plastic bag from Rowden's was dangling from her left wrist and that ridiculously large handbag of hers was swinging heavily from the other; every now and again it would bang against her right thigh. He gazed up beyond her as a weak sun broke through the drab November sky for a moment. A couple of bare branches on the huge trees at the end of the garden were black against the marbled background of greys and whites. Their trunks were barbed in ivy – like strings of broken lyres.

He had listened to a programme on Radio Four that morning about migratory thrushes – how they would fly south from Britain in November, only to be trapped and caught by hunters in eastern Spain and served as tapas in local restaurants. Birdwatchers were quite reasonably upset about this, but the Spanish were unmoved, claiming that their practice was an unbroken cultural heritage going back to Roman times – a tradition that must be encouraged, according to some EU policy about regional growth. 'Some blessed hope,' Mr Askew muttered to himself and shook his head before turning his mind to the lucky songbirds who managed to avoid the Spanish glue traps and flew on to North Africa; how, come spring, a handful of them would home in on those trees at

343

the end of his garden and travel thousands of miles to find this very spot again. Lucky birds, to believe in home, to have such an instinct for belonging. The whole thing baffled him.

He turned away from it and, with a long sigh, lowered his eyes once more to the outlandish figure of Mrs Ludgate – who was nowhere to be seen. She seemed to have disappeared into thin air, quite literally. He blinked. 'What the—' he began, greatly annoyed, but broke off abruptly as her face suddenly appeared right in front of him, pressed against the windowpane. They were inches apart, only separated by the glass. For an unsettling moment, he was forced to look straight into her eyes. They were of a peculiar violet blue and somehow angry, but there was something else, too, something which he could not quite place. 'Argh!' he barked, involuntarily. Mrs Ludgate looked equally perturbed, but she collected herself quickly and pointed sternly towards the front door, the plastic carrier from Rowden's swinging like a punchbag. Her face was an odd colour, he noticed, and blotchy like the bark of a beech tree, and there was a drop at the end of her nose. It glittered briefly in the weak sun.

He walked through to the hall and opened the door to her. 'For God's sake, woman!' The shock of seeing her face so close was still ripe in him. 'Why are you sneaking around like this?'

'I rang the bell, didn't I?' she yelled back, equally

frazzled. 'You gone deaf, or something? Or was your head in the clouds, as per usual?'

Had he really not heard the bell? Perhaps he *was* going deaf – or did he let himself drift too far away at times? 'Anyway,' he said in a calmer voice, 'it's not Friday, is it? I didn't expect to see you.'

'No, well, I'm not here to work.'

'Oh?'

'I've come on a matter of business.'

'Ah,' he said, and felt a thickening in his throat.

'A matter that concerns yourself.'

'You'd better come inside, then,' he said, stepping aside to let her pass.

To his alarm, she pushed right past him with unsettling determination and fell back into one of the armchairs by the cold fireplace with a great 'Humph!'

He stood for a moment, huge and mute, like a forest troll, before following her, hesitantly, into the drawing room.

'Well, then, is there any chance of a cup of tea?' she asked, and pulled her fleece jacket over her breasts. 'Or would that be too much trouble?'

He did not reply, but left the room promptly. When he returned, carrying the teacups and a few biscuits on a tray, she had settled into the chair with an air of importance. She was holding a folded paper in her lap. He placed the tray on a rickety side table and sat down in the chair opposite her. He considered the marble of the mantelpiece and the gilded mirror above it, reflecting their silence, and tried to think of something to say. 'Well, here we are . . .' he said softly, and smiled at nothing in particular. A dried twig with acorn, which he had picked up on one of his walks, was leaning against the little china clock on the mantelpiece; it was as brown and drab as the day.

She looked at him with something he interpreted as contempt, although it might just as well have been the opposite, before bending forward to help herself to a biscuit from the tray.

'I expect you know why I've come,' she said, at last.

'I have a good idea, yes,' he answered flatly.

'I know it's you – you have ruined us!' It was not what she had planned to say – certainly not – but a part of her was enjoying the drama of the situation, and her potential part in it. But 'us'? She heard herself use that word with disbelief.

'I object,' he protested, languidly, like some corrupted lawyer.

'You *what*?'

'I said that I object to such a simplified version of reality. I ruined your husband, but I gave you paid employment – reluctantly, perhaps, but I still think it ought to count in my favour. I didn't know who you were, at first – not until you told me your husband's name.' There's a certain comedy to all this, he thought to himself.

'Oh.' For a moment, she was dumbstruck by his straightforward confession. And a little disappointed – she had been looking forward to the interrogation part, to the drawing of blood as she presented her evidence, piece by piece. But he was right, of course. The document in her hand had nothing to do with her.

He stood up and crossed the room to turn on a lamp by the French windows. Outside, the wind was rising with the coming of darkness. Fallen leaves were whirling around the yard, riding their own dilapidated merry-go-rounds. Too fast; too fast. Sometimes a northerly gust would lift them away from their play and into the air, forcing some of them against the window, where they made a dry, scraping sound, like ghosts dragging their nails, wanting to make themselves known.

'I know you take me for a plain woman, an uneducated thug's wife,' she said to his back. 'Well, stupidity can be a great disguise, at times – but I believe in plain speaking.' She was calmer now. Steady.

A blood-red stain was spilling through the trees in the west. He turned his back to the window and looked about the room, wondering vaguely why it looked so unlived in. How could it be that he had not managed to make more of an impression? The furniture stood about like pieces in a stage set, or like extras in a drama about to commence: a stooped chair, ready to pull itself straight; a table on spindly legs, ready to leap; a book opened on the floor, waiting to say its lines.

'Are you listening?'

He nodded, unable to speak.

'So, you've quite deliberately ruined him, eh? I wonder how long you've been plotting it – five years? Ten? Well, there's no need to answer; doesn't matter much now, does it? There's more where this comes from, you know – a whole file of it,' she said, waving the piece of paper – a sound like the leaves at the window; the ghosts from the past, pressing against him.

'You were even behind the deal which made him have to give up the paddocks on the other side of the road to that holiday park . . . Those acres were part of the ancient tenement, you know. They have belonged to the farm for ever – it's mentioned in the Domesday Book. I suppose you thought it would hurt him, giving up the land?' She laughed softly, but then he thought he heard her sob. 'Well, you were wrong there; he couldn't care less about the land. Always hated it. Hated the farm, he did, but it was a convenient bolt-hole for a con man, wasn't it? That old barn, full of this, that and the other . . . It's quite clear that you did it all to get at this old pile, but what I don't understand is *why*? You don't seem like a man who has any need for . . . all this.' She flicked her plump hand at the room. Perhaps she noticed how empty it was. 'And then there's the question of why you wanted to hurt. And how did you know that the only way to get at him was to stab at his pride?'

'Hurt?' he interrupted. 'But you misunderstand . . . I never set out to hurt anyone – I just wanted to set things right. There was so much that had gone . . . well, wrong.' He turned back to face the French windows.

She ignored him. 'So that's when I remembered, didn't I? That the great professor used to know my hubbie, way back . . .'

He could feel her eyes on his back, intense, probing.

'And, anyway, as I said, I'm not as stupid as you may think; I can put two and two together. I knew from the time I saw that photograph of the little boy and his family at Oakstone that the Bradley boy was somehow related to you.'

He swallowed hard. She had known all along.

'So, once I'd found the file in the safe and read it word by word – all those transactions; I'm surprised he kept the documentation of such thorough failure on his part – I reckoned there must be something more to this story, a missing link, if you read me. And then I remembered you skulking around Edencombe on that rainy day. So I thought, hang on a minute, don't I know one of the nurses from up there . . .? Oh, yes, I do: Mrs Smith from the WI.'

His limbs were suddenly fluid. He staggered back to the chair opposite her. She was watching him, sucking her teeth.

'Of course the nurses aren't allowed – strictly forbidden, in fact – to disclose any information about the patients, seeing as it is an institution of a somewhat . . . delicate nature. However, Mrs Smith is a rather frail character, recently bereaved, and it didn't take me long to get her to spill the beans, the poor dear. It's not that she *likes* me – oh, no – and I'm sure she's, you know, moral and all that . . . I reckon she goes to that church on Sundays. But–' she fixed him with her eyes and there was something urgent in her gaze – 'but I suppose there are moments in *all* our lives, stripped, sort of colourless and, at least to the rest of the world, darned *dull*, when the nastiest, *bloody* agony—' she caught her breath and continued – 'I'm talking of proper pain here – heartache, that kind of thing – will make you go against yourself, I mean, go against who you are, your nature, right?' Her voice was softer now, almost tender, as if she was no longer talking about Mrs Smith and Edencombe, or, indeed, about the ruining of her husband, but about something altogether more personal.

They sat for a while staring past each other in glassy-eyed silence. How can I make her understand? he thought to himself. How can I make anyone understand why I had to do this, when I hardly understand it myself? Not compulsion, redemption, revenge – no. Setting the balance right. Joining things back together to make space for love. Nor would he be able to explain, he realised, why, now that he had recreated that place, he could not possess it. He could not unpack the boxes in the hall and he still hadn't opened the doors to most of the rooms in the house. The bliss to which he had aspired was still beyond reach, shielded from view by a sadness of cobwebs. He could no longer find a purpose. He was confused. He wanted somebody to whom he could tell the truth. But he could not think who such a person might be. He was a ridiculous figure, a freak, and they would be sure to laugh at him and his pathetic efforts. Bunny-boy, trying to set things right. The whole idea, the notion that everything would somehow be okay if only he got Oakstone back, was indeed laughable. If only he could return once more to Ithaca. To his own surprise, he started laughing. Leaning back in his chair, he laughed until he realised – oh, the horror of it, the shame – that he was crying.

But Mrs Ludgate, compact and contained in her chair, her feet not quite reaching the floor, looked at him calmly and, if it had not been so unthinkable, he might have thought that there was compassion in her gaze. She spoke again in her new soft voice: 'There are things – bad moments – which can change your life when it really matters. It's happened to me, you know. I sort of stepped out of myself and became a ghost.' Her cheeks had reddened a bit and she spoke quickly, as if embarrassed. 'It's like on all them chat shows on telly, when they keep telling you that you have to have ambitions in life and fulfil yourself and stuff like that. Well, it ain't always that easy, is it? You forget all those things you were dreaming of doing, all those pathetic, lousy hopes. You forget *yourself* – and then you have to spend the rest of your time trying to find your way back.' She stopped abruptly, looking away from him now.

Ah, yes, those moments she was speaking of – he knew them only too well and how inexorably linked they were with the search for love. Love. How truly helpless humans were in its hands. How it played upon our expectations. And yet, something else was at work here. However much one strove for it or against it, one's efforts were never enough; the cause and effect seemed always to be beyond one's powers. And the result – was it intentional or accidental?

Something – the fading disc of light from the lamp, which kept them in the dark, perhaps, or the unreal, Alice-in-Wonderland quality of their new world – stirred a memory in him of another time, so long ago now, in this room, when he had kept himself just out of the circle of light, here by the fireplace: Mr Bradley's funeral, when he had first understood that he was lost to himself and that it was all out of joint. Had he realised then how utterly overwhelming his task would be, and how wonderfully all-consuming?

On the road beyond the garden wall, a car passed; the beams from its headlights found their way through the forked trees and across the lawn, so that they finally hit the gilded mirror above the fireplace. Unruly shadows came to life and stirred around Mr Askew and Mrs Ludgate. Then these dancing shapes were gone and the room seemed darker than before. But there was something else;

352

yes, there was something quite new and they both sensed it. There was an odd mood in the chilly room, a sense of intimacy and understanding, and the possibility of it was strangely encouraging to them both.

'I am sorry, truly, that you got caught up in this. And I freely admit that I may have been prejudiced against you because of your association with *him*. It's only natural, after all.'

She looked up, with a genuine air of surprise. 'Oh, no, please don't be sorry. I wish he was dead!' she said with vehemence.

He stared at her for a moment and it was as if he had seen her for the first time. She was not all that ugly, he noticed. Quite pretty, really, if it hadn't been for that caked make-up. Her eyes were of such an unusual blue. 'That bad, was it? Yes?'

She said nothing.

'Why didn't you leave him?'

'We had a child. A daughter.'

He nodded. 'Yes, I remember now . . .'

'I was trapped, like a fly in one of them orange stones . . .'

'Amber.'

'Yeah, that's the one. And, once she had got away – once she was safe – I didn't really care. I was nothing to him; he left me alone for ages when he was out . . . roaming with Billy and those other friends of his. Or when he lived in London for weeks on end.' How she hated them all and their bloody 'business' – the stink of it, the rubbish they talked about it. 'There was some freedom then, which I enjoyed. I had the farm to myself. And I convinced myself it was all I wanted. That I mustn't rock the boat. That loneliness wasn't the worst of it.'

How come he had not seen it before, that extraordinary integrity in the face of her predicament? And then, in a flash, he recognised, behind her mask, the young girl in the pink uniform, serving in the pub on the moor, and he remembered her kind eyes from so long ago. Could it be that she had always been on his side?

'Why did you answer my ad?'

'Oh, several reasons, really.' She was blushing. 'I remembered you from all those years ago in the Moor Cross Inn . . . I felt bad for you that time. You were so helpless. It was quite brave of you to walk into that shit hole.'

He looked up at her quickly and saw that she was concentrating to find the right words, so he listened.

'I thought, at the time, that I had never seen anyone as alone. Then, when I saw you again at the trial – after all those years – I thought about all the parts of my life I had lost since I last saw you. And it stirred something in me. I thought perhaps we were rather similar – and I thought that, whatever we have lost, perhaps we could help each other find ourselves again.' She had reddened, he saw, before she added, 'Except that you're so bloody arrogant at times.'

He nodded, ignoring the last remark. 'Yes, I think you're right . . . I think we probably are, in some respects – alike.' He looked at her and smiled. What an odd turn of events. 'Oh, I almost forgot,' he said. 'I did force him to sign over the farm into your name.'

She looked at him and laughed in genuine appreciation. 'How very crafty of you, Professor!'

He rolled his eyes and waved a hand in mock smugness.

'But . . . there's something else, isn't there? Something to do with that . . . that person in Edencombe?'

He looked up at her in alarm and she let it drop.

'You still haven't told me . . .' she continued instead. 'I know he was awful to that boy, your friend, the one they called Fluffy, but what did he do to *you*?'

'My brother. *That boy* was my brother.'

He stood abruptly and crossed the room to the French windows, opening the doors. The cold night entered, smelling of burnt bracken and the coming of winter. As he turned back to her, the warm glow from the lamp embraced him, but the light had gone out in his face. 'What did he do to *me*? Oh, I don't know, nothing that you'd call criminal, I'm sure. He made me betray . . . everything.'

Gabriel's resolution to save Michael from Jim of Blackaton and *set things right* had been made in

St James's Park on a Saturday morning in summer, after his first year at university. It was a moment of perfect tranquillity and clarity. The sun was steaming the dew off the lawns and the two old spinsters living in Duck Island Cottage were already up and about, scattering feed for the early birds. A couple of geese flew in over the lake and landed in a sudden, spectacular show – a sequined crescendo. A rainbow formed briefly in their wake, but it disappeared before revealing its treasures. Hundreds of years previously, when the park was still no more than a swamp, two crocodiles had lived amongst the waterfowl. Imported from a warmer climate, they would yawn in bewilderment on a morning like this. Gabriel, his crumpled suit sodden with dew, yawned too as he sat up on the bench, where he had ended up after a night on the tear. He offered his face to the sun and smiled in revelation. It was obvious that he would have to treat his mission with great discretion, patience and perseverance. He had, at last, a *real* purpose.

The catalyst to this revelation was an ugly thing – a rather obscene episode – but, in reality, it was a series of unlikely events over the previous forty-eight hours which had led him to this park bench, where he had finally fallen asleep after walking all night until just before dawn.

It had all started with him overhearing a conversation in an Irish pub in King's Cross. Two thuggish-looking men in three-piece suits

356

and greased hair were discussing a new nightclub they'd been to in Soho. Something – a tone or the way their voices would hush deliberately at certain points in the conversation – made Gabriel listen harder. It was clearly a club where you could catch an act that was quite out of the ordinary. One of the men mentioned a dancer called Dolly May and her pianist, who was 'a bit of a daftie'.

Gabriel shifted closer to the two men under the pretext of taking a look out of the smudged window. The light had started to dim over the streets outside the pub and the taxicabs were putting their headlamps on. Suddenly he realised that the two men had stopped talking. He turned round, only to stare into the face of one of them.

The man looked him up and down, taking his time. 'Hey, this one looks as if he could do with a bit of excitement, don't you think?' he said, nudging his friend.

The friend grinned and turned to Gabriel. 'Enjoying our conversation, were you?'

Gabriel swallowed and nodded. 'Yeah, that club you were talking about sounded grand. Where can I find it?'

The two men stared at him for a moment and then one of them started to laugh. 'Well, *well*, aren't you a kinky one?' he said, and, turning to his friend, 'This guy clearly hasn't dipped his wick for a while . . . You'd better give him the address.'

'You run straight to the Pelican Club in Greek

Street, pal, and you may catch yourself some action tonight.'

Reddening, Gabriel thanked them and, leaving enough change on the bar, he stepped out into the street. It had started to rain. Buttoning up Uncle Gerry's tweed jacket, whose cuffs had started to fray, Gabriel set off towards Soho.

The Pelican Club was not easy to find and he walked past the entrance twice before spotting a narrow black door with an image of a pelican. The door opened on to an equally narrow stairwell, leading down into a large, windowless area with a long, curved bar and tables arranged in front of a small stage.

Leaning against the bar with a drink at his arm, he listened to the band rehearsing that evening's numbers. It was still early and the club was empty, save for himself, the barman, and a couple of men talking business in one of the leather-clad booths. Gabriel could only see the face of one of them – the other one sat with his back to the bar. For a moment, Gabriel thought there was something familiar about that back, but he let it go. Stripped of its clientele, the interior of the club looked shabby and dilapidated. It smelt of cigarettes and stale drink. The barman cleared his throat and spoke without warmth: 'You all right, there?'

'Fine thanks,' Gabriel said and turned around to face the bar. In the broken mirror behind the bottles, he saw his own split face and, behind it, multifaceted and fragmented, the duplicate profiles of the two businessmen. And then he saw the poster; it advertised a show – a burlesque show – and there, behind the long-legged young woman with black hair dressed in a corset and ostrich boa, was an image of Michael at a piano. It was definitely Michael. He was even thinner than when Gabriel had last seen him at the Moor Cross Inn, dressed in black-tie and half hidden in shadow, but it was Michael. The text on the poster read *Dolly May – Cabaret of the Damned*. He turned to the barman, who was drying glasses nearby. 'Hey, that guy at the piano—' he pointed at the poster – 'do you know him? Does he play here often?' The barman looked up with a dulled expression. He lit a cigarette and glanced at the poster. 'I dunno,' he muttered, blowing out the smoke.

'I'd like to get in touch with him, that's all.'

'Yeah?'

Gabriel ignored the tone of sarcasm in the barman's voice. 'Well, could you at least tell me when he played here last?'

The barman glanced over at the two men in the booth, but they were deep in conversation now; they didn't seem to have noticed Gabriel. 'They played here last Thursday,' he said, and spat into the glass he was wiping. 'That's all I know,' he added, curtly, and turned his back to Gabriel.

On realising that Michael might be close, Gabriel started a tireless, meticulous quest to track him down. He would hear snippets of information here and there – in the clubs and pubs in Archer Street, Wardour Street and Great Windmill Street, from the Caribbean musicians who set the rhythm of those streets and from the girls clustering like grapes in the doorways – but no one could vouch for any of the facts. No one could say anything for certain. And yet they all knew of him. He was remarkably handsome, they seemed to agree, although in a consumptive way. No one knew where he lived, but one man thought he sometimes slept on a mattress in a room above the Harmony Inn, and once under the grand piano at the Palladium. People said his mind was blown, and that sometimes he spoke in French.

This was all pieced together over the course of a week or two. Michael might have been mistaken for just another bum, another minor character in that incredible cast, but there was clearly a certain quality to him, something which made the low life of Soho's streets hesitate when asked about him, something intangible which would make them stop and smell the air, as if they expected the spirit of the elusive young pianist to be mingling with the stench of frying fat and alcohol. The secret of his attraction seemed to be his boyishness – it was as if he had never grown up – and his link to the owner of the Pelican Club. He was the club's mascot, said some; others used more sinister terms to describe Michael's ties to one of the most feared club owners in London.

He was simply called the Pelican, after his club,

and was well known for managing to stay out of the way of the law, in spite of some rather dodgy business tactics. Some said that he offered protection for the brothels throughout the West End. He had a number of police officers and judges on his payroll and no witnesses dared appear against him. His front-of-house staffer was Seamus 'the Clerk' O'Brien, a devout Catholic with a dingy office above a strip bar. The phone number printed on his visiting card rang in a phone box in Brewer Street.

'What do you want?' answered an irritated female voice when Gabriel finally called the number from a phone box in nearby Berwick Street.

'I want to meet the Clerk.'

The woman sighed and yelled to somebody nearby. 'Hey, it's another one for the Clerk!'

Gabriel listened down the line at the street life, which mingled with the noises outside his own booth.

Finally, a man's voice came on the line: 'What do you want to see the Clerk about?'

'I want to talk to him about my brother, Michael, the pianist.'

He could hear the man at the other end of the line breathe for a moment. 'Your brother?'

'Yeah.'

The man was silent, considering this. 'All right; go to Walker's Court and ask for the Clerk.'

This is a long way from Mortford, Gabriel thought to himself as he was led up a rickety flight of stairs to the Clerk's office. Seamus O'Brien was sitting at a large mahogany desk. His jacket was draped across the back of his captain's chair and the sleeves of his white shirt were held back with silver armbands. He might have been a typesetter, shaping the language of the day. A life-sized carved Madonna in sky-blue velvet robes was standing like a sentinel just inside the door. She wore a gold crucifix pendant, studded with red and blue stones – it looked real and very expensive. Gabriel entered and closed the door behind him. O'Brien looked up from his ledgers and studied Gabriel through half-moon glasses. There was a print of the Pope on the wall behind him.

'Yes?'

'I'm looking for my brother, Michael Bradley.'

'And what makes you think I could help you?'

'Well . . .'

'Don't be a weakling, boy. Spit it out!'

'They say he works for you . . . For the Pelican, that is.'

'No one works for me, do you hear? I deal with paperwork – I am a clerk!' O'Brien flared, his face suddenly blazing.

'I apologise.'

'Don't mention it.'

There was a moment of awkward silence.

'Well?' Gabriel dared ask, at last.

'Well, what?'

'Would you know where I could find my brother, sir? It would be—' he looked quickly around the room – 'a good deed, if you could help me.'

'Ah,' said the Clerk, and started looking distract-
edly through his papers. 'Yes, well, I keep a list of
names here, you see . . .'

Gabriel stood, frowning at his shoes, waiting.

Somewhere, a doorbell buzzed. A plastic Sacred
Heart in a gold frame started blinking on the
mahogany desk. O'Brien sighed and removed his
glasses to polish them on his shirtsleeve. His eyes
were tiny and red-rimmed. 'It's another one of the
bag men, bringing in this week's money.' He
nodded towards the blinking light. 'You'd better
leave through the back door.'

'But sir – a good deed, please?'

O'Brien sighed. 'All right, all right; come to the
club tonight. I'll make sure he's there.'

Gabriel hardly recognised the Pelican Club when
he returned later that evening. The shabbiness
seemed to have been transformed, at the stroke of
a wand, into glamour. A soft glow from uplighters
all around the walls picked out the sparkle in the
gold ceiling, which stretched like an oriental
canopy over the guests, seated at the small round
tables in front of the stage. Everyone was in
evening dress. A single couple was dancing; they
were beautiful – she pale, slender, almost green-
tinted, like the part of the flower stalk that never
sees the light; he golden, full of all that love, his
hand confident on the small of her back. There
was something rather dreamy – almost innocent
– about it all. Gabriel felt awkward in his old suit.

He smoothed his fringe to one side and wished he'd worn a tie. A jazz band was playing on stage and, for a moment, he was transported back to the safety and comfort of Uncle Gerry's cottage, where he had been able to dream of this allure. Put the blame on Mame, boys.

Keeping to the shadows, Gabriel moved around the periphery of the room, observing the guests. Waiters in white jackets and bow ties flowed around the tables, serving champagne cocktails from silver trays. The smoke from Cuban cigars and cigarettes formed tawny clouds around the tables, as if each one of them had its own weather system – or a volcano, ready to go off at any moment. Gabriel felt himself drawn towards the music. On the wall next to the stage was a large mosaic of a pelican, lowering its beak to its heart, where drops of blood stained its snowy white chest. Just below the pelican's beak, where real drops of blood would have fallen, Michael was sitting at a table by himself, his eyes fixed on the stage.

For a few minutes, Gabriel hung back, watching him. He was wearing black tie and his dark hair had been pasted back with brilliantine. Gabriel remembered Michael's cap of dark hair, the sandy smell of it and the way it used to sit so tightly on his head, like Pinocchio's. Michael's face was half in shadow and there were dark circles under his eyes. He was still and composed but, as he raised a cigarette to his lips, Gabriel detected a tremble in the elegant hand, a slight twitch in the pianist's fingers. Gabriel realised now why the descriptions he had had from the people in the streets had been admiring and at the same time rather vague; he was inconsolably handsome but in a slightly removed, fuddled way – as if he was an abstraction of himself, a character in a novel, a dark and brooding hero. There was something lacklustre, something wistful, about the way in which he stared at the band playing.

Gabriel hesitated in the shadows and, for a moment, he contemplated leaving, turning round quietly and sneaking out the way he had come, out of this world he had no place in, where he had ended up, as if by some great mistake. He could not recall why he was there at all and, in his frustration, he felt a wash of anger at having been trapped in this way, like a lobster who crawls greedily through the narrow passage, seeking fulfilment and satisfaction, and finding, at the far end of the creel, a shard of mirror tied to the frame, offering the seduction of company, but delivering only a reflection of himself. And that was at the heart of it: this feeling of loss and the fear of losing Michael once again, as he knew he must. He walked up to Michael's table and pulled out an empty chair.

Michael looked up as Gabriel sat down in front of him; if he had any feelings at that moment, his eyes did not reveal them. 'Gabe,' he said, flatly, without surprise, 'you look awful. What's happened to you?' Idly, he reached for the drink in front of him, the cigarette still clasped between his fingers. His face was pallid and gaunt.

'It's nice to see you, too.'

Michael laughed briefly. 'Irony never used to be your thing; didn't think you were cut out for it. Too much of a goody-goody; always so naïve.'

This hurt, but Gabriel did not let on. 'Yeah, well, I suppose I have grown up.'

'Can I get you a drink?' Michael motioned to one of the waiters.

'I'll have whatever you're having.'

'Two whiskies, Sam; water, no ice.'

The waiter bared his teeth at Michael and moved off.

They sat in silence, Gabriel studying Michael, who let it happen, pretending to watch the stage again. At last, the waiter returned with the drinks. They drank without looking at each other.

'*So*,' Michael spoke quietly, still looking away, 'what brings you to London?'

'Long story . . .' He wondered if Michael remembered the sideshow, Dr Buster and the twins, and contemplated making up a tale that might seem more credible. 'Well, after I saw you last, I finished school and joined a sideshow for the summer . . . and then I learnt that I had been accepted to university, so I came here to study.'

Michael looked at him properly for the first time and Gabriel thought he detected a glint of deference, a renewed admiration, in the brown eyes. 'University?'

Gabriel nodded. 'Yes, medical history, mostly. About mutants and stuff, you know.'

'Cripes!' Michael said and whistled.

They were silent for a while as they contemplated this. Then Michael spoke: 'So, you have come to me for money?'

Gabriel looked at him astonished. 'No! Whatever made you think that?'

'That's good, because I haven't got any.'

'But . . . what about your part of the inheritance?'

'Gone.'

'Oh.'

'George Bradley's darling boys – together again – only their fortunes seem to be somewhat reversed . . .' Michael slurred with a fatuous grin.

Gabriel looked at him, at the mask of his face, pinched and white like a young Punchinello's, but still so innocently handsome. A nerve started to twitch visibly under Michael's right eye and he lowered his face deeper into the shadows. Gabriel felt a surge of panic as the world seemed to shift and he searched his memory for something solid to grab hold of, something to moor him to the moment. Suddenly, he remembered: 'There's still Oakstone . . . We could let it and make some money – or even sell it – if you wouldn't mind, of course.'

Michael drank at a draught what remained in his glass and clicked his fingers at the waiter. 'Sam! Another one of these, please.'

'Seriously, Michael, it might not be such a bad idea.'

'Oakstone is already gone,' Michael said, in a voice that seemed to come from very far away.

'*What?* What do you mean, "gone"?'

'I had to get rid of it—' more remotely still – 'I had to get rid of Oakstone.'

'It's not possible; I still own half of it!'

'Well, it's complicated. I was in a bit of a bad spot. I had run into debt, if you like, and Blackaton offered to take Oakstone as part of the security. I forgot to tell him that you owned half of it . . .'

'You forgot to tell him . . .? This is madness. Crazy! You can't just give my part of a house away to some crook because of a stupid debt. Why didn't you speak to me first?'

Michael shrugged.

'I might have been able to help. I would have paid your debts, somehow.'

'Well, you did, in a way.'

'But why Oakstone?'

'It was the only thing he would accept. A class thing, I suspect – wanting to climb a step on the ladder.'

Gabriel sighed. He realised the feeling that had been nagging at him since he entered the club was one of suspension; it was as if his mind and limbs were tied to invisible strings – harmless enough, until someone tugged at them – and something else too, which was more like childish annoyance, a disappointment that things should be this way.

368

However, rather to his surprise, it was not the loss of Oakstone that upset him the most – his ownership had always seemed rather abstract, anyway – what infuriated him was Michael's detached, laconic behaviour. 'How much was it, the debt?'

Michael ignored the question, blowing a ring of smoke. He seemed to be miles away.

'How much, Michael?' Gabriel shouted, and shook him by the arm. A few people from the surrounding tables turned to look at them and the waiter called Sam sidled up to the table. 'Everything all right here, Fluff?'

'Yes, Sam, everything is hunky-dory,' Michael replied, icily, and added, with irritation, 'Is Mr D not here yet?'

'No; I said I'd let you know,' Sam answered, with a faint, derisive grin.

'Michael, just tell me how much,' Gabriel whispered, calmer now, when they were alone again.

Suddenly, Michael seemed to re-enter himself; his face opened a little and his eyes lit up briefly, as if somebody had turned on a switch. He smiled shamefacedly, in that old apologetic way, so that something stirred inside Gabriel. 'Not much, Gabe; not very much at all. It was my life we traded. I gave it to him once, as you may remember, and I wanted it back. And, as I said, Oakstone was the only prize he would accept to set me free.'

'The bastard!'

'Yeah, well . . .'

'Can nothing be done?'

'Not really, no; you see, there was more to the deal than I reckoned. I had been using his drugs, as it turned out – quite a lot of them, and for rather a long time, too. So, I wasn't quite free, after all.'

'Is that why you're here?'

He nodded, and gave a sort of laugh. 'But at least they pay me for my services here. And keep me in fine clothes . . . and recreational medicine, naturally.'

'What exactly do your services involve?'

He shrugged and smiled again. That charming smile. 'This and that, Gabe. This and that.'

Gabriel looked away quickly, for fear his eyes would give him away, the black bead of grief and shame shining through. And then suddenly he remembered: 'Why don't you turn to your mother?'

'Oh, I don't know . . .'

'Do you even know where she is?'

Michael shrugged. That infuriating vagueness.

'We seem spared from growing old together in our family, eh, Gabe?' Still ignoring the question. 'We are blessed.' The wit fell flatly on the table in front of them.

Gabriel felt a knot of pain in his guts as he thought briefly of his own mother. He pictured her reading the paper at the kitchen table, a towel spread out so as not to stain the oilcloth, and her unhappiness still filling the house, thrumming in the walls like some long-wave radio channel which one could never really tune into. He had loved Mrs Bradley, because of her soft touch. Perhaps more than his own mother. But was that love real or imagined? A young boy's muddled affections as he grows into his sexuality?

'Michael . . . she's your mother – she loves you.'

'Ooh, look who's talking.' But there was a tremor in his voice.

'Mr D has arrived, Fluff.' They were both startled by Sam's sudden reappearance.

'Thanks,' Michael said and stood up. 'Will you excuse me for a minute, Gabe?'

Sam remained behind for a moment, watching Gabriel. He was holding the silver tray, and a white cloth was folded over his arm. The light was behind him; Gabriel could not see his face.

'Yes?' Gabriel twitched involuntarily as he felt a shiver run down his spine.

Sam stepped into the light. 'Are you twins, or something? You look alike . . . except you're bigger. I like your moustache.' His smile seemed to insinuate something.

'No, no we are not,' he answered, in tight-lipped awkwardness.

'A shame, that,' Sam whispered, and smiled at him, before placing two large whiskies on the table. 'These are on the house, compliments of the Pelican himself,' he said, and winked, before moving away.

Gabriel felt like crying. He finished his whisky; his hand was shaking as he put the empty glass down. He looked around the room. It seemed different all of a sudden – shabbier and yellow-tinted.

Finally, Michael returned. His eyes seemed darker and there was something equivocal about him. 'Now, where were we?' he said, with a jaded smile, slurring slightly. As he reached out for his drink, Gabriel noticed that the cufflink on his right cuff was missing. He could have sworn it was there before.

'Just get out of here, Michael! Get out of London.'

'Yes, yes.' He sounded depressed, and tired.

'I'll get you out.'

Michael looked at him for a moment. 'It's not that simple, Gabe,' he said grimly.

'All right, all right, so it's not simple. Nothing is simple, but you have got to realise—'

'I *realise*,' Michael said, abruptly. 'Would you like another drink?'

Gabriel shook his head. They sat for a while, looking.

'You've got to understand,' Gabriel said, 'that I'd do anything to help you.'

Michael shrugged; it was not clear if he was listening.

'Are you listening?'

'Oh, hell!'

'You're drunk.'

'Not exactly.'

'Then you're just an idiot.'

'I guess so.'

'There are cures—'

'Yeah, yeah. Look, Gabe, can we stop talking

about me for a minute? It's so bloody *boring*. This conversation is fucking hurting my head. How are *you*?'

Gabriel did not know what to say. He wanted to cry. He sat there, biting his lower lip.

'Happy, are you?'

Gabriel shook his head. 'I'm fine, Michael, really. It's been a bit tough lately, but it's nothing . . . I could tell you about it . . . I am happy to have found you. I thought, perhaps, we could do something together. Start a business, perhaps, or you could sign up for university too. It's great fun, you know. You're clever; you could make something of yourself. Apply to a conservatory – something that would make you happy, now that Jim of Blackaton is out of our hair—'

'I'm happy where I am; never been happier in my life,' Michael interrupted.

'This – the drink, whatever – it will kill you.'

'It's the only thing that's keeping me alive.'

'It could be different.'

'Yeah? You sure?'

'Yes,' he lied.

'Happy. What a word.' Michael threw back his head and laughed an empty laugh. 'Oh, Gabe. You were always so gullible – you always refused to see life for what it really is.' He dropped his head into his hands and sat like that for a moment, rocking slightly from side to side, muttering unintelligibly until Gabriel thought he had fallen into some delirium.

'Michael?' He reached out to put a hand on his brother's shoulder, but Michael pulled away and looked at him, a dreadful haggard expression in his eyes.

'So vulnerable . . . So lonely. Don't you see? I had to save you from the world – it was my duty. I too saw the horror reflected in that pool; I too walked through the corridor of mirrors – or have you forgotten? I thought I'd make it – that I had it in me – but I was just as weak as all the others. I too am a coward.'

'You're talking nonsense, Michael.'

'Nonsense; yes, of course, I'm talking nonsense,' he mumbled with tenderness. 'What other language is left to me?' He closed his eyes and rested his cheek in his palm so that Gabriel thought he had fallen asleep.

'Michael? Michael? You should go to bed; it's very late. Where are you staying?' He stood up and pulled at Michael's arm.

'No, no; leave me alone. I want to stay here,' Michael slurred, without opening his eyes.

He tugged again at Michael's sleeve.

'Will you ever leave me *alone*?'

Gabriel felt desperate; he didn't know what to do. He had to get out; this was killing him. 'Perhaps we could meet for lunch tomorrow? When you're feeling . . . better. Would you like that?' Gabriel hesitated for a moment, looking down at Michael. 'Well, I'll come back tomorrow, then, and look for you . . .' he continued tentatively.

'Gabe,' Michael said then, with sudden clarity, 'stay away from me, will you? I'm no good; do you hear me? Promise me you won't come here again.' He reached up and took hold of Gabriel's face, pulling it down towards him. His hands were chilly against Gabriel's cheeks. There was a strange metallic smell around him. 'Promise me, Gabe.'

Gabriel could not say a word for the lump in his throat, but he nodded and closed his eyes so that Michael would not see the black thing, peering out at him.

'And would you do one more thing for me, please? Will you find Mother and check that she's . . . okay? Look after her for me?'

He nodded again and felt Michael's hands relaxing.

'That's my boy.' Michael patted him weakly on the cheek and let him go. 'Bye-bye, now.'

Gabriel pushed through the crowd towards the exit but, as he reached the bar area, somebody stepped out in front of him. Gabriel looked up into the face of Jim of Blackaton. He looked much the same as he had the last time they met at the Moor Cross Inn, but he had the puffed-up, pallid look of somebody who spent little time in daylight. He had taken off his black tie and his shirt was open at the collar.

'Well, well, well. I hadn't realised that we were going to have such fine guests tonight. Let me take a look at you.' His voice was darker and more guttural, as if he was trying to hide his rural accent, and he had the manner of speech of a man who was seldom interrupted. As he studied Gabriel's face, he lifted a big cigar to the soft lips, which seemed to kiss rather than suck. He blew the smoke away from Gabriel, like a gentleman, and smiled, almost sweetly. 'Who would have thought that Bunny-boy would grow up looking quite handsome, eh?'

Gabriel felt a cold sweat seeping through his shirt and looked around for the door.

Blackaton's smile broadened. 'What's the hurry? Come and sit down for a minute; have a drink with my associate and me. I'm sure he would *love* to meet you . . . absolutely love it.' He took hold of Gabriel's shoulder and steered him towards one of the booths. Gabriel did not have any choice but to move along. He recognised the man from the other day and straight away he realised that it was Jim of Blackaton he had seen from the back, talking to this man, who smiled as they approached. He was sinewy and with a ginger complexion; his gaze was at once roguish and cunning. His movements, the way he sipped his cocktail slowly, elegantly, seemed deliberate and calculated, as if it was a skill he had learnt quite recently.

'Ah, there you are, Bunny-boy—' that same west country accent – 'Sam told us you were here. I didn't actually recognise you when you popped in the other day . . . but then it has been a while.' That sniggering face – Billy Dunford – no longer a boy, but still cowering behind his master. An image of Billy's hairy cock pissing into the bucket surfaced in Gabriel's mind, but he managed to push it away.

Jim of Blackaton smiled. 'Sit down, please.' He gestured to the seat next to him. 'What can I get you?'

'I'm fine, thank you; I was just on my way home.'

'Very wise . . . But, tell me, where *is* "home" these days? My sources tell me that you have been living rather frugally lately. Student life is not so flush, is it?'

Gabriel blushed, but did not reply.

'There's no shame in it, lad, no shame at all; we all have to rough it at times, don't we, Billy?'

'Yeah, that's right; we do,' the lieutenant replied, cheerfully.

'And now you have come looking for your brother – to get a bit of help, eh? Is that it? No?'

'No. Michael can't help me. I came to take him away from . . . all this. From you.'

Blackaton laughed. 'Did you hear that, Billy? He's come to take Fluffy away from us.'

'Oh, *dear*,' Billy tutted. 'We can't have that, can we?'

'No,' Jim of Blackaton said, the smile gone from his face, 'we most certainly cannot, and you listen to me, pal—' he leant forward and stared into Gabriel's eyes, the mischief suddenly replaced by grit – 'if you want to help your brother, you'd better work for it; do you hear me?'

Gabriel swallowed and, without meaning to do

it, he pressed his finger against his upper lip. 'What kind of work, Jim?'

'Oh, a bit of this and that, lad,' Jim said, benevolently. 'Just a bit of this and that. Ain't that right, Billy?'

'Sure is, boss. A bit of this and that is all we're asking for.'

Gabriel felt a fevered rush inside his head. He realised he was caught. Closing his eyes, he tried to bring things into some kind of order, attempting to make sense of his situation. He looked up. Jim of Blackaton was studying him with those sly, cold eyes.

'Well, then?'

He took a deep breath and plunged. 'No, Blackaton; I'd never work for you – or for your echoing sidekick here—' he inclined his head towards Billy, his eyes fixed on Blackaton. 'Your business stinks. I'll get Oakstone back for my . . . my family's sake and I'll do everything I can to help Michael out of this shit hole,' he said in a level voice, his heart pounding.

Jim of Blackaton looked away.

'Oooh, Bunny-boy's stirring,' Billy mocked. But Jim remained silent; he only shifted slightly in his seat, the way a gambler might tense when a new hand is dealt. He took a drag from his cigar. Some ashes fell on to his trouser leg.

'And how exactly do you propose to do this?' Billy asked, sarcastically.

'Wait and see,' Gabriel answered, quite calmly

now, smiling to himself as Rey's voice surfaced somewhere in his mind. 'You just wait and see.'

'What the hell's that supposed to mean?'

Something in the way Billy's eyes flickered as he said this made Gabriel laugh.

'What's so bloody funny?'

'You're just *so* deluded, Billy, you know that?'

'What the fuck—?'

'Shut up, Billy,' Jim of Blackaton said, brushing the ashes from his trousers without looking up.

Gabriel got to his feet. For a moment, he thought he might have to steady himself against the table. But he didn't. He stood up straight.

'Hey, Gabriel?' Blackaton had never said his name before.

'Yes?'

'You make sure you don't stand in my way,' he said through his teeth. 'You fucking make sure.'

Gabriel left them, without looking back, and walked into the night.

'After that episode, I was quite determined,' Mr Askew told Mrs Ludgate, as he stood up and crossed the room to turn on the main light. 'I just knew that I had to get Oakstone back, for Michael's sake – and for Mrs Bradley's and even Mother's. It was like . . . like a way of reuniting the whole family. That's what I realised as I was sitting there, thinking it all through the following morning in St James's Park.'

The sudden brightness blinded them both for a

moment. She looked away, embarrassed, hiding her face, but he had stopped noticing. As he sat back in his armchair again, he might have smiled to himself, a bit smug now, as he remembered Jim of Blackaton spilling the ashes on his trousers.

'Their house of cards was bound to come down eventually – I didn't have to do very much. It was clearly rotten. They were getting quite fraught around that time. There had even been a couple of murders of rival club owners – covered up, of course, but the police were getting irked, just the same.'

She was listening to this with a withdrawn expression, eyes downcast.

'But, somehow, I think he realised that evening,' he continued, 'that I'd testify against him when the time came. I had nothing to lose, you see. I could no longer be scared into silence. For some reason, this dawned on him in the club that night.'

'Were you never scared for your life?'

'My life . . . no. I suppose I never thought . . . It's impossible to imagine those things.'

She nodded slowly. 'I never knew what he was doing up in London. I suppose that makes me an even bigger fool . . .'

He leant over and patted her hand. She twitched, but let it happen.

'What I needed was proof of an actual crime,' he continued. 'But where was I going to get that?'

They were both silent for a moment, before he

asked, 'One thing I've never understood is why Blackaton wanted Oakstone so badly.'

Mrs Ludgate grimaced and shook her head. 'It's hard to tell . . .' She hesitated. 'Perhaps he had a silly dream of another life too.' But, from somewhere in the depth of her mind's dark well, a memory surfaced, so faint and insubstantial that it might have been myth, of a spring day, early on, in those very first months when they had walked, arm in arm, in the sun, through the bright village. She had made them stop, briefly, by a low wall, peering through a screen of trees and bushes at the house that was Oakstone. She had teased him, laughing, saying that this was where she wanted to live one day – not with her parents-in-law on the moor, in that filth. He had laughed, too, and there had been happiness in his face – real happiness. She furrowed her brow now at the memory. *Vanity.* Where would such happiness have fitted in her life? What a fool she had been.

'Mrs Ludgate, are you all right? I haven't made you sad, talking like this about your husband? You must forgive me; I didn't mean to be so insensitive.'

She tried to smile, but managed only a wince. How could other people stand it, this helpless staggering into marriage, hoping to escape themselves by putting their trust in another person? She struggled to contain her feelings. 'Not to worry, Professor; I'm as perky as a pin,' she said, cheerfully.

'Oh – that's a relief,' he said with a laugh. 'I would never hold it against you that you married a bleeding bastard!'

'I should bloody well hope not.' Mrs Ludgate chuckled, feeling that dry ripple, like the tearing of old sheets, spreading from her breast towards her throat, so that, in the end, she could not help but let fall a sob.

Mr Askew stirred and looked up at her. 'Sorry, did you say something? I wasn't listening.'

'Humph!' she managed, grimacing again through her desolation.

He looked at her closely, sensing that something was wrong. 'Have you no sense of – of – of—' he stumbled – 'no feeling of – of anger towards me for what I have done – processing against him through the courts, that is?' He wasn't proud of what he had done, hunting like a bloodhound for intelligence and putting the case together, slowly, painstakingly. At first, he had only been able to gather evidence for tiny misdemeanours, but over time they added up until he had enough to make a case.

Mrs Ludgate ignored his question; it seemed too banal, under the circumstances; she only looked at him with a kind of sadness and asked, 'What happened to Michael? Did you manage to save him?'

'I . . .' He faltered, looking around the room, as if for a gesture of support and understanding, but the walls that stared back at him were numb, the furniture frozen. He looked suddenly old, dulled and defenceless. 'I was too late,' he whispered at the floor. 'He was beyond saving.'

'What happened?' she asked, breathlessly.

'An overdose—' he looked at her straight – 'self-orchestrated . . . only weeks after I met him that last time.'

'He died?'

He didn't answer. They could not have been torn apart so brutally if they had not been so closely entwined.

'So all this,' she gasped, 'all your . . . plotting, Jim's money, our fields – to get Oakstone back – all was in vain?'

He nodded his head slowly.

'Then you're as great a loser as I am.'

He looked up at her in surprise, gaunt with shadowed eyes.

'All things to all men and nothing to yourself.' She laughed, but sadly.

'I suppose you're right, yes.'

'Your own brother . . .' she said with a gentleness he hadn't heard in her before. 'Was there any other family?'

'Yes,' he remembered now, only too well. 'Yes, there was Mother, of course. In fact, it was she who gave me the evidence I needed to begin the search.'

'Ah?'

'She even talked about you, that time . . . I remember it now.' He wished he could remember more clearly; the young woman that Mrs Ludgate had been was still a rather pale reflection. But he smiled at her, encouragingly, as he thought about that visit to his mother, many years ago.

Most summer afternoons, the path that traced along the backs of the cottage gardens was left forgotten. It might just as well have been a track broken by deer, flitting through the woods at dawn, looking for water. The smells were secret and musky. It was clear that it was not frequently used. As a boy, he had sometimes been afraid of this undergrowth and the things that spurted out of it: stinging nettles, coils of barbed wire or the angry lids of rusting cans. Back then, the path had been outside the boundary of his enclosed world. But on that occasion when he came back, on that clammy summer afternoon, he had stood alone, looking back into the long, narrow garden, which had been brimming with enamel light.

He had left his office at the college in London that morning, abandoning his students, with no precise idea of where he was heading. He had woken early out of a dream of childhood, confused and tangled. What had made him come through the woods rather than walking down the lane? What was he doing here, skulking at the bottom of his mother's garden? The vegetable patch, which had provided the potatoes, cabbage, carrots, broad beans and peas in those early years after the war, was gone and, in its place, a small lawn had been planted, surrounded by neat flower beds. Tiny yellow roses climbed a trellis, which had been raised against the next-door garden. A wisteria twined over the top of the back door. From where he was standing, the pendulous flowers looked like water that had been arrested in its fall. It must have been there when he was a child, its scent waving through the curtains of his opened bedroom window on a day like this.

But it was no use thinking about that now, as he could no longer avoid the solitary figure, resting on the bench with the sun on her face. Under the bench, in the paving cracks, tiny purple flowers struggled. He had been standing there, not watching her, for quite some time and the sun had moved one notch, so that her feet were now in shade – her sensible shoes, the suede scuffed on the toes. She wore navy slacks in a cotton fabric and a mauve cardigan was draped over her shoulders. Her hands were spread on her knees, as if she was just about to stand up. But she wasn't; the hands were limp and unattended. The flesh of her face, under the greying perm, looked thinner than he remembered, as if it was slowly drying into bones. Her eyes were closed and she might have been asleep.

Gabriel shifted on his feet so that a small animal stirred in the undergrowth. Have we all grown older, quite suddenly? he wondered. Those of us who are still alive. He realised that he had been expecting some kind of prelude, like the beginning of autumn, which is softly scarved against the chill of winter.

'Hello? Is there somebody there?' Her voice was the same, only softer – it belonged to a much younger woman.

He hesitated and felt suddenly ridiculous, knowing that he would have to push through the shrubs to meet her – which he did, stepping into the light.

'Mother . . . it's me. Hello, Mum.'

The look of alarm on her face was quickly replaced by surprise and something else, which he could not quite read, but which might have been fear.

'Gabriel?' She stood up at last and he realised that she was about to embrace him. He had not been prepared for that, and yet he was the one advancing towards her out of the shrubbery, so that their bodies met – it could not be avoided – there, in full sun. He could not tell who decided to let go first but, when they stood apart, he swayed. He swayed and had to stand with his legs apart to steady himself. Mother was studying him carefully. He met her eyes and saw that she was blushing.

'If I had known you were coming,' she was saying, 'I would have been better prepared. I look a fright. What you must think . . .' She talked on, but he couldn't take it all in. He was dizzy with a surge of muddled emotions, which he couldn't express.

'Come—' her hand on his arm – 'let's sit down. I'll put the kettle on. Or would you like something stronger? Some sherry, perhaps?'

'Tea is fine, thank you.'

She stood back to look at him, almost shyly. 'You have grown since I saw you last. When was it? Five years ago? Six? Look at you. Aren't you handsome!'

There was an awkward silence.

He sat down on the bench with his hands spread over his knees, just as she had done a moment earlier, only his hands were gripping harder, trying to hold on to a solid part of himself. He breathed in deeply the sweetness of the wisteria and felt becalmed, like a ship after a storm, or was it before? Some tiny flies were moving about his head, but he let them be.

'Well, I'll just go inside to put the kettle on . . .'

He dared to look at her then, as she moved towards the pantry door. For a moment, he watched and listened for those movements and sounds her body used to make: the bounce and pace, some-times a terrible sharpness, which age had so abruptly transported into something frail and yellow – or perhaps, at best, into a dry kind of grace. Had she been alone all this time? Had she ever taken a lover? Dr Lennon, perhaps? She had been pretty once, he seemed to remember, if a bit too strict – and always very well turned out.

She returned with the tea tray, her lips notice-ably pinker.

'How uncanny.' She laughed, shaking her head. 'I was thinking of you only a moment ago . . . of how, when we first moved here from Oakstone, you used to follow me around the garden as I planted the seeds. You were only a toddler then . . . You would try to pick the seeds out to put them in your mouth, so that I had to do it all over again. I would get so frustrated.' She stopped abruptly and looked around, still holding the tray. 'Could you fetch that little table over there, please?'

He followed her gaze and saw a small pine table by the wall. Lifting it and setting it down again in front of the bench, he was struck by the apparent everydayness of their gestures. He took the tray out of her hands and put it on the table.

'Thanks.'

They sat down next to each other on the bench, and the wearied day settled around them with a sigh. She poured the tea into the blue and white china teacups, but hesitated with the milk jug. A brief look of confusion skimmed across her face, as if something precious and dear had been misplaced. 'I have forgotten . . . Do you take milk?'

'Yes, please.'

'Yes . . . yes, of course you do.'

He smiled.

'Where was I? Oh, yes – planting the seeds. I'd get so cross with you destroying everything. But you were just a little boy, starting to explore the world.'

He took a sip of his tea, not sure what else to do.

'Trying to be a single mother, proudly independent and all that, back in those days . . .' She
looked suddenly tired, as if the memory itself had
exhausted her. 'But you were just a small boy; you
couldn't understand why I was always vexed . . .
always so drained.'

His mind snatched at the end of another memory:
walking, hand in hand with Mother on grass, bells
ringing nearby – not just *ding-dong* but a proper
tune. It was a bright, blustery day and he was
carrying a bunch of crocuses. It was a happy
memory, he realised, and suddenly he felt a great
tenderness. It must have been inside him all these
years, this warmth at the heart, which had suddenly
made itself known to him now, like a revelation.
It must have been there all along, keeping the
embers alive. He had loved her, he realised – of
course he had – even when he didn't like her. Even
when he hated her. But then, he had never been
a helpful child, only bothersome.

'If only . . . If only I had been made in a different
way, things might have been all right,' he suggested
now, as the sun protected them both.

She looked up, perplexed. 'Whatever do you
mean?'

He said lightly, 'Mr Bradley . . . I mean, my
father and you might have stayed together, if it
hadn't been for my . . . you know, the way I turned
out.'

'But it had nothing to do with you. Your father
leaving me had nothing to do with you.'

He was uncovered, almost naked. He closed his eyes.

'He fell in love with another woman. It was that simple, really, only I was young and could not accept it. It was in the middle of the war – those were fraught times. Gabriel, look at me . . . Your father didn't leave because of you – he left . . . He left because of me. Do you hear me?'

He looked away, nodding. How terrifyingly opaque and incomprehensible his world had seemed back then. How misled he had been. Why had no one talked to him? If only somebody had talked to him, he might have been able to tell them about the horror he had witnessed that day and about the blackness that lived inside him. He might have been able to ask for help – for Michael, and for himself.

'And I suppose I loved him. I was terribly hurt. Terribly.'

'I heard you talk to Mrs Bradley, in the kitchen at Oakstone, after Mr Bradley's funeral.'

She considered him again. Her eyes looked sad; they were paler than his – light brown with specks of saffron. His own eyes were the colour of newly cut peat – the same as Michael's and Mr Bradley's.

'I'm sorry; you boys should never had been drawn into our mess. I wanted to keep you for myself. I thought I deserved to.'

'Michael is dead, mother. He killed himself.'

'Yes,' she nodded. 'Yes, I heard. I never knew him, of course. Gerry told me about him. He seemed such a lovely boy, but unfortunate . . . Such a frail mind, I was told.'

If only Uncle Gerry . . . But Uncle Gerry was long gone. He poured her some more tea; the pot felt surprisingly heavy.

'They say something bad happened to him when he was still quite young. That he was never right after it. Do you know what it was?'

A couple of swifts chirped high above them, feeding on the flies. The garden teemed with tiny noises. It felt like thunder in the air. No, it was too late . . . No use splitting himself open to tell her now. Yes, too late, at last. Best left forgotten.

'I have a job,' he said instead, 'at the university. I'm not a student any more. A proper job . . . A big international project about freaks.'

She nodded vaguely.

'The professor was so pleased with my dissertation that he offered me a studentship to work with him and to do a doctorate.'

'Oh?' She smiled mildly, the way one might smile at a young child bringing a new drawing.

'Mum, I'm sorry I have stayed away. There were things I had to work out on my own . . .'

How he hated his inner demons – that freak that still lived inside him, threatening to rip open the scar above his lip. But this job was useful. He was learning to control this need he had to project the demons on to others. The stillness of this sunny patch and the scent of the wisteria keep my mind from falling apart. Yes, I'm still here. Come, find me – bring me home.

She nodded, as if she had heard his thoughts and understood. He shifted a little on the seat so that his arm brushed against her side.

'By the way, I saw Jim of Blackaton in London a few years back. Remember him?' He couldn't think why he'd mentioned this to Mother.

The name made her flinch. He could feel her tense, deliberating some new thought – sharper, this time, not brought back from the velvet folds of memory. This was part of the present.

'He's a bad one, Gabriel. Stay away from Jim Ludgate, you hear me?'

'Why? What do you know?'

'It was criminal, the way he treated Mrs Bradley, her own son barely dead in the ground.' She shook her head.

He froze. 'What do you mean?'

'He ought to be behind bars, that one. And his poor wife, trying to raise a kid on her own, up on the moor . . . A lovely girl.'

Jim of Blackaton – married with a child? The thought had never occurred to him. Nor did it alter his resolve, now that he knew. Jim had never taken such considerations into account.

'Go on . . .'

'Well, after Michael's death, Amélie came back to Oakstone. I went to see her once, to offer my condolences. I felt ashamed of how I had behaved . . .'

He studied her with admiration. This was not the mother he remembered.

'When I arrived, that man, Jim Ludgate, was there, talking to her. She was terribly upset.'

'Really?'

'He was saying that he was a close friend of her son's and that Michael had given him Oakstone before he died.'

Gabriel made a sound like a snort.

'Well, luckily I heard all this as I arrived – the French windows were open, so I entered that way. At first, they didn't notice me . . .'

It made him shiver in the heat to think that Jim of Blackaton had been inside Oakstone, talking to Mrs Bradley.

'To cut a long story short, I told him to bugger off or I'd call the police, because he was on my son's property.'

She looked furious, even now, and Gabriel remembered how frightened he used to be of her at times.

'You know what he did? He laughed at me . . . that insolent peasant! Said I was wrong and showed me a paper where Michael had signed over the property to Mr Ludgate.'

'You actually saw the documents?'

'I said, "I'll show you papers . . ." and told him that Oakstone wasn't Michael's to give away – that half of it still belonged to you.' She laughed coldly. 'I've never seen a man so furious. He stormed out, cursing us like the Devil himself.'

Which one could well believe he was, Gabriel thought to himself. So Blackaton didn't know he owned half the house. Michael had never told him this. He wondered if Michael had been clever enough to know what he was doing, or whether he had just temporarily forgotten about it.

'Those deeds . . .' Gabriel said. 'The will and all that – do you still have them?'

'Of course . . . but why—?'

'I want to take them to a lawyer – to get Michael's share back so that Mrs Bradley can stay on in the house.'

'Ah . . .' she said, quietly, averting her eyes. 'I'm afraid that won't be possible.'

'No!'

'I'm sorry, Gabriel . . . I think it was the grief.'

'When?'

'Oh, she didn't die . . . but she will never be the same. Can't look after herself. I got her a place at the NHS nursing home, down the road.'

He stood up, abruptly, and paced the small patio.

'Not a very nice place . . . Local council's running it. Shame, really, that she should end up there . . . but there's no money for anything else.'

'Don't worry. I'll sort that out. I'll get money . . . somehow.' To think that Mother had been looking after Mrs Bradley when it should have been him!

'I'm sorry, Gabriel. I know you liked her very much.'

How was he going to find the money to get her out of there?

'Well, I've warned you about Ludgate . . . He might be coming after my cottage soon, for all we know,' she said, angrily. 'Mrs Bradley isn't the only widow he has turned out of a home, lately.'

He stared at her. 'Do you have any evidence of this?'

'I'm sure you could find it, if you talk to the local lawyers. All one needs to do is put two and two together . . .'

Something inside froze and hardened. He shivered, although it was still very warm.

'I've got to go, Mum.'

'Will you not stay for supper?'

He shook his head; he needed to get on with things. 'I have to get back to London. I'm teaching tomorrow morning.'

She nodded. They stood up and he felt suddenly very tall next to her.

'I'll come back soon,' he added, but without confidence, as he followed her through the pantry into the kitchen. Nothing had changed here. If anything, it looked uglier – more diminished – than he remembered it. His eyes fell on an almanac hanging on the wall above the table; it showed a picture of Dartmoor ponies grazing above the dates of the month of July. It was Sunday and tomorrow he would set the ball rolling that would finally knock down Jim of Blackaton and get enough money to find a better home for Mrs Bradley.

By the door, she put her hand to his face. It was an odd gesture, not quite complete, but he liked it. 'Come back soon,' she said. He smiled and kissed her cheek.

Just as she was closing the door after him, she saw him stop and turn round:

'Mother . . .?'

'Mm?'

'I'm very happy . . . that we got to know each other, at last.'

She looked at him. For a long time, she stood on the porch, looking at her son's back as he walked up the lane looking at the tall young man as a breeze streamed gently off the moor and rinsed his dark hair in liquid bronze. He had rolled up the sleeves of his white shirt and his jacket was swinging lightly from his hand, rousing vapours of tiny, tiny flies. Her boy, and once, in the beginning, her joy.

CHAPTER 14

The lights were turned down most agreeably in Mrs Chandler's drawing room. A couple of porcelain jar table lamps spread a warm apricot glow that contrasted with the year's first dark sparkling of frost outside. It was a couple of weeks before Christmas. Mr Chandler had moved some of the furniture – his easy chair and the oak coffee table – into the study before leaving for the pub, so that now, as they stood around, awkwardly, the ladies of the Mortford WI did not risk banging their shins or getting their skirts caught. A couple of wispy young girls were circling with tinfoil trays of canapés. A buffet of drinks had been put out on the sideboard; Mrs Chandler had been careful to dress the teak in an old tablecloth, so as not to mark it. Gin stains, especially, were so difficult to get out. Not to mention the stickiness of sherry.

'They are the Briggs-Beaufort girls,' Mrs Chandler explained to some of the ladies, 'setting themselves up as a catering firm. Isn't it wonderful! So *right* for a WI evening, wouldn't you say? I'm paying them a small wage out of the petty-cash fund.' The ladies nodded enthusiastically and cooed over the deliciously miniature toad-in-the-holes and figs wrapped in Parma ham. The members were all in their bests this evening – some in cashmere, because it was that time of the year. The less confident wore their pearls for safety and comfort. One of the women, called Maureen, wore blue eye shadow behind her turquoise-rimmed specs, in the hope that she might be perceived as slightly more risqué. In her mind she repeated, as she would on any social occasion, the mantra her mother had instilled in her from an early age: I must assert myself. I *must* assert myself.

Mrs Ludgate frowned suspiciously at the blob of salmon mousse, which threatened to slide off her crostini. How annoying, she thought, to be served such slippery things in such a beige room. Bending her head to her hand, she managed to gobble the pink mousse at the very last minute. She wiped her fingers on her mauve satin skirt, which stretched alarmingly at the seams. She had ordered it especially for this occasion, along with the matching scoop-neck jersey top. It had looked good in the catalogue. She did not want anyone to suspect that she had made a special effort, but, in reality, it was her most significant outing of the year: the WI Christmas do. And now she had a greasy spot on the new skirt. She swore under her breath.

Looking up, she met Mrs Sarobi's eyes from across the room. The foreign woman smiled and waved gracefully. She wore dark trousers in a soft fabric and a short jacket, embroidered in bright colours and inlaid with tiny mirrors. A red silk scarf covered her hair. Mrs Ludgate looked around once, quickly, to make sure the wave was really meant for her, before smiling back. And, as she did so, she was struck by the notion, improbable as it was, that Mrs Sarobi might be her only friend in this room. It was the same feeling of inevitability that she got once at school, when a boy that she had liked for a while had come up and pinched her from behind. 'Blimey!' she hissed silently through her teeth, and then, after a moment's pause, as if to emphasise, 'Cripes!'

'Yoo-hoo! Over here, everyone!' Mrs Chandler, the hostess, called from her position by the fire-place, as if the charmingly crammed drawing room was in fact a statelier place with chandeliers. The ladies stopped their whirring and turned to face the plump director, their slacking necks craning and their drooping jowls painstakingly rearranged into well-meaning smiles.

'You're all most welcome to this year's AGM and Christmas party. Aren't the Briggs-Beauforts' canapés just divine?' marvelled the director, and the ladies nodded and clapped their hands in agreement. 'Well,' Mrs Chandler continued, 'I hope you will eat, drink and be merry whilst we finish the business of the year. First, I suggest we discuss our next campaign. As some of you will remember, I attended the national AGM in London last month . . .' Here a few of the members crimped their mouths and bit at their lipstick. London and the Royal Albert Hall: such imagined extravagance was too outrageous to endure – the fact that she had been there, so close to Harrods, drinking chilled wine, perhaps even champagne, and not they. 'I had an excellent idea, after talking to my colleagues from Bedfordshire.' Her moon face was beaming. 'I suggest that our campaign for next year is—' a brief pause for suspense – 'multiculturalism! Wouldn't it be just *marvellous* if the WI could help our community to become more welcoming and inclusive?' She smiled and smiled, wrinkling ever so slightly though her powder.

But the ladies looked confused, suddenly. They were no longer making an effort. Some glanced at each other in order to form an opinion. Others looked at their hands, their fingers holding on tightly to the stems of plastic wine glasses – until one of them spoke up. As it happened, it was Mrs Briggs-Beaufort, the mother of the catering geniuses:

'Excuse *me*, but I was under the impression that we were going to continue the locally produced vegetable mission. It has been *so* successful and the interest in organic cooking has increased tremendously. Just look at my girls . . .' She, herself, could hardly take her eyes off them. 'Wouldn't it be *amazing* if other young people in the community could achieve similar success!' She looked around the room, but the ladies remained silent. '*Please* don't get me wrong, I *adore* foreigners,' she went on, and, by George, she meant it, except those who were really dark and smelt strongly of camel, 'but it's just that, well, oughtn't we to focus on a campaign closer to the heart of our community? Something that's of importance to *us*?'

Mrs Chandler's face stiffened ever so slightly and her doll's eyes looked very large and sad as she replied: 'But this topic *is* close to the heart of our community. Do we not read daily in the papers about globalisation? We cannot go on being some kind of local backwater – we are part of the larger world, are we not?' A handful nodded in agreement. 'Well, then, it's high time we overcome our cultural differences and open up to those who want to come and live amongst us.'

'But surely you're not saying that we are all the same – that *we* could ever be the same as *them*?' Mrs Briggs-Beaufort pressed on. 'I mean, the British culture is quite distinct, as I'm sure most people would agree. Everything we have done for democracy . . . Just think about the war – the old one and this new war-on-terror one. And the Empire. There might still not be any bridges in India, if it had not been for British engineering. And those trains they like to ride on – so many of them, at the same time – they just love their trains in India, and so they should!' Her face seemed to have developed a tic.

Some of the ladies felt uncomfortable at this and Maureen more than anyone, as she suspected the remark might be considered racist. I need to assert myself, she thought. This is when it really matters. 'I think it's a wonderful idea,' she squeaked. 'Multiculturalism, I mean. We could meet up every fortnight and cook our own cultural foods.' She was feeling the excitement rising inside her, and blushed. 'It would be a wonderful way of marrying multiculturalism with the local vegetable mission . . . We could cook mainly vegetarian recipes!'

There was a brief silence until Mrs Smith spoke up, to everyone's surprise: 'Yes, but there's only Mrs Sarobi who is, well, multicultural, if you like.' At that, everyone turned to look at Mrs Sarobi, who was retreating into the curtains by the bay window, as if she wanted to disappear altogether.

'Wasn't your mother from Lancashire?' Maureen said, sternly, in an effort to save Mrs Sarobi from the discomfort of being singled out.

'Yes,' Jenny Smith whispered, embarrassed, 'and John's people were Scottish.' Her eyes welled with tears and everyone bent their heads, as John had only been dead a few weeks. The discussion had taken a terribly unpleasant turn – it was absolutely ghastly.

Mrs Chandler cleared her throat, striving to save the day. 'That's an excellent suggestion, Maureen; thank you. Let's meet every fortnight and celebrate our differences through cooking.'

'Look,' Mrs Briggs-Beaufort insisted, not used to being passed over like that, 'I'm not a racist or anything, you must understand. All I'm saying is that people, by nature, prefer to live amongst their own kind and too intense mixing may not be natural. Animals always defend their territories against intruders, after all, don't they?'

'Yeah, but . . .' Mrs Ludgate snorted, to everyone's surprise. 'Yeah, but we're not animals – we're human beings, aren't we?'

Mrs Briggs-Beaufort fixed her eyes on something distant and slightly elevated, whilst Mrs Chandler smiled benevolently at Mrs Ludgate and murmured, 'Yes, my dear, we are all human, naturally.'

But Mrs Ludgate would no longer be put down by such considered kindness. 'What did I tell ye!' Her smile conveyed mischief.

The director felt that it was all beginning to slip. Turning back to Mrs Sarobi in frustration, she tried to bring back some order. 'Seriously, Mrs Sarobi, dear, what do *you* think – isn't multiculturalism a great topic for a new mission?'

Mrs Sarobi had been watching them all from her position at the bay window. Now she looked distinctly unhappy, as she unfolded herself from the curtains, and the smile that she managed to produce conveyed disbelief. Who were these people she had been watching?

'Well, if you really want to hear my opinion, I agree with Mrs Briggs-Beaufort that cultural diversity is obvious and inevitable. The fact that we are culturally different is indisputable; we have all been shaped by different experiences.' She stepped forward and looked around at the faces in the

403

room – the ladies who looked back at her were incredulous. 'But, more importantly, Doris—' at this, she smiled briefly at Mrs Ludgate – 'is absolutely right: we are not animals, and surely our shared humanity is more interesting than our cultural distinctiveness.'

Her statement was followed by dense silence as everyone tried to take it in and make some sense of it. Suddenly, Mrs Sarobi saw her chance – and grabbed it: 'As long as humans are on the move, cultures are fluid. Multiculturalism is a political idea, with good intentions, I'm sure, but in the end it will always seal people into ethnic enclaves where the borders are policed by well-meaning subsidies, community grants and by-laws. That's why we should see diversity as lived experience – not as a political project. Privately, we may be religious or secular, vegetarian or meat eater, farmer or banker – we may choose to adhere to whatever cultural expression we want in our own hearts and minds – but publicly, we are all citizens and should be treated equally; one perceived group must not be prioritised over another.'

The room seemed to be palpitating with discomfort. Hormones may have been playing their part, as some of the ladies started to steam, but, for the most part, the general uneasiness must be put down to such inappropriate linguistic gymnastics. At last, Mrs Chandler blinked, her face the perfect image of a doll's, and said, hesitantly, 'So, are you saying that cultural cooking evenings are *not* a

404

good idea?' She smiled again, making sure her disappointment did not show. She had suggested this mission almost solely with Mrs Sarobi in mind. It had been meant as a great kindness and a way to include the newcomer – and now the newcomer had turned out to be ungrateful.

'Well,' Mrs Sarobi said, quietly, 'you're all most welcome to carry on with the cultural cooking evenings, of course, but frankly, I find that kind of exercise terribly dull. Now, if you will excuse me, I have to go.'

'That's right!' Mrs Ludgate said, gleefully, as her friend walked out of the room. 'You carry on with your cooking evenings.' She knew now that she would never make it into their midst. Not properly. The way they had looked at her outfit . . . Still, for the moment, she was enjoying herself. 'Thanks for the nibbles.' What a relief it was to be the one to choose sides. On her way out, she stopped in front of Mrs Briggs-Beaufort. 'Congrats,' she said, lightly, patting the other woman's sleeve. 'Your daughters' success – absolutely brilliant. With such talent, they'd get a job any time, waitressing down the pub. *Any time*. Be great, wouldn't it?'

At the door, she turned round, waving her hand. 'Right,' she grinned, 'I'm off, then. See you girls later.'

Outside, snow had started to fall. In the glare of a streetlight, the thick, solid night was fragmented by the whirling flakes. Mrs Ludgate stumbled through the Chandlers' front garden, pulling on her coat. She swore as she tripped on the box hedge, neatly trimmed along the pavement, but soft now, under a white frosting. A section of it had been trained in a perfect kink around the wheelie bin. She wondered at this, at how the bin men would get at the Chandlers' bin, as she stopped to look up and down the street. A row of footprints led east, down the hill, towards the high street. She turned to follow.

'Oi! Mrs Sarobi!'

The figure ahead walked on.

'Hang on! Wait a minute. It's me: Doris.'

Mrs Sarobi stopped and waited for Mrs Ludgate to come within earshot. She was looking down at her shoes, which were not fit for the weather. 'I wasn't expecting anyone running after me,' she said, without looking up. She sounded bad-tempered.

'You were . . .' Mrs Ludgate was out of breath and had to pause for a moment. 'You were brilliant in there!'

'You're kidding.'

'Sorry?'

'I was a bloody disaster.'

'Nah, you said good things. That Briggs-Buffoon woman needed to hear those things—' she hesitated – 'and so did I, come to think of it . . .'

'Oh, what's the point? Why can't people ever think for themselves?'

There was a silence between them.

'Well,' Mrs Ludgate said, quietly, 'not everyone is used to thinking for themselves – at least, not aloud . . . Some of us were told our thinking was wrong, so we have been keeping it to ourselves.'

'I'm sorry; I didn't mean to sound arrogant. Gosh, I was a bit of a bitch in there, wasn't I?' Mrs Sarobi had stopped and was looking at Mrs Ludgate as if it was for the first time. 'Anyway, you never struck me as somebody who wouldn't speak her mind . . .'

'That's what I mean: just said what came into me mind. Never stopped to think – couldn't afford to – it might have killed me.'

'Yes, it can be painful . . .'

Mrs Ludgate smiled. 'Perhaps we are not so unalike, you and I.'

'Perhaps not.'

The snow fell softer around them and the cover was almost complete by now. The reflected light made the night feel warmer.

'I wish the professor had seen you in there,' said Mrs Ludgate.

'Why the professor?'

'He would have been proud of you, too.'

'I'm sure he wouldn't have cared,' she said quickly, looking down. But her voice was not so certain.

Mrs Ludgate looked at her with genuine surprise. 'Oh, I'm pretty certain he would've.'

They were walking now, side by side, in the middle of the road. The only sound was their footfall, muffled, almost to nothing. The flakes were getting bigger, softer; they settled on the women's coat sleeves and stitched into Mrs Ludgate's hair.

'It's so quiet,' said Mrs Sarobi.

'Yes.'

'I can never get used to the first snow – the way it transforms the world – especially at night.'

Mrs Ludgate nodded thoughtfully. 'When I was a girl, we lived by the sea and, when it snowed, it was as if the town and the sea merged. I used to imagine beasts walking with the snow out of the water – sea lions, unicorns, you know – leaving strange prints on the street outside my window.'

'When I grew up we used to put newspapers in plastic bags and slide down the banks of the old citadel.'

'There was snow where you grew up too?'

'Of course, sometimes.'

'What was your name then, when you were a little girl?'

'Nahal.' It felt strange to say it like this, here, after such a long time.

'Oh.' Mrs Ludgate did not know what to say, but knew the name had brought them closer.

Mrs Sarobi looked up at her and smiled. 'Would you like to come back to my place for a cup of tea?'

'All right, go on then,' she said, casually, feeling suddenly short of breath.

'I have got something I would like to show you

. . .' Now it was Mrs Sarobi's turn to hesitate. 'It's a letter.'

'Okay . . .'

'I found it, you see, in my cottage, when I moved in . . . This may sound odd, but I think it might relate to Mr Askew.'

'The professor?'

She nodded. 'But I'm not sure . . . I don't want to bother him with it, if it's not relevant. I can trust you, now, can't I?'

'Yes,' she said, and then again with emphasis, 'Yes, you can.'

'I thought so.'

The cottage had style, Mrs Ludgate realised as Mrs Sarobi turned on the lights and ushered her into the sitting room. The walls were painted light and a large Afghan rug covered the polished floorboards.

'Make yourself at home,' Mrs Sarobi said, removing her headscarf.

Mrs Ludgate stared for a moment at the thick, black braid, before taking possession of herself. 'Your face,' she said, shyly, 'it looks so different now that I can see you hair.'

But Mrs Sarobi laughed. 'Ah, well, you know . . .' she said gaily, as if such beauty was irrelevant and quite *ordinary*.

By the time Mrs Sarobi returned with the tea, her new friend had composed herself.

'Right,' Mrs Ludgate said as she accepted a cup

of tea, 'let's see if I can get this right. You're telling me that you have a letter relating to the professor.'

'Well,' Mrs Sarobi blushed, 'I think it might be . . . I found it in a bundle of letters – love letters – from the time of the war.' Her cheeks were aglow. 'But this one was different – it's from a later date.'

'And they had all been opened?'

'Yes.' She was surprised at her own dishonesty. 'No, actually – not this one. I opened it,' she admitted, staring down at the teapot in her hands.

'Did you, now?' Mrs Ludgate said, but let it be at that.

'Anyway, here it is.' Mrs Sarobi put down the teapot on a side table and pulled a letter from a pocket inside her embroidered jacket.

Mrs Ludgate looked at the broken envelope. *To my son, on his eighteenth birthday.* She licked her lips and pulled out the letter. It was written with a neat, dense hand, the letters sloping ever so slightly to the right.

Oakstone, May 1948

Dear Gabriel, dearest son,

I gave you both those names. But perhaps that doesn't matter now – because, if you read this letter, I have already forfeited my right to call myself your father. You see, I am writing these words in the unthinkable event that we may never get to know each other.

For a long time, I thought that sacrificing

410

you would hurt only me – that I would be no good for you anyway – but, at times such as this – late at night, when I am alone with my doubts and my fears – I realise that my actions may hurt you more than I could ever realise.

But your mother . . . No, that sounds as if I'm trying to shift the blame. Let me start again. I have the greatest respect for your mother and I trust – no, I know – that she has your best interests at heart when she tells me that I must have nothing to do with you now – that me coming back into your life at this stage would be too disruptive. I have to trust her – you see, she took on full responsibility for you – although, at times such as this, I feel in my heart that I should not . . .

Mrs Ludgate looked up. 'Are you telling me that no one, except for us, has seen this letter?'

Mrs Sarobi, who had been watching her closely, nodded. 'And the man who wrote it, of course. The father . . .'

Anyway, enough of my doubts. Your mother is a strong woman, Gabriel, perhaps stronger than you will ever realise. It takes some guts to bring up a child alone in a small village. She means no damn nonsense, I'll tell you that! I hope that you will one day learn to appreciate the strength of women, but I also hope that you will never have to suffer the fury of a thwarted wife.

Well, where do I begin? I have no way of knowing how much you have been told about your origins. Do you remember anything? Did you know that you were born at Oakstone – in the master bedroom, overlooking the lawn and the elms at the end of the garden? It was in July, as you know, just before dawn. I was outside, smoking and stomping around in the blue shadows, feeling as powerless as I have ever felt in my entire life. Dr Lennon was in the room with your mother and would not let me in for a while after you were born. I knew that you were alive, but they told me that something wasn't right. He did not realise, at first, that the hole in your face was just a cleft palate! A doctor! It's laughable to think that such a small defect should put such fear into a village doctor. Anyway, I got to hold you at last and that was one of my happiest moments. Unfortunately, I was not allowed to stay to get to know you. My leave was up the following day and I had to go back to the continent. I was moving in the shadows, in those days, alone behind enemy lines . . . but that's another story.

Things were not going so well between

your mother and me at that time. We got married too quickly before the war – it was the way it happened back then; people were nervous, I suppose. I reckon I just never realised that she loved me quite so much. I never really loved her, you see, or perhaps I did, in a way. But I want you to know that your birth was one of the happiest days of my life.

I am a weak man, Gabriel, and, in the eyes of the world, I have committed a crime. My offence: I fell in love with another woman. I fell in love with Amélie as soon as I set eyes on her. It was shortly after Germany invaded France, in May 1940. She was like a hook in my heart from then on – no, hook sounds wrong – something softer . . . Oh, sod it, I am not a poet, but she was there, in my heart. I swear I could feel it as a physical presence – the most tender, most alive, darling thing. Perhaps, one day, you will understand about that kind of love – I hope so. One thing led to another and, barely a year after you were born, Amélie gave birth to a little boy. I called him Michael, because he was your brother. You were two perfect parts.

Mrs Ludgate drew in her breath. 'Ah, now I get it,' she said, shaking her head. 'Poor, poor boy.'

413

And then, 'Poor Professor.' She folded the paper gingerly and put it back inside the envelope. 'I think you ought to give this letter to the professor straight away – I don't want to read any more . . . You read it all?'

'Yes.' She was ashamed, but not altogether sorry. She felt closer to him than before and, at once, she was grateful to Mrs Ludgate for not reading on. She took the letter from her hands.

'You should take it to him straight away,' Mrs Ludgate repeated. 'He needs to see this letter.'

'I'll bring it over tomorrow.'

'No, you should go now.' She stood up, looking at her watch. 'I need to catch the last bus, anyway. Let's walk together to the top of the lane.'

As they reached the bus stop, Mrs Sarobi said, 'I was just thinking, perhaps you would like to come over for Christmas dinner?' The thought had only just occurred. 'I'll invite Mr Askew, too,' she added quickly.

'I'd love to.'

Mrs Sarobi started walking away, but turned after a few paces. 'You will be all right, Doris?'

Mrs Ludgate looked up. 'Of course.' She smiled, her eyes dazzled already by the glow and tinsel of their Christmas. For a long time she stood looking after Mrs Sarobi, who walked into the snow, towards Oakstone. This is like living again, she thought, as she heard the bus coming up the high street.

As he took her fare, Mr Carpenter, the bus

driver, noticed that Mrs Ludgate's eyes glittered. For some reason, it made him think of the ingenuity of a magpie – a survivor. It pleased him.

'You're looking jolly tonight, Doris. Had a good time at Chandler's party?'

'What? Oh, that. Nah . . . I'm just looking forward to Christmas.'

'Jolly good,' he muttered, somewhat embarrassed. Everyone knew by now that her husband would spend Christmas in jail. In fact, he would be in prison for quite a while, if you were to believe the rumours. 'Jolly good.' You had to give it to the old bag – she was quite a fighter.

By the time Mrs Sarobi reached Oakstone, the snow had stopped falling and the lawn in front of the dark house lay silvery beneath a pattern of winter stars. She stopped abruptly, regretting coming here at this hour. But then she saw a slit of light in the curtains and walked on towards it.

He helped her out of her coat and led her through to the sitting room. Their shared awkwardness seemed to fill the large room, which would otherwise have been quite sparse. If he was surprised, he did not show it. They talked a little, too shy to really listen to each other, and all the while she was trying to get to the point. How did you hand somebody a letter like that? But, at last, he was reading it – reading the letter that should have reached him forty-five years ago. Silently, she removed her headscarf, in an effort to bare herself

415

like him – to help him cope with this new exposure.

Gabriel Askew read the letter that confirmed what he already knew, but he had never known it in so many words. At one point, he looked up and saw that she had removed her headscarf. He smiled at her, at all her beauty, and read on:

People will tell you that I did wrong in abandoning you and your mother in order to marry Amélie. But I see it differently. War changes us – it brings out the best and the worst in people, and it shows humanity in its most naked form. One does good deeds and bad deeds; one can be a hero or a coward, all in the same day. And a day is all you get on this earth. War shows you that life is a short race. The bravest thing I ever did was to follow my heart. That was my most heroic deed. And yet, to the rest of the world, it will have made me look like a weak, selfish coward.

I will put this letter in an envelope now and write on it that, should I die before my time, this letter shall be handed to you on your eighteenth birthday. By then, you will be old enough to make up your own mind about your parents. You and Michael will inherit Oakstone eventually, of course. My greatest wish is that the two of you will find each other and that your love will make up for the wrongdoings of your parents.

Blessings, my son –

From your loving – albeit absent – father,
George Bradley

Post scriptum

I watched you today, like I watch you most days when I am in Mortford. Hiding behind some shrubs, like a common thief, I watched you and Michael walking together in the lane towards Gerald's house. You looked so incredibly vulnerable and I had to bite into my hand not to cry out to you. On my knees, cursing myself. I hear they tease you about your face. You are a beautiful boy. You and Michael are so alike. My little angels.

CHAPTER 15

O n Christmas morning, he drove to Edencombe. The day was extraordinarily still, a northern day, silenced by the cold – a Brueghel day. Up here on the higher lands, the snow had drifted into ditches and pressed against stone walls. There was a fresh sugaring of frost where the sun had not touched the heather, a few yellow gorse flowers sharp against the sky. As he crested the last hill, the sea lay deadpan before him, offering a flawless reflection of the sky, as if the world was sinking into the sea – or growing out of it. The white house on the cliffs looked like a seaside hotel or a luxury villa on the Riviera. Or the Berghof. It was not a bad location for a private nursing home. Not bad at all, he reckoned.

On entering the double glass doors from the porch, he was pleased, and a little relieved, to see that Ms Turpin was on reception duty.

'Ah, Ms Turpin – merry Christmas,' he said, somewhat exuberantly, opening his arms like a priest. He still held the car keys in one gloved hand, a net carrier bag in the other.

'Mr Askew – have you been tasting the port already?'

'Oh, no, no, my dear – it's far too early for that kind of nonsense, wouldn't you say? I'm just in a good mood. 'Tis the season to be jolly, after all.'

'Fa, la, la,' Ms Turpin replied – but managed a smile.

'Here—' he reached into the net bag – 'I brought you some chocolates – from the deli.' He was glad, now, that he had spent that little extra on the posh box.

'How lovely of you to think of me!' Her dull cheeks pinked and revealed, for an instant, that stubborn young girl who never would settle for less.

'Ah, it's nothing, really. You deserve a knight-hood. How is she today?'

'Much the same.'

Mr Askew nodded.

'Here, give the stuff to me. I'll take it in to her later and let her know you were here.'

'No – no, I would like to go in myself today. I . . . I have something to tell her.'

'Of course . . .' If she was surprised, she hid it well.

'Will she hear me, do you think? I mean, will she understand?' He looked at the brooch on her chest – a sparkling bow, or a butterfly – away from her watchful eyes and their solid grey. Too honest.

She shook her head, letting something surface in those grey pools, something he could not bear

419

to interpret. 'I have told you this before, Mr Askew; the doctors say it's unlikely that she understands anything at all. She's almost ninety, for Christ's sake – it's quite something that she's still here at all . . . It's as if she's waiting for something.' A brief pause. 'But one can never be a hundred per cent certain . . .'

'No?'

'Look, you know the odds as well as I do . . . All I'm saying is that there has got to be some room for doubt in all our lives. Otherwise we'd be a sorry lot, us humans.'

How well they understood each other. They accepted it all. As close as any two strangers looking unflinchingly at the world could be – and as alone. But the day, at least, was bright. One must not stoop into a mood.

'We certainly would, Ms Turpin,' he said, cheerfully, knowing for sure that uncertainty could never be quite destroyed. 'We most certainly would.'

The room, when he entered it, was a painting – a bright seascape of blues and specks of white. Diamonds of sunlight. There were three large windows, all facing the sea, although, because Edencombe sat high on the rocks, it was the horizon that could be seen rather than the waves themselves. The image was fixed in its frame, forever caught in the moment. There was no flux, nothing stirred, apart from the plankton of dust filtering slowly down. A bed in the middle of the room, its head

420

against the wall to the left: white, standard-issue with a lifting device. A tartan rug had been spread over the washed-out white sheets. This unexpected blotch of colour seemed slightly out of place, too bold, almost reckless. *Twelve ships with bows red painted.* Next to the bed was a stool and small table, untidy, cluttered, as if a small child had, briefly, been let into the best room with its toys; there was a box of latex gloves, a couple of packets of tissues, a blue plastic pill organiser, a glass of water (half full), some browning grapes on a plate, a biro and an abandoned Sudoku puzzle, ripped out of a magazine and left behind by a yawning night nurse, perhaps. A scene within a scene; a still life, at once symbolically explicit and unbearably private. A television set had been pushed into a corner. It was unplugged and somebody – a cleaner? – had draped the lead over the top of the screen. A door on the opposite wall from the bed led into a bathroom large enough to accommodate the wheelchair that was parked, for now, by the door. That was it, apart from the large leather armchair, which had been drawn up to the window, its solid back facing the visitor.

Mr Askew, who had stopped for a moment inside the door, watched the crown of the head of the woman in the armchair. Amazingly, the thick hair still had some brown in it; the overall impression was muddier, perhaps, but not yet altogether grey. It was almost as if her aging had stopped when she was placed here – or as if her life had been suspended. There's life in the old dog yet. What an absurd expression, Mr Askew thought to himself as he picked up the stool by the bed and carried it over to the window. It made him contemplate his own life. *When* was his life? Was it in the beginning? Was it now? Would there be a future? Ah, all those questions. Those questions . . . When young, we are in such a hurry to experience, he thought now as he sat down and looked for a moment at the sea outside, to free ourselves from the dredge of the present, that our gaze is already ahead of us. Should we, at any point, look over our shoulder at our own past, we would be surprised to find ourselves still there, in real time, but already fading. There's something so vague, almost dull, about it all – in spite of the extraordinary setting.

'Yes, the setting is extraordinary,' he said aloud, with emphasis, and then, leaning in, he said, 'Happy Christmas!' His voice seemed somewhat too loud and it carried that awful tone of a sickroom. He cleared his throat.

The old woman in the chair did not stir. The skin of her face was pale, finely lined, but not unhealthy. Her eyes were dead, fixed. Someone, probably Ms Turpin, had set her hair and dressed her in proper clothes: a dark green dress of soft wool, which he thought he might have seen before, thick stockings and felt slippers. Her wedding ring was hanging on a gold chain from her neck. Proper, but not accurate – she would

422

never have worn such stockings and slippers. She had always been very elegant. But Ms Turpin wasn't to know that. For a moment, Mr Askew wondered if Ms Turpin had bought the warm stockings and slippers herself. He suspected perhaps she had. Dignity mattered to her. And warmth. An expensive-looking grey woollen shawl had been draped loosely around the woman's shoulders. She seemed to be watching the horizon. Mr Askew smiled; she still had that soft beauty.

'I brought you something special from Oakstone . . . to brighten this place up a bit,' Gabriel said. 'Better than grapes, at least. Found them in a box in the attic. Now, hang on . . .' He stooped to reach the net bag at his feet and pulled out a small bundle. Ever so carefully, he untangled strips of red and yellow fabric.

'Ta-da! Do you remember these?' The streamers were flowing from his hands like Christmas tinsel. 'I made them for Michael. Did he ever tell you? Mother was very cross.' He laughed. 'I'd cut up some precious old nightie of hers. I think he liked them, though, no?'

Mrs Bradley's blank eyes were fixed on the horizon. Could she even see the ribbons?

Gabriel gave them a last shake. 'I'll put them over there, on your bedstead,' he said, indicating. 'That's if you don't mind, of course . . .' He sat back on the stool and stole a sideways glance at Mrs Bradley's face – such familiar territory and yet so uninhabited. 'I made them for Michael to say sorry for something awful that happened to him . . . I didn't know what else to do at the time. We were just kids . . . None of us should blame ourselves.

'Ah, well, no use crying over spilt milk, eh?' He nudged her ever so slightly with his elbow. And then, after a moment's hesitation, he reached out his hand and put it over hers, which lay folded limply on her lap.

'There was something else I wanted to tell you . . . I've been asking Ms Turpin to fill you in on things that have been happening over the years, since you moved here. Well, as I was saying, I have some pretty great news for you . . . Blackaton got ten years. That'd be enough to finish him off, I'd say. Old Jim is not as strong as he once was . . .' He gave Mrs Bradley's hands a squeeze. They were dry and not very warm. 'I finally got to testify against him, as I knew I would. It was a long time coming, but, in the end it was my testimony that brought him down. I'm not saying that to brag, just to . . . well, just to say that he's nothing to us any more. To you and me and Michael – and Mother and Mr Bradley and Uncle Gerry. To our family.' He was silent for a moment, thinking, remembering that day the previous year at Exeter Crown Court.

The first thing that had struck him as he saw Jim of Blackaton being led into the courtroom was how insubstantial he seemed these days. Once the black-faced Harlequin, roaming the moor with his demons, Blackaton had been reduced to somebody you might glance at through the smudged and sooty window of a train slowing into a station – a figure of blurred edges, of drizzle and strips of plastic bags, moving vaguely this way and that.

Documents had appeared in the court proceeding, pieces of evidence retrieved from Blackaton's secret files. In amongst them had been a note for Gabriel on a scrap of paper. His name and the address of his department had been written at the top, perhaps at a later date. It was impossible to know when, of course, as it was never posted, or if there had been others like it over the years that had never reached the recipient. This one, Gabriel Askew calculated, must have been written shortly after they met in the Pelican Club for what proved to be the last time. Michael had written:

. . . These days, I sometimes surface with a tune in my ears – a slow, dragging song, dawdling this way and that, pulsing through smoke and chatter. It's not clear to me whether this music is supposed to be a comfort or a threat. Is it the singing of angels I hear, or is it the monster under my bed humming our tune? Whether tramping the corridors of a labyrinth or roaming the bounds of the Mappa Mundi, the monster is the evocation of all our phobias and fears. You think you're a rational being, and yet you feel uneasy when you swim across a black pond or when you're trapped in an unknown, windowless room. Can monsters be human? Do they have souls? Aristotle thought that a monster was a failed human, one that was never fully formed. He said that humanity was a fragile mantle and that everyone had the potential to become monstrous. You and I have both known such monsters, Gabe. Once we were halved, we were split in two. Now I want you to be whole again – for my sake. We did as well as we could, only I got lost inside the corridor of mirrors. There are corridors here, too, in this anteroom, I know, and many rooms filled with stale air. And there are others like me, brought here from the edge of the world by heroes. We are all slumbering now in these rooms where acceptance becomes like a long sleep. I am tired, Gabe, but you must stay awake. We are brothers. I'm going away – you must return to our home . . .

Why had Blackaton kept the note? Could it be that he had actually been jealous of their friendship – their closeness – back then, in the beginning?

'I think I am free now,' Gabriel said to Mrs Bradley. 'I mean, really free. We can start living, for real.' Was there a movement in one of the dry hands? A twitch? A lizard blinking once on a hot stone. At once, he regretted the absurdity of his remark. 'In our hearts, I mean.' Mrs Bradley's eyes stayed level on the horizon.

'Anyway, I've got to go now. I'm invited for Christmas dinner . . . at a friend's house. In fact, it's Mother's old house. She lives there – this friend, I mean. You'd like her. She's a bit like us. Quite a coincidence, eh?'

He stood up, but hesitated for a moment. Then, without knowing quite why, he bent down and put his cheek to Mrs Bradley's, breathing in the smell of her neck, of her hair, just behind the ears. She smelt of very little, he was surprised to find, except for a faint, old woman's muskiness and woody iris and a hint of something familiar, but very distant . . . like butter frying in another part of the house. But perhaps that was just his imagination. He straightened himself up, his face quite flushed.

'I'll be coming to see you more often from now on. To speak to you, like this. And there's this note I'd like to read to you, if you'd care to hear it . . . You know I have been here every week, don't you? It's just that I couldn't face staying for very long; I find it terribly upsetting, seeing you like this. And the shame of it . . . I promised Michael, you see, to look after you when he died. But, as usual, I was too late.' He stopped talking for a moment and the sealed room was so quiet that he could hear his own heart – or was it hers?

'Oh, dear – I expect you don't wish to hear that all that much – I'm sorry.' He wanted to escape,

427

but felt compelled to linger. Why? Was it guilt? 'Perhaps you'd be able to come back to Oakstone one day. Yes, why not? I'll speak to Ms Turpin about it. She can come, too. Quite a girl, ain't she? Stand and deliver, eh?' He chuckled and looked, for a moment, into Amélie's brown eyes. He looked right into the black pupils and saw, in all that dark, an amber glow – a faint flash of a coded message. Then he pulled back. What was that? He was sure he heard Amélie say something. 'What did you say?' He laughed briefly at his own folly, shaking his head. 'All right then, my dear; see you next week.' As he left the room, the door seemed to close on a vacuum.

Ms Turpin was still at the reception desk, reading a paperback novel. She looked up as he approached. 'Well?'

'Have you ever heard her speak?'

She looked at him sharply through her reading glasses.

'Well, have you?'

She sighed. 'Yes, I suppose so, but it doesn't necessarily mean that she's aware of things. You mustn't—'

'Ms Turpin, for the love of Christ, I'm asking you straight: do you think she's in there? Might she actually have understood what I said to her?'

She took off her reading glasses, pinching the bridge of her nose while looking past him out of the glass doors. Then she turned her eyes back to him. 'Yes,' she said. 'Yes, I'm quite certain of it.'

It was not until he was on the road, driving back towards the moor, that he realised what he had heard Amélie say: 'Gabe' – and then another word – was it 'life'? Or 'live'? Or could it have been 'love'? Or was it all just a fantasy, brewed amongst this new lightness he felt inside his head?

As the road left the sea behind and started climbing towards the moor, he passed a rambler who stopped at the roadside and raised his hand in greeting. It was an oddly familiar gesture. And that head of hair . . . Those copper curls . . . Did he really see the man wink? He glanced in the rear-view mirror but, to his surprise, the rambler was already gone.

He slowed down when he reached the edge of the village. He drove in second gear past the old school and the willow by the river, where he used to hide as a child. He crept past Rowden's and the church, passing the lane with the cottage where he grew up. He drove even more slowly up the drive to Oakstone and parked to the left of the front steps. After killing the engine, he sat for a moment with his hands on the steering wheel, staring up at the big house – the house that had started to become his, not because of its history or because he tried so hard to acquire it, but simply by him coming back here after a visit to a loved one, by him parking the car in its usual spot. Because this was the kind of comfort one could dare to draw dreams from.

He stepped out of the car, his legs a bit stiff from the cold and the drive. The gravel underfoot could be anywhere but it gave him consolation to think that it was here. Here, outside Oakstone: his home.

CHAPTER 16

An hour later, Mr Askew set out again, this time on foot, wearing his best suit under the tweed coat. He had decided, against his own better judgement, on the shoes with the leather soles. He carried a bottle of Amarone in a canvas bag and two gifts wrapped in brown paper. It was still very cold – colder now, as the sun was setting – and the grass was spiked, each blade pared and ready. There was something solid about the way they stood to attention. He stepped off the gravel drive, on to the lawn, enjoying the way his feet crushed and sank, leaving behind a march of ghostly footprints. Dusk was gathering over the short day, a blue shadow tumbling silently from the moor, descending like the seventh wave, its force softened by its own advance. This was the same darkness that he used to hug against his chest at night as a child. Still a friend, it touched his hands now, and his face, pressing softly, coyly against its hollows, finding its way into the hole that had been mended. What was he ever, in his own life? A memory – a ghost – always at the periphery of his own story, stroking the shadows.

Being stroked by the shadows. But now the tautening imprints on the frosted grass gave him a sense of being there. Yes, he was here.

As he passed through the gates into the road, his hand reached, out of habit, for his upper lip – checking, making sure. But tonight the skin was smooth under his fingers, and unnaturally white, apart from the scar pinking in the sharp air, an arrow ready on his cupid's bow. He did not know what had made him do it but, coming back from visiting Amélie at Edencombe, he had gone straight to the bathroom and shaved off his moustache. As he had searched for his reflection in the steamed-up mirror, he could not be sure what he was looking at. He had stood there for a long time, staring, as the steam dissolved slowly without bringing him closer to himself, until, at last, when the heat had gone out of the bathroom and the skin on his naked torso was goose-pimpled, he had looked into his own eyes. He had leant forward, resting his hands on the sink, and looked deep into himself. He had been surprised at what he found and he had kept staring in amazement, until he retrieved himself from the corridor of mirrors. He must not forget.

Few cars passed along this road on Christmas Day and the frost had spread like white fur over the tarmac. It was slippery and he walked, instead, on the gravel edge of the road, avoiding stepping into the puddles that wore only a gloss of thin ice. A few stars had come out overhead and the frost glimmered in the blue light. He listened to his footsteps as they pinged in the tight air. He walked with the hedges high on either side until the road climbed into the village, joining the high street, past the pub, which was lit up like a cruise liner, past Rowden's, which was quiet and dark now, for once, past the post office and the rows of chocolate-box cottages, past the looming church, where the Christmas service was over. A forgotten candle was still flickering behind one of the stained glass windows. He stopped for a moment to watch its single beauty. It would burn down eventually and no one would ever know that the health and safety regulations had been breached; no harm would have been done.

He set out again through the landscape of his mind, and walked a hundred yards to the mouth of the lane, which had swallowed him up on so many nights in the past. Here, he hesitated and a shiver went through his body as a cold gust sneaked its way up from the valley and stroked its tail against him. He took a deep breath, stretched his back and walked on, negotiating the slippery cobbles with the emphasised carelessness of a lover approaching a tryst.

The nicer cottages at the top of the lane stood empty – they were only used as holiday homes in the summer, these days. But further down the dark lane he could see the light from behind the drawn curtains in the front room and knew that somehow it would be all right. In this light, the harsh façade of the cottage looked less uninviting. He could smell the peat smoke on the air, familiar and comforting. Out of habit, he reached for the brass handle, but stopped himself at the last minute, remembering this was no longer his home, that somehow the many twists and turns of life had stood him here once more outside the house where it all began. Second comings were like second glances: risky, unpredictable, thin as ice. As he knocked on the door, he was aware of his knees weakening, possibly bending. He could hear gay voices from inside.

'Ah, there you are! We were beginning to wonder . . .' Mrs Sarobi smiles at him with her warm eyes. Her hand is on his arm, pulling him in by the sleeve – 'Come on inside; don't let the cold in—' closing the door behind him. Her hands are lifting his coat off his shoulders, releasing him from his pelt. He pulls out the bottle and the gifts and drops the empty canvas bag on the floor by the door.

Mrs Ludgate is sitting by the fire with a glass in her hand. The peat is burning high. 'All right, Professor? I poured you a drink from the posh bottle.' She nods towards a second glass on the table beside her. 'Reckoned you would need warming up after your walk, knowing the way you're likely to stray and walk off in your mind.'

Mrs Sarobi's hands are again holding both of his, lifting them up towards her lips, blowing. Her hair is free, falling on either side of her face as she bends it towards his hands. He wants to hold her face, cup its fine bones, kiss her.

'You're freezing! Come, sit by the fire.'

Would it be wrong to love Mrs Sarobi's hands? Her lips? Would they laugh at him, if they knew?

'Move over, you; give him the best chair.' The hostess's cheeks are flushed.

'Okay, okay; you're the mistress of the house.' Mrs Ludgate smiles, pushing herself out of the chair.

But Gabriel Askew stands by the door, his newly released hands still suspended in front of him. He's distracted, for a moment, by the confusion of a childhood memory – of Uncle Gerry sitting by the fire, looking into his glass, the world no longer in his sight. And of Mother standing nearby, looking straight at Gabriel, for once, frowning at everything that's wrong and ugly in her damaged child. Or is she wondering in perplexity how she will be able to protect her beloved child from the rest of the world? Ah, but it's time to leave it behind. Memory is the safest place to store such images. He shrugs and looks up at Mrs Sarobi. 'What was that?' he asks. 'I was reminded of something from long ago.'

'I said, you look great without the moustache.'

'Oh, thanks.' Reddening.

'How was your Christmas so far? Did you talk to Amélie?'

'Mm-hmm; I'll tell you all about it later,' he says,

looking into her eyes. Braver than ever before, he's strengthened by the knowledge that there's somebody, at last, who will listen.

Mrs Sarobi – Nahal – sees all this and at once she feels better about the gift that she has wrapped for him. He will understand, she is certain; he will somehow understand why it is beautiful and significant, although it's only a silly old vase, pieced together from a thousand shards of blue glass, revealing the tiny flowers, a cluster of forget-me-nots. She will give it to him later, when they are alone.

'What are you two on about, skulking by the door?' Mrs Ludgate has moved to the chair further from the fire. 'Are you going to sit down, or what?'

Laughing, rubbing his hands together, Gabriel moves into the room. 'Now, where is that drink you promised me, Doris? We have a lot to celebrate, haven't we?'

'Drink's still here – come and get it, before it goes off.'

Later on, the three of them sit there around the table, playing out their *fête galante*. The oilcloth has been replaced by a beautifully embroidered tablecloth. The Rayburn's heat is picked out by the tiny blue flames of many candles, flickering in the draught like leaf shadows on a summer's day: shy, tender, delicate.

This is our world, he thinks. Together and alone, just the way we prefer it; three outsiders, each of us finished, each of us at our beginning. This is the tightrope we walk, a void opening on either side as we simply place one foot in front of the other, never looking down. Never looking back. No need to look back. Life stretches in front of us and yet it's contained in this moment. He looks at his watch. It's nearly six o'clock. The hands – the heart – balanced, slotted into place. I have caught up with myself.

There is still time, he thinks to himself, smiling at Nahal across the table, realising now he has never known this happiness.